MY FAIR
Duchess

EM,

It was great to meet you at HRR!

All the best,

Julia Johnston

Al,

It was great to

meet you at HER!

All the best,

Nik Johnston

My Fair *Duchess*

Julie Johnstone

My Fair Duchess

Cover Design by Lily Smith

For more information: juliejohnstoneauthor@gmail.com
www.juliejohnstoneauthor.com

ISBN: 1503305465
ISBN 13: 9781503305465

Dedication

For my wonderful Duchesses, Debutantes and Demi-mondes:

Davina E. Bell
Crystal Coe-Benedict
Molly Bishop
Ginny-Beth Brady
Simi Chatterjee
Lesia Chambliss
Mary Chen
Anne Durward
Sharon Fournier
Sally Hanoush
Rhonda Jones
Jenna Kenote
Rhonda Kirby
Nicole Laverdure
Debbie McCreary
Molly Plant
Katie Vines Poole
Lisa Schmidt-Ringsby
Lindsey Ross
Mary Schabaker
Patricia Turner

Thank you ladies for cheering me on, helping me make decisions, making me smile and being the very reason I love being a writer! You're the most wonderful fans a gal could have!

Smooches ~ Julie

Prologue

St. Ives, Cambridgeshire, England
The Year of Our Lord 1795

The day Colin Sinclair, the Marquess of Nortingham and the future Duke of Aversley, entered the world, he brought nothing but havoc with him.

The Duchess of Aversley's birthing screams filled Waverly House, accompanied by the relentless pattering of rain that beat against the large glass window of Alexander Sinclair's study. The current Duke of Aversley gripped the edge of his desk, the wood digging into his palms. He did not know how much more he could take or how much longer he could acquiesce to his wife's refusal of his request to be present in the birthing room. He knew his wish was unusual and that she feared what he saw would dampen his desire for her, but nothing would ever do that.

Camilla's hoarse voice sliced through the silence again and fed the festering fear that filled him. She might die from this.

The possibility made him tremble. Why hadn't he controlled his lust? After six failed attempts to give him a child, Camilla's body was weak. He'd known the truth but had chosen to ignore it. Moisture dampened his silk shirt, and Camilla screeched once more. He shook his head, trying to ward off the sound.

He reached across his desk, and with a pounding heart and trembling hand, he slid the crystal decanter toward him. If he did not do something to calm his nerves, he would bolt straight out of this room and barge into their bedchamber. The last thing he wanted to do was cause Camilla undue anxiety. The Scotch lapped over the edge of the tumbler as he poured it, dripping small droplets of liquor on the contracts he had been blindly staring at for the last four hours.

He did not make a move to rescue the papers as the ink blurred. He did not give a goddamn about the papers. All he cared about was Camilla. The physician's previous words of warning that the duchess should not try for an heir again played repeatedly through Alexander's mind. The words grew in volume as the storm raged outside and his wife's shrieks tore through the mansion.

Alexander could have lived a thousand lifetimes without an heir, but he was weak fool. He craved Camilla, body and soul. His desire, along with his pompous certainty that everything would eventually turn out all right for them because he was the duke, had caused him to ignore the physician and eagerly yield to his wife's fervent wish to have a child.

As Camilla's high, keening wails vibrated the air around him, he gripped his glass a fraction harder. The crystal cracked, cutting his hand with razor-like precision. Yanking off his cravat, he wrapped it around his bleeding hand. Lightning split the shadows in the room with bright, blinding light, followed by his study door crashing open and Camilla's sister, Jane, flying through the entrance. Her red hair streamed out behind her, tears running down her face.

"The physician says come now. Camilla's—" Jane's voice cracked. She dashed a hand across her wet cheeks and moved across the room and around the desk to stand behind his chair. She placed a hand on his shoulder. "Camilla is dying. The doctor needs you to tell him whether to try to save her or the baby."

Pain, the likes of which the duke had never experienced, sliced through his chest and curled in his belly. A fierce cramp immediately seized him. "What sort of choice is that?" he cried as he stood.

Jane nodded sympathetically then simply turned and motioned him to follow her. With effort, he forced his numb legs to move up the stairs toward his wife's moans. With every step, his heartbeat increased until he was certain it would pound out of his chest. He could not live without her, yet he knew she would not want to live without the babe. If he told the doctor to save her over their child, she would hate him, and misery would continue to plague her and chafe as it had done every time she had lost a babe these past six years.

He could not cause her such pain, but he could not pick the child over her. Outside the bedchamber door, Jane paused and turned to him, her face splotchy. "What are you going to do? I must know to prepare myself."

Alexander had never been a praying man, despite the fact that his mother had been a devout believer and had tried to get him to be one, as well. His father and grandfather had always said Aversley dukes made their own fate and only weak men looked to a higher power to grant them favors and exceptions. Alexander stiffened. He was a stupid fool who had thought himself more powerful than God. The day his mother had died, she had told him that one day, he would have to pay for this sin.

Was today the day? Alexander drew in a long, shuddering breath, mind racing. What could he do? He would renounce every conviction he held dear to keep his wife and child.

Squeezing his eyes shut, he made a vow to God. If He would save Camilla and the babe, he would pray every day and seek God's wisdom in all things. Surely, this penance would suffice.

A blood-curdling scream split the silence. Alexander's heart exploded as he shoved past Jane and threw the door open. The cream-colored sheets of their bed, now soaked crimson, lay scattered on the dark hardwood floor. Camilla, appearing incredibly small, twisted and whimpered in the center of the gigantic four-poster. Her once-white lacy gown was bunched at her waist to expose her slender legs, and Alexander winced at the blood smeared across her normally olive skin.

Moving toward her, his world tilted. His wife, his Camilla, stared at him with glazed eyes and cracked lips. A deathly pallor had replaced the healthy flush her face usually held. Blue veins pulsed along the base of her neck, giving her skin a thin, papery appearance. Even the sour stench of death filled the heavy air.

Only seconds had passed, yet it seemed like much longer. The physician swung toward Alexander. He appeared aged since coming through the door hours before; deep lines marked his forehead, the sides of his eyes, and around his mouth. Normally an impeccably kept man, his hair dangled over his right eye and his shirt, stained dark red, hung out from his trousers. Shoving his hair out of his eye, the physician asked, "Who do you want me to try to save, Your Grace?"

Alexander curled his hands into fists by his sides, hissing at the throbbing pain the movement caused his cut palm. His mother's last words echoed in his head: *Great sins require great penance.*

The duke glanced at his wife's face then slowly slid his gaze to her swollen belly. "Both of them," he responded. Fresh sweat broke out across his forehead as the doctor shook his head.

"The babe is twisted the wrong way. Even if I can get it out, Her Grace will be ripped beyond repair. She'll likely bleed out."

Anger coursed through Alexander's veins. "Both of them," he repeated, his voice shaking.

"If she lives, I'm certain she'll be barren. You are sure?"

"Positive," he snapped, seized by a wave of nausea and a certainty that he had failed to give up enough to save them both. Rushing to Camilla's side, he kneeled and gripped her hand as her back formed a perfect arch and another cry broke past her lips—the loudest scream yet.

Alexander closed his eyes and fervently vowed to God never to touch his wife again if only she and his babe would be allowed to live. He would do this and would keep his sacrifice between God and himself for as long as he drew breath and never tell a living soul of his penance. This time he would heed his mother's warnings. Her threadbare voice filled his head as he murmured her words. "True atonement is between the sinner and God or else it is not true, and the day of reckoning will come more terrible and shattering than imaginable."

Alexander repeated the oath, coldness gripping him and burrowing into his bones.

Moments later, his throat burned, and he could not stop the tears of happiness and relief that rolled down his face as he cradled his healthy son in his arms.

Then in a faint, but happy voice Camilla called out to him. "Alex, come to me," Camilla murmured, gazing at him with shining eyes and raising a willowy arm to beckon him. He froze where he stood and curled his fingers tighter around his swaddled son, desperate to hold onto the joy of seconds ago, and yet the elation slipped away when realizing the promise he had made to God.

That vow had saved his wife and child. As much as he wanted to tell Camilla of it now, as her forehead wrinkled and uncertainty filled her eyes, fear stilled his tongue. What if he told her, and then she died? Or the babe died?

"You've done well, Camilla," he said in a cool tone. The words felt ripped from his gut. Inside he throbbed, raw and broken.

He handed the babe to Jane, and then turned on his heel and quit the room. At the stairs, he gripped the banister for support as he summoned the butler and then gave the orders to remove his belongings from the bedchamber he had shared with Camilla since the day they had married.

As he feared, as soon as Camilla was able to, she came to him, desperate and pleading for explanations. Her words seared his heart and branded him with misery. He trembled every time he sent her away from him, and her broken-hearted sobs rang through the halls. The pain that stole her smile and the gleam that had once filled her eyes made him fear for her and for them, but the dreams that dogged him of her death or their son's death should the vow be broken frightened him more. Sleeplessness plagued him, and he took to creeping into his son's nursery, where he would send the nanny away and rock his boy until the wee hours of the morning, pouring all his love into his child.

Days slid into months that turned to the first year and then the second. As his bond with Camilla weakened, his tie to his heir strengthened. Laughter filled Waverly House, but it was only the child's laughter and Alexander's. It seemed to him, the closer he became to his child and the more attention he lavished on him, the larger the wall became between him and Camilla until she reminded him of an angry queen reigning in her mountainous tower of ice. Yet, it was his fault she was there with no hope of rescue.

The night she quit coming to his bedchamber, Alexander thanked God and prayed she would now turn the love he knew was in her to their son, whom she seemed to blame for Alexander's abandonment. He awoke in the morning, and when the nanny brought Colin to Alexander, he decided to carry his son with him to break his fast, in hopes that Camilla would want to hold him. As he entered the room with Colin, she did not smile. Her lips thinned with obvious anger as she excused herself, and he was caught between the wish to cry and the urge to rage at her.

Still, his fingers burned to hold her hand and itched to caress the gentle slope of her cheekbone. Eventually, his skin became cold. His fingers curiously numb. Then one day, sitting across from him at dinner in the silent dining room, Camilla looked at him and he recoiled at the sharp thorns of revenge shining in her eyes.

The following week the Season began, and he dutifully escorted her to the first ball. Knots of tension made his shoulders ache as they walked down the stairwell, side by side, so close yet a thousand ballrooms apart. After they were announced, she turned to him and he prepared himself to decline her request to dance.

She raised one eyebrow, her lips curling into a thinly veiled smile of contempt. "Quit cringing, Alexander. You may go to the card room. My dances are all taken, I assure you."

Within moments, she twirled onto the dance floor, first with one gentleman and then another and another until the night faded near to morning. Alexander stood in the shadows, leaning against a column and never moving, aware of the curious looks people cast his way. He was helplessly sure his wife was trying to hurt him, and he silently started to pray she would finally turn all her wrath at how he had changed to him and begin to love the child she had longed for...and for whom she had almost died.

Chapter One

St. Ives, Cambridgeshire, England
The Summer of 1812

The dinghy creaked and dipped to the right as Colin leaned back against the knotted wood and kicked his boots up on the middle bench. Crickets chirped a pleasant sound that tickled his inner ears.

"Watch it," Philip de Vere, Viscount Rhetford snapped, gripping the sides of the rocking boat.

Colin chuckled at the pinched sound of his best friend's voice. "You really weren't joking when you said you don't care for the water, were you?"

Rhetford flashed a pained grin from his seat on the other side of the dinghy. "You're clever. I see now why you're at the top of our class."

Colin shot him a grin in return and eased into a sitting position before carefully placing his hands on either side of the small boat. "Remember last week when you tricked me into drinking vinegar?"

Rhetford laughed. "How could I forget? Your face turned the most hilarious shade of pea green."

"Yes." Colin purposely eyed the water. "I did say I would be sure to pay you back when you least expected it, remember?"

"Don't even think of it," Rhetford growled. His dark eyes had grown wide.

Colin snickered. "Oh, I'm thinking of it. Would it bother you if I did this?" Ever so gently, he rocked the boat until the water lapped with a soft slap against the hull.

Rhetford's pitiful groan caused Colin to burst into laughter, but he also stopped shifting the boat. It was one thing to tease his friend, and it was quite another to be cruel. After a moment, the sound of the water sloshing against the boat died away to be replaced with the more distant notes of orchestra music flowing out the open terrace doors, across the wide expanse of meticulously manicured gardens, and down the rolling hill to the lake. It always amazed Colin how far music carried in the silence of the countryside when there was no other noise to compete with the beautiful melody. The soft notes seemed to carry even farther in the warm summer air, but that was preposterous.

Colin sighed, welcoming a rare peace, until a burst of feminine laughter filled the starry night. He cocked his head toward the boathouse where his mother's drunken tittering had come from. Under the glow of the lights his father had recently had installed, his mother stood with her arms around the neck of her latest lover, the Marquess of Farnsworth. Colin's gut clenched as he stared at Farnsworth, who apparently had captivated his mother's attention but would certainly never have her love, since she was devoid of the emotion. Farnsworth had his hands resting on Colin's mother's hips, and Colin narrowed his eyes. His nostrils flared, and a rattle of disgust filled his throat. He swallowed down the useless emotion.

"Say—" Rhetford's voice was like a horn in Colin's ears.

He jerked and cut his gaze to his friend. "Keep your voice down. I'd hate to interrupt the lovers' tryst."

Rhetford frowned. The pucker on his smooth young skin was perfectly visible in the bright moonlight. "Isn't that your mother?"

"Yes," Colin said, striving to keep any emotion out of his voice even as his gaze trailed back to his mother just in time to see her and her lover scurry inside the dark boathouse. The door clicked shut. No light came from within, but that didn't surprise Colin. His mother was twisted and liked to pretend to hide her affairs, though everyone knew of them. What Colin would not give to row to the boathouse, throw open the door, and drag his mother back to the house and to his father's side where she belonged. Yet that would cause a scene that would only serve to further humiliate his father, and Colin would never want to do that.

Sickened, he looked away and into the dark water. He knew better than to hope his father would appear and separate the lovers. Colin suspected his father was too afraid he'd drive his duchess completely away if he demanded she stop her affairs. Colin growled deep within but forced the sound to silence, though he could not control the muscles of his shoulders, which tightened considerably. He had not wanted a seventeenth birthday celebration, because he'd known it would provide the perfect opportunity for his mother to slip away and further torture his father with her continued dalliances. The only consolation, though it bothered him to think of it as so, was that his birth had left her barren and there would never be a worry of a child from one of her dalliances. Colin scrubbed a hand across his face. He should not have agreed to this party, but his father had insisted and had seemed briefly happy while planning it with Colin's aunt.

As wood creaked and the boat rocked, Colin remembered he was not alone. He glanced across the space at Rhetford. What must he think? "I did warn you when you accepted my father's invitation to this celebration that you needed to be prepared for anything."

"That you did," Rhetford echoed with a note of disbelief, his words a hushed whisper. "Is that why you didn't want me to come? Because you were worried I might see your mother and her lover?"

"Hardly. That"—he waved his hand toward the boathouse—"is nothing. You can see my mother with a lover on any given visit to this house when there are men besides my father in residence. What concerns me is that she may try to slip away with *you*."

"I'd never do such a thing," Rhetford murmured, his face turning the same shade of red as his hair.

No. Rhetford would not, and that was one of the reasons Colin especially liked and trusted him. His friend was one of the few truly good people he knew. Bitterness clogged his throat, but he cleared it and leaned back against the wood once more to rest his head in his interlocked fingers. He looked up at the bright stars. It would be nice to recapture that fleeting moment of peace he had felt before his mother had appeared, but the prospect was doubtful at best.

"Scarsdale was the last friend I brought here, and as you well know, he departed no longer a friend."

"I gathered there had been a falling out when you refused to speak to him at school, but when I asked him what had happened he would not say, and well, you know what happened when I asked you."

"Sorry about that," Colin immediately replied, remembering how Rhetford had broached the subject of Colin not speaking to their classmate. Colin had snapped and told Rhetford that if he ever mentioned Scarsdale's name to him again, Colin wouldn't speak to Rhetford anymore, either. "Now that you know, I expect you to take the secret to your grave."

"Of course," Rhetford said. "But I think I should point out that I would never sleep with your mother. She is married for one. Your mother, for another. And most importantly, I don't love her."

Colin sat up, the boat swaying as he did and leaned against his knees. "By God, you are a dreamer. I wish I could be like you, but in my world, love has nothing to do with sex, or marriage for that matter, which is precisely why I'll never bother to find it. My father is miserable because he loves my mother and she could care less about him. I'd rather be an eternal bachelor and blissfully happy."

Rhetford snorted while plunking his booted feet on the bench between them. "My parents love each other and are incredibly happy when my mother isn't harping. Someday I'll marry and find a wife who loves me as much as my mother adores my father. The only difference is I'll have plenty of blunt so I won't have to listen to any harping."

"Really?" Colin quirked an eyebrow. "Is your father's land now profitable?" Rhetford had confided several months ago that bugs plagued their land. The infestation combined with too much rain had hurt their holding's worth.

"Father has a plan. When I graduate, I'm going home to help him institute it. It's my dream."

"I wish you the best of luck," Colin said, meaning it. The only dream he had was not to end up like his father, at the mercy of a wicked woman.

In the distance, Lady Farnsworth, his mother's archenemy, and the wife of the man currently bedding his mother, appeared at the edge of the lake embankment. Even with the distance separating them, Colin could make out her green silk gown fluttering gently behind her in the summer breeze. She raised a long slender arm and waved.

Colin grasped his oar, angled it against the side, and slid it into the water where it dipped beneath the dark surface with a swoosh and a ripple. Rhetford sat up from his reclined position and grabbed his oar. "Are we headed back to the celebration now?"

"You are," Colin said. "I have a prior engagement." Lady Farnsworth had passed him a note after dinner tonight expressing a wish to see him in private to give him a present. He knew all about her idea of a gift. The idea of bedding Lady Farnsworth tonight did not excite him as it had the first time, however. She was out for revenge, and he was her chosen instrument. The lady was foolish to think his mother would care, but who was he to point it out again. He'd explained this already several months ago after learning what she was up to. He no longer got a bitter taste in his mouth at the memory of her confessing that she'd used him.

"What do you think you will do in the future? I mean, when we eventually graduate, that is." Rhetford's question captured Colin's attention.

He hadn't given it much thought. He had two more years at Cambridge and really, what was there for a future duke to do but dutifully learn all about his land and the people who relied on him? His father, though weak in backbone, was healthy enough in his body and no doubt had plans on exactly what he wanted Colin to do, and Colin would do everything in his power to live up to his father's expectations and give the duke a bit of the happiness he so richly deserved. In fact, Colin had a sudden idea of how he could help his father now…

A plan formed in his mind. One that would aid his father and provide the gossipmongers more to talk about than the pathetic way his father continued to be cuckolded. He took a deep breath of the jasmine-scented air. "I do believe I shall work on becoming a notorious rake."

Chapter Two

NORFOLK, ENGLAND
THE HARTHORNE HOME
THE SUMMER OF 1812

"Amelia de Vere, if you do not come down here ready to go right this instant I will insist your father not give you any pin money this month," Amelia's mother called shrilly from the foot of the stairs.

Reluctantly, Amelia put down the novel she had been reading. *Sense and Sensibility.* She was almost done, which made her sad because the story was so grand and wonderful. But what would be far more depressing than ending a great book you wished would go on and on was having her pin money withheld and not being able to buy another novel next week. No novel meant she would have to live in the real world for a while without the luxury of pretending for a brief time that she was someone else.

She scrambled off the bed with one last look at her book. Not being able to purchase another one would be infinitely worse than having to survive going to town to be fitted for a new dress with her mother today. The fitting would be short, but a new book could last her several days. At least Mother had said Constance could go with them. That way Amelia did not have to suffer the seamstress's pitying glances when Mother went on and on about how Amelia had still failed to blossom and then said dramatically—and with her hand pressed against her forehead—*Maybe next year.*

Amelia snorted. She'd given up on becoming a beauty and decided she was perfectly happy being plain. As far as she could tell, beautiful women were not sensible. Her mother was a perfect example. She was a Marianne, like in the novel, beautiful yet senseless, though intelligent, which made the senseless part so infuriating. And Amelia was an Elinor, sensible and witty but unremarkable in looks, except people were constantly remarking on her height. If only she were not so tall, she was quite sure she would get Charles just as Elinor had just captured Edward's love with her unwavering devotion to him. She practiced slouching, just in case she should see Charles in town today. It was embarrassing in the extreme that she could look him directly in the eye. He really did need to hurry up and grow taller.

"Amelia!" her mother shrieked, a voice she usually reserved for Philip when he was home from school and plodded through the house with muddy boots on.

"Coming," Amelia called. As she made her way down the stairs and noted the faded carpets and peeling wallpaper, she could not help but wonder what Philip was looking at this very moment. How lucky her brother was to have been invited to the Duke and Duchess of Aversley's country home for a birthday celebration for their son. A pang of jealousy at the beautiful artwork and gardens Philip was probably getting to see streaked through her, but then she reminded herself jealousy was not sensible and forced her mind to think of other things. Such as how her name would sound when she was one day married to Charles Stanhope, Baron Worthington.

"Lady Worthington how are you today?" Amelia asked the air with a giggle.

"Not that again," her mother moaned from the bottom of the stairs. A small, albeit exasperated smile, played at her mother's lips. "Amelia, if we should run into Lord Worthington in town today, please do remember not to call him Charles. It's unseemly, and now that he's seventeen, he's practically a man. You really cannot call him by his given name. Do you hear me?"

Amelia blinked as her mother snapped her fingers in front of Amelia's face.

"I hear you," Amelia murmured and made her way out the door and toward the carriage. She'd not seen Charles since he had turned seventeen. For some reason, she had not been invited to his birthday celebration, which she only knew of because Constance had been invited, but Amelia was quite sure her lack of invitation was because of Charles's mother and not Charles. Amelia tried not to take it too personally. If she were a mother that had a son as beautiful as Charles, she would probably hope he found a stunning girl to compliment his golden beauty so they would produce striking grandchildren. Amelia would someday give birth to smart, sensible grandchildren for the woman. The thought made her face warm.

"Amelia, do you feel unwell?" her mother asked as she sat across from Amelia in the carriage. "You're flushed."

Amelia pressed her hands to her cheeks. "It's awfully hot today, that's all. Perhaps in town I can get a glass of lemonade with Constance before my fitting?" Then she could have a moment alone with her dearest friend to learn who had been at Charles's party, and if he had paid special attention to anyone, specifically any girls. She had to stay abreast of who her competition was.

"That seems like a good idea," her mother agreed as the carriage started to roll down the driveway. "I can have my fitting first, which will put Mrs. Pickard in a pleasant mood before she does yours. She does so love to fit me."

Amelia eyed her mother's perfect figure. She had lovely womanly curves and was not tall at all. Fate must have been in a bad mood the day Amelia was born. With a sigh, she glanced out the window and watched the scenery, perking up when they arrived at Constance's home, and Amelia saw her friend standing on the front porch waving at her.

"You must tell me every detail," Amelia insisted not long later as she sat at the bakery with Constance and sipped her lemonade.

Constance shrugged. "There honestly is not much to tell. The celebration was rather unexciting, and I would never have gone after the way you were snubbed if my mother had not insisted I go."

"Thank you for being my champion, Constance, but I assure you Charles did not forget me. I am positive it was his mother."

"If you say so," Constance said dubiously.

Amelia did not have time to quarrel over who was right. Her mother had only given them ten minutes alone to drink their lemonade. "Did he pay special attention to any of the girls?"

Constance shook her head. "No, though Lady Georgiana did try to monopolize him. I actually saw him sneak away from her!"

"See," Amelia said triumphantly, "Charles's heart belongs to me. Ever since he saved me from—"

"I see your knight and shining armor out the window," Constance interrupted.

Amelia's heart leaped, and she swiveled in her seat to glance toward the street. Charles stood by his carriage with two friends, one of whom was a rather mean boy who had started referring to Amelia as "Tree Trunk" and had convinced half the boys in town he knew to do the same. She hesitated where she sat, desperate to go out there and talk to Charles but wishing wholeheartedly he were alone.

He opened his carriage door, as if he was about to leave. Her heart thumped wildly. This was nonsense. She was sensible and brave. Rising, she glanced down at Constance.

"I'm going to talk to Charles."

"Lord Worthington," Constance corrected. "I'd hate to see you get into trouble again for a breach of etiquette."

Amelia laughed at that. Breeching etiquette and getting in trouble for it seemed to be a daily problem for her. "Lord Worthington," she agreed. "Will you come with me?"

"Of course," Constance said, rising and then linking her arm with Amelia's. "However, you owe me a huge favor, which I will demand repayment for sometime in the near future. I cannot abide Lord Worthington's friend, Lord Donahue, and if it were not for you, I would not give that barbed-tongued baboon the pleasure of my presence."

"You are a wonderful friend," Amelia whispered in Constance's ear as they strolled across the street toward Charles's carriage.

At the halfway point, Amelia saw Charles starting to climb into his carriage. "Lord Worthington," she called, desperate not to miss him.

Beside her, Constance groaned. "Really, Amelia, are you trying to get your mother to come out of the dress shop?"

Amelia bit her lip while hurrying her steps and praying her mother had not heard her. Perhaps she was making a mistake? Her step faltered, but then Charles turned and grinned at her and stepped back onto the street.

Her heart soared. He cared for her. *He must*!

"Lady Amelia, it's a pleasure to see you."

Amelia practically skipped toward the three young men, dragging Constance behind her.

Lord Donahue started to laugh and then he pointed at her. "Look at Tree Trunk run! I'd have never thought a gangly legged girl could run so fast. Would you have thought so, Barrett?" Lord Donahue asked the other boy standing beside him.

"Never," Lord Barrett said with a whistle. "Tree Trunk, I bet you could outrun me."

Amelia stopped skipping and pulled herself into a dignified slow walk, though she felt about as dignified as a bug.

"Tree Trunk, Tree Trunk," the two boys began to chant.

Her steps faltered altogether, though. She wanted to march up to them and slap them both silly, but that would not solve anything and that was, therefore, quite insensible. She clung to the notion that she needed to behave practically and like a proper lady, even as she blinked away the angry tears stinging her eyes.

"Tree Trunk, Tree Trunk," the boys kept chanting, except for dear, sweet, golden Worthington. He looked appalled. The smile of greeting had slid off his face, and he was glancing between her and Lord Donahue, but that was expected. As kindhearted as he was, he was probably stunned by his friend's cruel display.

Constance surprised Amelia by pulling away and marching ahead to the three lords. The sound of a long, drawn-out hiss of words floated back to Amelia, but she could not distinguish what Constance had said.

Whatever it was, Charles seemed to stand taller. He threw Amelia a look as he faced Lord Donahue.

"If you call Lady Amelia Tree Trunk one more time I will plant you a facer."

Amelia's heart soared. He was championing her!

"Tree Tru—"

Charles raised his fist. "I'm warning you, Donahue," he snarled.

Lord Donahue shrugged. "I was merely teasing her."

"Well, don't," Charles growled. "Ever again."

"Lady Worthington," she murmured under her breath as she once again began to stroll toward Charles. The sound of her name combined with his was perfect. *He* was perfect. She didn't care how long it took, she was going to capture Charles's love and his request for her hand. *Eventually*, her sensible mind reminded her. She was only fourteen, after all.

Charles winked at her—he actually winked!—and then said pointedly to his friends, "I'll see you both later."

Guffawing, the boys took off across the street and into the bakery. This was her golden opportunity; she may never get it again. She touched Constance on the arm and prayed her friend would play along.

"You better go back to the dress shop and have your fitting. Just wave out the door when my mother is ready for me." More like when her mother was coming for her.

Constance, brow creased, looked on the verge of disagreeing, but Amelia gave her a little shove. "Do hurry, Constance."

Pressing her lips together in unspoken protest, Constance nodded, albeit jerkily, and fairly stomped off in the direction of the dress shop. Amelia stood by Charles and watched her best friend march away.

Charles nudged Amelia in the arm. "Lady Constance should take lessons from you in grace."

"From me?" Amelia could not have heard correctly.

"Yes, you. Lady Constance strides like a man, but you're graceful, especially when you ride your horse."

Amelia's heart tried to beat out of her chest. Had he been watching her? This was wonderful. "You're very graceful, too," she said and tried to make it a purr like her mother did when she wanted something from Amelia's father. It always seemed to work for her mother, and Amelia did want something—Charles's heart.

He quirked his mouth and furrowed his brow. "What's wrong with your voice?"

Maybe she'd overdone it. "I had something caught in my throat. I wanted to tell you happy birthday."

"Thanks. It's too bad you weren't feeling well. My mother told me of your note of regret. I was disappointed."

"You were?" His admission made her so happy, she could not hold on to her anger at his wretched mother.

He nodded. "I just finished reading *Children's and Household Tales* and couldn't wait to talk to you about it. I know how you love to read. Have you read it?"

"No, but I'd love to."

He grinned. "Just a minute."

He scrambled into his carriage and then came out holding a book that he then extended to her. "You may borrow it, and next time there's an opportunity, we shall discuss it."

Would it be ridiculous to dance around in glee? Amelia snickered. *Undoubtedly so.*

"Amelia!" her mother screeched from behind her.

Amelia just grinned, though she knew her precious time with Charles was up. Charles wanted an Elinor, and if Amelia was anything, it was an Elinor.

Chapter Three

LONDON, ENGLAND
1820

Colin was about three seconds from finding his release when the widow Lady Diana leaned down, her bare breasts grazing his chest, and whispered in his ear, "Happy twenty-fifth birthday, Your Grace."

And just like that, the potential for a pleasant ending to the stormy afternoon disappeared. There was nothing happy about his birthday. Each one brought another year that his discontent grew. With himself. With life. His choices. His mother. Even his father who had been dead for a year. Colin had intended to forget this year's birthday, devil take Diana.

When she drew away and glanced down at him with a coy smile, he grasped her smooth hips and lifted her off his body to place her gently beside his thigh. A small frown puckered her lovely forehead, and her green eyes briefly narrowed before widening. She must have realized her pretense of pretending to care for him had slipped. Colin almost laughed. She lay by his side then curled her body against his like a cat would before trailing her long nails back and forth across his chest.

He tensed, unable to help himself, and grasped Diana's hands to still her motion before carefully putting much-needed space between their bodies. Never one easily deterred, she pressed herself alongside him and brushed her lips against his. Heavy French perfume that reminded him too much of the gaudy scent his mother favored filled his nostrils all of a sudden and made him want to shove Diana far away. Out the door preferably. It was definitely time to end this affair. Whenever he grew to dislike his partner's touch, it always helped to find a new lover. Pity the prospect did not bring a flicker of anticipation or thrill today—just as it had not in quite some time.

A sigh rumbled from his chest, mirrored by Diana's irritated exhalation. Colin smiled as he glanced at her. Her red lips were puckered in a perfect pout. She sat up and frowned over her shoulder before spearing him with a scathing look.

"I care not if you're sick of me. You'll not discard me before taking me to the Stanhope's ball."

Colin tucked his interlocked hands behind his head to prop himself against the down pillow before speaking. "I'm afraid you've mistaken me for an obedient dog. Tread carefully, my dear. The only thing canine about me is my ferocious bite when cornered."

She smiled wickedly. "Your strength is exactly why I sought you out. My late husband was a weakling in every sense of the word, and I wanted to bed a man who knew his mind. And his power. You have quite a reputation, you know."

"Yes, I know," he replied. The absurd sense of satisfaction that acquiring and building his reputation had brought him had died with his father. Yet, here he was doing exactly the same thing, though the need to divert gossip from his father was long gone. For a split second, he allowed the pain of losing his father to break the surface of his mind, but then he immediately willed his thoughts back to the woman in front of him.

Colin thumped his fingers against the wooden headboard behind him. "Seeing as how you are well aware of my reputation, I admit to confusion as to why you think you can make demands of me."

Diana raised her arms over her head and arched her back in a stretch no doubt meant to display her voluptuous breasts. "I spoke hastily," she said with a pointed look. "I'm making a plea more than a demand. I'm desperate, you see, and though you can be quite wicked, I've also seen you take pity on the wallflowers and dance with them when no one else would."

Colin grunted. No good deed ever went unpunished. Taking pity on a few wallflowers did not make him kind. Even the wicked could possess annoying consciences that kept them awake. Gritting his teeth against the pity awakening in him, he sprung up, swung his legs over the side of the bed to grab her corset, and then remembered she had come without one. At the time, he had been aroused, now he was annoyed as he was sure this was a ploy. Locating her chemise, he snatched it up and thrust it toward her. "Time to go."

She took the garment, slipped it over her head then gathered her gown and donned it, only pausing to turn her back to him. "Hook me, please?"

He reluctantly moved toward her and started fastening the hooks of her peach silk gown. When he was done, he turned her toward him, feeling compelled to say something. "Thank you for these months together. I have enjoyed our time."

Diana's shoulders sagged. "I will be subjected to no amount of catty comments from your other past lovers if I fail to arrive on your arm at the Stanhope's ball. Have I not suffered enough with the rumors swirling around me regarding my husband's preference for his assistant Mr. Dunn's company over mine?"

The tears filling her eyes and the throbbing notes of desperation in her voice made him pause. Something stirred deep within. He knew better than to trust a woman, yet she seemed so vulnerable and in need.

"Aversley, please."

Her quivering voice pierced him. His own voice used to tremble like that when he was much younger and would beg his mother to stop her affairs. She never acknowledged his pleas but simply looked through him as if he was not there. He opened his mouth to agree to Diana's request, but she stomped her foot and thrust her hands on her hips.

"I can see disagreement written all over your face," she snapped. "I don't like to make threats, and I have tried to be nice but you are forcing my hand. You *will* take me to the Stanhope's ball tonight and dote on me. That way other eligible lords will line up to court me. If you do not agree to my terms, I'm afraid I will have to whisper in several gossipmonger's ears that your mother is up to her old scandalous behavior and has recently taken a commoner as her lover. You would not want that, would you?"

Every muscle in his body tensed. "Who?" he asked, struggling to keep the shock out of his voice. As far as he knew, his mother had not been with another man since his father had died. Ironic, considering how she had tortured him with her infidelities during his life.

"Your father's old solicitor and now hers. What a scandal that shall create!"

In a barely controlled voice Colin said, "Careful, Diana. You are angering the hound."

Diana cocked her head. "The what?" She waved a hand at him. "Never mind. What time will you collect me for the ball?"

Anger pounded at Colin as he reached down and grabbed his trousers and shirt. After quickly tugging them on, he walked past Diana and opened his bedroom door. At the threshold, he motioned her to come closer. Damn his mother. After the years of pain she had caused Father, she deserved to feel the heat of the *ton's* scorn for taking a lover they would consider beneath her, but he could not quite make himself be that cold. God alone only knew why. She had always been heartless to him. Even still, he would not bend to any demands either.

Diana sashayed across the floor and sidled up to him then curled her hand around his arm. "I'm glad you understand."

Colin grasped her gently by the chin, though he wanted to shake her senseless. He drew her face close to his. "I do understand you," he murmured. "You are as calculating as I thought you were. I wish I could say I'm surprised."

Her face, turned up to him, tightened into a scowl. "I'm only taking care of my needs."

"Yes, I see that." He released her chin and glanced down, narrowing his eyes. He may not like his mother, but he damned sure would prevent this woman from hurting her. "Have you ever seen what happens to a dog protecting one of its own from attack?"

Her eyes widened slightly, and she shook her head.

"The dog becomes vicious. Ferocious and unstoppable." He purposely raked his gaze slowly over her. "It's a bloodbath really for the foolish creature who attempts to harm one of the dog's pack."

"I don't think—" she burst out before he pressed a finger to her lips.

He nodded. "I agree. You do not think. Neither clearly nor thoroughly before you spout threats. I do, though. If I hear one whisper about my mother, I'll destroy you. Make no mistake about it. I won't touch one pretty little hair on your head because I won't need to. I know all your secrets, my dear. I made it a point to learn them. They were shocking even to me, and that is saying something."

Her mouth gaped open.

"Yes," he said slowly. "I see you understand me now, and we can now go our separate ways. Permanently."

She nodded, even as her lips pressed into a thin, hard, white line. God, how he hated to threaten her, but he could not allow her to disparage his mother further than she had already managed to ruin herself, no matter how much she might deserve it.

"You're a beast," she muttered before stomping out the door.

Confident that his butler Bexley would see her out and safely into her carriage, Colin closed his door and ambled over to his bed. He dropped backward onto the mattress and stared up at the ceiling tiles. Was he really only twenty-five today? He felt eighty. Weary. Tired of his life. He needed a change. What sort, he had no idea. But everything seemed dreary. Depressing and predictable. Almost everyone he knew was banally disappointing in his or her debauchery, including himself. His father had been the only good person he knew, and look what that had gotten the old duke.

"Your Grace?" Bexley called while scratching on the bedchamber door.

Colin sat up. "Come in."

The door creaked open, and Bexley plodded in, his dark wooden cane clicking against the hardwood with each step he took. Even though it had been six months since Bexley had fallen down the stairs and broken his leg, Colin still sometimes forgot that the imposing butler who had served his father for years was not so sturdy anymore. By the whiteness of his knuckles gripping the handle of his cane, the man's leg must have been causing him pain. Bexley was too stubborn and proud to admit such a thing, however.

"Bexley, I'd like you to closet yourself today and take inventory of the staff's wages. I do believe it's time I give them a raise."

Bexley's bushy black eyebrows shot up over his keen brown eyes. "You gave them a raise two months ago, Your Grace."

"Did I?" Colin moved past his butler toward his riding boots, which had been discarded haphazardly by the door. He knew damn well the servants had recently been given a raise, but it was the first task that had come to mind that would force his obstinate butler to sit and relieve his leg pain.

He shrugged. "Well, I think I was too tightfisted. It's been keeping me up at night."

"Yes, Your Grace. I could hear the trouble you were having sleeping last night when I strolled by your bedchamber before I retired."

Colin paused, bent over with one boot in hand. Heat seeped up his neck and for once, he wished he had a cravat on. "I know you don't approve of Lady Diana. Rest assured she and her shrieking will not be returning to this house."

Bexley hobbled toward Colin, the movements jerkier than they had been moments before. He glanced down, and when he did, a thinning lock of peppered hair fell forward. In one fluid motion, he flicked the hair out of his eyes and back into its position then reached into his pocket and handed a letter to Colin. "It is neither my place to approve nor disapprove of the company you keep, Your Grace, but I do feel obligated to remind you that your father would not have liked her."

Colin grinned. Bexley always felt obligated to remind him of who and what his father would have liked and not liked, and Colin let him because Bexley had been loyal to his father all his life, and now he was loyal to Colin. The pain of his loss once again gripped him, tightening his shoulders, but he rolled them, stood, and took the cream-colored envelopes. He flipped the first one over and clenched his jaw. His mother's overly flourished handwriting was not hard to recognize. He was tempted to throw it in the trash without reading it, but what if she was ill or hurt? Damnation, he hated that he cared at all.

He ripped the missive open, scanned the contents and handed it back to Bexley with a frown. She was summoning him. He barely contained an irritated grunt. They both knew he never adhered to her summons, but this time he would actually go. It was clear she needed to be reminded of the need for discretion.

"Tell Lawrence to pack my bag for a four-day trip. I've a need to visit my mother."

"Certainly, Your Grace," Bexley replied while handing Colin another envelope. This one brought a smile. He ran his thumb over Rhet— Colin stilled his finger. He was still making the mistake of calling his school chum *Rhetford* even though the man's father had been dead for well over two years.

Colin would save the Earl of Harthorne's letter to read when he was alone. His friend was a wordy fellow, and his letters were usually several pages long and sprinkled with windy, comical descriptions of whatever scrape he had pulled his younger, hoydenish sister out of, or sometimes Harthorne's letters would be rather sobering with news of the declining state of his properties. "Tell Lawrence to have everything ready by three. I'm going to go for a ride and then head out after lunch."

"And cake," Bexley said, his mouth pulling into a smile.

"No cake," Colin said firmly.

"If I may be impertinent, Your Grace, when will you allow your staff to show their appreciation for you by permitting them to celebrate your birthday as we used to? I know it's unseemly for me to suggest such things to you, but I feel I must tell you that making new happy traditions in the present can help erase past memories."

Colin winced. That last part sounded close to advice his father had given him, and Colin still thought it an unsound recommendation. "I simply don't want to celebrate my birthday, but if the occasion ever arises that I do, you will be the first to know." He could never explain how his mother had screamed at him on the day his father had died, which was the day before Colin's birthday last year, that everything had gone wrong with their marriage the very instant he had been born.

"Go on, now," Colin said, his words clipped because of the harsh memory.

Bexley nodded and disappeared out the door. Without hesitation, Colin ripped into Harthorne's letter, hoping there was a humorous tale of his sister's antics inside. He needed something bloody cheerful in his life, even if it really had nothing to do with him.

Dear Aversley,

I hope your birthday finds you not in the arms of any widow but of a young woman who adores you. I wish for you some dreams of what may come. To help you see what true love looks like, I am inviting you to my wedding to Lady Mary Treveport, which is to be in one week. I expect to see you at my home post haste so we may visit before I wed and am a bachelor no more.

Colin groaned. Lady Mary was a well-known strumpet. Leave it to that dreamer Harthorne to fall under the spell of a woman who was about as virtuous as Colin was. He was sure Harthorne had no clue. "Damnation," he muttered. "Bexley!"

After striding over to his desk, Colin pulled out a piece of foolscap and jotted a note to Harthorne letting him know of his impending arrival in Norfolk in three days. He would see his mother first and then head straight to Harthorne's After a few minutes, the *clack* of the cane echoed in the hall and Bexley appeared, red-faced from his efforts to get there. Guilt stabbed at Colin. He should have gone to find Bexley and not made the poor man trudge back up the stairs to him.

"I'm going to be gone longer than expected. Tell my valet to pack my bag for a week and then draw my bath, if you will. I'll be leaving shortly." The sooner he got on the road, spoke with his mother, and headed toward Norfolk to save Harthorne from the mistake of marrying a strumpet—or even marrying at all, as far as Colin was concerned—the better.

Once Bexley had gone to speak with the valet, Colin scanned the rest of the letter and laughed. Only Harthorne's sister would climb a tree to spy on the man she was obsessed with and fall on top of said man and the woman he was kissing. As usual, Colin tried to picture Harthorne's younger sister but got no further than his friend's long-ago description of the girl who looked like a skinny branch with two overly long knobby sticks for arms and legs and a mass of unruly pale hair on her head.

His mood improved, picturing the girl, despite Harthorne's ridiculous news of his impending marriage. As he recalled different stories about the sister, Colin chuckled, and even as he left to lecture his mother, he kept a tiny slither of that lighthearted feeling with which his friend's young sister's antics always filled him.

Chapter Four

St. Ives, Cambridgeshire, England

Colin strode through the sunny portrait gallery of Waverly House with his mother's butler, Fletcher, on his heels like a yapping dog.

"Your Grace, Your Grace," the man implored in a high-pitched voice tinged with the vibrating notes of unmistakable tension. "Please, Your Grace, allow me to announce you first. As I explained, your mother is in a meeting with Mr. Nilbury."

With a temper that had gone from a simmer to a boil with every jostling bump from his London home, Colin jerked to a halt, ironically in front of his father's portrait, and swung around to demand the butler leave him be. Drops of perspiration slid down the man's forehead as he puffed out short, gasping breaths. Colin clamped his mouth shut and heaved a sigh. He could feel his father's gaze on him and hear his father's words of wisdom. It was not this man's fault that Mother's idea of a business meeting with the solicitor had nothing to do with actual estate business and everything to do with her pleasure. Consequences be damned, as always.

Determined to tread in his father's unusual footsteps and treat the servants exactly as he would want to be treated, Colin clamped a hand on the man's shoulder. "I promise you, Fletcher, I will ensure my mother understands I barged past you and there was no stopping me. You will suffer no consequences of failing to announce me, but if you feel you do, I will bring you to my home and make you head of all my servants there. Is this acceptable to you?"

"Yes, Your Grace. Thank you."

Colin nodded, and with a sideways glance at his father's portrait, he continued down the hall, leaving the problem of the butler behind him but not the hollowness he still felt from losing his father. Colin dismissed those emotions as he walked and focused on the strategy he'd use with his mother. He needed to get on the road to Norfolk to stop Harthorne from marrying Lady Mary, and the best way to cut through his mother's lies in an efficient manner was to catch her in her lover's arms. His gut twisted at the thought. He paused outside the closed parlor door and said a silent prayer that both parties were fully clothed. The last thing he wanted to do was find his mother in the nude—again—with yet another man. Once was enough.

Carefully easing the door open, he stepped into the gold-and-green parlor. His chest tightened, and a surge of disappointment filled him. He wasn't sure why, since he had expected the scene, but seeing his mother with her forehead pressed against Mr. Nilbury's chest made Colin want to cross the room, rip them apart, and remind the man he had a wife at home. Damn it all.

Long ago, he'd given up hope that she might change, but the sharp ache in his chest was unmistakably familiar to the pains that had plagued him when he had first learned of his mother's dalliances.

"It's always so nice to see you, Mother," he called while striding through the room toward her.

She jerked her head up and swiveled to face him while Mr. Nilbury stumbled back a step, a deep flush covering his fat face as he gaped. Colin stopped in front of his mother and took in her appearance. Not a hint of a blush tinged her skin. At least Mr. Nilbury had the decency to look embarrassed. "I see you are up to your old habits again."

Finally, a flush stained her cheeks. "I'm not, darling. I swear it."

The endearment caused him to pause. He could not recall his mother ever calling him anything but *Nortingham* and then *Aversley* upon his father's death. Nothing resembling love had ever been part of their relationship. What the devil was she up to?

"I have somewhere important I need to be. I simply came here to tell you to cease carrying on with Mr. Nilbury unless you want to once again become the talk of the *ton*."

"Your Grace," Mr. Nilbury rushed out, "you've the wrong of it. This is not what it appears and whoever has told you otherwise is mistaken. I'm a married man."

Colin flicked his gaze to his solicitor. "I'm glad to hear you've remembered it. You'll forgive me, though, if I find it hard to believe you, given my mother's past history and the fact that I walked in on such a cozy scene."

Mr. Nilbury's face deepened in color. "I was only comforting her."

This was exactly the sort of thing Colin did not have the time or the patience for. "Give up the ruse," he snapped. "You two were seen together in public by someone other than me, and it must have been quite a sight for my informant is convinced you are lovers."

"We are no such thing," Mr. Nilbury retorted. "Whoever this informant of yours is he or she is incorrect. Two weeks ago, I was on my way to deliver a letter to your mother that she was to deliver to you once she read it. She happened to come upon me in town and insisted on reading it immediately. The contents made her upset, and I do recall offering her comfort as anyone would."

"A convenient excuse," Colin said. He had heard his mother's lovers spout ridiculous lies many times before, but he had somehow expected more of Mr. Nilbury. He had respected and trusted the man.

"Don't bother trying to persuade him of the truth," Colin's mother said with a sigh. She turned on her heel and strode toward her escritoire while still talking. "All he has ever known is me at my worst." Wood sliding against wood filled the quiet room as his mother opened a drawer, rummaged through some papers, by the sound of it, and then shut the drawer with a click before facing him. She grasped an envelope in her hand that she slowly held out as she advanced and finally stopped before him.

"Your father instructed Mr. Nilbury to give this to you on your twenty-fifth birthday, *after* allowing me to read it."

Shock slammed into him. "What?"

His mother cocked her head. "We were just discussing how to tell you, but I suppose the best way is simply for you to read it."

He struggled to control the emotions suddenly coursing through him. A letter from his father. It was an unbelievable gift.

He glanced at his mother and stilled. She was nibbling on her lip, and a frown puckered her brow. Uneasiness curled inside him. He'd never seen her act concerned about a thing in her life, and she truly did seem anxious now. With his heartbeat thumping in his ears, Colin unfolded the foolscap and glanced down at his father's scribbled handwriting:

Dear Colin,

Since you are reading this letter, it means you are now twenty-five, still unmarried and, I fear, as jaded about women as the day I died. I know this attitude stems from the problems your mother and I faced, but what you do not know is that I was the cause of your mother's heartache. As for you, my son, I wish for your happiness, which I know you cannot attain on your current path. You might be surprised to learn that I truly believe only a marriage of love will bring you contentment. I want you to take the next year to let go of your anger and find the sort of love I always held for your mother. Since I know you will refute this wish, I am making it a demand with a steep stipulation. If you are not married within one year's time of reading this letter—and your mother must deem the marriage one of love—then I have instructed Mr. Nilbury to strip you of all my unentailed land, which effectively means you will be penniless since the entailed estate, unfortunately, has never been profitable. The only advice I have to give you is to be careful of your wording when you give a vow to God.

My love is with you,

Father

Staring down at the foolscap, Colin swallowed hard and folded the letter while fighting to slow his speeding pulse. What the devil did he mean by being careful of his wording when giving a vow to God? What vow? His pulse jumped another notch. He took a deep breath. Becoming angry would not help. How could his father think he could force Colin to fall in love?

Colin curled his fingers around the letter, the paper crunching in his hand and stabbing at his flesh. He would never be so stupid as to allow himself to become like his father, but he was not foolish. He was not going to lose everything by refusing to take a wife. Colin stared at his hands. His mother was to judge whether his marriage was one of love? He choked back a laugh. His father must have been delirious near the end.

"Colin, are you all right?"

His mother's soft words, so filled with what sounded like concern, made him frown. He glanced up from the letter and met her soft brown gaze. Her eyes held a look of sorrow he had never seen before, or maybe he had simply never noticed it. Foreign guilt stabbed him. Had he grossly misjudged her?

His mind rebelled against the possibility. Whatever his father thought he had done, Colin could not comprehend what sort of deed would drive his mother into the arms of other men if she loved his father.

He swallowed again, feeling as if someone had filled his mouth with sand. Trailing his gaze to the fidgeting Mr. Nilbury, Colin cleared his throat. "I'd like to speak with my mother alone."

Mr. Nilbury nodded his head vigorously. "Yes, of course. If you wish to talk about the legality of the letter—though I assure you it's all very legal—you know where to find me."

Colin nodded and motioned his mother toward the green velvet settee as Mr. Nilbury showed himself out. Once seated, Colin faced her. "I cannot be forced to fall in love. You above everyone should know that."

"I do," she said, her voice trembling.

Colin was at a loss for what else to say. He drummed his fingers on his thigh as the silence in the room grew. A sideways glance at his mother confirmed what he suspected. She was just as uncomfortable as he was, or else she was supremely unhappy with the dress she was wearing because she appeared to be trying to rip it by the way she was twisting it. He let out a sigh. He and his mother never talked about anything personal. Really, they rarely spoke at all.

"I suppose I better be going."

She stilled her hands then started wringing them again with vigor. "Colin, nothing excuses what I did to your father. I—" She pressed her hands to her face then lowered them slowly. "I loved your father. You must believe me."

Colin struggled to remain aloof as his blood rushed through his veins. Damn her. After everything she had done to Father, she had the nerve...He ground his teeth together. At least she seemed to recognize that what she had done was inexcusable. That was something new.

He drew a long breath. He was too tired to hate her anymore. "I wish I could believe you," he said. "Obviously Father wished to believe you loved him, since he blamed himself for your behavior on his deathbed." The moment the words were out of his mouth, he regretted them. "Devil take it. I'm sorry. That was unpardonably rude."

"No." Her voice was a choked whisper. "I knew it was foolish to hope you were ready to hear anything I have to say. It's no more than I deserve."

His mother's shoulders sagged a bit. He had the most surprising urge to reach out and pat her on the arm or offer some show of affection. Before he moved, however, she stood.

Looking down at him with the detached expression she'd worn for so many years, she lifted her chin in a defiant gesture he had seen her give many times before. She swiped at her face while staring at him. "I do hope you find someone you love to marry, but I promise to deem your marriage worthy no matter if it's for love or convenience."

"How thoughtful of you, Mother," Colin said. Whatever moment they might have shared was obviously gone. Something deep within him twisted, but he refused to care. Standing, he offered her a smirk in return for her unblinking gaze. "Are you concerned I'm incapable of falling in love and may lose my fortune?"

"I know you're capable of it by the love and devotion you showed your father. What concerns me is that you will never trust a woman enough to allow such a thing."

She was positively right. Only a fool would willingly offer his heart only to get it ripped apart. But despite every hurt his mother had ever caused him, he had no desire to torment her with the truth.

"I have to leave, Mother." He turned on his heel and headed toward the door. As he strode back through the portrait gallery, he paused in front of his father's portrait once more. "Well played, Father. But you of all people should know that just because two people are married does not mean they are both in love."

His chest tightened suddenly, in a way that reminded him too much of the soft emotions he worked to keep at bay. He had to get out of here, but even more importantly, he needed to go save Harthorne. There was time enough to find a wife who would want as little to do with him as he would her. And he had to admit, a marriage would certainly settle the problem that had been needling him lately. He needed a legal heir.

Chapter Five

Two Days Later
Norfolk, England

Lying atop her bed, Amelia squinted at her novel through the flickering candlelight, her heart racing with the twist of the plot. She finished the page and reached to turn it when a loud knocking came from below.

"Mother," she yelled with enough volume to wake the servants, *if* there had been any left in their employment to rouse. Cook was the only help they still employed, and she was away on a trip. "Mother, Philip is home." She glanced at the longcase clock and laughed merrily. Raising her voice, she called, "I have won the bet! Philip is not so distraught that he stayed out late and imbibed too much! I told you he had more sense than that!"

Blasted Lady Mary. It may not be sensible for her brother to have gone to the inn to drown his sorrows in ale, but Lady Mary breaking their betrothal mere days before their wedding was excuse enough for Philip to act without a lick of sense for one night. At least in Amelia's book. But sweet Philip was home.

The knock below became louder. Amelia frowned. "Mother, please get the door," she called, wanting nothing more than to find out what was about to happen to the heroine of the story. She started to look down again but the banging drew her gaze back up. "Mother, can you not hear that Philip has forgotten his key?"

Amelia craned her neck to listen for a reply that never came. She released a disgruntled sigh and set her book down. Once standing, she slipped her feet into her slippers and moved toward the door, catching a glimpse of her unruly hair in the looking glass. She frowned at her reflection. She'd quite imagined she would see long, shining black locks like the heroine's. Amelia shook her head. It was entirely too bad that reality did not match the fantasy in her mind. With a snort, she descended the steps while struggling to grasp the hair falling in her eyes and obscuring her vision.

"Oh, to cut off all this blasted hair," she muttered, making a big pile on top of her head and then tying it into a knot. She patted the lumpy thing with grin. Mother would roll her eyes the minute she saw the masterpiece.

She rounded down the last of the stairs while busily tightening the knot of hair and then collided with a warm body as she reached the bottom. "Mother," she gasped, the air swooshing out of her lungs with the force of the collision.

"I'm sorry, dear," her mother murmured in a distracted voice.

Amelia dropped her hands and frowned at the sight of Lord Huntington standing behind her mother. Each time she saw her father's one-time friend it rankled all over again how he had called her father a bumbling fool. No matter she had been eavesdropping when he had said the cruel words to her father—it did not change his comment. She would never forgive Lord Huntington, but nevertheless, she dipped into a proper curtsy.

"Lord Huntington, whatever brings you here at such a late hour?" She left the *inconvenient* part out.

"Amelia!" her mother exclaimed, clutching her arm and drawing her firmly against her side before giving her a hard squeeze. "I'm terribly sorry, Lord Huntington. Even at two and twenty, Amelia still forgets to curb her tongue."

Lord Huntington roamed his gaze over Amelia. "A lesson you well need learn, Lady Amelia, if you ever expect to catch a husband."

Catch a husband, indeed! The only husband she would ever want was Charles. Careful to keep her tone neutral and not scathing, she said, "What surprise brings you to us tonight?"

"I happened to be in town and ran into your brother at the Pigeon Inn. He appeared to be well into his cups, and as I know of his recent misfortune, my concern sent me here to inform your mother of his whereabouts after Harthorne refused to leave as I suggested."

Amelia's mouth fell open in shock. She whipped her gaze to her mother's face, noting her eyes seemed a bit too bright and her hands fidgety. Egads! She glanced between her mother and Lord Huntington while a sickening sensation built in her stomach. She could not have been so preoccupied with getting Charles to notice her that *she* had failed to notice that her mother was developing a tendre for Lord Huntington. Knots formed in her stomach, and she had to press her hand to her side to stop the sudden ache.

Surely her mother did not care for this man who had refused to write a letter on Father's behalf to the bank Father had owed a great deal of money. It would have been a simple task for Lord Huntington, as a board member of the bank, to vouch for Father. Amelia swallowed, her throat too dry to speak. Trying to focus on the worry at hand, she frowned. But why else would Mother betray Philip's privacy by revealing that Lady Mary had broken their betrothal and his heart?

Despite her pounding temples, Amelia cocked her head at her mother and prayed her ability to understand what Amelia was silently asking had not faded. When her mother discreetly shook her head, Amelia breathed out a half-sigh. Why did good news always seem to be followed immediately by bad lately? This turn of events could only mean Philip's recent disgrace was spreading through town. Amelia bit her lip to stifle a cry. Poor Philip!

She pulled away from her mother, concern for her brother overwhelming her. "I must go to Philip," she murmured and started for the front door.

"Dearest, no!" The high notes of panic in her mother's voice caused Amelia to swing around once more.

"Amelia, you cannot go to a pub!"

She stiffened. There was no one else to help Philip but her. Father was gone. And under the stress of the past year's estate debt, the strong mother she used to know had disappeared before her eyes. "Mother," she started soothingly, a habit she'd only recently adopted. "I—"

"Certainly, your mother is correct," Lord Huntington cut in. She faced him, and the hairs on the back of her neck stood on end. Something about the way he was ogling her so intently made her uncomfortable.

She moved back a step just as someone banged on the front door. "That has to be Philip!" she cried, her heart pumping with relief. She flew to the door and threw it open, only to have her brother's name die on her lips.

"You're not Philip." She could think of nothing more to say, at least nothing sensible. By his looks, the towering man could have been the hero in the current novel she was reading. She felt oddly dazed. His sun-kissed skin was showing above his cravat and peeking out from under the golden whiskers on his face. She sucked in her lower lip under her top teeth, her thoughts tumbling one over the other. Maybe it was his great height or the fine-drawn bones making her thoughts scatter. Or perhaps it was his startling hazel eyes and sinful black lashes that muddled her wits. Yes, that was most certainly it. And heavens...that wavy hair gleamed like the dark gold of Adonis. Yes, yes. Each of those things muddled her head, but mostly it was his eyes—assessing, slanted, amused, accentuated by the fine lines suddenly crinkling around the edges.

Blast! She was not a silly, senseless girl, but he was too handsome to be real, and his wide chest rose and fell with each breath proving her most assuredly silly. "You're not Philip," she murmured again, suddenly hot and her tongue thick.

"I am not," he agreed, surveying her with interest. He scrubbed a large hand over his face, and a massive gold crest ring on his finger caught the candlelight and glinted as he moved.

"Who are you?" Amelia demanded, sounding shrewish and feeling foolish for the way he had affected her. He could not be from here. She knew almost everyone in this town, and she did not recognize him. No man who filled out a kerseymere coat as exquisitely as this man did and who stood several inches taller than all other men she knew could avoid being the talk of the town. There were far too many single ladies here. Amelia set her hands on her hips as her mother and Lord Huntington came to stand behind her.

The stranger raised his brows at her question. "Who am I? Don't you recognize me?" His mouth twitched with an almost smile.

Amelia furrowed her brow and shook her head. "No. Should I?"

His eyes raked over her from head to toe, traveling with a sort of insolence over her gown. She glanced down with a frown, suddenly oddly aware that she wore a drab, gray, dirt-smudged gown. She grasped at the material, irritated that she had noticed at all. Raising her gaze, she meant to meet his and show him her indifference, but his gaze lingered on her hair with an odd look of amusement. Amelia raised a hand to her head and grimaced. Her knot had come partially loose, and soft strands of hair poked out in every direction.

He smiled, and the way it lit his eyes to a brilliant green made her breath catch. Offering a partial bow, he said, "I suppose Harthorne didn't regale you with stories about me as he did me about you. I'm undecided whether I should be offended or grateful." The rich deepness of his voice made Amelia smile, despite the fact she still had no idea who this man was.

"I'm Aversley. Judging by your hair, I'd bet my entire fortune on the fact that you are Lady Amelia."

"My hair?" Amelia had her hand halfway to her head before realization struck. She knew this man. Well, she did not really *know* him, but she knew *of* him. Philip had mentioned his friend but truthfully only from time to time and not in specific details. And the Duke of Aversley, though invited by Philip to visit them on several different occasions, had always declined to come. Apparently, he was too busy.

And rude! He was staring at her hair still. Blast Philip! He must have made quite the show in describing her unruly hair. Heat flooded her cheeks. "Philip is a pain in my—"

"Amelia!" her mother interrupted sharply, nudging her aside and stepping forward.

The Duke of Aversley's gaze finally left Amelia, and when it did, it was as if an invisible lock on her mind had been sprung and she could once again think properly. She gasped, eliciting a sharp glance from the duke before he returned his attention to her mother, who curtsied at him as Amelia belatedly realized she should have done.

"I'm Lady Harthorne."

Amelia faced her mother as she made the formal introductions between the Duke of Aversley and Lord Huntington. The conversation between the three faded in her mind with a sudden remembrance that made Amelia's heart race.

The Duke of Aversley was the gentleman who had salvaged Constance's disastrous beginning of the Season last year by coming to Constance's rescue and dancing with her when no other gentleman had. This was according to Constance, since Amelia had not yet had a Season due to lack of funds. She studied the duke from under her lashes. The sardonic quirk of his full mouth could almost lead her to believe he was hopelessly jaded, but his eyes appeared kind and he had done a great service that surely had not benefitted him in the least.

Guilt niggled at her. She could now understand why Constance had developed a secret tendre for His Grace, though on the day of her marriage to Lord Lindley, Constance had confessed the duke had gently dissuaded her from pursuing him by explaining he had no wish ever to marry.

"Amelia, dearest, did you hear me?"

She blinked and, taking care not to ogle the duke again, looked at her mother. His Grace probably thought her a silly nitwit who stood around daydreaming. Which she was. *Tonight.* In the past, daydreaming had only been a problem when she thought of Charles and the life they might share. "I'm sorry, Mother, I was woolgathering. What did you ask me?"

"Will you head upstairs and open the guest room for His Grace?"

"Why?" The question was out before she could stop it.

Beside her, the duke's chuckle tickled her ear. Her mother did not appear as amused. She frowned, shaking her head. "His Grace will be our guest for a few days. Philip invited him to come stay with us for the wedding."

"But—"

"I know. I know," her mother rushed out. "Philip should have told us so we could properly prepare for our guest."

That was not what Amelia had been about to point out, but her mother's narrow-eyed warning communicated clearly that she knew. Perhaps Mother thought it best if Philip relayed the news of his cancelled wedding himself.

"I'll see to it right away," she murmured, glad to leave the room and take a moment to compose herself. Curtsying to both gentlemen while keeping her eyes cast downward to avoid further embarrassing herself, she turned to flee and smacked into the entrance-hall table.

The letters on the table went flying to the ground, and Amelia watched in horror as the last gift her father had ever given her mother, a beautiful black-and-gold vase, teetered sideways before tumbling off the table. Her mother's gasp filled the room. In a blur of motion, the duke lunged for the vase and snatched it out of the air right before it hit the ground. Amelia let out a ragged breath, too dumbstruck to move. Instead, she stared while he effortlessly bent over and scooped up the mail in one swoop. The man moved with utter grace. Envy streaked through her.

Standing once more, he set the vase on the table, glanced down at the letters clutched in his hand and laughed. Amelia scowled. Was he laughing at her? Being the brunt of cruel merriment was all too familiar to her. Being less than graceful tended to be the cause of it much too often, but she had been working very hard at becoming more graceful ever since Charles had commented that he required a wife who possessed the utmost poise.

The duke looked up from the letters, and when his gaze met hers, his smile faded. He took a deep breath and stepped toward her, holding out one of the envelopes. "Here is the letter I sent Philip to let him know I would be arriving today. My apologies, Lady Amelia, if you misunderstood my amusement. I vow it was directed solely at myself. I would not dare laugh at you for knocking over a vase. You should see all the broken vases in my home that I have accidentally run into."

"Really?"

"Truly," he replied in a deep, sensual voice that sent a ripple of awareness though her. The man was lying. He moved with the grace of a thoroughbred, though she suspected no one would ever tame him.

As wild as he may be, he was very kind to try to soothe her feelings. Not at all the utterly selfish, wicked duke she had imagined after Constance relayed the rumor that he was known for his ability in the bedchamber. Amelia blushed at the memory.

He smiled gently and turned toward her mother. "If I may be so bold as to inquire where Harthorne is?"

Amelia took the opportunity to quit the room before she embarrassed herself again. When she got to the top of the stairs, she leaned against the wall and inhaled another ragged breath, which did nothing to stop her racing heart. Why did this man affect her so? She had loved Charles ever since she was eight years old and he had rescued her on her runaway horse. Amelia shook her head as she moved toward the guestroom. She was not about to become fickle hearted just because the Duke of Aversley had shown her a kindness. Charles had offered her many kindnesses in the years they had known each other. Of course, he had never spoken to her in a voice like silk that held the promise of a thousand wondrous kisses, but she was positive he was going to. *Soon.* The other possibility was unacceptable.

Chapter Six

Colin wasn't certain why he couldn't put Harthorne's sister out of his mind, but thoughts of her were stubbornly still in his head like a plague. Frustrated with his inability to control himself, he shifted in his seat as the carriage headed over cobbled streets toward the Pigeon Inn. He'd much rather be in bed than on the road again, but he never had been able to say no to a desperate woman, and Harthorne's mother had seemed distressed when she'd asked him to collect her son and bring him home.

The question was why? She'd been tightlipped when pressed, and he'd not had the opportunity to speak with Lady Amelia alone to uncover the details before he'd departed. Though, he had caught a fleeting glance of her bare feet and shapely ankles peeking out of her fluttering nightgown as she'd dashed from her hiding place at the top of the stairs. No doubt, she'd positioned herself there to eavesdrop on his conversation with her mother. Naughty little chit. A smile tugged at his lips.

Devil take it! If he could not get her out of his head, he might as well allow himself free rein to contemplate her. He never had been one to deny himself, so why start now? He leaned back and closed his eyes, enjoying the soothing rocking of the carriage. Lady Amelia was not the stick thin girl with colorless frizzy hair he had expected. Of course, his vision of her had been painted years ago by her mischievous brother. She was tall, though. Very tall and could appear rather elegant if she would stand up straight.

Colin frowned. Maybe she was self-conscious? As best he could tell from her drab, ill-fitting gown and strange, lopsided chignon, she had developed into a young woman who either did not care about her appearance or had no idea how to properly dress and present herself. The latter begged the question of why her well-dressed, rather pretty mother would not have demanded her daughter take an active interest in her appearance.

He grunted. The answer to his question showed itself. The mother was jealous. He'd seen it before. The mother was commonly petite whereas Lady Amelia was strikingly tall. There were other attributes to consider, as well. The curves he had detected in blurred outline under Lady Amelia's thin gown danced tantalizingly across his mind.

Colin glanced out the window into the bright, star-peppered sky. The carriage rattled over Bishop Bridge, and in the distance, Norwich Cathedral came into view. He scrutinized the architecture from afar. He'd never seen a spire that tall before. Interesting and different, just like Lady Amelia. By God, that was it! He'd found it intriguing the way she had boldly assessed him one minute, had become flustered the next, and then in the ensuing space of a breath had shifted to vulnerable and distracted. She'd changed like the winds of a storm, yet for some reason, he had not detected the destructive nature most women hid from men behind a sensual smile.

Growling, he shook his head and straightened in his seat. What was he doing? Sitting here contemplating the goodness of a woman he did not know—likely never would—was a waste of his time, let alone unwise. He knew better than to entertain the notion that any woman did not have ulterior motives for everything she did.

The carriage came to a swaying stop, and within seconds, the door opened and his coachman lowered the steps. Colin descended into the dark street and took a deep breath of the countryside air. Things were fresher here than in London. Maybe it would rub off on him. A few scattered, burning oil lamps lit the pebbled walkway to the inn. He whistled as he took in the one-story gray-and-red brick building with two pitiful windows and a narrow door. It was a far cry from White's. The chimney on the left side of the building had PIGEON INN painted on it.

The shabby appearance of the building made him smile. He was just as tired of the polished exterior of White's as he was his life. Both seemed a front to him. Perhaps his time here would give him perspective on his life. Deep within, he felt something about himself had to change, but he wasn't certain where to begin or even what it was he needed to alter. He caught the notes of a raucous tune pouring out from the bar and soon was whistling along as he sauntered through the open door and into the small pub. The room smelled of stale ale, and a faint scent of smoke lingered in the air.

He stopped in his tracks, shocked at the sight of his normally reserved friend balanced precariously on top of a barrel, surrounded by a group of ragtag men. The one-room bar was empty except for the small cluster of men gathered around Harthorne. Distracted as they were by the earl leading them in song, no one appeared to have noticed Colin enter, not even the barkeep, who sat behind the counter on a round stool drying glasses.

It was a nice change not to have all eyes turn to him when he entered a room, watching for what he would do, who he would talk to, and what sort of tantalizing gossip his actions might create for the night.

He leaned his right shoulder against the cracked and dusty wall, and released a long breath that felt as if it had been pent up for years. Drawing the *ton's* attention away from his mother's scandalous behavior and to his titillating affairs, for his father's sake, had taken a toll.

His thoughts swung back to Harthorne, who waved his hands in the air as if he were leading a grand chorus. A large smile spread across his friend's lips. Harthorne had the look of a man full of happiness. Colin had everything money and title could offer, and he'd wager it all on the fact that his friend had felt more joy in the last five minutes of singing than Colin had felt in his entire life.

The notion that something—no, *he*—needed to change struck him again. With his father gone he had no reason to continue accepting the many invitations to bed whatever woman wanted to use him that week whether to make a suitor jealous, or seek revenge on an unfaithful husband, or simply to see if he was as good in bed as gossip hinted.

Colin clenched his jaw. He felt dirty, and damn it all, he was sick of it. And now that his father was forcing him to find a bride or be left destitute, he had all the more reason to quit playing the eager rake. He would never give his wife his trust, but he would damn sure give her his fidelity, and he expected no less in return. He wanted to feel clean and optimistic about life. He snorted. Optimism was too much to hope for. *Clean*. He'd settle for feeling clean.

Relieved he finally understood what he needed to do, he pushed away from the wall and made his way the few feet across the dank, candlelit room toward Harthorne. Before Colin reached his friend, though, Harthorne's eyes widened and an ear-to-ear grin broke out on his face. *Spotted.*

"Gentlemen, gentlemen," Harthorne said, abruptly ceasing his song. He waved his hand with a flourish, palm up, toward Colin. "We have amongst us, in these most humble surroundings—"

"Eh!" the bartender bellowed as he stood. "Dinnot insult my inn! These here surroundings may be humble, but the ale flows jest the same out of these here kegs as it does the fancy gentlemen's clubs those fops in London frequent."

"Here, here!" A jovial roar resounded from the small group of men who had been surrounding Harthorne.

Colin crossed his arms over his chest as he studied the barkeep. He was a large man, with a thick reddish brown beard and dark searching eyes, but the smile that crinkled his eyes and twitched at his lips showed his humor. Colin relaxed his stance. "Since I'm one of those fops who frequent the fancy gentlemen's clubs in London," Colin called across the small room, "I'll take a mug of ale and let you know if it satisfies my thirst as well as the whiskey at White's does."

The bartender tossed the white rag he'd been drying the glasses with over his shoulder and laughed, a low rumble that built in volume. "You've got yourself a deal, Mr....?"

"He's no mister.!" Harthorne bellowed. "He is Aversley."

Colin raised an eyebrow, only now realizing by the swirl of Harthorne's words that the man was foxed, an unprecedented state for him. As Harthorne swayed dangerously on the wooden barrel, causing it to rock back and forth with a creak, Colin stepped nearer to steady him, only to have Harthorne wave him away. "I'm in absolutely no danger of falling, Your Grace."

"Your Grace, eh?" a deep voice came from behind Colin's back at the same moment a mug of ale was thrust in front of his face. "I should've known ye 'twas a real gentleman by yer fancy clothes. We dinnot get many of your kind in here, 'cept Lord Harthorne. But he bade us long ago not to treat him as a better."

Colin met the bartender's friendly dark gaze, eye to eye, an unusual occurrence since he was normally a good deal taller than most people. To his surprise, the bartender thudded him on the back. "How shall we treat ye in yer time here with us? Like one of us or one of them?"

"One of you, most definitely," Colin said, glad to shed his identity so completely for a while. He understood perfectly why Harthorne came to this damp, disgusting pub, as Harthorne's mother had put it in a tight voice earlier. Here, his friend could likely forget who he was and all the responsibilities and problems that went with it for a while in this cozy, candlelit, albeit dusty, room.

"Then raise yer mug to yer friend. He's had a hard day with likely more hard days to come by the way he's handlin' it."

As Colin raised his mug, he studied his longtime friend. Harthorne had appeared happy initially, but that was from a distance and with the shadows somewhat masking his features. Closer now, the dark circles under his eyes were visible, as well as his rumpled appearance and the reddish stubble covering his chin and cheeks that showed the normally fastidious Harthorne had not shaved. Colin held his silence, waiting for Harthorne to speak and give a clue.

"I thank you for your kind words, McNair," Harthorne mumbled, offered a leg, and tipped right off the barrel as he did so.

Colin lunged for him at the same time the barkeep did. Together, they caught Harthorne on either side and hauled him upright before he landed on his backside. Harthorne rolled his head to the side and with one eye open and one eye squeezed shut gazed at Colin. "I'm glad to see you."

The stench of liquor on his breath reminded Colin of the way his mother used to smell in the mornings before she took to sleeping in until two or three in the afternoon. Colin leaned back enough to breathe fresh air. "It's good to see you, as well."

Harthorne switched which eye was open and which was shut while frowning at Colin. "I see two of you. How many of me do you see?"

Colin met the barkeep's stare behind Harthorne's back. *Woman trouble* the barkeep mouthed. Colin nodded. Woman trouble could be a very good thing in deed if it meant his friend was not going to marry the conniving Lady Mary. "I see only one of you," Colin finally replied. When Harthorne didn't respond, Colin asked, "Shall we sit and talk?"

"Splendid idea," he said on a hiccup. "This room is spinning. Need to steady myself."

With McNair's help, Colin got Harthorne situated in a wooden seat at the nearest table. The barkeep rapped his knuckles on the chipped wood. "I'll leave you two to your private conversation."

Colin nodded and then thought of the ale. "One moment, please."

McNair raised his eyebrow. "Aye?"

"I need to sample your ale first." Colin turned the tankard up as the man steadily watched him. The ale had a bitter taste that made Colin want to spit it out. Instead, he drank down every drop, swiped his hand across his mouth, and held out his tankard to McNair. "Excellent. I'll take one more." That should be enough to make the barkeep think Colin truly loved it. He did not want to wound the man's pride.

The man laughed, his chest heaving with the force of it. "Yer an excellent liar, except for yer nostrils did flare a wee bit when ye drank the ale. 'Tis all right, Aversley. I would'na expect a gentleman like ye to appreciate hearty Scottish ale."

"Bring me two more tankards," Colin replied in a steady voice. "And I'll show you just how tender I am."

Both of McNair's eyebrows quirked high on his forehead. "Ye just might have some Scottish in ye. We Scots are famous for never turnin' away from a challenge."

"My mother is Scottish," Colin replied, feeling odd speaking about his mother. He never talked of her to anyone, but it seemed a safe enough topic here among people who didn't know her, except for Harthorne. And he trusted Harthorne with his life.

"Aye." McNair nodded. "I see the Scottish in ye, now that I look close into yer eyes. There's a wee bit of a devil twinklin' back at me. We Scots always have a tad of a streak that we have to keep constrained."

Colin furrowed his brow. That sounded like his current problem. He'd let the devil in him loose, and it was time to tame him. "Ever seen a Scot or part Scot who didn't keep his devil constrained?"

"Oh aye. Seen plenty. Makes a man jaded and miserable."

"Any cure?"

McNair grinned. "Ale. Or the love of a good woman."

Colin snorted. "I don't believe in good women."

"That be yer devil talkin'. 'Til ye come to yer senses, I'll bring ye three more tankards, and if ye still be standin' after the third, yer drinks are on the house any time ye be here. Ye keen?"

"Indeed, I do."

As McNair walked away, Colin realized he'd not heard a word out of Harthorne. He glanced across the table and chuckled. His friend still sat in his chair, but his head was tilted back, his eyes closed and his mouth hanging open with a line of spittle running down the side of his cheek.

"Wake up, man," Colin snapped, rapping on the table.

Jerking his head up, Harthorne gaped at him. "I'm terribly sorry, Aversley. Was I out long?"

"Not long. I must say I was surprised to find you standing on a barrel, singing, and having imbibed so heartily."

"Now see here," Harthorne slurred, his face coloring a deep red.

Colin held up his hand. "You misunderstand me. I'm not judging at all. Just surprised. Care to tell me what the trouble with Lady Mary is?"

Harthorne's shoulders sagged. "The trouble is me. I'm poor. And I told her the truth."

Colin tensed. Women and their black hearts. They cared more for money than love and more for pleasure than fidelity. They were all the same, every damned one of them. "I take it the plan to turn the estate around has not gone accordingly."

"It's going as I hoped but too slowly. The creditors are hounding me, and I don't yet have the blunt to repay everyone." Harthorne plopped his head against his crossed forearms. "I know I can make the estate profitable again"—his words were muffled in his prone position—"given enough time, but time seems to be the very thing I'm running out of." He rolled his head sideways and looked at Colin with one eye open. "Mary started talking about redecorating the house here and in London once we were married, but I sold the house in London. It was the only property I had that wasn't entailed. When I told her the state of my affairs, how tight things would be for a while, she told me in no uncertain terms that she would not marry me."

There were no less than a thousand scathing comments Colin could make about Lady Mary, but Harthorne likely would not want to hear any of them now. Tomorrow was soon enough to point out the merits of avoiding marriage, especially to a known lightskirt. McNair appeared at the side of the table bearing a metal tray teeming with six pewter mugs. He eyed Harthorne, raised an eyebrow at Colin, and then tilted his head toward the mugs. Normally, Colin was not one to encourage someone to imbibe to excess but tonight was an exception. Harthorne deserved to forget his heartbreak for a time.

Colin nodded and gestured for McNair to put the mugs on the table. Once the tankards were settled and McNair started to turn away, Colin grabbed the bartender by the forearm. The man turned back, his brow creased. "Did I forget something ye need?"

"You forgot the challenge. Don't you need to drink with us to ensure I consume all three mugs myself?"

"Wha's that you say?" Harthorne slurred, raising his head and staring, with bloodshot eyes, at both men.

McNair pulled out a stool. "Yer friend here thinks he can drink three of my best tankards of ale and remain standing."

At this pronouncement, Harthorne raised himself upright and propped his chin against his left hand. With the other hand, he grasped a tankard and slid it, liquid sloshing over the side, close to his chest. "Then I shall drink a tankard with you, Aversley. After all, what are friends for?"

"Indeed," Colin agreed, supremely glad to see a lopsided smile on Harthorne's face. Tomorrow morning would undoubtedly bring regrets for drinking the bitter brew, but helping Harthorne forget his woes tonight was worth it.

McNair was the first to raise his tankard. "Ta keeping the wee devil in us all constrained."

"To capturing the love of a good woman," Harthorne added.

Colin rolled his eyes. Helping Harthorne to accept the reality of women was not going to be easy. The man was too much a romantic. Time to plant the first seed of truth. Colin lifted his tankard toward the others while catching McNair's gaze. "To Scottish ale. The far wiser choice to tame a man's demons than a beautiful yet volatile woman."

Amelia pressed her nose against the glass pane to get a better look at the magnificent ducal carriage ambling up the drive. The dark night made it impossible to properly distinguish the details, nevertheless, she squinted, trying to do just that. Botheration. She could not make out much. As the conveyance rolled under one of the burning torches, it cast tall shadows against the stone walls that rose up on either side of the courtyard entrance. The carriage was surely breathtaking and overwhelming in size —quite like the man who owned it.

"Stop, stop, stop," she hissed, mortified that she had not shaken the impression the duke had made on her with nothing more than his looks to recommend him. Well, that wasn't quite true. He had gone back out into the night after just arriving to get her brother. For that she would be eternally grateful.

Mayhap the Duke of Aversley was just as honorable as Charles. "Impossible," she muttered. Charles was the finest man she had ever known, besides her father. Never mind she did not really know any other men. As the carriage drew to a stop in front of the estate, Amelia unfolded her legs and slid on her slippers. With a fluttering heart, she raced out of the sunroom toward the library. She could hide behind the door and still hear what the men were saying as they came in. A little niggle of guilt prickled her, but she pushed it away. Better to eavesdrop and position herself to help Philip if he needed it than to remain ignorant. Philip would never admit the depths of his devastation to her or anyone else, for that matter. Other than his best friend.

Amelia scurried down the hall on her tiptoes, darting a glance toward the stairs, half fearing and half hoping to see her mother descending the steps. At the sight of the empty staircase, Amelia sighed, regret and relief filling her chest in an odd tangled up mixture. Clearly, mother had not bothered to stay up as Amelia had to see if Philip returned safely. On the bright side, at least Amelia would not be commanded to return to her room without learning of the precarious state of Philip's heart. The small comfort didn't quite make up for the fact that Mother had been acting increasingly withdrawn and uncaring.

Amelia skirted behind the library door just as the front door creaked open and loud jovial singing filled the room. Pressing her nose to the crack between the door and the wall, she stared into the candlelit foyer and could not help but smile. Philip stood—if one could call what he was doing standing—between the duke and his coachman. Her brother looked more like he was hanging like a wet noodle than actually using his legs. His arms were flopped over both men's shoulders and the men, in turn, each had their hands clasped around Philip's as if to hold him up.

Despite Philip's obviously foxed state, she smiled. She knew her brother. He had a tender heart and felt things deeply. No doubt, Lady Mary's breaking their engagement had wounded him severely. He'd been in a black mood since it had happened this morning, but now he was singing.

Singing! The fact registered in her brain. Philip did not sing. He was serious, almost always. She turned her gaze to the duke, who sang rather lustily right along with her brother. Her breath hitched in her throat as she drank in his appearance. Somewhere along the road to retrieve her brother and the road to bring him home, His Grace had lost his coat. And his cravat. She blinked and fanned her hot face, very glad to be in a dark room alone.

It was not a betrayal of her love for Charles to stare at the duke. She repeated the affirmation in her mind as she gazed at his corded neck muscles and lower still to the top of his chest that was visible without the cravat on, his shirt pulled open at the collar. The man's skin appeared beautifully flawless. A little sigh escaped her, and in that instant the duke's gaze seemed to be on her through the crack in the doorway.

Impossible.

A smile pulled at his lips even as he continued to sing. Surely, he could not see her. To be safe, she moved back several inches and pressed her body against the wall. She'd seen enough to know that Philip was not too terribly devastated and that was all she needed see for now she supposed. Once the men retired upstairs, she would be free to make her escape and tiptoe up to her own bedchamber, no one the wiser that she'd been here.

Surely the song could not be much longer and the men would indeed retire? As if on cue, the singing ended, and her brother spoke in a rather slurred tone. "Let me show you to your bedchamber."

"There's no need," His Grace replied. "Your mother showed me where it is earlier and also directed my groom to his sleeping quarters."

The duke took a step toward the library. Amelia tensed and caught her breath.

He took another step and spoke. "I think I will have a look around in the library for a book, if you don't mind. If you recall, I sometimes have trouble falling asleep and reading usually helps that."

Amelia tensed. This could not be happening. The duke could not mean to come into the library at this hour. It had to be close to midnight.

"I recall," Philip slurred. "Browse freely. I'd stay but my head is spinning."

"Not necessary at all," the duke said. "Barnes will help you to your room, if you think you can make it without me."

"Of course I can," Philip boomed. "Between Barnes and the railing I'll be upright all the way."

Amelia rolled her eyes before glancing at the only door out of the room. She was trapped. All she could hope for now was that His Grace would be quick about obtaining a book and would not find cause to come near this side of the room. She fingered the thin cotton of her night rail and wished she had taken the time to don a wrapper.

Her heart began to pound as her brother and the duke's coachman started up the stairs with loud clopping steps. She forced herself to breathe in slow, long measures that hopefully made no sound. It would be more than embarrassing to be caught in the library dressed as she was. She could think of no possible way to explain her presence here, and then His Grace would know she was not only an eavesdropper but a liar when she inevitably tried to conjure some excuse.

The duke's footsteps tapped across the tile of the foyer and grew louder as he drew nearer. Flickering candlelight filled the room. She rubbed her sweaty palms on the sides of her gown and then fisted the material in her hands to help her keep from fidgeting out of nervousness. If she was lucky, the man would leave the rest of the candles unlit.

He paused in the middle of the room, as if deciding whether to do just that. She sent a silent prayer upward. The duke suddenly turned on his heel and marched straight toward her.

He stopped so close she could smell the scent of smoke and spirits on him. The aromas appealed to her in a rugged, raw way. Her belly clenched as he moved a step closer, and the heat emanating from his body surrounded her. When his fingers brushed the sleeve of her dress and the door beside her swished away and closed with a soft *click* she almost yelped, but light illuminated between them as he raised a candle. His humor, visible by the crinkles at his eyes and smile on his lips, took away her momentary fear.

Whatever could she say? Her mind raced, but her thoughts tripped over themselves as a slow, sinful smile spread across his face. "If you wanted to get me alone all you had to do was ask."

She didn't know whether to be outraged or amused, but her thoughts would not cooperate to form a proper rejoinder as she stared into his hazel eyes.

Chapter Seven

Colin had never kissed a woman who didn't want something from him, and despite the fact that Lady Amelia probably did, since she had not responded to his question, the way she stared at him made him certain he wanted to kiss her. As he returned her gaze, his body warmed in a way it should not. She was not a classic beauty. Well, perhaps...He glanced at the slant of her high cheekbones. Maybe she was. It was hard to tell from the way she presented herself to Society, though certainly she possessed features that hinted at beauty.

Regardless, the smart thing to do would have been to turn around, walk out of the library and pretend he had never spied Harthorne's sister with her nose pressed to the crack of the door. He trailed his gaze down the gentle slope of her neck, to the hollow between her collarbones where her pulse pushed frantically against her skin. His reputation must have preceded him. It had happened before. It would be no hardship to take Lady Amelia to his bed, if he weren't tired of his reputation and that particular life.

He stepped back, putting a safe distance between them. "Were you waiting in the shadows for me?"

She gaped then squared her shoulders and drew herself a good two inches taller. "Certainly not."

"Really?" He quirked his eyebrows. "Then what exactly were you doing hiding in the doorframe conveniently dressed in a thin, white cotton night rail far too easy to see through in flickering candlelight?"

Gasping, she crossed her arms over her chest and glared. "Are you always this arrogant?"

He nodded, but his usual sense of confidence in judging women felt off with Lady Amelia.

"If you must know," she said, each word clipped, "I waited up to make sure Philip was not too heartbroken over Lady Mary."

Convenient excuse. "Why you and not your mother?" There, let her come up with a reasonable sounding explanation for that.

Lady Amelia looked away from him and toward the floor. "Mother has not been herself lately. She retires early quite frequently due to megrims. She went to bed and told me to do the same." Returning her gaze to his, she set her hands on her hips. "Hence, my night rail, if you were going to ask."

He had been, but he'd never admit it. For some inane reason he halfway believed her. "Why didn't you simply come to the door when we arrived home and talk to your brother instead of lurking in the shadows?"

She smiled at him, and the gentle beauty of it tightened his chest. "You have no siblings, do you?" she asked.

"No." He was not about to explain all the nasty details of his birth and how it left his mother barren and how she blamed him.

"Philip would never tell me if he had a broken heart, and wrong as it may be, I hid because I simply had to know. I thought he might mention something to you. He is my brother, and I love him dearly. I would do anything in my power to help him."

By God, he believed her. He really did. Envy, because the pull in his gut could be nothing else, snaked through him. It was absurd to be envious of Harthorne having a sister who cared deeply for him, but nevertheless he was jealous and regretful at having misjudged her. The two emotions were foreign to him when it came to the fairer sex. He ran his hand through his hair, vastly uncomfortable and aware that Lady Amelia deserved an apology. "I'm terribly sorry."

She shrugged, making her night rail stretch tight across her delicate shoulders. "It's all right. I suspect you have encountered a great many women who lurk in shadows waiting for you. My friend Lady Constance, who you probably don't remember from last Season—"

"I remember her," he interrupted, fascinated with the way Lady Amelia seemed utterly unaware that she should have been greatly offended by his accusing her of wanting him.

"Do you?"

The skepticism in her voice was hard to miss.

"I do." He leaned against the wall, amazed with the moment. It was not every day he carried on an innocent conversation in a dark library with a woman in nothing but her night rail who only wanted to talk. Hell, it was never the case. He cleared his throat. "She had red hair, brown eyes, and is about"—he raised his hand to his shoulder—"this tall."

"That describes at least a dozen women I know in London," Lady Amelia murmured, though her smile had grown wider.

"Perhaps," he agreed, enjoying their easy banter. "But I would never forget a woman I've danced with."

"I'm not sure I believe you, given I'm certain you've danced with an awfully lot of women." Lady Amelia cocked her head to the side, and the movement caused a few tendrils of blond hair to fall out of her haphazard chignon. They curled gently around her neck and trailed down her bodice. One even nestled between the shadowy valley of her breasts.

Colin's blood thickened as he stared. He shifted and forced himself to look strictly at her face. "She was unforgettable, believe me." Lady Constance, with a dreamy look in her eyes, had come right out and told him he was beautiful as they danced.

Lady Amelia's pure, rich laugh interrupted the memory and heated his blood further. Her forehead puckered with an adorable crease before she spoke. "I'm not sure you should go around saying that. She's married now."

"Wonderful for her," he said, meaning it. "A delightfully unique creature and definitely not deserving of wallflower status." Though, perhaps because she had been a wallflower she had still been rather sweet when he met her. No telling what she might be like in another year, now that she was married. All women seemed to develop an unpleasant nature once they were married, wallflower or not. "Is there a reason you mentioned her?"

Lady Amelia sucked her upper lip between her teeth as she had done earlier today after knocking over the vase. It didn't escape his notice.

"I probably shouldn't have."

Here it came. The unkind remark. Some caustic way to make her friend look bad so Lady Amelia could cast herself in a more favorable light. One that shined brighter than Lady Constance. He pressed his lips together. If Lady Amelia was waiting on a sign from him to encourage her to be spiteful, she would be waiting all night.

She fidgeted where she stood and licked her lips repeatedly before speaking. "Well, it's only that she told me how very kind you were to her and the great service you did by sweeping her away from the wallflower line and dancing with her. I know she wanted to thank you in person, but she said every time she tried to approach you, you had a beautiful woman on your arm—"

"On my arm?" he repeated, stunned by what Lady Amelia was saying.

She finally blushed, a lovely pink color he could just make out with the candle he held.

"Well, she actually said *clinging* to you." Lady Amelia's brow creased and she pressed a hand to Colin's arm. "Don't worry. She didn't mean it cruelly. She said they were all very beautiful, and she felt rather awkward approaching you to thank you in that situation and because she had made a cake of herself, so I'm doing it for her."

He had to force himself to ignore the odd, rather pleasant sensation her small hand created and focus instead on what she had just said. "You are thanking me for your friend?"

She nodded, causing another lock of hair to slip from her chignon. He had the urge to pull the last few pins out and see exactly what her hair looked like cascading around her shoulders. Instead, he gently removed her hand from his arm and said, "It was nothing. I was in the right place at the right time and saw a woman in need."

She curled the hand that had been on his arm into a small fist before dropping her arm to her side and clutching at her night rail. Had he somehow hurt her? Even if he had, it had to be this way. Nothing good could come of the strange attraction he was feeling to her. He was sure she was an innocent, and as debauched a life as he had led, it had never included deflowering an innocent or his best friend's sister.

"You're too modest, Your Grace. Many men likely saw Constance standing with the other wallflowers that night and none of them made a move to dance with her or any of the other women." Lady Amelia studied him for an unaccountably long moment. "She also told me of her words to you on the dance floor that night and how you gently and kindly dissuaded her from pursuing you."

"Did she really?" He glanced down at his hands, not comfortable with Lady Amelia painting him as some sort of knight in shining armor. He was far from it. If Lady Constance had been married or a widow, he would not have dissuaded her from pursuing him and using him for his body because then he could have used her in return. He was not a good man, and Lady Amelia needed to understand that. "Did she tell you why I told her not to pursue me?"

"Of course. You told her you were not interested in marrying and never would be."

He glanced up to find her scrutinizing him. "And you find that disturbing, I'm sure."

"Not particularly," she said breezily. "Rather, I think it's well done of you to know your heart and not give false hope to the women who find themselves in the unfortunate position of being enamored with you."

"I believe you just complimented me." He could hear the shock in his own voice and realized he could not remember the last time a woman had shocked him in a good way. Lady Amelia was the first woman who had ever seemed to understand that it was better to be upfront than to play the liar.

"I did," she chirped, dashing past him. "I'll bid you good night now, before my mother or Philip discovers us alone down here. That wouldn't do at all."

Holding back a smile, he said. "Really? Come now, don't tell me you wouldn't like to be married to a duke."

She paused at the door and turned back with a frown. "Your conceited nature is coming out again, Your Grace. Good night." With that, she dashed out the door, the edges of her white night rail fluttering behind her.

A reluctant smile of admiration pulled at his lips. Lady Amelia had no qualms about putting him in his place. It was refreshingly honest of her. Or was it? Every part of him rebelled against trusting her.

Early the next morning, Amelia woke and rushed to get ready for the picnic at Lady Georgiana's. The woman was a continued—and bothersome—rival for Charles's affection. The Prichard's ball was in two day's time, and she refused to endure one more ball watching Charles dance with everyone but her. She was going to make him realize he loved her if it was the last thing she did.

After struggling with her riding habit, she forced herself to face the looking glass and grimaced. If resembling a man dressed in a dull brown doublet buttoned snugly across his too-flat chest to right under his chin was the look she had been going for, then she had accomplished her goal in spades. Groaning, she grasped the full skirt in her hands and turned side to side to judge if it was really as bad as she thought. Unfortunately, it was.

If it wasn't for her petticoat dragging under the longer coat no one would be able to tell she was a woman. Women were not supposed to be as tall as she was. *Tree Trunk.* The old nickname the other children used to tease her with rang in her head. Stubbornly forcing the memory away, she glanced over her shoulder and eyed the offensive hat that went with the riding costume. She didn't give a fig what custom demanded, she was not putting that thing on *and* wearing a riding habit two years out of fashion.

Pausing, she giggled. She had just worried about fashion instead of when she could get back to reading her latest novel. That had to be a first. Books had been her way to escape all her life. It was far easier to worry about what was going to happen to some poor character than what was going to happen to her.

Grabbing her hairpins and her mother's ribbon off the dresser, she marched out of her bedchamber and to her mother's door. The house was especially quiet this morning. No doubt, the men were still sleeping after all the spirits they had consumed. When she felt a smile pulling on her lips and her thoughts drifting to the way the Duke of Aversley had looked last night, minus his coat and cravat, she shook her head and forced his image away. The duke was nothing like Charles. He was a conceited scoundrel, even if he had done good deeds for Philip and Constance. They were probably executed to ease his guilty mind.

She tapped lightly on her mother's door, not wanting to wake anyone else. "May I come in?"

"I'm still abed," came her mother's muffled reply.

Amelia frowned. Her mother was sleeping later and later with each week that passed. Making a decision, she opened the door and went in without an invitation. A sweet stench assaulted her at once and caused her to wrinkle her nose. The room, oddly dark for the hour because of the tightly drawn curtains, contained an oppressive, almost smothering feel. As she made her way to her mother's raised bed, she eyed the bottle of laudanum on the bedside stand and forced herself not to snatch it away and throw the thing down with enough force to break it. Lately, Mother acted like the bottle of laudanum was her most prized possession.

Keeping herself under control made her stomach clench in protest. The sleeping aid was but one more thing her mother had started doing that was not at all like her. Amelia pushed the covers down enough to place a hand on her mother's forehead. It was cool to the touch—not clammy, simply normal. Sickness was not the thing keeping her in bed. Still, accusing Mother of hiding from something would not help matters. She gently brushed back her mother's hair. "I'm sorry to intrude, but I am worried about you."

"I've a megrim, dearest. That's all. I'll be up shortly and join you for brunch."

"Did you take laudanum for your megrim?"

"Goodness, yes, but it does not seem to be working as well lately. I need to speak with the doctor about that."

"Perhaps you are taking it so much your body is getting used to it."

"What nonsense," her mother rallied enough to exclaim. "One cannot get used to laudanum just as one cannot get used to being a widow or having a daughter who says disrespectful things."

Amelia bit the inside of her cheek to stop herself from arguing further. "I've the picnic, remember? You promised to do my hair with your ribbon." Amelia waited, her shoulders tensing with the hope that her mother would rouse herself from bed...and from the melancholy that had taken hold of her.

She did not even stir. "I'd forgotten," she murmured, her voice muffled from the coverlet that was pulled up to her eyebrows. "It must be all the laudanum I'm taking." Her words dripped with sarcasm.

"I'm sorry," Amelia said, meaning it.

"That's better, dear. I feel my megrim retreating just a tad with your kindness."

At least her mother had not lost her sense of drama. So much of the old her was gone that Amelia was pleased to cling to any familiar ways Mother acted. "Will you help me with my hair, please?"

"I'm not accustomed to you giving one fig about your hair."

Amelia raised a hand to her head, her fingers grazing silky strands and then what felt like a tangle. She frowned. "Neither am I."

A throaty chuckle came from the petite cocoon that was her mother's shape. "Where is the picnic?"

"Lady Georgiana's. Remember?" Worry prickled Amelia. She had stated this at least four times. Maybe she shouldn't go. "If you need me to stay—"

"No," came her sharp reply. Her mother rolled over and shoved the coverlet down to her chest. She reached out and grasped Amelia by the hands, the strength of the hold startling. "You must go to that picnic and be your most charming. Will Lord Worthington be there?"

"He's supposed to be," Amelia replied, unable to take her gaze off her mother's hands. When had they grown so bony, her skin so paper-thin? The blue lines visible beneath the delicate skin made Amelia's stomach turn. "Mother—" Her throat tightened and made it impossible to finish the sentence. She pressed her head to her mother's chest and hugged her. "What's wrong? Please tell me. Is it our lack of funds? Philip swears things will get better soon."

"No, no. Nothing like that. Sit up, dear, you're crushing me."

Amelia immediately complied and stared down at her mother. Her fine-boned face had new lines of age, but even still, she was incredibly beautiful with large, doe-shaped blue eyes, high cheekbones, and lovely smiling lips. Amelia twisted her own lips. If she had even a fraction of her mother's beauty Charles would have already noticed her.

Shush! She chided her inner voice, hating when she allowed doubt about herself to assault her. Lately, it had been quite a lot, rather like when she was younger. Despite her best efforts to remain positive that Charles would prefer a smart, not-quite-as-pretty wife to a petite, beautiful one who knew more about fashion than the world around her, Amelia had started to become concerned.

Her mother pushed herself into a sitting position and held out her hand for the hairpins and ribbons. Amelia passed them over and turned to present her hair. Immediately, her head was tugged back as her mother began to pull and twine the strands of hair. "I'm missing your father more than usual, as I always do in April since we were married then. This month is always especially hard. That's all. I will recover soon, I promise."

Amelia's throat tightened further. "I'm sorry, Mother. I should have realized. I'll stay with you today."

Firm hands came to Amelia's shoulders and turned her around. "No, dearest. The best thing you can do for me is go to the picnic and catch Lord Worthington's eye."

"Mother—"

Her mother pressed a finger to Amelia's lips. "Shh. I know what you're going to say. I have never encouraged you to change who you are. In fact, I was rather glad you cared more for books than gowns and ribbons, especially since your father's death, but now I want you married and out of this house."

Amelia's stomach plummeted. "Am I such a burden?"

"Yes. Yes, you are. If I did not have to support you I could purchase more laudanum."

Amelia gaped, and her mother flashed a smile that Amelia had not seen in ages.

Mother patted her hand. "See. I still have enough wits about me to tease you. Now as to your being a burden, you are not. Of course you are not, darling. You—" She gulped.

Amelia could have sworn tears were just behind her mother's dark lashes, but when she blinked, they were gone.

"You are at the age I was when I started to blossom. Soon, you will change and become beautiful no matter whether you care to be beautiful or not."

Amelia laughed. "I never said I would not like to be beautiful. I just said I thought Lord Worthington was smart enough to see past a pretty face and expensive gown. The laudanum has made you daft."

"One can hope," Mother said, smiling again. "But in all seriousness, men sometimes need to be shown what is beyond the outer shell by being enticed to look within, and that is not deception, Amelia dear, it is self-preservation. It's time you get married and have a house of your own. And soon, before—" She abruptly quit speaking and pressed her hands to her chest. "Never mind. I'm babbling nonsense. Hurry and go before you miss the fun."

Amelia glanced out the window at the bright blue sky. She did need to be going, but she felt as if she were missing something here and that if she stayed she might uncover what that something was. "I'll stay."

"No." That one word was hard. "You will go, and I will permit no more arguments from you. Get Philip to accompany you."

Amelia nodded and stood. There was absolutely no point in worrying Mother by telling her Philip was still abed. She would simply take one of the horses and ride it up the road to Constance's home. No one would see her on the lonely road, and Constance would be more than glad to let her tag along to the picnic with her and her new husband.

After pressing a quick kiss to her mother's cheek, Amelia made her way out of the house and to the stables to ready one of the horses. Rounding the corner on the pebbled path, she jerked to a halt and stared in amazed wonder. The Duke of Aversley was not in bed nursing an aching head. Well, he might have an aching head, but His Grace was not nursing it. He stood at the edge of the wheat field in a flat plane of bright-green grass, surrounded by blazing-red flowering poppies. The sun shined down on his golden hair and glittered off the sword he was slicing through the air. The metal made a high-pitched sound against the air as it went.

An odd tingling started in the pit of her stomach and spread to her chest. She glanced at the stables. If she slipped behind the row of tall bushes, she could get to the stalls without being noticed. Before she had time to talk sense into herself, she scooted behind one of the bushes and watched him. He moved with the fluid grace of one who had been expertly trained in the sport of fencing or who was simply a natural athlete. Both, she suspected. As he lunged and swung the sword high above his head, his white shirt pulled tight across his broad chest and his tan buckskins hugged the curves of his chiseled leg muscles.

She allowed her gaze to travel slowly up his long legs and powerful chest to his neck where he was once again without his cravat and showing more skin than was descent. She smiled. He was a rule breaker, and, Society had turned a blind eye because he was a duke, no doubt. She needed to turn a blind eye, as well, and quit ogling him. He was not the hero in one of her books, but a man of flesh and blood and very near. Gathering her skirts so she would not show up to the picnic with a soiled habit on top of looking like a boy, she hurried away toward the stables.

Once there, she panted from her mad dash and drew a deep breath to gather the strength to yank the heavy stable door open. It creaked on the hinges, and to her ears, filled the mostly silent morning with deafening noise. Hurrying, she made her way inside, the smell of horses and fresh hay filling her nose. Sun flooded into the stables and made her squint as she prepared to feed and water the horses.

She glanced around the stable with a frown. The watering bucket was not where she usually left it. Grumbling to herself, she spent the better half of ten minutes looking for the blasted thing before it occurred to her that she had probably left it in one of the stalls. Opening the first stall, she searched in vain for the watering bucket and then did the same in the second stall. Blast Philip! He had probably left the watering bucket outside again. She closed the stall door and twisted to make her way outside to search for the missing bucket. As she did, she came face-to-face with the Duke of Aversley.

He towered in the stable doorway, his hair slicked back with perspiration and an easy smile on his lips. He held a bucket of water in one hand. "Going somewhere?"

His question had a trace of amusement, and his gaze, she noticed, was locked firmly on her head. Self-conscious, she raised her hand to her hair and patted it with a frown. Egads, she should have peeked in the looking glass after Mother had done her hair. It felt rather odd, and Mother had seemed drowsy still.

Dropping her hand, she cleared her throat. "I'm going to a picnic." She eyed the bucket of water. "Whatever are you doing? Surely, you do not intend to water our horses."

"Why not?" he demanded with a chuckle as he swooped past her toward Buttercup's stable.

She could not help but stare at his powerful body as he walked. The squeak of the stall door opening brought back her senses, and she tore her gaze away and followed behind him, intent on taking the bucket, but he was in the stall and pouring out the water before she was close enough to reach it. "Please, let me."

He swung around and faced her, so close she could see the golden whiskers, yet unshaved, and smell the sweat from his swordplay. Her heart thumped in her chest, and she took an unsteady step back only to bump into the side of the stall. Heat singed her cheeks and neck, but she met his eyes straight on. "You should not be watering our horses."

"Because I'm a duke?"

"No. Because you are our guest." She stretched to grab the bucket from him, but he held it out of her reach.

"I enjoy the work. It takes my mind off things."

"What things?"

His stare travelled slowly down her body and then back up to her face. A scowl replaced the easy smile of moments ago. "Things I should not be thinking about. If it makes you feel less concerned about propriety being trampled on, my coachman fed the horses. I insisted on watering them myself. I used to do it as a child with my father and our stable master, and it was pleasant to do it once again. I hope you can forgive me for making you uncomfortable."

She shifted, wishing she could shake the absurd notion that he might have been thinking about her. How utterly ridiculous the thought was. "There's nothing to forgive," she murmured and brushed past him to unhook Buttercup.

He halted her with a light touch to her arm. The intimate caress made her skin tingle and her heart flutter unnaturally. "Is there something else I can help you with?"

"No. I'd like to help you."

She bit down hard on her bottom lip. Did the man know that every time he looked at her she felt as if he was undressing her with his eyes? Or that his voice held the promise of all sorts of deliciously scandalous moments? He'd probably been seducing women for so long he didn't even realize when he was being seductive. She was quite certain a man like the Duke of Aversley would never try to beguile a woman like her. Not that she wanted him to seduce her. She certainly did not.

"Lady Amelia?"

She blinked. Drat it all, she'd been lost in her thoughts again. She focused on His Grace and a shudder heated her body. Sometime during her daydream, he had raised his arms to grip the beam above him. His shirttails touched the edge of his trousers so that the smallest sliver of glistening skin showed between the bottom of his shirt and the top of his trousers. She gulped and forced her gaze back to his face. "I'm terribly sorry. My thoughts drifted."

"And here I thought the one thing I was good at was holding a woman's attention."

His gaze was locked knowingly on hers. Blast him. He knew perfectly well she had been thinking of him. The least he could have done was pretend not to notice her staring. She scowled. "I'm sure there are some women whose attention is easily held. I am not one of them."

A delicious sort of gleam came to his eyes. "Now you have me imagining what it takes to hold your attention."

"A good book," she clipped, struggling to control her racing pulse. She took a deep breath. "How would you like to help me?"

"Please take my carriage to the picnic. I'd feel much better if my coachman attended you and I knew you were protected. He will be glad to have a break from serving me. He can wait there for you until the picnic is over and bring you home afterward. And if you lift up the seat box you will find several good books."

She barely resisted grinning at him. "That's very kind of you," she said and impulsively squeezed his arm. The way his eyes immediately darkened a shade made her breath hitch in her throat. She drew away and nervously patted her hair. When her fingers grazed a particularly large lump, she frowned and dropped her hand. "If I asked you a question would you give me an honest answer?"

"That depends on the question," he said, the trace of humor back in his voice.

"What does my hair look like?"

"Lovely," he immediately replied.

"You're lying!" she exclaimed, watching the twitch at the right side of his jaw. "That's kind of you, but I need the truth. Should I try to fix it?"

He cocked his head and surveyed her hair. "Well, what were you intending with this creation on top of your head?"

"Not to scare anyone," she joked, not wanting to admit the truth that she was becoming desperate that the man she loved might never notice her and she was therefore succumbing to giving a fig about unimportant things such as the state of her hair and the cut of her gowns. "My mother put it up for me."

"That explains a great deal," he said with a frown.

Before she could ask whatever he meant, he made a slight gesture with his right hand toward her hair. "I think perhaps you better repair it."

"I'm not very good with hair," she admitted. The last thing she wanted to do was stand here struggling to put her hair in order with this man watching her. She was terrible with hair for one thing. For another, no matter what she did to it, she highly doubted her efforts would look presentable in his eyes, given the beautiful women he was used to. Grasping the only diversion for him she could think of she said, "Perhaps you ought to see to your coachman and let him know he will be taking me to the picnic."

The duke nodded while dragging his gaze to her eyes. "That's probably a good idea. He's just past the stables."

"Take your time," she answered.

With a tilt of his head, he strode away, not looking back. As she pulled the hairpins out she moved to the door of the stable and opened it enough to see outside. His Grace walked toward the house with long assured strides. It was no wonder at all Constance had fallen for him after one dance. He exuded confidence. She was not Constance and would never be so silly, but she *could* see how his looks might make one feel entranced.

Lady Amelia truly baffled him. Her blushes over her family's state of affairs and her honest blunt question regarding the god-awful creation atop her head made her seem vulnerable and without guile. Maybe she was the finest actress of them all, though at this moment he was disinclined to believe that. Unsettled by his thoughts, Colin jerked a hand through his hair as he strode toward the tree he had left Barnes dozing under. He stopped in front of his coachman and, with the tip of his boot, tapped him on the foot.

Barnes opened his eyes and sat up. "Your Grace?"

"I need you to take Harthorne's sister, Lady Amelia, to a picnic."

"Certainly, Your Grace. Will I be bringing her home, as well?"

Colin nodded, an idea forming in his mind. "Watch the lady as close as you can and let me know if she pays particular attention to any gentleman and how she acts if she does."

"How she acts?" Barnes's brows drew together.

Bloody hell. Colin rubbed the back of his neck. This was idiotic. What did it matter if she was coy with other men? He didn't care. But he was curious. Intrigued. It was perfectly fine to be curious since she would undoubtedly prove herself like all other women. Barnes was staring a hole through Colin. Damnation.

"I want to know if she pretends to be helpless or perhaps bats her eyelashes a great deal or walks too close to a particular gentleman or even disappears into the woods with him. That sort of thing." The sort of trickery women used to bait men before they reeled them in and showed them they were not a pretty little fish but a shark.

"If you say so, Your Grace."

Colin felt damn ridiculous, but it was too late now. He wanted to prove to himself that she was not as good as she seemed, but then again, he didn't want that at all. This confusion was annoying in the extreme. He missed the certainty he had held about all women just yesterday before he had met Lady Amelia, even if it had depressed him to be so sure of the fairer sex's duplicitous nature. He detested this wavering.

"Come on," he clipped and turned on his heel to stride back to the stables. Once there, he flung open the door and was about to call Lady Amelia's name when she stepped into the walkway from a horse stall. He clamped his mouth shut and stared at her glorious hair. With the sun shining behind her she appeared to be surrounded by a golden mist. Wisps of hair framed her face, but the rest tumbled in careless waves over her shoulders. She may look like a boy in her brown riding habit buttoned to her chin—it did nothing at all to stir a man's lust—but one look at her hair would ignite a man's passion. And to touch the silk tresses and let them run between his fingers—

He ruthlessly shoved the thought away. "Are you ready?" His voice was husky to his own ears.

She nodded, her gaze finding his under her lashes. "Is this any better?" she said, indicating her hair with her hand.

By God, it was more than better. It was a phenomenal difference. It made him consider what she would look like with the right clothing and the knowledge of how to truly comport herself to capture a man's attention, if she didn't already know. Perhaps this was all a game.

"It's lovely," he said. If he said anything more his tone would give away the absurd effect her transformation had on him.

Within moments, Lady Amelia was riding off in his coach, and as the coach rounded the bend and disappeared out of sight, he realized he had stood there like a green boy and watched her leave. He'd not observed a woman leave his presence in years. He was always the one to go. Yet, here he was, and though Lady Amelia was gone, he could call up a perfect picture of her in his mind. Odd, that. Particularly since he could not even remember what color Diana's eyes were and he'd slept with her less than a week ago. But Lady Amelia's eyes a man could never forget—luminous, striking as the prettiest bluebell flower he'd ever picked, and enchantingly slanted with sooty lashes he suspected veiled as many secrets as he himself hid. Except he doubted her secrets were near as vile as his were.

Pulling his thoughts away from Lady Amelia's lovely eyes, he made his way to the house to rouse her brother. There was no time like now to set Harthorne straight on the true nature of women and exactly how carefully he should chose a bride if he insisted on doing so.

As Colin passed the dining room, a groan came from within that he recognized as Harthorne's. His friend likely felt bloody awful this morning. Colin pushed through the dining room door and smiled at the sight of Harthorne sitting in a high-backed chair with his head tilted back and his eyes closed, dressed in the exact same clothes he'd worn the night before, right down to his scuffed Hessians.

"By the rumpled picture you present, I feel certain I don't need to be concerned about my lack of cravat when we break our fast."

Harthorne opened one eye and slowly, as if the action took tremendous effort, shook his head. "Your time would be better spent worrying about when and if my mother is going to drag herself from bed. Unless we can find Amelia, though I already tried."

"Your sister left moments ago for a picnic."

Harthorne groaned again, much louder than before. "My stomach does not like me at this moment, Aversley. Say a prayer that my mother rouses soon."

Colin frowned. "What does that have to do with breaking our fast? Does your mother insist we wait on her?"

"Something like that," Harthorne answered and rose slowly to a wobbly stance. "I think I'll go lie down until Mother is up, if you don't mind. There is a thunderstorm going on in my head."

"Actually," Colin said, "I'd like to talk to you for a moment." He preferred to have this conversation alone, so this was the perfect opportunity.

"What is it?" Harthorne asked, plopping back into the chair and burying his head in his hands.

"I think you need to be much more selective in choosing the next lady you propose to, assuming you are going to seek another bride."

Harthorne raised his head enough to glance at Colin. "I was hoping Lady Mary would change her mind about not wanting to marry me."

Colin snorted. "This is exactly why you need to listen to me."

"Says the man who has never for one second in his life contemplated marriage."

Colin wasn't quite ready to tell Harthorne about the predicament his father's will had put him in, so he ignored the barb and said, "I've contemplated ladies' duplicitous natures plenty, and I've plenty of personal examples of how coldhearted women truly are and a sterling example of the folly of ever allowing yourself to fall in love with a woman."

"Your father." Harthorne was sitting straight in his chair now, though his skin did hold a definite green tinge.

"I don't want to see you end up like him."

Harthorne took a long breath and winced as if it hurt him. "I hope I don't offend you when I say this, but not all women are like your mother. They are not all calculating creatures who will throw love over for money or pleasure or—"

"Simply because they are cruel," Colin said, thinking now of only his mother and what she had incomprehensibly done to his father.

"Yes. And simply to be cruel."

The note of pity that tinged Harthorne's voice made Colin stiffen in his chair. He never talked about his family life, and this was exactly why. It made him feel shame, and up until recently, he'd been supremely good at avoiding the emotion.

"Name one woman you know who isn't calculating," Colin said.

"My mother," Harthorne replied with a triumphant grin.

Colin waved a dismissive hand. "Your mother does not count."

"And why not?"

"Because you are blind when it comes to your mother." As well Harthorne should be. Most mothers showed their children love and affection, so the children forever thought them perfect, even when the youths grew into adults that should know better.

"I won't bother arguing the point about my mother," Harthorne said, "because I know I would never convince you otherwise."

"How very astute of you," Colin said. "Are you willing to concede that you cannot name a woman?"

"Absolutely not. Give me a minute."

Harthorne pressed his fingers to his temples, but by his ever-whitening pallor, Colin couldn't decide if his friend was really trying to think or was trying to rub away the pounding in his head.

"My sister," he finally said. "There is not a conniving bone in her body."

"You cannot name your sister," Colin said, trying to block out the memory of how luscious she looked with her hair tumbling around her shoulders. "You are biased to her, as well."

"The devil I am. That little minx has driven me crazy my entire life with her mischievous ways and dreamy head. I'd be the last person in England to be biased about Amelia."

"Because you look as if you are about to keel over, I won't argue with you about your sister—for now—but I guarantee you if your sister had a dozen beaus who offered her marriage she would pick the lord with the greatest title and wealth."

"Your words just prove you don't know my sister in the slightest," Harthorne said, standing. "I've got to take my leave, Aversley. I feel certain I'm about to lose the little bit of food left in my stomach."

With that, Harthorne dashed out of the dining room, leaving Colin with nothing but his thoughts, which devil take it, were firmly stuck on Lady Amelia—the way she had hidden in the library to make sure her brother was all right, her complimenting the fact that Colin was smart enough not to give women false hope, the way she looked in her night rail, the lovely craziness of her luxurious hair, and the way she slouched in an obvious attempt to appear shorter.

Groaning at his inability to get the woman out of his thoughts, he stood and made his way outside, determined to practice with his rapier until he was too tired to think about Lady Amelia, his mother, and most especially himself.

Chapter Eight

While sitting beside Constance on a picnic blanket, Amelia watched Lady Georgiana and Charles stroll arm in arm around the perimeter of the lake. They curved around the far corner near the woods and headed back toward the group of forgotten picnickers, which Amelia was unfortunately among. Amelia sighed and turned away from the noisy conversations of the ladies on the blanket to her left and glanced at Constance. Her friend was staring at her husband, with the besotted look of a new bride, as he stood some five feet away with the other gentlemen.

Amelia nudged Constance's side. "I vow I never thought I would say this, but I have to do something to get Charles's attention. At this rate, he will ask Lady Georgiana to marry him before he even thinks to consider me."

Constance frowned. "Perhaps Lord Worthington is not your true love."

Of course Charles was her true love. But he certainly was taking his time realizing it. *Shouldn't he instinctually feel it*, an inner voice whispered. She'd been hopelessly in love with Charles for years; now was not the time to give up.

"You are not being helpful. I have loved Charles since the day he rescued me from certain death. You remember. My brother's stallion took off with me on it and Charles—"

"I remember," Constance interrupted. "Lord Worthington helped you."

"Helped me?" Amelia frowned. That was not at all how she would phrase it. *Because Constance is right* Amelia's annoying inner voice said. She gritted her teeth. She was only doubting Charles because she was doubting herself. "That is not the way I see it." Amelia stared at Constance, waiting for her agreement. Her friend opened her mouth, gave a little shake of her head, and snapped her mouth shut once again.

"What is it?" Amelia asked. Having known Constance her entire life, she knew her friend was usually not one to voice her opinions.

"Truthfully?"

The question reminded Amelia of earlier when she had asked the duke to be truthful. A picture of the sinfully handsome man filled her head. Why ever was she thinking of him now? She shoved the thought away. "Truthfully, *of course.*"

"And you won't be upset?"

"Egads! Since you've said that I'm now naturally worried." Amelia pressed a hand to her stomach to quell the butterflies. "Tell me anyway though. Remember we swore to always be truthful with each other."

"No matter the pain," Constance said with a nod. She sighed. "Very well. I think..." she said, dropping her voice low even though the nearest blanket was a foot away and the talk loud and lively. "That is...What I want to say is perhaps your memories of that day Lord Worthington helped you on the stallion have been exaggerated by your mind and the way you feel about him."

Amelia did not like where this conversation was going, especially because she had wondered this same thing before, but that had been more of her not believing in herself. Hadn't it?

She swallowed. "Exaggerated in what way?" she said quietly.

Constance picked nervously at her dress, until Amelia reached over and stilled her friend's hand. "Go on."

"As I remember it, the stallion ran off and raced beside Lord Worthington, spooking his horse, which in turn ran after yours in more of a panic than pursuit."

"Nonsense," Amelia grumbled, even as she quickly searched her memory. She was quite sure she was correct. "Charles came after me to save me. If it weren't for him I would have fallen and broken my neck."

Constance compressed her lips for a moment before taking a deep breath. "You saved *him*. His horse galloped after you in a fright and when he passed you and nearly collided with a tree limb, you yelled for him to duck. Both of you did so, and he flailed his arms out, nearly knocking you off your horse! You are nimble, always have been. You landed on your feet, and he landed beside you."

"That's not the way it happened at all," Amelia retorted, her heart pounding. Could she have twisted the memory so much? How pathetic and lonely, if so. "I do not love him based solely on one day. He has always had a ready smile for me, treated me with kindness, sought me out to talk to at various social occasions."

"Because you are intelligent and interesting, Amelia."

Amelia smiled. "You have just proved my point. If he cared to simply be with a lady because she was pretty, he would never bother to talk to me. And he is my champion." She had gotten that notion right out of her favorite novel. "If it was not for him everyone would still be calling me Tree Trunk."

Constance groaned. "Amelia, I swear you are either blind or you simply do not see what anyone else does when they look at you."

"You are my best friend," Amelia said. "You are naturally biased. I am gangly and far too tall for a woman, and if Charles had not demanded they quit calling me Tree Trunk, the name would still haunt me."

"I refuse to argue," Constance said, though her stern tone suggested differently. "Charles only demanded it because I called him a weak follower."

Constance's words were like a slap across the face. "You did?"

"Yes. I'm sorry I did not tell you sooner. Honestly, I thought you would grow out of this childhood obsession with him. He is not a hero from one of your books, Amelia."

"Well, of course he isn't," Amelia said, a trifle irritated. He was too good to be a hero. The heroes in her books always had wicked streaks that had to be tamed or demons that had to be destroyed, and only the perfect woman, the heroine, could help the hero do it. The Duke of Aversley could definitely be a hero. All he needed was the right heroine to come along. Appalled with her straying thoughts, she cringed.

"Are you terribly upset with me?" Constance whispered. "You're flushed."

She was upset with herself. Reaching out, she patted her friend's hand. "No. Just thinking." Her pulse dipped right along with her stomach. If she had misconstrued that Charles had tried to save her and then come to her rescue out of love, then her love for him was based on a lie. Maybe he would never love her. *Impossible.* Charles was the only man who had ever done anything chivalrous for her in her entire life. "He kissed me that day he saved me. Did I ever tell you that?"

"No. Where was the kiss?" Constance asked.

"My right cheek."

"Amelia de Vere, I cannot believe you withheld such important information all these years."

The kiss had been so special to her she had wanted to keep it her secret. "You didn't tell me of your first kiss with your husband."

"You've got a point," Constance said. "And I hate to say this, because in my heart I honestly don't feel Lord Worthington is for you, but he does seem to watch you in a special way. And the kiss changes everything! Still, there is something else you should know."

The grave tone of Constance's voice made Amelia's stomach clench. "What is it?" she whispered.

"Lord Worthington is going to London for the Season. He told Steven so."

Amelia felt as if her heart were suddenly beating entirely too fast. It had to be true if Charles had told Constance's husband, as they were good friends. Amelia bit down on her lip and found the object of her desire strolling directly toward them with Lady Georgiana still on his arm. Charles looked especially handsome today in his navy-blue jacket and dark buckskins. His brown hair was a bit short for her taste, but it did serve to display his nice strong jaw to advantage. From where she sat, she could not see his coffee-colored eyes, but that cocoa color was forever committed to her memory.

She should be in London for the Season, but they could not afford it, not that she had minded missing the Season one bit—until this very moment. He'd probably meet a nice, short lady there, a Marianne. "This is awful news. At least Georgiana is not going to London."

"But she is," Constance said.

Amelia whipped her gaze to her friend. "Whatever do you mean? She told us specifically she was not allowed to have her Season until her eldest sister was betrothed."

"Elspeth was betrothed yesterday."

"But there isn't enough time for Georgiana to have gowns made for the Season." Amelia knew her voice was too loud, her tone too high, but she was upset.

Constance shrugged. "You know as well as I that Georgiana's family can spare every expense. Likely they will pay to rush the gowns. She leaves next week. Rumor has it that her father wishes her to find a husband by the end of the Season."

Amelia trailed her gaze to Charles. He threw his head back and laughed at something Georgiana said. Her stomach turned and twisted, making her feel sick. "When did Charles decide he was going to London?"

Constance's hand closed over Amelia's and squeezed. "Yesterday. Steven said he made up his mind to go yesterday, after he learned Georgiana was going." Constance pressed her lips near Amelia's ear. "Steven says Charles must marry for money."

"That's his mother's doing, I'm sure of it," Amelia grumbled. "Look at Georgiana."

Amelia continued to stare at the lady and didn't bother to see if Constance had obliged her request to glance that way. Georgiana had on a gown of fine mint silk. On her head was a beautiful hat, perched perfectly to display her lovely hair, which was atop her head in a perfect chignon with the exact right amount of tendrils hanging around her peaches-and-cream heart-shaped face. Amelia raised her trembling hand to her own disheveled hair then self-consciously ran a smoothing hand over her ugly brown riding habit. She may not be able to compete with tiny Georgiana on appearances, but she doubted Georgiana had ever read an entire book in her life. The thought made Amelia feel good for a moment until she felt snide, blasted scruples. Georgiana was a beautiful flower with the perfect petals of adornment. Amelia's throat tightened. *She* wasn't even a flower. More like a long weed.

The need to leave rose up so strongly she felt as if she would choke, but she refused to scamper away defeated. "I have to make Charles remember he wants me, an Elinor."

"Who?"

"Never mind," Amelia hurriedly replied, knowing Constance would chide her for being silly. "He thinks he must settle for fluff and feathers in a woman's head to please his mother, but he would hate that sort of wife. I know him. He needs a wife whose head is filled with interesting information because he is so intelligent. I need to make him remember this. Or realize it, though honestly I think deep down he knows."

"You are babbling, but I think I'm following. What is your plan?"

Amelia scanned the picnic area. There were flowering bushes, large beautiful trees with low-hanging branches and winding pebbled paths. Nothing she could use to her advantage. "I cannot think of a thing. Can you?"

Before Constance could answer, Georgiana clapped her hands together. "Time for the games! Everyone get a partner!"

A swirl of activity commenced at once, and within seconds, Amelia found herself standing without a partner while everyone else had paired up. She caught herself glancing uneasily around the group, hoping she had missed someone. Her gaze locked with Georgiana's and the lady offered a venom-tinged smile.

"Poor Lady Amelia. It seems you are without a companion. I must have counted wrong when making my guest list. I could have sworn I had an even number." Georgiana twined her arm through Charles's and beamed up at him before focusing back on Amelia.

Since it wasn't likely the ground would crack open and mercifully swallow her inside, Amelia straightened her spine, a thing she rarely did since she was tall enough without doing so, and met Georgiana's smirk. "That's quite all right, Lady Georgiana. Counting can be so very tedious for some people. I can play the games by myself."

"Amelia, no!" Constance blurted and moved toward Amelia and away from her husband.

"I have to concur," Charles said, stepping toward her and bringing the clinging Lady Georgiana with him. It won't do at all for you to have no partner." He gazed at Georgiana. "You don't mind if Lady Amelia joins us, do you?"

"If she must," Georgiana said with a brittle smile and cool tone.

Amelia clamped her teeth down on the hot words scorching her tongue. Georgiana had obviously planned to humiliate her. Smiling so wide her cheeks quivered, she inclined her head to Charles. "Thank you for being so generous, Lord Worthington."

"Not at all," he replied while extending his free elbow to her.

Elation welled within her as she linked her hand around his arm. The group moved toward the lake where the games were set up under a large cluster of trees. As they walked, chattering commenced around Amelia, and

Georgiana prattled some nonsense about the weather to Charles. Amelia could have been strolling in the clouds for as light as her feet felt. Charles had come to her rescue once again, or was it for the first time? Blast Constance for making her unsure. Whichever it was, Charles was noble, kind, and he clearly cared for her. Fat little Constance knew.

"Lord Worthington," Amelia said, interrupting Georgiana's complaining about the heat and the effect it had on her hair.

"Yes, Lady Amelia?"

"I want to thank you for coming to my rescue."

"Think nothing of it," he replied. His arm suddenly pulled inward having the effect of pressing her hand firmly to his side. A little thrill coursed through her. He wanted to be closer to her, but secretly. That was perfectly understandable, given the circumstances. From under her lashes, she gazed sideways at him, half expecting to find him looking slyly at her, or with a glint in his eye like the duke had, but Charles's gaze was focused on Georgiana.

Irritated at herself for the twinge of disappointment, for her once again straying thoughts to the duke, and for Charles's continued attentions to Georgiana, Amelia concentrated on the positive. She would have the next hour to remind him of his heart and to capture his attention and get him to look past her exterior—as her mother had put it. She eyed the hoops ahead in the distance. She was good at this game.

"Are we playing hoops, Lady Georgiana?" she asked as they neared the lake.

"How very astute of you," Georgiana replied.

"Lady Georgiana," Charles said in a chiding tone.

Amelia tried to stop the smile that spread across her face, but really, it was hopeless. Maybe she would not have to worry about Georgiana, after all. The woman was so mean spirited. Surely, Charles would see it.

As they turned onto the narrow dirt path that would take them around the lake to the trees they would play under, Charles moved ahead. "I'll go first to make sure it's not slippery."

Amelia nodded and expected Georgiana to move behind Charles and force Amelia to the rear of the line. The three of them trailed a good distance behind everyone else, and she could not imagine Georgina being willing to be last at anything. Instead, the woman surprised her by indicating, with a wave of her hand, that Amelia should fall into step behind Charles. She glanced at Georgiana, sure she must be up to something, but all Amelia got in response was a false smile.

The pebbly path was rather slippery, undoubtedly due to the rain of the night before. Amelia slowly picked her way across the stones, each sharp rock digging into her rather worn kid boots. Wincing, she slowed her steps and fell even further behind Charles. Georgiana, on the other hand, was so close to Amelia that she was assaulting her ears with her tsking and sighing. Was she trying to rush her? Make her trip and look a fool?

Amelia scowled. "Please don't walk so close."

"Do you swim, Lady Amelia?"

"Of course." Amelia wrinkled her brow. What an odd question. Unless— Her heartbeat galloped ahead like a racehorse coming out of the gate. She glanced to her left at the dark, murky pond water. "Don't you dare—"

With a hard shove into her back, her warning words were lost as she bit down on her tongue and tumbled sideways into the pond. Cold water hit her skin, causing her to gasp and let out an outraged cry just before the heavy weight of her riding habit dragged her under the surface.

Instantly, her vision clouded and her lungs screamed for release as she clawed her way back toward the glimmering sunshine above. Suddenly, fingers clamped like a vise around her arms and jerked her upright, bringing her out from underneath the water to the glorious sunlight and fresh air. She gulped in greedy breaths, caught between a haze of panic and relief. The smell of fish and mud clogged her nose and grit filled her mouth. She barely resisted the urge to spit, but her body heaved in protest.

"Stand up, for pity's sake," a hard voice said in her ear.

"Stand up?" she sputtered, kicking out wildly.

"Ouch!" Charles barked as she felt herself being hauled even farther up and then plunked downward.

Her boots sunk into squishy mud. With shaking hands, she wiped the water and muck out of her eyes. When she opened them, she almost wished she hadn't. Everyone, including Charles, was staring at her with either gaping mouths or embarrassed smiles. Everyone except for Georgiana. She gave Amelia a cold look of contempt.

"You poor dear," Georgiana purred, placing her hand on Charles's shoulder as he knelt at the edge of the pond embankment. "You tripped. I tried to stop your fall, but you're much bigger than I am."

Standing on shaking legs, Amelia looked from Charles's tight face to Georgiana's now smiling one. Amelia had the urge to dunk under the water, but that was no escape. She forced her shoulders back and prayed she did not look as undignified as she felt. It was useless to accuse Georgiana of pushing her. It would only serve to draw more attention and make her look foolish, as if she was trying to falsely blame the host.

Charles thrust a hand out to her. "Grasp my hand, and I'll pull you out."

As some creature—*please God, a fish*—brushed her leg, she disposed of her mortification and quickly complied. After a moment of grunting and struggling on Charles's part as he tried to pull her out to no avail, Constance's husband came over and grasped Amelia's other hand.

Constance peered over the edge of the pond, her nose wrinkled with worry. "They'll get you out Amelia. It's the weight of your skirts that is making it difficult."

Constance was only trying to make it better, Amelia knew, but despite the cool water soaking her to the bone, the heat of her embarrassment burned her skin. "Yes, I know," she forced herself to answer in as cheerful a tone as possible, though every doubt she possessed had wrapped itself around her like a tight, merciless vise.

With one great tug, the men lifted her out of the water and onto the embankment, a soggy, dirty mess. A few of the women giggled behind their fans, and the men shifted from foot to foot, looking as if they would rather be anywhere else than staring at her. She felt the same way about the anywhere else part.

Georgiana did not spare her a glance as she turned away. "Well, now that Lady Amelia is rescued, let's proceed to the hoops."

With amused backward glances and snickers, everyone in the picnic party except Constance, her husband, and Charles, followed Georgiana away from Amelia. She glanced down at her dripping, muddy gown and sighed. On the bright side, she would never have to wear the tragically ugly riding habit again. Of course, they could not afford another, so there was that problem to consider, but she would face that another day.

"Are you all right?" Charles asked, gripping her elbow.

"Yes," she quickly replied, since being mortified to the bone did not count for being hurt. Not physically, anyway. She gathered a handful of her sopping, wet skirt in her hands and twisted it gently. Water immediately splashed the ground near her feet. "I suppose I better go home since I am soaked." She glanced hopefully at Charles. This would be the perfect opportunity for him to be gallant and offer to accompany her. Or better yet, say she should not go, then she could explain she had to, and then he would offer to go with her.

Amelia's stomach fluttered as he looked over his shoulder toward the picnickers and then back at her. "Lady Amelia, I—"

"Lord Worthington!" Georgiana's voice rang in Amelia's ears. The woman sounded like a frantic goose squawking to get attention. Amelia gritted her teeth.

"Lord Worthington, come quickly! I need you as my partner."

Charles's face tightened as he looked at Amelia. Her stomach constricted in response. He was going to go. She knew it. He was not going to offer to go with her. She was not one of the heroines in her novel any more than he was a troubled hero. If she wanted a happily ever after it was up to her to make it happen.

"I better get back to the picnic." He cleared his throat. "Will you be all right to return home alone?"

Amelia nodded, a lump of disappointment making it entirely impossible to answer without sounding hurt.

"She won't be alone," Constance said, stepping near Amelia and twining her arm through hers. "Steven and I will go with you."

Lord Lindley furrowed his brow. "We will?"

Amelia almost laughed when Constance gave her husband a murderous look. Constance's heart-shaped face made it almost impossible for her to appear angry.

"Yes, yes," her husband quickly amended. "Of course we're going.

Amelia shook her head. "You two stay and enjoy the picnic. I'm fine, really, and the Duke of Aversley's coachman will see me home safely."

Charles—who had already taken three steps away from Amelia and toward the awaiting picnickers—swiveled back around on his heel, his brows raised. "Did you say the Duke of Aversley's coachman is waiting for you?"

"I did," she replied. Why was Charles looking at her so oddly? "His Grace is a school chum of my brother's, and he came for the wedding."

"I know Aversley," Charles said, his voice holding a curiously flat tone. "I may have been a year behind your brother and the duke at school, but everyone who attended Cambridge knew Aversley's reputation with the ladies."

Amelia frowned. "I would not have thought you to be the type of person to put any stock in malicious gossip." She didn't know why, but she felt inclined to defend the duke since he had helped her brother and Constance.

Charles scowled. "I put no credit in gossip, Lady Amelia. Aversley and I used to be friends. I know the man personally and what he is capable of."

"Used to be? Did he do something to offend you?"

"Nothing I'd like to discuss," Charles said, his tone hard and unwavering. "What is Aversley doing here?"

"As I said, Philip invited him to come and stay with us for the wedding."

"*With you?* Aversley is staying at your home?"

Amelia smiled, scarcely controlling her desire to grin. Charles sounded almost jealous. The Duke of Aversley was not the least bit interested in her, but Charles did not need to know that. She batted her eyelashes, hoping she looked flirtatious and not as if an insect had flown in her eye. "Really, Lord Worthington, you almost sound jealous."

"I'm not," he growled, but his gaze stayed firmly on her. "Your brother's wedding is not even going forward."

Amelia shrugged. "Yes, but the duke did not know that."

"Well, now he surely does," Charles snapped. "I'm going to speak to your brother and—"

"Lord Worthington!" Georgiana called in a high, grating voice.

Amelia glanced over Charles's shoulder and grimaced. Georgiana strode their way, her jaw thrust forward in determination. Amelia turned her attention back to Charles, hoping he would finish what he had been about to say. "You were saying?"

He shook his head. "Never mind. I'd better go. Good day to you, Lady Amelia."

"Wait!" Amelia called, a nervous pressure exploding inside her chest. "Will you be at the dance in two night's time?"

Before Charles could answer, Georgiana came up beside him and smiled up at him before leveling Amelia with a glacial stare. "Of course he will, silly. He has already asked for my first and last dance."

"I see," Amelia forced out, trying to keep her voice light but steady. "How lovely for you. I'll see you both then." Anger and hurt bubbled inside of her. Clearly, it was going to take a bit more doing to show Charles the way to her and away from Miss Fluff and Nonsense. "I better be going home now," she chirped, though her voice sounded brittle to her ears.

She swiveled away, desperate to get to the coach before she did something rash like stay, sopping-wet gown and all. She had a mighty urge to shove Georgiana into the lake, too, and she was not all certain she could control herself if provoked further. As she strode toward the carriage, footsteps rustled behind her in the grass and then a hand touched her shoulder.

"Amelia," Constance murmured. "Are you all right?"

"Perfectly. Of course, I'd like to slap Georgiana and smack Charles upside the head for acting so dull witted when I know he's not, but other than that I feel perfectly well. Why do you ask?"

"You are headed away from the carriages."

If it were possible to make something come true simply by wishing it, then at this moment Amelia would disappear and reappear at her home away from the embarrassment of having to turn around and march back past everyone. Since that was pure and simple desperate hopefulness on her part, she, for once in her life forced herself to her full height, drew back her shoulders, notched up her chin, and strolled as gracefully as she could back in the direction she had just come. As she passed Charles and a smirking Georgiana, Amelia recalled something her mother had once said to her. If someone laughed at you, the best thing to do was to laugh with them. She offered Charles the largest smile her unwilling cheeks would muster.

"Just drying off a bit." She waved her arms up and down while piercing Georgiana with an accusing look. "There," she said, turning her gaze back to Charles. "Dry enough to leave now, I do believe." Without waiting for a response, she strolled purposefully away—in the right direction this time—and turned her attention to the problem of Charles. There was no time to waste. The problem was the annoying voice in her head that kept interrupting her thoughts about how to get Charles to remember he wanted an intelligent woman for a wife. That blasted voice! It kept asking why she should have to help Charles remember anything. If it was his mother swaying his mind, should he not be man enough to stand up to her for Amelia? Was that asking too much?

As she neared the Duke of Aversley's coach, she was no closer to answers regarding Charles than before and she had to push the problem away for another moment or else she would babble nonsense to the duke's coachman, who was reclining in his seat with his feet propped up, and that would not do at all.

"I hate to interrupt you," she called to the man who had his face turned to the sun and eyes closed, "but I wish to depart now."

The coachman's eyes flew open, and he scrambled to sit up. "My lady, is the picnic already over?"

She shook her head. "No, but I need to return home."

The coachman was by her side startlingly fast. He offered his hand to help her up the steps. "I did not realize swimming was part of your plan today," he said in a gentle voice.

"I did not realize it, either," she said.

Once the carriage was underway, Amelia wrapped her arms around her waist to ward off the slight chill her damp clothes were causing. Her time was ticking away with Charles. Soon he'd be gone to London, and then he'd likely be lost to her forever. The painful fact seemed to be that he was apparently lured by the pretty picture Georgiana presented. Amelia rubbed her arms as she shivered. She could not recall having the opportunity to speak to Charles like she used to about books in the last five months. If she could create that opportunity, she was sure he would realize he needed an intelligent wife and not that nitwit Georgiana.

Chapter Nine

"That's odd," Harthorne said, rising from the iron bench where he had only just sat and heading to the edge of the balcony.

Colin frowned and stood, certain Harthorne was trying to come up with some excuse not to finally continue the conversation they had started earlier about marriage. After waiting around for a good part of the morning for Harthorne to come back downstairs, Colin was not in the best of moods.

He was famished. They had no cook at this house, and he had no idea how to prepare a thing, but even if he had, it was not as if he would rummage in the family's kitchen. On top of his growling stomach, he could not quit thinking about the way Lady Amelia had looked with her hair tumbling over her shoulders. It was blasted frustrating, especially given he was usually in such control of his thoughts.

Presently, all he wanted to do was convince Harthorne to take an immediate loan from him with an indefinite payback date, change his friend's mind about the need to marry, and then depart for London with a stop at a nice inn for a hearty lunch.

Colin strode to the bottom of the long steps that led up to the front of the house and followed Harthorne's gaze to the stables. Frowning, he raised a hand to shield his eyes from the glare of the sun and surveyed his carriage coming down the drive.

"I told Barnes to wait at the picnic for your sister."

"I thought that's what you said."

Harthorne strode across the grass toward the stone path that followed the line of bright green bushes.

Colin caught up with his friend at the stone path. "You don't suppose anything is wrong?"

"That's exactly what I suppose. Amelia would not leave the picnic early unless something was amiss."

Colin's chest tightened oddly. "Perhaps she told Barnes not to wait."

"No." Harthorne shook his head and pointed ahead of him. "There she is."

"What the devil?" Colin studied Lady Amelia as she descended the steps of his carriage. Her hair was still down but did not appear to look the same from this distance. He could not yet make out the expression on her face, but a quick scan of her body showed no apparent injuries. Her skirts hung oddly as if plastered to her legs, and as they drew closer, he realized her skirts did cling to her legs. "She's wet."

"Yes." Harthorne's voice held a note of distraction.

As Harthorne picked up his pace to reach his sister faster, Colin slowed his own steps to allow them privacy, but his gaze locked on her face. She looked burning mad with her hands on her hips and her eyes narrowed and blazing with anger. She also looked beautiful. Perhaps it was the way her hair was swept back to reveal the slope of her high cheekbones. Definite, undeniable lust stirred in his veins.

He held back for the space of another breath before closing the remaining distance and standing in front of her. It took all his concentration not to allow his gaze to remain on the swell of her pert full breasts to which the wet material of her riding habit clung. She definitely did not resemble a boy now. She gazed at him from under hooded lashes for a moment before looking away. He wanted to ask her what had happened, but he doubted she'd be willing to share with him.

Maybe Barnes knew something. Colin inclined his head to Lady Amelia and Harthorne. "I'll give you two a moment of privacy," he said, moving toward his carriage where Barnes was unhooking the horses. "What happened, Barnes?" Colin demanded as the coachman worked to untether the horses.

Barnes halted in his task and turned to face Colin. "Do you want the version the lady told me or the one I saw with my own two eyes? I crept through the woods and spied on the lady as you told me to do."

With a grin, Colin clamped his coachman on the shoulder. "The one you saw, of course."

"Lady Amelia was pushed into the lake by another lady. From the side and rather slyly."

"Pushed?" Colin rubbed the whiskers on his chin, belatedly realizing he had not shaved in two days, and trailed his gaze to Lady Amelia. She was waving her hands in the air as she talked to Harthorne. "Why would a lady push another into a lake?" Colin asked, more to himself than his coachman.

Barnes leaned close. "I do believe it was over a gentleman."

That figured. "Did you recognize the gentleman?"

"Yes, Your Grace. It's Lord Worthington."

"Worthington?" By God, Colin had forgotten Worthington was from Norfolk. Probably because he had striven to forget Worthington, his accusations, and his anger since the accusations were partially true. His hatred of the man he had made himself into welled within him. So Lady Amelia thought she wanted to catch Worthington…?

Colin glanced at her in time to see her turn from her brother and stalk away. Five steps into her departure, she stopped and cried out, bending down toward her foot. She came up hopping, one leg slightly raised. "Oh," she groaned as Colin reached her right side while her brother was on her left. She gripped her brother's arm.

"What is it?" Harthorne asked. "Did you twist your ankle?"

"No. I've a stone lodged in the soul of my kid boots."

"May I?" Colin waved a hand toward her foot.

"No, no." Her cheeks turned a brilliant shade of red. "That won't be necessary. Philip can help me to the house."

"Don't be ridiculous," Harthorne grumbled. "You are not hobbling all the way to the house. Aversley is not a delicate flower. Are you, Aversley?"

"Not the last time I checked." Colin kneeled down and held out his hand for Lady Amelia to hold out her foot.

"I don't suppose this day can get any worse or more embarrassing," Lady Amelia mumbled under her breath.

"I would not say that," Colin replied as he struggled not to slide his hand up her delicate ankle to her inviting slender calve. "Whenever I've declared a day cannot get worse it invariably does." With determination, he focused his gaze on the sole of her shoe, which was in a sad, threadbare state. Damnation. If it was the last thing he did, he was going to get Harthorne to borrow some money from him. Better yet, if he could think of a way to give it to his friend and make it not seem a gift, so Harthorne would take it, Colin would. He gripped the stone lodged in Lady Amelia's shoe and yanked it out before gently setting her foot down. As he released her ankle, his fingers brushed across her silken skin.

When he raised his gaze, he found her staring at him, mouth parted slightly and eyes wide. Heat rose in his body. Clenching his teeth at the reaction, he rose and held the stone out to her. "I believe this is yours."

"Yes, it's my favorite stone. Silly of me to try to keep it there," she said with a laugh that made him smile in return.

"I fear the stone left a hole in your boot. You may want to get rid of that pair."

She bit her lip, confirming his suspicion that it was likely her only pair. Releasing her bother's arm, she shook out her skirts and raised a hand to her half-dry hair, a frown tugging at her lips. "I must look a fright. I'll go make myself presentable."

"You look lovely," Colin said, meaning it. He couldn't believe he had not recognized her beauty right away. Here in the bright sunlight there was no denying her exquisite bone structure.

"I do believe your eyesight must be deteriorating, Your Grace," she said, turning to leave.

"I see perfectly," he said to her back and chuckled when she faltered in her step but then continued on.

He turned to find Harthorne studying him. "What?" Colin demanded, feeling as if he had just been caught flirting like a school boy with Harthorne's sister, yet Harthorne's face held an inquisitive look, not an angry one.

"You're slipping, Aversley."

"I don't have any idea what you mean," Colin snapped, though he suspected it had to do with Lady Amelia.

Harthorne grinned. "You just showed your kind side to my sister. Your act as a cold-hearted duke is slipping."

"It's not an act," Colin replied. "My heart is cold, but my bed is warm."

"I see you're back to your performance, but I suspect the play of the Tortured Duke will end soon. I see flaws in the script, and I know you do to. And eventually a woman—probably one exactly like my sister—is going to come along and sweep you away and make you want to step out of that role you have embraced for so long and take on a new one of the Besotted Fool and eventually the Worshipful Husband."

Colin scowled. He was going to have to be a husband thanks to his father, but he'd never be besotted or loving. Loyal, yes. Besotted, no. "It's entirely too bad you were born a lord, Harthorne, and have lands to be tended and women to be fed. You and all your sappy thoughts are much more suited to the life of a poet."

"For once, I could not agree more. But then, we all have obligations that dictate our lives, don't we?"

Colin immediately thought of his father's damned will, which he did not want to discuss right now.

"What happened to your sister?" he asked, wishing to hear the details and to turn the subject. "She looked livid."

"Oh, she is. She says Lady Georgiana shoved her in the lake at the picnic and then pretended she had not. It seems the two of them both have their hearts set on catching Worthington, and Amelia is fuming that Worthington—in her words—is acting like a puppet, allowing his mother to pull his strings and forgetting that he is better suited to have a wife with brains than a lovely face."

"All men are fools," Colin replied. "Worthington more than others. And apparently he is blind if he does not see how lovely your sister is."

"You are slipping again, Aversley. Before long, everyone will know you for a good man like I do."

The muscles in Colin's neck bunched under Harthorne's words and not-so-hidden scrutiny.

"You know," Harthorne said, "we could pay Worthington a visit. Perhaps the two of you could clear the tension between you."

"I'd rather have my eyes gouged by a vulture."

"That's harsh," Harthorne said. "He may be more inclined to believe you now than he was when we were all foolish young Cambridge men."

"I was never foolish or young, and I doubt Worthington would be more apt to believe me now. Besides, he was correct in his accusations, so there is nothing left to say. I'm not a good man. I've told you that for years."

Harthorne stopped walking toward the house and faced Colin. "The simple fact that you say you are not decent makes you so. I know you never slept with Lady Eleanor, as Worthington accused you."

"I did sleep with her," Colin said, rubbing the back of his neck where his muscles were twitching. "But when I realized she was the lady that Worthington cared for, I immediately put a stop to our affair."

Harthorne gripped Colin on the shoulder. "Still. You did not know he cared for her, and it's not your fault she fancied you over him."

Colin laughed. "She fancied whoever had the most blunt and best position in Society to offer her. When she realized I was offering nothing but a temporary spot in my bed, she no longer fancied me. Unfortunately for Worthington, I learned she was also sleeping with another fellow at the same time as she was warming my bed, and magically, he quickly took my place in her heart. Worthington never stood a chance with her."

Harthorne suddenly stopped, and Colin realized they stood in the threshold to the dining room. Dare he hope they were going to be fed?

Harthorne motioned to a chair. "Our cook's mother took ill, and being the only servant left in my employment we have had to make due for the last week."

Colin nodded, not sure whether he believed his friend still employed a cook at all, but prying and embarrassing him was out of the question. "Has your Mother been doing the cooking?"

Harthorne frowned. "Amelia mostly. She can cook eggs. Cook taught her the night before she left. To see to her mother," he added hastily, almost as if an afterthought.

At the sound of pans being clanked together in the kitchen, Colin asked, "Your sister?"

"Undoubtedly. She is just as graceless in the kitchen as she is everywhere else. Yet somehow, her eggs turn out delicious."

Colin leaned back in his chair and crossed his ankle over his leg. "I want you to take a loan from me."

"No," Harthorne replied, his tone dark, his face even darker.

Colin had expected this, so he was prepared to argue his case. He leaned forward and rested his elbows on the table. "Listen to me. You cannot even afford to buy your sister a pair of kid boots that do not have holes in them. How will you afford to keep the estate running and pay your debts until your crops are ready to be sold?"

"I'll afford it somehow," Harthorne snapped. "I don't want to hear another word about you loaning me money. If you cannot abide my wishes I'll consider that your way of telling me you no longer want to be friends."

Colin locked gazes with Harthorne, positive his friend was recalling, as Colin was, the time years ago on the boat at Colin's birthday when Colin had uttered similar words, except his had been in reference to Harthorne never mentioning Scarsdale's name to Colin again. Harthorne had abided Colin's wishes, but this was different. Harthorne needed help.

His friend was a stubborn and proud man. It was something to be both pitied and admired. Leaning back, Colin sighed and rested one ankle over the other as he thought. This tactic wasn't going to work. Harthorne would never take money from him, no matter the terms. He had to find a way to make Harthorne think he was not taking the money for himself. "I have something else to say."

Harthorne raised his eyebrows. "Is this another lecture regarding Lady Mary?"

"Does it need to be?" Colin inquired, praying his friend had come to his senses about Lady Mary.

"No. I decided while I rested that I don't want a woman for my wife who prefers money to love."

"Then you should not take a wife," Colin replied with a scowl. "All women prefer money to love. Or at least women who think they can capture a man with plenty of blunt."

"No," Harthorne growled. "You're wrong. My mother married for love. My sister will marry for love."

Anger flared through Colin at Harthorne's willful ignorance. If his friend kept this line of thinking, it was going to be all too easy for a woman to wield power over him. "Your sister cannot afford to marry for love. Damnation, man, do you even have a dowry for her?"

Harthorne grew still, and a twitch started at the right side of his temple. After a moment, he rubbed it while shaking his head. "No. Devil take it. Nor can I afford to send her to London for a Season so she can chase after Worthington and win him over. He'll likely marry Lady Georgiana and then Amelia will be heartbroken. She thinks she loves Worthington and has thought so since she was eight. Silly girl would pick him even if—"

Harthorne tugged a hand through his hair, his gaze settling firmly on Colin. "—even if you offered for her."

Colin's mind raced at the pronouncement, and like a flash of light the best plan came to him, all laid out nice and simple. He knew how he could help Harthorne. Quickly, he thought through the idea. If he could not convince Harthorne to borrow money, the way around it was the man's sister. Colin had to marry unless he wanted to be poor, and marrying a woman who fancied herself in love with another man, or who likely would end up showing she cared more about titles and money than love, after all, would be perfect.

Lady Amelia would not want any love from Colin in either circumstance, which suited him, since he didn't intend to ever love his wife. He was so pleased with himself for his idea that he wanted to pat himself on the back, but that would look rather odd.

Now, getting Harthorne to agree to his plan, which would provide Harthorne a great deal of money from Colin so his friend could pay off his debts was going to be the tricky part. He chose his words with precise care. This plan had to take an exact course. "I *could* marry your sister. I recently found out my father dictated in his will that I marry by a certain date or lose everything. You'd have one less mouth to feed, too, if I married Lady Amelia."

"Your father did what?"

Colin waved a negligent hand at Harthorne's shocked face, though he was positive he'd looked the same way when his mother had told him. "He left a will that states that if I'm not married by twenty-six I will be stripped off all the land that is not entailed, which as luck has it, would leave me destitute. If I marry your sister"—saying the word *marry* out loud really did make him feel ill, but he forged ahead—"I can meet the terms of my father's will and you can have one less person to worry about caring for."

"How generous of you, but as I said, she thinks she loves Worthington, so she'd never agree, and I'm not inclined to force her hand."

Predictable answer, Colin thought smugly. Harthorne was too soft and tender when it came to his sister and mother. "Then let me lend you some money to provide your sister the Season she so richly deserves."

"Absolutely not. I don't borrow money."

Colin almost grinned. This was like teaching his horse to jump fences. Creel had not wanted to leap the tall fence and had kept going around it. At least, he had until Colin had not given him anywhere to go but over the barrier. Carefully, Colin was leading Harthorne to the fence, and he was going to show the man that he had to jump it.

"If you won't borrow it, then let us make a wager." And there was the bait. Harthorne had never been one to pass up a wager, if he thought he could win.

Harthorne cocked his head. "What sort of wager?"

"I'll provide your family enough blunt to allow your sister to have a grand Season. And I will personally help give her the polish she needs to capture Worthington. I doubt she'll end up marrying him, because I propose that your sister is like all ladies, and that once she is transformed into a graceful beauty and realizes she can capture a gentleman with more worth than Worthington, she will forget all about him and turn her sights to greater prizes. If she does indeed become, shall we say, more concerned about blunt than love, then I win the bet and she marries me."

Colin almost grinned. He'd managed to find the solution to save Harthorne and if Harthorne happened to lose the wager Colin had in mind then Colin would have the perfect wife, without ever looking. If Colin somehow lost the wager he'd proposed, he doubted it would be too much of a hardship to find another suitable woman to be his loveless bride.

Harthorne studied Colin. "And if you lose and my sister remains determined to marry Worthington? What do I get?" Harthorne asked in a mildly interested voice.

"I will pay off all your debt."

Harthorne whistled. "All of it? That's quite a fortune, my friend."

"Then it's a good thing I have quite a fortune. I would pay ten times my worth to discover a woman who had a true heart, but sadly, I tell you I know I will win." Either way Colin would get what he wanted. If he lost he'd get to pay off Harthorne's debts to save his friend, and if he won, then he'd not have to bother searching for a wife who would not expect love because Lady Amelia would have shown herself to be the perfect candidate. Moreover, he would still be able to help Harthorne, as he would then be family.

Harthorne cocked an eyebrow. "If, and it is a big *if*, I agreed to this wager, I would only do so under the express conditions that the terms were laid out in writing and that it is stated clearly that if you won and married Amelia, you would not try to give me money to pay off my debts."

"I'd agree to those terms," Colin said smoothly. He'd simply give the money to Amelia and tell her to help her brother. He knew she would, too, by the love she had shown for Harthorne that night she'd hidden in the library. "Do we have a wager?"

Harthorne drummed the table with his fingers as he stared blankly down at his empty plate. When he looked up, he had an odd sort of gleam in his eyes. "I'm not sure. On the one hand, the wager could provide Amelia with the chance to win Worthington that she desires, but I'm not positive I really want her to win him. I'm not confident he deserves her." Harthorne speared Colin with an intense look. "What do *you* think? Is Worthington worth my sister?"

"Absolutely not," Colin replied. "Your sister has far too much spirit for a man like Worthington. If they married, it would not take long for him to try to control her, and a woman like Lady Amelia should not be controlled."

Colin wasn't sure, but he thought he saw a small smile playing at Harthorne's lips. What the devil was the man smiling about?

"What is it?"

"Nothing at all," Harthorne said smoothly.

A bit too quickly and with a false ring, to Colin's ear, but Harthorne was not the sort to mince words and the man was honest to a fault, so it must've been Colin's imagination.

Harthorne glanced down, seemingly examining his fingernails, and when his gaze met Colin's again, he leaned forward. "Setting the wager aside for the moment, I wonder what sort of gentleman Amelia should marry, if not Worthington."

"That's easy," Colin said, reclining against his chair. Harthorne simply needed to consider everything, and Colin would help him. "She needs a man who can match wits with her. Who appreciates her quirkiness and who is confident enough in himself to sit back and simply let her be herself and enjoy the outrageous but pleasurable havoc she brings to his life."

Harthorne let out a deep, almost satisfied-sounding sigh. Somehow this conversation had gotten off track, and Colin needed to refocus it, but before he could speak, Harthorne said, "Whether you and I think Worthington is the right man for her or not, Amelia does. She believes she loves him, and she's rather stubborn when she has set her mind to something, much like you."

Colin's chest tightened. It sounded like Harthorne was not going to agree to the bet, and Colin could not think of anything else to say to convince his friend and save him from ruin. "Are you refusing the wager?"

Harthorne shrugged. "I suppose I have no other good choices, so I'll accept your wager."

Odd, but for a man who had just said he had no good choices, Harthorne sounded awfully cheerful. Maybe it was nerves and not cheeriness.

"Well, tentatively. I agree, but before we can proceed, Amelia will have to consent as well. I won't use her as a pawn without her understanding the repercussions of her decisions."

"That's fair. Shall we call her in here and talk to her."

"After we break our fast." Harthorne grinned at Colin but then suddenly frowned. "I almost feel bad for you that I agreed to the bet, but yet, I don't."

"Because you think I'm going to lose?"

"What?"

"The bet," Colin said slowly, unsure why Harthorne seemed suddenly confused. "You feel bad for me because you think I'm going to lose the wager and have to part with so much blunt?"

"Oh, yes, certainly, the wager. Why else would I feel bad?"

"Exactly," Colin replied, a certainty that he'd missed something lodged in his gut, but what the devil he'd missed he was not sure. "Don't be concerned or so sure," Colin quickly inserted, not wanting Harthorne to overthink the situation and change his mind. "I vow if I win and your sister changes, I will respect her and I will be faithful. And in the end, you will have ensured she marries well and without the nonsense of love."

"No need to make vows about perfect marriage matches," Harthorne said, that same odd smile tugging at his lips. Before Colin could demand an explanation, Lady Amelia came into the dining room, balancing a tray with three steaming plates of delicious smelling eggs and ham.

"Mother refuses to come down to luncheon, or rather to break our fast, very late." Lady Amelia set the tray on the table. "Philip, you must try to reason with her after breakfast. I fear she's in another dark spell."

"I'll speak to her," Philip replied.

"Excellent. Now that we have settled that, who is making a brilliant marriage match?" Lady Amelia's hand accidentally brushed Colin's as she moved the plate into place before him. He could have sworn he felt a tremor on the surface of her delicate skin.

He glanced up at her and caught her gaze. "You are making the brilliant match, Lady Amelia."

"And who, pray tell, am I to be brilliantly matched to?" Amelia asked, desperately trying to keep her voice steady, but given that His Grace stared at her with that unblinking hazel gaze, it made it rather difficult. As she set her plate on the table, she prayed to God Philip had not been so dimwitted as to tell the duke about Charles. Her morning had been embarrassing enough, but if the duke knew of her problems, that would just be the cream on top of the pie. Too much!

The duke set his fork down without taking a bite of his food. "We are speaking of your possible marriage to me, Lady Amelia. What do you think?"

"Aversley!" Philip shouted, spitting out a mouthful of egg as he did so. "I hardly would have asked my sister that way."

Amelia's stomach clenched and then a rather strange, warm sensation flooded her. She couldn't help but stare openmouthed at the duke. He was handsome, shockingly so, reclined casually back in his chair with that devil-may-care smile on his face, his golden hair mussed and bronze stubble-glazed cheeks. Being married to him would be no hardship except for the fact that she didn't love him and he didn't love her. Oh, and he loved to sleep with women. Indiscriminately, so rumor would have it. She gave herself a mental shake to clear her head.

She decided to address her brother and pretend for the moment that His Grace was not there. Not staring at her as if she were utterly fascinating, which of course, she was not. "Philip, whatever is going on? You know very well I, um, er…" However did one say they had already given one's heart to someone else when that someone else didn't, as of yet, know?

Philip set down his fork, a deep-crimson blush creeping across his face. "I'm sure you are aware of our financial hardships."

Amelia would have laughed if she did not feel so sorry for her brother. "I'm aware," she said simply, keeping her gaze on Philip even though she could feel the heat of the duke's stare on her face.

Philip tugged on his neck cloth until the perfect snowy knot came undone and the ends of the material hung from his neck. "Aversley and I have made a gentlemen's bet, but if you don't wish for me to go through with it, Emmy, I won't."

Amelia sucked her lower lip between her teeth. Philip never called her Emmy unless he was very worried or nervous, and she could never recall him using the pet name in front of persons other than their parents. "Perhaps you better tell me the wager…?"

"Of course. Well, you see—"

"Darlings!" her mother called out cheerily as she swept into the room in a swirl of pink silk.

Amelia spit out the large sip of water she had just taken. Droplets flew across the table and, to her horror, splattered on the duke's face.

Without a word of acknowledgment about her social blunder, he wiped off his face and graced her with a grin. She could have gotten lost in his smile, but her mother's perfume, mixed with the sweet stench of laudanum, reached her and reminded her what had caused her to spit out her water in the first place—shock.

When Amelia had checked on her mother before coming down to cook, her mother had refused to get out of bed and now she was completely transformed and apparently gay. "Mother, I'm so glad to so see you feeling better."

Her mother jerked her head in Amelia's direction. "I remembered it was Tuesday."

Amelia frowned. That was an odd response. Perhaps it was the laudanum talking. "And Tuesdays make you feel better?" Amelia inquired, not wishing to point out the illogical statement and upset her mother.

The bright smile pasted on her mother's face faltered for just a moment and her hand fluttered at her neck. "I would not say that. No, I would not say that at all, but Lord Huntington is calling on me to take me for a ride and to visit with his sister, and I could not cancel that."

Amelia could swear her mother flinched when she said Lord Huntington's name, but then that too large smile was back on her face. Something very odd was afoot. "Why not?"

"It wouldn't be prudent, dear."

Before Amelia could say more, someone knocked at the front door.

"That would be Lord Huntington!" Mother announced in an almost shrill tone.

Amelia started to push her chair back to join her mother in greeting the man—and perhaps to ascertain a clue as to what was going on—but her mother speared her with a stern look.

"Stay seated," she commanded, as she used to do when Amelia was a young, wiggly child.

Amelia would have protested, but Philip discretely shook his head and rose. "Mother, I insist on saying hello to Lord Huntington."

"If you really must," she murmured, wringing her hands.

"I'm afraid I must," Philip confirmed to Amelia's relief. Philip was not near as attuned to picking up clues people were trying to hide, but hopefully he would discover something.

As they quickly departed the room, Amelia turned her gaze to the duke and was startled to find him staring at her again. She swallowed and forced herself to speak. "Since Philip is now occupied, perhaps you ought to go ahead and tell me what nonsense the two of you have concocted."

The duke nodded, a smile tugging at the corner of his lips. "I wagered with your brother that I could transform you into a woman of grace by providing personal lessons and the appropriate blunt to purchase gowns and other necessities that would assist in the transformation."

He spouted out the ridiculous wager with a straight face, as if delivering news of the weather. The heat of humiliation warmed Amelia's cheeks. To her utter shock, His Grace reached across the table and grasped her hands. She realized as he held them tightly between his for a second, that she had been wringing them together. Once she stilled, he quickly released her, yet his hands remained flat on the table, the breadth of them displaying a hint of the strength and vitality he possessed. The crest ring gleaming on his finger was a potent reminder of the title he held, which clearly made the man think he could do or say anything.

She swallowed her mortification, determined not to show she was hurt that he thought she needed transforming. Of course he thought so. After this morning's disaster, it was hard to think otherwise. She pushed the hurt away and tried to be logical. It was her best trait, after all, and one had to use their best qualities whenever possible. Perhaps he had an idea that would help her win Charles, and for that information, she would set her pride aside for a bit. "Do continue."

"That's one thing I like about you, Lady Amelia. I have known you less than two days, but I already see you are a woman of strength. Then again, most women are. It's how they use their strength that's so disturbing."

"My gracious," Amelia said, allowing a note of sarcasm to spill over. "Your compliments do so make my heart flutter. If winning my affection is part of the bet, I daresay perhaps you need lessons on flattery more than I need lessons on grace."

"Is it flattery you want?"

His voice had pitched low, with an undercurrent of something beckoning.

She started to shake her head but caught her breath when his fingers stroked slowly down her hair.

"One look at you with your hair down made me want to lose myself in you."

She gulped as flames licked not only her face but everywhere she most certainly should not be hot.

"Are you flattered?" he asked on a husky whisper.

She had to think about that. She was shocked. Thrilled. Perhaps flattered, but she'd never admit it. So instead, she stubbornly shook her head.

A low chuckle rumbled from him. "Excellent. I like a woman who makes me work for what I want."

"And you want to win my love?"

"Love is not part of the bet," he said, all traces of the rake gone and replaced with a no-nonsense tone.

"Then how am I to end up married to you?"

He leaned across the table toward her. His eyes had taken on a dull look. "You will end up married to me, Lady Amelia, because I wagered with your brother that once I transform you, and you are labeled an Incomparable by the *ton*, you will no longer have any interest in marrying Worthington but rather turn your attention to capturing a gentleman of greater worth and title. And once you do that, I win the bet."

"So I'm to simply be a prize in a silly wager?" she asked, pleased with how blasé she sounded while her stomach twisted violently and her heart pounded.

He grimaced and shook his head. "Don't think of it that way. I need a wife, but I'd prefer a marriage of convenience to a love match. Your brother needs to see you married well but does not have the means to give you the Season you require to capture the man you desire. With this wager, I will provide you the means. If you stay true to your feelings for Worthington, when I'm through transforming you, I guarantee you that he will offer for you. Once you accept, Philip wins the bet. But if you have a change of heart regarding Worthington, as I have wagered, then I win, and I get a bride who will suit my needs perfectly."

He stopped, reached for her hand, and pulled back. "Risking that I might anger you, I'm going to be as honest as I can. You do not love me. I do not love you. We won't bring false expectations into the marriage that will lead to betrayal or years of bitterness on either of our parts."

A cold chill raced through Amelia. She clenched her teeth against showing any reaction. The marriage he was describing was exactly the sort she would never want. She longed to marry for love and have a life filled with great hopes and expectations. She licked her lips, trying to sort out what she had learned and what she needed to know. "What does Philip get if he wins the wager?"

He leaned back in his chair once again, his expression one of complete lack of concern. His gaze held hers while his lips showed a trace of the slightest smile. "I will pay off all your brother's debt. Every last pence."

"And if you win all you get is me?"

He nodded, though he evaded her gaze.

"That doesn't seem a very good wager on your part," she said, dryly. "True, if I change you gain a bride who has proven love does not matter to her, as you have so clearly stated you want, but you will gain nothing else. I have no dowry."

She leaned forward and tried to catch his gaze once again, but he avoided her. "Why not simply find a rich lady who you know does not care to marry for love. I'm sure you know dozens."

"This way is more entertaining," he said, meeting her gaze briefly before looking away.

She nearly snorted. What poppycock he was spouting. He was putting up a front of a cold, indifferent man, but she'd already seen a few glimpses of his kind side. He had done good deeds for two people she loved, for goodness sake.

She already knew she'd agree to this outrageous wager. Her participation would guarantee Philip's debts were paid off, and she would do all in her power to help her brother and mother. Besides, there was no danger to her since she would not change, but the duke did not need to know it until she learned the whole truth of his motivation. "What if I refuse to participate in the bet?"

"You won't."

His tone was so self-assured she wanted to refuse, just to prove him wrong. "I might," she said with force. She was rather pleased with how sincere she sounded. "I don't think I need to transform myself to capture Lord Worthington's attention." She may not think she should have to, but she clearly needed to...*Foolish man.*

His Grace raised an eyebrow. "Be that as it may, it's my understanding that Worthington will be leaving for London shortly to follow a certain young lady that lives here in town. It will be hard for you to capture the attention of a gentleman who is not even present."

Blast Philip for blabbering.

She hoped her expression appeared as unconcerned as the duke's. "There is a dance in three day's time, and I plan to make an impression on Lord Worthington then," she said, revealing what she had known she wanted to do but had been unsure how to do it. When the duke simply stared at her, she thrust out her jaw and added in a cool tone, "One he won't forget."

He shot her a twisted smile as his gaze raked over her body making her acutely aware that she had changed from a drab brown riding habit to a dull gray cotton gown that made her look like she was dressing more to become a nun and less to bedazzle a gentleman. He grinned at her. "Do you plan to make the same sort of impression you did today at the picnic?"

"Oh, do be quiet," Amelia snapped, her temples suddenly aching. She reached up and pressed her fingertips to them while staring at the insufferable man. "I'm willing to admit my gowns and grace could use polish, and I'm not going to lie and say I have never imagined obtaining both, but I desire a man to love me for me. Every tarnished bit." Her temples were really pounding now, and she expected the duke to laugh at her. Instead, he nodded.

"I couldn't agree more, Lady Amelia. But I'm afraid the world does not work that way."

Amelia sighed. She was tired of bandying words. This wager was ridiculous. It held no benefit for him. "Did you create this bet to help my brother? You must know in your heart of hearts I won't change, and therefore know you will have aligned yourself to be able to pay off his debts without him feeling he borrowed it."

"Clever, but not true," he said, yet she saw him stiffen. She was right! She knew she was. Gratitude flooded her.

"You are lying. Why don't you want people to know you have a good heart?"

For a moment, the only sound in the room was the tick of the longcase clock, until the duke, who had been frowning ferociously, grumbled, "I do not have a good heart. I'm so certain that you will change and I will end up married to you, that when your brother insisted the terms of the wager be written out to include that I will not be able to give him so much as a pence if I win, I immediately agreed. Because I realized I could get around his terms by giving the money to you. Then you, in turn, could help him. See how deceitful I am? I will do anything to get what I want, and your brother is so honorable he would never consider I'd circumvent the terms he dictated."

She smiled smugly. "I told you, you had a good heart."

He simply gaped at her, then slowly ran a finger back and forth across the golden stubble on his jaw, saying nothing. As the moment stretched on, Amelia's thoughts raced. Had she gone too far? She prayed she had not. If she'd ruined her chance to help Philip and Mother, Amelia would beg the duke to reconsider. He stood, placed both palms on the table, and leaned so close that when she breathed in, all she could smell was him—a faint scent of earthy maleness mixed with the tang of fresh grass and clean air.

His gaze captured hers so she felt no more than a prisoner to his will. "You tricked me."

She nodded.

"You knew you'd participate all along?"

"Of course," she replied sweetly. "I'm in no danger of changing, and I will rescue my family from financial disaster."

The duke nodded, causing a lock of his golden hair to fall over the right side of his forehead. He reached up and pushed it back off his face. Amelia sat, spellbound, watching the way his body moved with effortlessness and grace. He laid his hand open-palmed on the table. "I've been duped by a woman before, but I must say, this is the first time the woman had good intentions and was trying to help someone else."

"I'm sorry I tricked you, but I had to know the whole truth." She scrutinized him. Had he just flinched at that statement? "There isn't anything else I should know is there?"

His gaze locked with hers, making her heart flutter oddly.

"Like what?"

"I'm not sure," she admitted. "Anything that would change the outcome of the bet?"

"No. There's nothing you should know will change the outcome of my wager with your brother."

His confirmation sounded true but carefully worded. Perhaps, he was simply hiding some other secrets of his past. She wasn't going to try to force the man to tell her anything else and risk him deciding helping Philip was more trouble than it was worth. Plus, she felt sorry for him. It was sad that he was so sure a woman could be swayed from the man she loved by title and money.

Amelia rubbed her sweaty palms against her dress and stood. His Grace straightened to his full height and looked down at her. The power he exuded made her feel safe, and she tilted her head back to meet his gaze. "I daresay it will take quite a bit of your blunt to set my brother's affairs to rights."

He offered a devilish smile. "I'm not concerned. I'd rather spend my fortune helping a man I admire than wasting it on the worthless pastimes I have been."

A lump of gratitude lodged in her throat, but she swallowed it and spoke. "Shall we begin our lessons today? Will you stay here for a bit or shall we figure out a mutual place to meet? How will this work? Will I—"

Chuckling, he held up his palms. "I don't know. Let me speak to your brother about the details. In the meantime, why don't you go rest a bit?" He frowned and brushed a hand across her forehead, making her jerk back in response.

"I'm sorry," he said, his tone serious. "Your face is flushed, your eyes a bit glazed, and your forehead hot. Do you feel unwell?"

She did feel tired, but who wouldn't after the morning and early afternoon she had experienced. "I'm a bit fatigued. Perhaps I'll go lie down. When my mother returns we will have to speak to her about the wager and get her agreement."

"Of course," he said, pressing a firm, warm hand to her back and waving her forward through the doorway and toward the stairs. It was strange how his touch caused her pulse to skip a beat. Charles had never put his hand on her back to lead her from a room. She was sure if he had, her heart would have raced uncontrollably.

She paused at the steps and turned to him. Her head was rather light, but after a second, it passed. "I will never forget the kindness you have shown by creating this wager to help my brother, and I vow to repay your kindness."

"Really?" He quirked both eyebrows. "How do you plan to repay this so-called kindness?"

"It's my secret," Amelia said and turned away to ascend the stairs so he would not witness her silly grin. If he could transform her, then she could transform him. He would make her passably pretty, and she would show him that all women were not coldhearted schemers. He would give her the chance to obtain her dreams, and she would teach him how to trust women so he could love and be loved.

Amelia headed straight to her room, her head spinning as she walked. By the time she lay down, she could hardly keep her eyes open. As she rested on the bed, her body becoming heavier, she imagined herself married to Charles and then on a whim she replaced Charles with the duke. Oddly, the thought did not totally disturb her, and the fact that it did not bothered her. She squeezed her eyes, counted to one hundred, and slowly forgot everything.

Chapter Ten

Amelia woke to absolute darkness. For a moment, confusion swarmed her. It had been early in the afternoon when she had lain down to take her nap. *Good heavens!* She blinked and sat up with a groan. She had slept the entire day away, and a fat lot of good it had done her. Her head ached worse than ever and—she sniffed, or rather she tried to—but her nose was so congested she could barely take in any air.

Muttering, she swung her legs over the bed and padded over to her looking glass, instantly wishing she had not bothered. Her hair was an absolute disaster. It hung wildly around her face and over her shoulders. She reached for a brush to try to set it to order, but the moment the bristles touched her skin she winced. Her head ached so badly her scalp hurt!

She set the brush down with a sigh. Their houseguest would just have to suffer her bedraggled appearance tonight. A warm sensation filled her chest at the thought of the duke and how he had orchestrated the entire wager simply to help Philip. The man had a good heart whether he believed it or not, and she was supremely glad she had thought of a way to pay back his generosity.

She glanced at the longcase clock with a frown. Six in the evening. Surely her mother was home from her carriage ride and visit to Lord Huntington's sister by now? Though, Mother could talk for hours, once she got started.

Tugging on her gown and giving her pitiful appearance one last glance, Amelia forced herself to quit her bedchamber and head to her mother's. After knocking on the door and getting no response as usual, Amelia cracked the door open, and peered into the empty bedchamber, glad to see her mother was not lying in bed. Excellent. Even if Amelia did not like Lord Huntington, she was glad his calling on Mother had gotten her out of bed.

Amelia moved toward the stairs to go in search of her mother. She sighed as she descended the stairs and then hesitated when a sharp pain jabbed her temple. Her stomach rolled in protest. Goodness, she'd not eaten all day. Perhaps she ought to grab a slice of bread before finding her mother and talking with her. Yes, that was the best course. Turning toward the kitchen, Amelia hurried her steps. As she neared the room, she frowned at the unexpected sounds of clattering pans and— Was that *humming*? She quickened her step, a smile tugging at her lips. Was Mother actually cooking dinner? Joy and relief filled her, but when she pushed through the kitchen door, she paused at the sight of a rather rotund but seemingly cheerful woman stirring a pot.

The woman stopped mid-stir, withdrew the spoon, and set it down. She faced Amelia and curtsied. "Good evening, my lady. You must be Lady Amelia."

"Yes, I am," she said coming to stand in front of the woman. "Who might you be? Did my mother hire you?" Amelia could scarcely believe Philip would let them spend money on an interim cook or that her mother had rallied herself enough to take such an interest in helping to run the household, but surely both things had occurred. Happiness bubbled in her. Perhaps things would be all right after all.

The woman shoved a stray lock of brown hair behind her ear and smoothed her hands over her starched white apron. "Yes, my lady. I met her several hours ago along with Lord Harthorne and the Duke of Aversley. After your mother approved of my qualifications, your brother arranged for me to work here for the next week."

"That's splendid," Amelia cried out, thrilled she would no longer have to eat eggs for every meal and that they could afford to pay another servant. Perhaps they were not as purse-pinched as she had previously thought. "What are you cooking?" Amelia took a deep breath and caught a whiff and her mouth immediately started to water.

Cook grinned. "Goose and braised ham for the meat. Peas and asparagus as sides. Turtle soup to start. But my specialty"—the woman waved Amelia over to the oven—"is pastries." The cook opened the oven door, and Amelia inhaled the delicious aroma of baking sweet treats.

"Apple tarts?" she asked hopefully.

The cook nodded. "Especially for you."

"Did my mother tell you they were my favorite?"

"No, my lady. Actually, it was the Duke of Aversley who mentioned it."

"That's odd," Amelia mumbled. His Grace had no way of knowing apple tarts were her favorite, nor was it his place to recommend to the cook to make special dishes for her. It would look particularly odd if he went around doing such things and people assumed they held a tendre for each other only then for her to become betrothed to Charles. She was going to have to set the duke straight on a few boundaries of this wager.

"I look forward to dinner," Amelia said, grabbing a piece of bread off the counter and departing to find her mother.

Amelia headed to the drawing room, and grinned at the sight of her mother sitting on the settee, still dressed in her frothy gown. She looked very fresh, except for the dark circles under her eyes. With a swift look around the room to ensure they were alone, Amelia strode over to the settee and returned Mother's wan smile as she sat. She grasped her mother's hand and was baffled when her mother flinched at the touch. "Is everything all right?"

"Certainly. Why do you ask?"

"You seem a bit nervous."

"Not at all," Mother assured, though the wringing of her hands was rather the opposite of reassuring.

They had always been able to speak openly to each other, but something seemed to have changed in her mother. Amelia chose her words with care. "I'm glad to see you are feeling well enough to go out for rides and visits and join us for supper. How was your time with Lord Huntington and his sister?"

"Lovely," her mother replied, her voice somewhat strained.

"Are you sure?"

"Yes, Amelia. These questions are tiresome, though. There is no need to be concerned about me. I haven't even had one drop of laudanum today."

Amelia pressed her lips together on pointing out that she had smelled laudanum on her mother earlier. Instead she said, "I was pleasantly surprised to find you and Philip decided we could hire a temporary cook until Uriah's return."

Her mother tugged her hand away. "The duke insisted on the cook. His Grace was adamant that you have proper meals to ensure you look your best when you go off to London next week. The cook is only here until we all leave for Town, thanks to the duke's generosity."

"Mother, do you mean to say they already spoke to you about the arrangement and you have given your consent?"

"Certainly," her mother said, patting Amelia's hand. "I jumped at the suggestion, truth be known. I have been desperately trying to find a way to get you out of the house and wed as soon as possible, and I had almost given up hope until this solution fell into my lap. His Grace must be rather bored indeed to take an interest in remaking you."

Amelia let the comment about the duke go unremarked upon. It was the furthest thing from the truth to say His Grace's interest in her was born from boredom, but perhaps it was better to let her mother think so. If she explained the duke had concocted the whole plan to ensure he could help Philip out of debt, Mother might let the secret out while under the influence of her laudanum.

Amelia focused on her mother's comment about needing to get her out of the house. "I did not realize you wanted me gone so badly." She tried to keep the hurt from her voice, but when her mother grasped her hands and squeezed, she knew she had failed.

"Amelia, darling, things are not as they seem to you. I'm trying to protect you."

"Protect me from what?"

"Good evening, ladies," a deep voice called from the door.

Perturbed at the untimely interruption, Amelia glanced toward the drawing room entrance where His Grace glided through the door. The bottle-green superfine coat he wore fit him to perfection and enhanced the broad expanse of his chest, but it was his eyes that captured her attention, melted her annoyance, and held her bewitched. From her spot on the settee, she could see the happy crinkle around his hazel eyes. He stopped in front of her and took her hand—ungloved, she belatedly realized. He brushed his lips to her skin, and an undeniable tremor ran through her.

It amazed her that a man she knew perfectly well had absolutely no interest in love whatsoever could so easily cause such strong reactions in her. And all this time she had thought herself so very sensible. Of course, she had enough sense to know she would never marry a man who did not want her love and plan to give it in return, which in addition to the fact that she already loved Charles was precisely why she would never marry the duke. He wanted to marry for convenience. She wanted a marriage of supremely divine inconvenience full of passion, devotion, laughter, and joy.

He smiled, almost secretly as if he had noticed her body's response to him, but he quickly moved away from her and repeated the same kiss on the back of the hand to her mother. Amelia felt daft. She was not special. He kissed every woman on the back of the hand. He had probably kissed a thousand hands in his life.

"It's good to see you finally up." His tone was jovial even as his gaze travelled over Amelia and lingered on her hair.

She glowered at him. "My head aches or I would have set my hair to rights."

"I can fix that."

"Beg pardon?" she said sharply. Immediately, her mother gently nudged her in the side.

Amelia cleared her throat and strove for a more conciliatory tone. "Do you mean to say you can fix my aching head or my hair?"

He laughed, and the low, smooth sound curled around her. "I've no experience whatsoever fixing women's hair, but I have a great deal of knowledge on how to help an aching head."

"Truly?" she quirked an eyebrow, and he nodded solemnly in response.

"Truly. If you will but come with me to the kitchen, I can prepare you a tonic that you can drink before dinner. It works faster on an empty stomach."

Amelia glanced to her mother, sure she would protest Amelia traipsing off to the kitchen with the duke, but her mother was vigorously nodding. "Do go, dear. I'm fine to sit here alone until Philip comes down for dinner."

Things were becoming odder around here by the minute, and it had all started when the Duke of Aversley had arrived. Before that, Mother never wanted to be left unaccompanied, even for a moment, unless she had taken to her bed for one of her long sleeps. Amelia stood and locked gazes with His Grace. He waved her toward the door and fell into step directly behind her. As they entered the long hallway that would take them around back to the kitchen she said, "I suppose I am in your hands now."

Fingers came to her arm and stopped her progress. She glanced back over her shoulder, her heart jolting at the way his gaze softly caressed her. "You were already in my hands, Lady Amelia, but I'm glad to hear you accept it."

"You presume too much, Your Grace. I am in my own hands, but I am allowing you to help me so that I can assist my brother and mother."

He winked at her. "I like your independence."

"Good. Then we shall rub along nicely while we are working together." Turning on her heel, she made her way toward the kitchen, but as they passed her brother's study the duke once again stayed her with a hand to her shoulder. Her skin tingled with his touch, and she fought to keep the odd reaction at bay while slowing turning toward him.

"Yes?"

"I'm going to need some whiskey."

Amelia quirked an eyebrow and smiled. "Do you mean to cure my megrim by getting me foxed? I daresay my mother will not like that."

"I daresay she wouldn't," he concurred. "The whiskey is for the cooling wash I'm making for your head. I only need a bit. Does your brother have some in his study?"

"Yes." Amelia entered Philip's study and led His Grace to the sideboard. "How do you know so much about curing megrims? Do you get many?"

"Not a one," he replied, rather evasively. He took up the whiskey bottle and tucked it under his arm. "Come with me."

With a frown at his commanding tone, Amelia reluctantly followed him to the door and stopped when he did, at the end of the hall where you could turn left or right. He faced her with a grin. "I just realized I've no idea how to get to your kitchen. Serves me right being so high-handed."

His smile was so infectious that she grinned back. "I'm pleased to see you can admit your flaws."

"Are you?" His voice had taken on a low, silky tone that made her heart quicken.

When he tucked a lock of her hair behind her ear, she froze. The moment his fingers grazed her skin, it was as if electricity raced from the point of contact and spiraled out through the rest of her body. He leaned in a fraction, but that little bit was all it took for the heat radiating off his body to surround her. His eyes took on a dangerous glint. "Do you know you make disheveled hair look quite lovely?"

His softly spoken compliment made her belly flutter. Was he going to kiss her? Heavens! Where had that thought come from? She scrambled back a step and blurted, "I am in love with Lord Worthington."

He shrugged dismissively. "Yes, I know you think you are. It was a compliment, Lady Amelia…and your first test, which you failed."

He said one thing with his words, yet his voice vibrated with an odd note of tension. She had a suspicion he was not being completely honest again, yet she certainly could not say that. "What sort of test?"

Colin tensed. Lady Amelia's question was an excellent one, and normally, he would have a quick and ready answer for the lie he had just told—not so this time. The compliment had fallen from his tongue and had been the absolute, astonishing truth. He thought her lovely just the way she was. She was untarnished. Or he thought she might be. Or maybe he was acting the fool falling for her ploy. Yes, devil take her, that had to be it. Her strategy had to be to play the part of the utter innocent, and he was acting like a green lad entertaining her ruse. "I was testing you to see if you know how to flirt, and you failed."

Her crestfallen look made his gut clench, but he continued. "We will have to allot some time for your learning to effectively play the seductress."

She blinked and her eyes widened while her cheeks turned bright pink. "If you think so."

He did think so. In fact, too much. He was getting hard simply imagining the lessons.

Pulling his thoughts in order, he asked, "Where is the kitchen?"

"Follow me."

As Amelia walked ahead and her hips swayed gently back and forth, his thoughts set his blood to fire once more. He forced himself to look higher, at her head. There. Much better, when he focused on her hair—long, luxurious, inviting— He groaned and moved past her to barrel through the door. He came to an abrupt halt as he faced the cook he had hired and had no intention of dismissing when he left for London in a week. He was positive their cook was never coming back, and he was not going to let them live forever on eggs, no matter Harthorne's pride.

"Ms. Darlington, would you be so kind as to bring me salt, vinegar, water, and a cup. Lady Amelia has a megrim, and I'm going to make her a tonic to cure it."

To Ms. Darlington's credit, she clamped her gaping jaw shut and bobbed a curtsey before issuing a quick, "Certainly," and scurrying around the kitchen to collect the items.

A few moments later, Colin handed the cup to Lady Amelia. She took the drink, sniffed the contents, and shook her head while thrusting the tonic back toward him. "I'll not drink that." Her nose had wrinkled adorably, and he had to fight the desire to smile.

"I insist. We cannot have our first lesson tonight if your head is still bothering you."

"It's better," she murmured and cast her gaze down.

Ah, so Lady Amelia did not like to lie. He was rather glad of that. He hooked a gentle finger under her chin and raised her face until her gaze met his. "Let's be honest, shall we?"

Her chin notched up in a rather defiant gesture that both amused him and made him oddly proud at her show of backbone. She jerked her head in agreement. "Fine, let us be truthful. If you tell me how you know how to make a tonic to cure megrims, I'll drink the nasty-smelling concoction."

"My father taught me how to make the tonic."

"Oh, I see," Amelia said slowly, a frown puckering her brow. "Was your father plagued with megrims?"

Colin nodded. "Yes, a rather big megrim about your height with long brown hair."

"I don't understand."

"You wouldn't," Colin said, raking his hands through his hair. Why had he not simply lied? Why was his tongue—so silent all these years—suddenly loose with this woman he barely knew?

"I'm told I can be a very good listener if you care to explain it to me."

Tension drained from Colin like the rush of a river breaking a dam. Not one woman he had slept with had ever offered simply to listen to him. They'd offered a multitude of things, but understanding had never been one of them. He took Amelia by the elbow and led her out of the kitchen and away from the prying ears of the cook.

Once they stood alone in the hall, he spoke. "My mother loved to drink about as much as she loved to breathe. Because of her habit, she was plagued with megrims, and my father did his best to hide her shameful state from everyone. Part of his efforts included being the one to always to fix her special tonics to cure the megrims. Later, when he fell ill, he begged me to do it, and I agreed."

He had glanced down at his hands while he spoke, but when he finished he forced himself to look up, though he did not want to see the pity that would be in her eyes. Her matter-of-fact expression surprised him.

"My aunt drank too much," Amelia blurted with a decisive nod of her head. "Though she passed away some years ago, it is still a family secret, but given what you just told me, I feel safe revealing it to you. I did not have to live with her. Thank goodness," Amelia said, a shudder coursing through her slender body. "That must have been dreadful if your mother behaved anywhere near as bad when in her cups as my aunt did. I bet you were counting the days you could put distance between the two of you." Amelia paled and put her hand to her lips then slowly lowered it. "That was unaccountably rude of me to say that. I'm terribly sorry. I simply meant I'm sure her drinking drove you to want to leave."

"It did." But not near as much as watching how her indiscretions killed his father. Colin scowled.

"Does she still imbibe?"

"No."

Amelia smiled. "That's wonderful. Have the two of you reconciled?"

"No. It was not simply her drinking that drove me from her."

"Oh dear." Lady Amelia sighed and cocked her head. "Do you care to talk about it?"

He would have thought his reaction would have been a violent *no*, but something about Amelia was pleasantly disarming and luring. Yet the habit of hiding his mother's infidelities was not so easily let go of. Perhaps someday. He glanced at her open, expectant face. Little minx. Did she think he was so easily wrapped around her finger? It was time to get her to cease her questions. He brushed his hand across her pale, silky cheek.

"Perhaps I'll tell you one day after we have been married for many years." The comment was meant to goad her. Nothing more. He did not really want to win. Did he? No, of course he did not. That would prove he was right about women, and he would frankly love to be proven wrong, as doubtful as it was. Though he would be left with the problem of finding an indifferent wife to marry if Philip won the wager, but Colin would welcome the loss.

She pursed her lips prettily. "I would never marry a man who kept secrets from me."

He chuckled at the stormy look that crossed her face. "Then you better make sure not to change, because one thing I will never be, Lady Amelia, is an open book."

"I'll not change, so there is no need for this discussion. I've given my heart to Lord Worthington, and no amount of money or lofty title is going to alter that." She grasped the cup out of his hand and gulped down the tonic with a terrible grimace. "I do believe I need to be excused for a moment before dinner. Will you be all right to make your way back to my mother and Philip alone?"

"I've been making my way on my own all my life, Lady Amelia. I'll be splendid."

With a nod, she turned away, but her muttering floated back to him as she strode down the hall. He could have sworn she said something about that being *terribly sad* and *needing to change.*

He stood in the hallway and watched her depart, her hips doing that luring gently swaying motion as she went. When her gray skirts fluttered out of sight, he moved to find Harthorne, yet a thought caused him to pause. She was intriguing, and when he was through with her, she would be beguiling. Then she would learn the power she could yield over a man, and her desire for true love would be replaced by the desire for true wealth and status. The thought made his chest tighten, yet oddly enough, the idea of her wedding Worthington did not sit quite right, either.

Chapter Eleven

Amelia awoke the next morning rather late and found the duke had gone into town but had left specific instructions for her to be prepared for her first lesson, which was to be instructions in dancing. Muttering to herself, she crumpled the note he had left for her and tossed it on the stand by the entrance to the door. He could not have picked a weaker accomplishment for her to start with if he had tried. Why it was almost as if—

"Philip!" Amelia screeched.

Within a moment, her brother came strolling down the staircase and bowed to her. "You called?"

"Did you tell the Duke of Aversley of my dancing abilities?"

"He did not," her mother said from the top of the stairs where she appeared blessedly dressed in a light-green and white striped carriage gown. Her hair was swept off her face in a lovely chignon, the emerald earrings Father had given her twinkled at her ears, and light rouge graced her cheeks. Yet even dressed in finery and having taken obvious efforts with her appearance, the dark circles under her eyes were evident, and as she drew nearer, the tight lines around her mouth were also hard to miss.

Her mother stopped at the foot of the stairs and stared at Amelia. "I told him. He asked me where you needed the most work and I told him dancing, flirting—"

"Mother!" Flames licked Amelia's cheeks.

"It's true, dear. I've never taught you how, and you just don't seem to be one of those young ladies who innately knows how to flirt. If you're going to capture a husband you must learn to flirt."

Philip coughed discreetly, but his red face gave away his discomfort. "I don't think I'll be needed here today. Will I?"

Amelia quickly shook her head. She certainly did not want her brother as an observer while she made a total cake of herself. "Where are you off to?"

Philip settled his hat on his head before answering. "To see the bankers. I'm going to try once more to get an extension on the payment of our debt. The crops look good, and all I need is more time."

"Do you think you can manage it, Philip?" their mother asked.

The question was perfectly normal and had been on the tip of Amelia's tongue, as well, but it was the desperate note in her mother's voice that gave Amelia pause.

"I hope so, Mother," Philip replied. "Try not to worry."

Her mother's shoulders slumped, but she nodded. Amelia said nothing as Philip gave them both a quick hug and departed, but when the door closed, she turned to her mother. "Is there more happening than you are telling me? Or telling Philip? Is there something else we should know?"

Her mother bristled. "Certainly not."

There was no point in arguing because her mother's gaze had dropped and she had balled her hands into fists by her side. Whether she was concealing something or not, she was not going to be forthcoming about it. Amelia glanced over her mother's fine carriage gown. "You are not planning to go out, are you? What if His Grace comes back?"

"Oh dear. I had not thought about that when we let Philip go. Lord Huntington"—her voice cracked on his name—"will be here shortly to collect me."

Amelia frowned. She didn't understand what was occurring. This was the second time her mother had allowed the man to take her riding in his carriage, and she had not looked happy about it either time. "Are you sure you want to go? You just saw him yesterday."

"Yes, of course," her mother replied in a tired, broken whisper.

A thought occurred to Amelia. "Mother, are you considering allowing the man to court you because you think to save Philip? You don't have to do that, you know. Philip will win this wager, and everything will be fine."

Her mother's face had drained of all its color, and she pressed a hand to her chest. She glanced away and then back at Amelia. "That's not it at all." Her voice wavered as she spoke.

"I don't understand," Amelia began in slow, faltering words. Her heart squeezed a bit within her chest. She supposed she had thought Mother would love Father forever. It wasn't fair to expect that, though. She should be happy that her mother was out of bed and dressed so nicely, even if she was going on a carriage ride with another man.

It should not come as such a shock, anyway. Lord Huntington's visits here had become more frequent with every passing month, but Amelia had not wanted to believe her mother could care for that man. Seems she had been incorrect. "I, well..." She floundered for the right words. "That's nice if you really do like him, Mother."

Her mother swallowed audibly. "Never say that, Amelia. Never think it."

"Now I'm afraid I really don't understand. If you don't care for him why are you letting him take you on a carriage ride, and why do you constantly let him call on you?"

"I'm glad you don't understand, and I pray you never will," she replied, her features drawing closed.

Amelia frowned. "Do you mean because you hope I never lose my husband?"

She jerked her head in confirmation. "Yes. That's what I mean."

What a falsehood. Amelia sucked in her lower lip and fought the urge to question further. "I'm sure if you don't want to go, Lord Huntington will understand that you cannot leave me here unchaperoned with His Grace."

"No!" her mother snapped. "I must go when he comes. I must."

There it was again. That note of desperation. "What would you have us do, then?" Amelia asked carefully, afraid to upset the situation more.

The wild-eyed look her mother gave her did not make her feel one bit better. "The cook can chaperone you."

"The cook?" Amelia asked blankly. At her mother's nod, Amelia opened her mouth to protest, but a knock resounded on the front door, and her mother fairly shoved past her.

"That must be Lord Huntington. Go on now, dear. Find the cook and tell her to chaperone you. I'll be home by nightfall. I'm going to visit Lord Huntington's sister again, as well."

Amelia did not move. Something very strange was happening, and she was not about to go anywhere, whether commanded to or not.

At the door, her mother glanced back at her with a worried frown and hissed, "Go, Amelia."

Amelia shook her head.

The knocking increased, and with one last scowl, Mother opened the door to Lord Huntington.

His gaze passed over Mother with a slight smile then landed on Amelia. Something in the way he insolently studied her made her skin crawl. She took a step backward, preferring distance. She had never liked the man, but now she cared for him less than ever.

He stepped toward Amelia, grasped her hand, and kissed it before she could snatch it away. A rather lecherous smile tugged at his lips. "You look lovely in blue, Lady Amelia. Much lovelier than my daughter. That thing does not have the slightest clue how to dress in colors that suit her, but then again, none do, pathetic woman."

"Oh, Lord Huntington," her mother crooned in a high-pitched tone. "How complimentary you are of Amelia."

Amelia narrowed her eyes. It was so wholly unlike Mother to ignore someone besmirching another, but for Mother to pretend Lord Huntington had not spoken cruelly of his own daughter was astonishing. It was almost as if Mother were afraid to stand up to Lord Huntington. That was ridiculous, though. The man had no power over them.

Amelia set her hands on her hips. "Mother, I'd really like for you to stay."

"Oh, silly girl," her mother twittered in a false voice and clutched Lord Huntington's elbow. "We better get going." Her mother's gaze landed on her as she pulled Lord Huntington toward the door. "Make sure to concentrate on your lessons, Amelia."

Too dumbfounded at the odd scene before her to say anything, Amelia nodded. Within seconds, the door closed and she stood alone and confused in the entranceway.

She had no idea what had just occurred, but she had to somehow solve the mystery. She would talk to Mother again tonight to try to force her to tell her the truth. If that did not work, she would threaten to tell Philip. Maybe that would do the trick. Mother never wanted to burden Philip, since he had so much on his shoulders already. However, this might be one of those instances where Amelia would have no choice but to involve her brother.

It did not take long to find the cook and ensure she would be on hand to chaperone once the duke returned. With nothing more pressing to do, Amelia made her way to the courtyard since it seemed the best place to practice dancing. The weather was perfect today. Not too warm but with a nice burst of sunshine. Though she knew she would not be doing the waltz at the country-dance tomorrow night, she had always dreamed of when she would waltz. She felt rather silly, but she raised her arms to the correct positions, closed her eyes, and began twirling around the cobblestone terrace, humming.

Colin's chest tightened at the sight of Lady Amelia twirling in the sunshine with her eyes closed and her arms raised in the air. Was she dancing with an imaginary lord? No doubt, it was Worthington. For some inane reason the thought irritated Colin, but the annoyance slid away as he watched her waltz around the terrace. Her unbound hair swayed as she moved, and the slender column of her neck beckoned to be kissed. Devil take it. He desired Lady Amelia, and he had not even recreated her yet.

Behind him, something shifted, and he got a whiff of perfume. Damnation, he cast his gaze over his shoulder, remembering that the new lady's maid he'd hired in town for Lady Amelia stood behind him. He pressed a finger to his lips to signal Lucy to remain quiet before he turned back and studied Lady Amelia as she danced. Though her movements were somewhat stiff, he could detect a bit of grace. Practice would give her confidence and lend her poise.

Turning, he pointed to a bench at the top of the stairs and waved Lucy toward it. She nodded and moved quietly back up the stairs the way they had just come. Years of practice of moving around his parent's home so as not to disturb his mother made it easy for Colin to approach Amelia without making a sound. A smile tugged at his lips as he positioned himself to take her in his arms. She twirled left, and he stepped toward her, sliding one hand around her waist and clasping her other hand with his.

Her eyes flew open as her body tensed. Her steps faltered then stopped altogether. When she moved to step away, he held tight and stared into her beguiling blue eyes. "I'm pleased to see you have some skill at dancing."

She blushed but did not lower her gaze from his. "Were you watching me?"

"I was studying you to see what needed to be worked on." That was partially true. He had enjoyed watching her—another first when it came to the fairer sex. He had, in the past, only ever taken the time to watch a woman he was planning on seducing or who he knew was attempting to seduce him. What was between him and Amelia was innocent.

She cocked her head. "And did you find there is much I need to learn?"

"A bit. You lack confidence, which effects how you appear. First, you must learn to stand up straight. You slouch as if you are embarrassed of your height. All that hunching over makes you appear inelegant."

Amelia stood straighter and regarded the hand that still clasped hers. "If you'll release me, I will go get Cook so she can chaperone us. Mother and Philip are both out."

He inclined his head toward the bench at the top of the stone staircase. "I went into town to secure you a lady's maid. She will also act as your chaperone in London for the Season."

Lady Amelia glanced at Lucy then back at him, her eyes swimming with what appeared to be gratitude. "Thank you," she whispered, her voice hitching.

Colin's own heart seemed to fill immeasurably. He did not like it. Not one bit. Making her happy should not have such an influence on him. Allowing someone to affect you meant they could hurt you. "No need to thank me. I did it for myself. If you end up as my wife your reputation needs to be sterling." That was utter rubbish, but it sounded good. He would will himself to believe it.

"I see," she said slowly, but she shot him a look of disbelief. "Well, whatever your reasons were, I appreciate the lady's maid. Getting all those torturous back hooks fastened on your own is rather hard."

An image of her naked flesh flashed in his mind. He gritted his teeth, but a groan escaped him.

"Is something wrong? Are you in pain?"

He was in pain—the agony of lust. "Nothing's wrong. Just considering all the work we have ahead. Let us begin the lesson, shall we?" The sooner he was not holding her in his arms the better for both his uncomfortable state and her innocence.

She nodded but sucked her lower lip between her teeth again, showing her nervousness.

"Quit sucking on your lip," he said gently.

Immediately, her lower lip—pink, plump, and begging to be kissed—popped out from between her teeth. The desire coiling inside of him was a bloody nuisance. He gripped her hand and started counting off the steps of the waltz for them. After a moment, they began to move around the terrace. "Pick up your pace a bit."

Instantly, she glanced down at her feet and stepped on his right foot. "I'm sorry," she mumbled, still looking at the ground.

Pausing, he hooked a finger under her chin and raised her gaze to his. "Never glance down at your feet. It will always cause you to misstep. Stare into your partner's eyes. You won't get many chances to be so near Worthington, so use the waltz to your advantage."

"What do you mean?" she asked.

"Hold his gaze. Lean toward him as you dance. Allow your chest to briefly brush against his."

"I couldn't do that!"

He chuckled at the bright scarlet of her cheeks. Her innocence was wonderful. And refreshing. Still, she could not be naive and still win Worthington. Colin shrugged. "All right. Don't employ my suggestions. But I bet Lady Georgiana uses such tricks."

"Of course she does." Lady Amelia grinned wickedly. "There's not much in the way of interesting talk for her to offer, so she has to resort to batting her lashes and swaying her hips."

"Well, I know firsthand you have plenty of witty things to say, but if you want Worthington to notice you, I suggest you bat your beautiful lashes. Otherwise, you will have no audience for your clever rejoinders."

"Oh, all right," she said mulishly. "I'm sorry to be fussy. I know what needs to be done, Your Grace. I've come to terms with the fact that I need to lead my pig to the trough."

Colin laughed at her odd comparison. "I like that Worthington is a pig in your mind."

"That is not what I meant, Your Grace," she said in a grave tone, though a smile played on her lips.

Colin paused in their steps. "I think since we will be working so closely together you should call me Colin in private."

Her eyes widened, but she nodded. "And you may call me Amelia."

"Well, Amelia," he said, enjoying the way her name rolled of his tongue. "Shall we dance?"

"Of course we shall, Colin," she replied with a giggle then pulled him into a turn.

Laughing, he tugged her back. "Though I am positive you would have no trouble leading any man, you should let your partner lead. It's customary, and we men like to think we are in charge."

Her grin flashed briefly, dazzling as it lit her eyes. "Then by all means, lead me."

"Careful what you say to a man, Amelia," Colin growled as he tugged her a bit closer and started counting off the steps once again. After a bit, when he realized that she was actually dancing with ease. He left off counting, and she did not miss a beat. He studied her when she looked elsewhere. She stood taller than he'd ever seen her, and her shoulders and hands were relaxed. When Amelia forgot about being concerned about her height, she acquired a bit of confidence that gave her grace. He squeezed gently on her hand. "When you relax, you dance quite well. And since we don't have much time before your first social appearance as my prodigy, we need to work on other things."

Her gaze found his and held it. "Such as?"

"Flirting," he said, his blood heating with the thought. He longed to see her eyes light with desire. "Use your eyes."

"Like this?" She fluttered her eyelashes rapidly.

"That's a good start," he said, holding his laughter at bay. He did not want to hurt her feelings. "Try doing it a bit slower."

Slowly, she lowered her lashes, the fringe casting a shadow on her cheeks. Then with slow, sensual care of a courtesan born and bred for seduction, she opened them once more, her gaze, dark and beckoning, froze on his lips. An intense desire to capture her lips with his strummed through him. "I do believe you've already mastered the art of flirting with your eyes."

"What shall we try now?" She cast a glance in the direction of Lucy then leaned close. "Shall I try to brush up against you?" The question was whispered with breathless earnestness.

"The fact is," he said, his voice breaking as his blood thickened in his veins, his hands sliding to her waist of their own volition and molding against the gentle curves, "you are pressed against me now."

The tiniest gasp escaped her as she glanced down. He looked too, though he knew damn well they were chest to chest. Despite his shirt and overcoat, he could have sworn he felt the heat of her body, her heart pounding in a steady rhythm, and the hardened peaks of her nipples. Fierce need pummeled him. Inhaling slowly, he gently set her away. "No need to practice this anymore. You've mastered it, as well."

She grinned. "What shall we work on now?"

"The art of conversing," he immediately replied. No more touching her or else he would take that kiss he neither had right to take nor want near as much as he did.

"I know how to talk perfectly well." Her statement was punctuated with a snort of sorts that made him laugh.

Gripping her elbow, he led her to a bench across the cobblestone terrace and in front of a trickling fountain. Once seated, he faced her. "There is a difference between talking to your family or the ladies you know and talking to a gentleman in whom you are interested."

"I know that," she said with a dismissive wave of her hand. "I have a mother, after all."

She did indeed, but her mother had already confirmed that she had been negligent about informing Amelia exactly how to capture a man's attention. The question remained as to why, though Lady Harthorne did appear willing to allow Amelia to learn now that she knew a marriage would be forthcoming no matter what.

"Let's see what you think you know." The anticipation that strummed through him surprised him. "Let's pretend you are interested in capturing my attention."

Amelia's cheeks immediately pinked. "All right."

"How would you respond if I said I want nothing more in a wife than one who looks pretty in a gown, can play the pianoforte expertly and will be adept at planning the perfect grand dinner party."

She wrinkled her nose. "I'd say you were in for one boring marriage."

For some reason her answer pleased him immensely, though it was entirely wrong. He struggled to school his features, but he could feel a smile of appreciation pulling at his lips. "You cannot say that, or you will have no eligible gentlemen offer for you."

She shrugged. "I would rather end up alone than married to a man who could never love the woman I truly am. I detest the pianoforte. And frankly, I loathe large dinner parties. You can never truly talk to the attendees and get to know them or what they really think. On most occasions, the conversation is meaningless and revolves around the weather, at best, or cruel gossip at worst. I'd much rather marry a man who prefers small intimate gatherings with true friends rather than large ostentatious affairs given only to show off one's wealth."

Colin knew he was staring at her, but he could not help it. Who was this creature? Was this truly how she felt or was she far better at the art of telling a man what he wanted to hear than Colin had ever suspected? Her words had echoed his sentiments almost exactly.

"Worthington is the sort of man who will want to have a great many large dinner parties."

"You're mistaken." Her voice had raised a notch.

Colin tensed. Worthington had always been too self-conscious of the fact that his father was not nearly as wealthy as many other lords, and Worthington's mother was an incredibly scheming woman. Colin was sure he was right about the man and what he wanted. He should let it be. If she had a false impression of Worthington, what did Colin care? He didn't want to marry her. Hell, he didn't want to marry at all. He had to. He'd simply find another apathetic woman to put in her place. The need to speak was like an itch he couldn't scratch. *Damnation.* Drumming his fingers on his knee, he attempted to let it go, but he could not. If there was any chance she was as true as she seemed, he could not let her go on thinking Worthington was a paragon of goodness.

"I'm afraid I'm not mistaken. I went to school with him, and I know him well. He will want dinner parties. He will desire you to play the pianoforte, titter when he tells a joke, inane or not, and look stunning in a gown."

"He will love me for me," she snapped. "Not those silly things you mentioned."

"Perhaps," he replied, evenly. It was a struggle not to let the strange anger building in him seep into his tone. His eyes captured her wide, beautiful gaze. What would it be like for her to speak of his character with such confidence and assurance? The thought stunned him. Why did he care? He did not. Could not. Standing, he held out a hand to her. "Come, I have a surprise for you."

Her gaze and her movements bespoke her hesitation, but she took his elbow and allowed him to lead her into the house with Lucy trailing behind them. With an unaccountable sense of excitement, she stopped in front of the three boxes he had brought from the seamstress. He picked up the first package and handed it to her. "A gift for tomorrow night's dance."

Her eyebrows rose in an expression of amazement. "You should not have."

"Why not?" he said with an ease he did not feel at the moment. "I want you to ensnare Worthington if that's what you truly want."

Her lashes lowered as she glanced down at the box and opened it. An exclamation of delight came from her that filled him with instant pleasure. With trembling hands, she carefully set the box on a table and gathered the gown out of it.

"It's exquisite." Her eyes tilted to meet his, and his heart jerked at the tears glistening there. "I've never been given such a beautiful gown," she whispered.

"I've never given such a gown." Actually, he had never bought a gift for any woman in his life, save his mother. He had given plenty of blunt but never a personal gift. "I have to confess I enjoyed dress shopping much more than I ever thought I would."

"Oh?" She pursed her lips in an irresistible smirk. "I now have a secret to lord over you."

"I suppose you do," he teased back, a foreign light-hearted feeling coming over him. "Try it on for me."

Her eyes widened.

"I mean so that we can ensure it fits you properly." Really, he wanted to see her in it.

"I suppose we do need to know that. I'll be quick," she said with a grin and dashed off before he could respond.

Colin barely had time to prowl the room before soft footsteps tapped against the hardwood stairs and two slippered feet appeared, followed by a peek of swishing rose skirts and finally, Amelia. She was stunning in the silk gown he had chosen for her. His breath snagged in his chest. "The color is perfect for you, just as I suspected it might be with your light hair and bright eyes. The contrast is magnificent."

"Thank you," she said, descending the last of the steps to come directly in front of him. She tilted her head up as she assessed him. "I'm astonished how well this gown fits me, considering that it must have been a sample or perhaps one that was never picked up."

Smiling, he shook his head. "I had it made today." He tapped her back lightly and quickly. "Stand up straight."

She complied while studying him. "You couldn't have possibly had it made today."

"Anything is possible when you have enough blunt, Amelia." He swept his gaze over her body. The gown hugged every curve exactly as he had expected, and this garment was not even made by the finest dressmakers in London. When he got her to Town and had her fitted for the Season...His blood thickened as he considered the alluring picture she was going to present when she made her debut. No man she wanted would be able to resist her tomorrow night. Really, any man who even used half his faculties would not be able to resist her.

"Did my mother give you my measurements?"

"No. I did not need her to."

Amelia frowned. "Is your accuracy in judging women's measurements due to all the women you have known so intimately?"

He stiffened at the caustic remark. Not because it was not accurate. It was. Yet he wished it wasn't. His choices, however well meaning they had been, had made him miserable and dishonorable. "I suppose that's a true enough remark. Do you want all the sordid details of my life? It could provide you quite the risqué education."

She pressed her hands to her cheeks as all the color leeched from her face. "No. You may keep your details. They are not mine to know, unless you need a friend with whom to share them."

"I have enough friends," he lied.

She cast her gaze away, wringing her hands in front of her. "I'm terribly sorry. That was a horrid thing to say. I don't know what came over me."

The last sentiment he understood perfectly. He was confused about what was possessing him lately, too. He had a desire to tell her why he had done the things he had, but he didn't understand why. He wasn't supposed to care what she thought, but a part of him did. He drew a breath and released it slowly as he glanced out the window toward the driveway where Harthorne's carriage ambled up the path. "Your brother is home. Why don't you go change so you can surprise him with how lovely you look in your new gown tomorrow night?"

In truth, Harthorne and he needed to sign the wager paper, and Colin didn't want to chance his friend saying something to Amelia about his father's will and the fact that Colin had to marry or lose his fortune. When she'd asked him if there was anything else she should know about the wager, he had considered telling her. But then he'd thought better of it. Right now, her head was full of fanciful ideas about love, and she might have refused to participate in the wager, despite her family's predicament, if she'd known in actuality he had to marry. Women were too unpredictable to chance complete honesty.

Chapter Twelve

Amelia's nerves were twisted into one big tangled knot that sat in the center of her stomach. Lively music swirled around her, along with the oppressive heat from all the eager bodies crammed into the Stanhope's ballroom for the annual country-dance that kicked off the departure of everyone going to London for the Season. She was going, therefore she should be ecstatic, but she was not. Far from it.

This night should have been perfect—a fairy tale beginning to her very own happily ever after. She had on a beautiful gown, thanks to a generous gift from the wicked, or was that wickedly handsome, duke.

Couples cavorted down the line of dancers with happy smiles on their faces. Amelia forced that same expression to her lips, though she was positive it had to look false. She tapped her foot in time to the music to appear as if she were having a grand time, standing there absolutely alone. Well, throngs of acquaintances surrounded her, but the only person that mattered might as well not have been there, given he had not exchanged a single word with her yet tonight. What was wrong with her fairy tale?

A tittering of especially grating female laughter came from her right. She cast her glance toward the punch bowl where it landed on her blue-gowned rival for her knight in shining armor. Georgiana batted her eyelashes at Charles as he led her to the parquet dance floor.

Oh yes, now she remembered what was wrong with her story. Her knight had failed to notice her. Well, that was not entirely true. She had seen Charles gape at her when she had come into the ball on her brother's arm. Despite the gloomy mood that had pervaded because of her mother's earlier refusal to talk to her, excitement had bubbled in her chest when Amelia had entered the ballroom and her sadness had vanished with Charles's look. She had been sure by the raised eyebrows and appreciative smiles of men who had known her all her life that her moment had finally arrived. That was, until Georgiana had swept up to Charles's side and *poof* Amelia's chance had disappeared before her eyes. No magic involved there. Georgiana was simply more beautiful and apparently more interesting.

Amelia steeled herself against the unhelpful thoughts. She was not ready to give up quite yet. She just was not sure what to do now. Across the ballroom, Constance and her husband appeared in the doorway, and Amelia breathed a sigh of relief. Maybe her friend would have an idea of how to get Charles to notice her. She raised her hand to wave Constance over, but before she got it halfway in the air, a hand clamped on her elbow and pulled her arm down.

Jerking her head around, she blinked at the sight of Colin standing directly behind her. He looked…She struggled to find the words to match what she thought…He looked stunning. Could one use that word to describe a man? No matter. It fit.

His black coat and trousers molded to his powerful body in a way that displayed his muscles to perfection. His crimson cravat, tied in the most exquisite knot she had ever seen, should have made him look foreboding, but he appeared tamed by societal rules temporarily, which she was sure was not accurate. He simply knew how to play the game.

He cocked an eyebrow at her, a knowing smile spreading across his lips. "Has my appearance rendered you speechless?"

She caught herself about to nod and instead shook her head. "Don't be silly. I'm just surprised to see you here." He had been languishing in the study with a book when she and Philip had left.

"Excellent." He grinned. "I do so love the upper hand the element of surprise can offer."

She returned his infectious grin. "That, *Your Grace*, does not surprise me."

"Already you know me so well," he said huskily.

Heavens, but she was suddenly hot. He seemed to have a way of doing that to her. She swallowed, wishing for a fan. "If you were intending to come tonight, why didn't you ride with Philip and me?"

"Because it would not do for everyone to realize I was staying at your house. As I said before, if you end up as my wife, I want no hint of rumor attached to your name."

She pressed her lips together. "You should have remained home with your book. I'll never end up your duchess."

He regarded her quizzically for a moment before slowly smiling. "I do so like your strong mind. However, you should know I plan to be at every social function you attend from here on out."

"Whatever for?" she managed to ask in a steady voice, though her pulse had begun to gallop at his words.

He moved to stand beside her. "Why to help make you an Incomparable, of course, so Worthington will realize he simply must have you as his wife or so you will realize that you simply must have a duke. That cannot happen if you are standing all alone on the side of the dance floor with the other wallflowers." He gave her a cheeky grin.

She scowled at him. Blasted man. He thought he knew women so well. She was going to show him. "I'm not standing with the other wallflowers."

He looked over his shoulder and back at her. "I beg to differ."

Darting a quick look behind her, she sucked in a sharp breath at the sight of five women loitering near the plotted plants and looking decidedly abysmal. Wretched man. He was right but she'd die before admitting it.

"I'm strategizing on how to get Lord Worthington's attention."

"How is that going?" he asked, a smirk pulling at his lips. Her chest tightened as she followed the direction of his gaze to where Charles and Georgiana were still twirling on the dance floor.

"Not very well," she begrudgingly admitted. She could have lied, but what was the point? The truth was too apparent to deny.

Colin turned his head toward her, his gaze softening and the smirk disappearing. "Worthington is a fool."

"Be that as it may, he is a fool who stole my heart long ago,"

A strange glint came into Colin's eyes but was gone before she could place it. His fingers grazed momentarily over the bare skin of her arm before disappearing. Gooseflesh covered the surface where he had touched her. Automatically, she ran her hand against her skin to rub away the bumps.

He leaned near her. "I have an idea. Do you trust me?"

His husky voice vibrated in her ear, and the sensitive skin of her lobe tingled from his warm breath against her tender flesh. "No," she said, irritated with the way her pulse sped every time he drew close to her.

A deep chuckle rumbled from him. "It's good to be guarded, especially with a man that has a reputation like mine, but you *can* trust me."

She glanced sideways at him, and he grinned, showing his gleaming white teeth, much like a wolf. "I can trust you?"

His smile widened. "For tonight anyway."

She snorted. "Do you know you have a predatory look in your eyes?"

"Do I? Some habits are hard to break." He wiggled his eyebrows. "Enough about me. Listen to my plan."

"Yes, all right," she said, trying and failing to wipe the grin off her face. Colin's humor and willingness to joke about himself surprised her and, she realized, put her at ease. "What's your plan?"

"We are going to make Worthington jealous."

"How are we going to do that?"

"Simple, my dear," he said in the silkiest voice she had ever heard. Colin took the dance card she had been fidgeting with and read it with narrowing eyes.

"Bunch of fools," he muttered under his breath, yet she heard him.

"Who?"

He glanced up sharply then swept his gaze across the dance floor. Raising his hand, he pointed to Lord Belford. "He's a fool. And there." He jabbed his finger in Lord Cooper's direction. "Definitely lacking wits." He jerked his head toward Lord Herbert who walked in front of them and smiled at her but did not stop. "He may be the biggest idiot of them all," Colin practically snarled and none too quiet. Lord Herbert glanced back at them, his forehead creased in puzzlement.

"Lower your voice," she hissed. "Whatever is the matter with you?"

His gaze, now dark and dazzling with fury, pierced her. This time her pulse did not simply speed up, it raced ahead, so that she felt as if catching her breath might be impossible.

"There is nothing the matter with me. It is the lot of men here who have dull wits or else your dance card would be full."

A sudden ache blossomed in her chest as she gazed at him. "You are angry on my behalf? Because my dance card is empty?"

"I'm more than angry. I'm livid." He glanced down the length of her dress and then slowly inched back up to her face. "You look ravishing, and I know personally that you have more intelligence in you than any other woman I've ever met."

The warmth that had been building rapidly in her chest exploded and flowed through her. He thought her ravishing and intelligent. It took only a second to realize she was grinning like a ninny and that his words had made her incredibly happy. But why? She did not love him. Why would she care what he thought? But he was handsome. And interesting. And titled. And— She gasped.

The wager had barely started and she was already allowing her gaze to stray away from Charles to another man. And worst of all, she was ogling a man who so happened to believe all women wanted nothing more than to marry the gentleman with the greatest title. She swallowed hard. If she did find herself interested in him, it certainly would not be because of his status, but he would never believe that.

"Thank you for the compliments," she finally said. "Are you trying to bolster my confidence?"

His brows came together. "No. I mean, yes." He swiped a hand across his face. "Do you know you confound me, and I've never met a woman that does that?"

Her cheeks quivered with her smile. She was grinning again, blast him. "You confuse me, as well, but frankly, all men confuse me."

He threw his head back and laughed. Once the rich sound died away, he glanced at her, a sober expression on his face. "Either you are the most truthful woman I have ever met or you are the best actress I have ever come across."

She shrugged, dismayed and alternately amazed at how much she was enjoying bantering with him. "I'm quite sure it's the first, but I don't suppose you can simply tell someone you are truthful and expect that person to believe it."

"No, I don't suppose you can," he murmured. "I do believe my plan is working," he said, looking over her shoulder at the dance floor.

She blinked. His plan? Oh, yes! She started to twist in the direction she had last seen Charles, but Colin put a staying hand on her arm. "Never search out the object of your affection."

"Never?"

He shook his head.

"Is this part of my lessons on how to become an Incomparable?"

"But of course. By my account, we are on lesson number three."

"What was one and two?" She hated to ask, but her wits felt absolutely addled tonight, and she wanted to remember everything she was and was not to do.

"Number one was dancing and number two was conversing."

"Well, at the rate this night is progressing, *teacher*, I'm afraid this pupil will not have a need for either of your previous excellent lessons."

"Ah, my dear," he murmured in a velvet voice. "Never underestimate yourself...or me. Your prey has been watching us for the last five minutes."

She arched her brows. "He has?"

Colin nodded. "Yes. And now we are going to teach *him* a lesson."

"We are?" Her stomach tightened, whether from excitement or apprehension she was not sure. "What sort of lesson?"

He gave her an exaggerated wink. "That he will lose you if he does not pay you the attention you deserve."

That sounded good to her. The attention part, that was. Not the loss part. Though, what if Charles turned out to be the sort of man who could never truly see into her heart and appreciate her mind, as well as the outer picture? She did not want a life filled with games played out day after tedious day to keep her husband's interest. She wanted a man who felt he could not breathe without her. Like in the novels she read. Before she could contemplate it further, Colin grasped her hand and drew her close.

"He's coming this way. Throw your head back and laugh, and when he requests a dance, tell him you do not have one left."

She tried to jerk away, but Colin's hand came to her back and kept her near him. "But none of my dances are taken," she whispered.

"They will be." His words came out clipped, urgent and unbending.

"But I want to dance with Lord Worthington. How else will I make him fall in love with me?"

Colin blew out a sigh that tickled her neck. "By not dancing with him, my dear. Allow the master to show you."

Giggling in earnest, she glanced at his face and was startled by the way his gaze seemed to caress her. She blinked, and the moment was gone. "All right. I'll do as you say, but what if no one asks me to dance? I'll look the fool."

"I will never allow you to look the fool. Trust me." His gaze, as well as his voice, lowered. "Once I'm finished, the gentlemen will be climbing over each other to request a dance with you."

She nodded, unable to speak since her heartbeat had taken up residence in her throat. She really didn't want to be the star in this play, but it seemed she had no choice, unless she wanted to lose Charles. Behind her, something rustled, and then Charles sidled up to them, his gaze trained on her and not sparing a greeting or even a glance for Colin.

Amelia stiffened at his rude behavior. This was not what she expected of him.

"Lady Amelia, you look lovely."

"Thank you," she murmured. Hadn't Colin called her ravishing? She preferred that word. It held so much more emotion. Oh dear! Whatever was wrong with her? Colin was truly addling her wits with his presence, and no wonder, he was an expert seducer, even when he was not trying to seduce.

"Might I have the next dance?" Charles asked.

"I'm frightfully sorry, but the next dance is taken." Gracious, she could hardly believe she had gotten the lie out without giving herself away.

"Taken?" Charles's eyebrows shot up in what looked to be surprise. Heat instantly flamed her face. It irritated her to no end that he had the power to make her feel bad about herself.

"Yes, Worthington," Colin drawled lazily beside her. "The lady said her next dance is taken, which means she is spoken for. I guess you did not pay enough attention in school if the meaning of the word *taken* escapes you."

Amelia wanted to kiss Colin for putting Charles in his place.

Charles's eyes narrowed. "Why are you still here, Aversley? There is no wedding for you to attend. Shouldn't you be getting home to all your *activities*?"

"Lord Worthington!" Amelia exclaimed. Were his words inspired by jealousy or a cruel nature? The sudden doubt in him made her stomach clench.

"Lady Amelia, don't fret yourself on my account," Colin said smoothly. "I'm quite used to Worthington's contempt." Amusement flashed across Colin's face. "You know, I thought to leave immediately, but once I started getting to know Lady Amelia I quickly decided to stay in Norfolk for a visit."

"Lady Amelia," Charles said through clenched teeth. "Might I have the dance after this one?"

"Taken," Colin fairly chirped before she could open her mouth to respond. She glanced at him to warn him with her gaze not to carry this too far, but the challenging smile on his face made her reconsider. He had asked her to trust him, and she would. Plus, it was rather fun, this turning the tables on Charles.

"How the devil would you know which of the lady's dances are taken or not?" Charles snarled.

"I'll have to ask you not to speak vulgarly in front of me," Amelia added, throwing herself into the game.

Charles's neck reddened. "I'm sorry, Lady Amelia."

"I forgive you." She allowed a small smile. *"This time."*

His jaw clenched, and she could see him working it back and forth. After a moment, he spoke. "Do you have an open dance?"

"I'm afraid I don't. I'm so sorry. But perhaps we will run into each other in London for the Season, and we can dance then."

His eyes rounded in surprise. "I did not realize you were going to London."

"Of course she's going to London," Colin inserted, moving so close to her that his arm brushed her ribs. He proffered his elbow, and without hesitating, she slipped her arm through the open crook. If Charles's narrowed eyes and pressed lips were any indication, Colin's plan to make the man jealous so he would take note of her was working. Colin was a genius. He glanced down at her with eyes filled with what appeared to be adoration. What a silly thought. It was simply an act for Charles's benefit.

The first notes of the next dance started and Colin began to pull her toward the dance floor, but Charles grabbed her arm. Beside her, Colin growled under his breath and his muscles jumped under her fingertips. She had to bite down on her lip to keep from laughing. He was truly putting everything into pretending he was besotted by her. She gave him a grateful squeeze while quirking an eyebrow at Charles. "Yes?"

"Please let me call on you in London."

Amelia allowed a small smile. This was more like it. "I suppose that will be all right."

"Excellent. Where will you be staying?"

That was a good question…and one she did not know the answer to since Philip had sold their London townhome to pay some of their debts.

"Just follow the line of suitors, Worthington, and you'll find her," Colin barked as he tugged her forward. "Now if you don't mind, you are taking valuable time away from my dance with the lady."

Amelia allowed Colin to lead her to the dance floor and through the first round of steps to make sure she had mastered them before she spoke. "That was brilliant, thank you."

"No need to thank me, Amelia. I have to be truthful. There is not much love lost between Worthington and myself, so I rather enjoyed making him jealous."

"You certainly played the part well."

His hazel eyes met hers. "You make it easy."

"Are you still acting?" she blurted. Heavens! Why had she asked that? Yet, one glance of his smoldering gaze answered her question. She knew why. He stared at her with a strange hunger, much like the look she had dreamed Charles would wear when gazing at her.

But then Colin blinked and the look was gone. "Yes, I'm sorry. It seems once I'm in the role it's hard to break it."

~

Why the devil had he just lied? Colin gripped her around the waist a little tighter as they danced down the line and then came back together face-to-face. Confusion swarmed him. He had been jealous when Worthington had asked to call on her and livid when he had seen her empty dance card. He wasn't sure why he cared so much, or even at all. He didn't want a wife, let alone one who made him jealous. Yet, the fact was that if Philip did lose the wager this woman would be his wife, and even though he would never allow himself to feel love for her, he did not care for the idea of his possible future duchess in another man's arms or with another man's lips pressed to hers. He had never had to share a thing in his life, and he was not going to start with her. *Especially not her*, a voice in his head added.

He needed to help her while ensuring she remained chaste per chance Philip lost the wager. That was going to make a very thin line for him to walk.

"If anyone else should ask you, you can tell them you are staying in Town at my aunt's home. Lady Langley is her name."

Amelia quirked her lovely eyebrows at him. "Will your aunt approve of this?"

He nodded. "Aunt Jane is a spinster. She'll welcome the company."

"Why did she never marry?"

"She did not need to. Her mother's aunt left all her money to Aunt Jane. She is a very wealthy woman in her own right, therefore rendering the need for a man useless."

"I suppose you imagine that proves your point about women."

"But it does. The money is all she requires. She cares nothing for love."

Amelia smirked at him. "Did you never think that perhaps your aunt simply never found love or she did but it slipped away from her?"

"That's absurd," he replied but missed a step as he did so. Amelia's eyes widened as she teetered. He reached out and grasped her arm, pulling her closer than needed, to rescue her. She had imbalanced him by offering an observation that he had never considered. The desire to do the same to her overcame him, but he could not think beyond the overwhelming awareness that she was crushed against him—all soft and womanly.

He glanced at her face and need stirred restlessly within him. Her lids had become heavy, and her gaze had darkened. Heat rushed through him. By God, she desired him. Her lashes fell but not before a blush of awareness stained her cheeks. She may think she loved Worthington, but her body had never craved a man as she wanted Colin. That much was evident by her embarrassment.

A sharp pain assaulted his chest. If Amelia were his, he would be her first everything and, in a way, she would be his. He shoved the thought away as ice crept into his veins. Already, he was becoming a weak fool like his father had been.

"Please let me go," she whispered hoarsely.

With numb fingers, he complied. Around them couples moved off the dance floors while others poured onto it. One particular gentleman caught Colin's attention. Huntington stood at the edge of the dance floor with his gaze fixed on Amelia, though Colin saw Huntington's daughter swirl by in the other direction. The lecherous look on the man's face did not sit well with Colin.

"Amelia, what do you know of Huntington?"

She looked past him, and her face became pinched. "I do not care for him in the least."

"Neither do I. Something about the way he stares at you does not seem right." He would have said more, but Belford strode their way with an eager look on his face. Colin clenched his teeth. He had known if he'd danced with her and showed her special attention the fools here would notice her. Colin nodded toward Belford. "The gentleman beating a path this way like an eager puppy is a harmless, though none too entertaining, chap I know from Cambridge. As I predicted, your dance card is about to become full."

Amelia's chest rose with her sharp inhalation, but he had to give her credit, she did not turn in the direction of his gaze. She was a fast learner. "Belford is about ten paces away and fairly foaming at the mouth. He'll ask you to dance. Do so. Then I imagine Cooper and Herbert will want to claim a dance. Those three fools compete with each other for the attention of one woman every Season." Colin swept his gaze around the room. "After that, I suspect Denton and James will fill out your card."

Her lips were parted as if to protest, but she closed her mouth and nodded. "You seem very sure about who will do what tonight."

His chest did that odd tightening thing again. "Unfortunately, I am sure," he said. It was the first time he had not wanted to be certain of something because that confidence meant that tonight would be the beginning of Amelia's change. Tomorrow, she would wake with the smallest knowledge of the power she had over men. She would greet him at breakfast, and he would see the change by the knowing slant of her eyes and the beguiling notes in her voice or perhaps she would purposely sway her hips.

Belford reached them on the last thought. Colin surveyed the man's foppish dress clothes, elaborate cravat, and rings shining from more fingers than not. The man was not for Amelia, but that was for Amelia to decide.

"Belford," Colin said by way of greeting.

The man's squinty eyes focused on Colin. "Aversley, what brings you to Norfolk?"

Colin allowed his gaze to trail to Amelia, linger for a moment, and then he pulled it back toward Belford. "I have an interest in someone here but that someone will be leaving tomorrow, so I will, as well. Though, I have found Norfolk quite entertaining."

"Don't tell me the infamous Aversley is searching for a bride," Belford said with a chuckle.

Normally, anyone asking Colin what he was doing or implying they knew what he was about would have sent him in the other direction with a clipped answer, but this night was not about him. It was about Amelia, and for her, he would endure the boring Belford's prying. "All right, I won't tell you, but I do suppose you should mention what it is you want. Or did you stroll up to simply offer your greetings to me?"

Splotches instantly covered Belford's face. His gaze darted from Colin to Amelia. "Lady Amelia, I was hoping you might have this dance free?"

Amelia nodded, though Colin would swear she did not look overly pleased, and unless he was wishful hearing, she had sighed.

She turned to him. "Until later, Your Grace."

"I do hope there will be a later, Lady Amelia," he said.

As Belford led Amelia into the throng of dancers, Colin stood there fighting the urge not to go after her and snatch her away from the man. Finally, he turned away and searched the room for an inconspicuous place to stand and keep watch over her in case she should need him. His gaze landed on Harthorne, lingering very near the terrace doors. He waved Colin over.

A few moments later, Colin strolled up to him. "Why are you standing alone in the shadows?"

Harthorne shrugged. "Keeping an eye on Amelia. Same as you judging by the way you were staring at her as she walked off with Belford."

Colin tensed at the knowing lilt in Harthorne's voice. Amelia's brother turned to him. "I can understand perfectly why you insisted on being here tonight and at future events she attends. And I even understand why you don't want her to be alone with Worthington, unless I have a formal offer from him. I happen to feel the same way about that."

"I'm glad we concur," Colin grated out. He did not like where he sensed this conversation was going, but what he liked even less was how Amelia had just batted her eyelashes at Belford and thrown her head back as if the man had said something funny. Colin had taught her that flirtatious trick, but now he was wishing he had not. What the devil was wrong with him?

"Aversley, are you listening to me?"

Colin snapped his attention to Harthorne. He had not heard a bloody word the man had said. "Sorry, I was concentrating on your sister's progress with Belford."

"I see that," Harthorne said with a smug smile. "And that is exactly the point I just made. You seem overly invested to me, as if you are a man who truly cares for my sister and is not simply interested in her because of our wager or even because you have to marry. Do you care for Amelia?"

The question was like a punch to the gut. Did he care for her? His stomach clenched as she smiled at her newest dance partner, Cooper. The man slid his hand too low for Colin's liking.

"Do you think Cooper is taking liberties with your sister?"

Harthorne glanced from Colin to Amelia and Cooper. Turning back to Colin, he grinned. "No, I don't. Do you know what else I think?"

Colin absently shook his head, finding it hard to care what Harthorne thought. His blood rushed in his ears and all his muscles tensed in preparation to plunge in the dance crowd and rescue Amelia from the lecherous Cooper.

"I think only a man besotted would construe an innocent dance as an attempt at seduction."

That got Colin's attention. He narrowed his gaze on his friend. "I am not besotted with your sister. Not only do I hardly know her, but I am not a man to become besotted. Ever."

With a hearty chuckle, Harthorne clapped a hand on Colin's shoulder. "If it makes you feel better, keep telling yourself that, my friend."

Irritated, Colin shrugged Harthorne off. "It is the truth. My interest in your sister may seem keen, but it is because I know you are going to lose the wager. I do not want her reputation besmirched. I will not be made a laughingstock as my father was."

Harthorne grinned at him. The man actually had the gall to grin! "I predict things will turn out splendidly. Exactly as they should for two people who mean the world to me. I do believe I'll go play a game of cards in the other room."

"I thought you were going to keep watch over your sister."

"I'm confident you won't let her out of your sight," Harthorne replied.

That was perfectly true. For the next hour, Colin watched Amelia dance with suitor after suitor and with each new partner the strange tension within him grew. By the time the night was over and he could take his leave, he felt just as exhausted as when he had been in the boxing ring at Gentleman Jackson's for hours. The difference was he felt happy now. Fighting at Gentlemen Jackson's had always managed to push the gloom down somewhat, but it had never made him feel *happy*. Yet, simply watching Amelia made him happy. The thought scared the devil out of him, because if she could give him happiness, she could just as easily take it away and then all that would be left was misery.

~

The next morning, Colin rose before the sun with an odd sort of tension running through him. He did not like the fact that Amelia made him feel anything. What had been so perfect about the wager was that even if he lost and Amelia became his wife, he had been sure he could remain aloof for a lifetime and thus, safe from pain. He dressed quietly, so as not to awaken anyone else in the household, and made his way outdoors to practice fencing to relax.

On the way to the open field he had trained in the day before, he was strolling past a garden when the sound of Amelia singing reached him. He stopped to listen. Her merry tone made him smile, but seeing her bent over a vegetable garden, her dress sleeves rolled up, and her hair shoved haphazardly on her head in that beautifully messy style of hers released his tension in a way nothing in his life ever had. He frowned at that.

"Amelia," he called, certain a short conversation with her would confirm that her change had already begun.

She paused with her tool raised high in the air, sat up on her knees, and craned her neck around to look at him. A large splotch of dirt covered her right cheek, and the urge to walk over to her and wipe the grime off her lovely skin nagged him. He strolled over with his arms crossed. The last thing he bloody needed to do was touch Amelia.

"Last night went splendidly," he said.

Amelia frowned and swiped a hand across her sweaty forehead, which put another dark streak of dirt on her skin. That was it. He couldn't stand it. He dropped to his knees, whipped out a handkerchief, and held it in the air between them. "May I? You have dirt on your forehead and cheek."

"Does it bother you?" she said with a laugh.

"Only because it covers your pretty face." *Bloody idiot.* Why was he saying such syrupy nonsense?

Her eyes widened, but much to his relief, they rounded in what appeared to be delight and not guile. "Go ahead," she said, her voice low and wavering.

With care, he cleaned her face and then stuffed the handkerchief away. "Were you pleased with the way things went last night?" He tensed as he waited for her gushing to begin.

"Who wouldn't be pleased spending hours fluttering her eyelashes and pasting on false smiles. It was almost as much fun as playing the pianoforte."

Colin suppressed a smile. "I thought you didn't play."

"Exactly," she huffed. "Because it's mind-numbingly dull."

"And you find flirting dull?"

Her gaze locked on his then strayed to his lips before coming back to his eyes. "I suppose one has to have the right partner."

Did she think he was the right partner? Devil take it, he should not care. "Well, you're certain to find it entertaining when you flirt with Worthington, since he has your heart."

She nodded, but her brow was puckered.

"Are you doubting your feelings?" He didn't care for the way his pulse surged all of a sudden.

She rested her hands on her knees. "No. Not that."

She sounded uncertain, by God, she did.

"Part of me knows I need to catch Lord Worthington's attention so he will have the chance to fall in love with who I really am, but there is another part of me that is frustrated because he has previously failed to notice me as I am. Graceless or not, gowned in shiny silk or drab cotton, if he is meant for me, would it really matter to him?"

Her words caused his heart to pound harder. He wanted to tell her it should not matter one damn bit and to forget Worthington, who really was not worthy of her, but the same fear from last night reared its ugly head. He was becoming too involved and caring too much about what she did. "Worthington is a man like any other."

"Like you?"

"I'm no better," he said dully. "In fact, I'm worse."

"So you care about all that, as well? I would not have thought—"

"I don't care about anything," he interrupted, needing to sever the connection he suddenly felt to her.

The hurt that flashed across her face made him want to take back every bloody word he had just said. Instead, he sat in stony silence. Already, she was wiggling into his heart. He could not allow it. Hell, he was *afraid* to permit it.

She stood and brushed off her skirts while piercing him with eyes that seemed to know too damn much. "You're lying, again. You care about my brother, and I vow you care about me."

His heartbeat thrashed in his ears. "What makes you think I care about you?"

"Because of the way you've treated me with such patience at kindness. We could be friends, you know. I bet you've never had a woman as a friend. Have you?"

"No, I have not." His words came out stiff. He could not bloody help it. The turn of this conversation was making him uncomfortable.

"I'm going to be your friend," she fairly growled then flashed him a smile. "We will be friends, whether you like it or not." She plunked her hands on her hips. "In fact, you will not be able to stop it. One day you will wake up and realize you could not imagine your life without my friendship." She tossed down her tool and speared him with narrowed eyes. "Think on that, Colin. Now, I am going to wash up and start packing for the trip to London." With that, she whirled on her heel and walked away.

There was no sway in her hips whatsoever, but damn it all, it was the most provocative stride Colin had ever seen—purposeful and unchanging from the day before. It was perfect.

Chapter Thirteen

London England
Lady Langley's home

After three long days of traveling from Norfolk to London, Amelia wanted nothing more than to sink into a bath to wash the grime of the road away. Instead, she stood alone before Colin's aunt, Lady Langley, and felt very much like a horse being inspected for purchase. Finally, the lady stopped in front of Amelia, one haughty dark-red eyebrow raised. "Aversley said in his letter that your mother would be joining you."

Heat crept up Amelia's neck, along with a pang in the pit of her belly. "She fell ill just before we left and will follow once she's better." The lie made her stomach knot. Yet, it was the same lie her mother had uttered when she had told Amelia she would not be coming with her right away. Amelia had recognized the falsehood by her mother's wringing hands and her darting eyes. She had tried, without success, to get her mother to tell her the truth.

When that hadn't worked, Amelia had said she would stay until her mother felt well enough to accompany her, but Mother had ordered she go. She hadn't wanted to come alone, but the more she'd argued the more insistent and upset Mother had become, until Amelia felt the arguing was only making matters worse for her mother's already fragile state. So she'd relented but had stopped at Constance's and gotten assurances that Constance and her mother would check on Mother every day. Philip was with Mother too, but he was a man, after all.

Lady Langley waved her hand, and a kind smile came to her face. "No matter. This will give me a chance to really get to know you and decide if you are worthy of Aversley."

Amelia blinked. "You misunderstand, Lady Langley. I'm here to make my debut, not to marry your nephew."

The woman's eyebrow quirked higher. "I misunderstand nothing. Colin wrote me about the wager."

"He did?" Amelia felt her mouth gape open.

"Of course he did. He may be a lot of things, my dear, but a liar is not one of them. He would never ask me to sponsor you for the Season under false pretenses. He disclosed everything to me as was proper, but rest assured, I'll not whisper a word of it."

"Thank you," Amelia choked out.

"No need to thank me. When I started to read his letter my first inclination was to deny his outrageous request, but then I thought about the fact that he had bothered to make the request of me."

"I don't understand your meaning."

Lady Langley motioned her over to a settee and took the chair opposite Amelia. Once seated, Colin's aunt continued. "Colin has never asked me for anything in his entire life, so you must be very special to him."

Amelia shook her head. "No, not me. My brother. He is doing all this for my brother."

"I don't think so. If this were simply for your brother, Colin would not have asked for my help. He involved me to make sure everything is perfectly proper. I do believe he's quite sure you will become his duchess."

"Well, he's wrong," Amelia retorted more sharply than she intended.

Lady Langley cocked her head. "You may be the first debutante I have met that did not have designs on marrying my nephew. Do you find him displeasing?"

"No. He's very easy to talk to. And kind, generous, and good, though I vow he does not think so."

"I vow you're right," Lady Langley agreed with a soft smile. "You seem to think very highly of him."

Amelia nodded. "I do. I truly do."

"That pleases me to hear. I worry about him."

The flash of pain that crossed Lady Langley's face tugged on Amelia's heart. Impulsively, she grasped the woman's hand. "I'm worried for him, too. That's why I have a plan."

"A plan?"

"Yes. I intend to show your nephew that he's wrong about women. I mean to help him fall in love."

Both Lady Langley's eyebrows arched high. "I daresay you will accomplish your goal, Lady Amelia."

The sound of a throat being cleared behind her made Amelia tense. She instantly turned in her seat and froze. Colin leaned in the doorway with the oddest expression on his face, almost one of wonderment

Dear heavens. Had he heard what she said to his aunt? She jerked her gaze back to Lady Langley, and the woman gave a slight shrug as if in apology. Amelia dug her nails into the velvet of the settee. Colin's aunt had known he was standing there and had not said a word while Amelia blurted her intentions for Colin.

There was no hope for it now but to face him. Amelia straightened her spine and turned back around. "How long have you been standing there eavesdropping?"

"I was not eavesdropping," Colin said, in a smooth tone. "I simply did not want to interrupt. I came to see how the two of you were getting along, make my apologies for being detained and not being here to properly introduce you."

"How long have you been standing there?" Amelia asked again. She simply had to know.

Colin shrugged. "Long enough to know you harbor false hopes."

"Aversley!" Lady Langley cried out.

Amelia kept her attention trained on Colin. "Which part is false, Your Grace?"

~

Colin yanked on his cravat as he stared at Amelia. Her hands were on her hips, and she had a challenging glint in her eyes. By God, she was already changing his views on women. Or at least one woman—her. But that did not mean he wanted any part of love or that he would share any of this with her. "Likely both, but most definitely the latter. However, I did not come here to talk about me."

He strode across the room and gave his aunt what he hoped was a stern look of warning. He did not like that she had tricked Amelia into spilling her secrets while he was standing there, though he had to admit hearing Amelia say she thought he was kind, good, and generous pleased him. In fact, it pleased him more than it bloody should.

He had never been close to his aunt, but he knew she had never approved of how his mother had treated his father, and that simple fact alone made him like her and had caused him to think he could trust her not to meddle in his affairs. She never had before.

Glancing between his aunt and Amelia, he said, "If you are done discussing me, I've come to collect Lady Amelia to take her shopping for gowns. She only has two nights before her first ball, and she needs to be properly outfitted."

"You're going to take her shopping?"

He chuckled at the disbelief in his aunt's voice. "Yes. To Bond Street. I've scheduled an appointment with Madame Laurent."

Amelia gave him a puzzled look. "But if we go to Bond Street together, even with my lady's maid as chaperone, won't people whisper that there is something between us?"

"They will," he replied, watching her face. "That's part of my plan, Lady Amelia. The gentlemen will want you because it seems I do. We men are simple creatures. We always want what we think we cannot have."

Amelia rose slowly and faced him. "I only care if one man wants me, and as long as you're certain of this plan I will go along with whatever you say."

He grinned wickedly and held out his arm to her. "You've no idea how I've dreamed of a lady telling me she'd go along with whatever I say."

Amelia smirked at him. "I've no doubt you've met plenty of women willing to do exactly as you bid, but let me clarify that my willingness to act like an eager puppy extends only so far as the boundaries of decorum allow."

"I do so like you, Lady Amelia," his aunt said with a snicker. "You're feisty."

Amelia inclined her head toward his aunt, but Colin caught the mischievous twinkle in her eye. When Amelia slipped her slender arm into his, Colin was struck with how right it felt to hold her so near. "Incomparable women don't adhere to the boundaries of decorum, my dear. That's what makes them unique. And when I am finished recreating you, you will be in a class of your own."

Amelia snorted.

"Personally," his aunt said from behind them as they strolled toward the door, "I don't see that there is any need to recreate Lady Amelia at all. From the short time I've spent with her, she seems perfect to me. A smart man will want her exactly as she is."

"I couldn't agree more," Colin said. "But the man she wants is a fool." Amelia's sharp intake of breath was not lost on him, but he did not say another word as he led her out of the house and into the awaiting carriage.

Several hours later, Colin sat in the world's most uncomfortable chair, but that was not what had his anger mounting with every second that passed. Amelia had come out from the dressing room with at least twenty different shades of material draped cleverly around her, apologizing each time for how awful she looked. He had responded repeatedly that she looked lovely. It was true. Amelia could have been wearing a sack, and she would be ravishing. Why he had ever thought she needed a beautiful gown to enhance her already stunning appearance now mystified him.

Damn it all, he had contributed to her doubts about herself along with every other foolish gentleman she had come across.

Amelia strolled into the center of the waiting room, this time resplendent in azure. The color of the gown enhanced her eyes perfectly and left him speechless.

She eyed him, as did Madame Laurent who hovered behind Amelia. "Well?" Amelia said, repeating the same process she had been for the last two hours. "What of this color?"

"It looks perfect on you."

"You've said that about every hue I've been draped in for the last two hours! I am sure I look inadequate. I always look wretched."

"May I have a moment alone with Lady Amelia, Madame Laurent?" Colin asked in as steady a voice as he could muster with the anger at himself simmering within.

"But of course," the seamstress replied and hurried to the opposite corner of the room to busily toy with swatches.

Colin rose, walked over to Amelia, and grasped her by the elbow to lead her to the looking glass. "You do not properly see yourself, Amelia," he said staring at her.

She furrowed her brow. "I see perfectly fine, and what I see is tall, gangly and graceless.

He wanted to run the pad of his thumb over her skin and remove the lines of worry. Instead, he took a deep breath and continued. "The color of the gown does not make you beautiful, nor in truth, does the opulence of the material. It is correct both can enhance beauty, but unless beauty is there it cannot be revealed." He gripped her shoulders and turned her until she faced the looking glass. "You already possess beauty. It's here." He brushed his finger down the silken skin near her shining eyes. "Real joy comes from your eyes. I also see beauty here." He ran a finger perilously close to her full lips. "When you smile, it's genuine." The tremor that he felt course through her made him want to spin her around, tilt her head back and claim her delectable mouth for a kiss that would make her forget who the devil Worthington was. The problem was the kiss might make him forget who the devil *he* was.

Appalled at the desire she inspired in him, he forced it under control, inch by painful inch, until the detachment that had always been a part of his life when it came to women descended over him like a fog blanketing the countryside. He forced his fingers to release her arms and break the contact that made him feel tethered to this woman who was supposed to mean nothing to him. Yet, words that needed to be spoken still burned his throat. "Never forget that a dress cannot make you beautiful because you are already heartbreakingly so."

Her mouth parted, but before she could say a word, he turned on his heel and stalked toward Madame Laurent. "Make her a gown in every color she wore for me today, but the first one must be made of the color she is wearing now. Have it sent to my aunt's home in two day's time."

It was no surprise that Madame Laurent nodded vigorously. Colin had offered her a small fortune to assure him Amelia would have a new dress for her first ball in two days. He felt Amelia's quiet presence behind him. The very air seemed to shift when she drew near. He turned to her. "If you'll please go change. I have somewhere I need to be shortly. I'll drop you off at my aunt's." He had absolutely nowhere to be, but he knew he needed to get away from her and clear his head.

As she wandered off to change, he paced the room, his mind turning. He was beginning to question his plan, his wager, and devil take it, his sanity. If Philip lost the bet, Amelia would be his wife, and that had previously been an acceptable outcome to the unescapable situation his father's will had left him in. It had only been tolerable because he had assumed he would never have any feelings for Amelia other than indifference, as one has to a rather bland cup of tea. One drinks it because it's there, but really, one could take it or leave it.

Except, damn his father, Colin *had* to take a wife.

What the devil was he going to do? He could find another wife. A dull-witted, ugly thing he'd never desire or think witty, but then he would be unable to help Philip, assuming Philip would even let him out of that part of the wager. Colin paused and placed his hands on the back of the settee, digging his fingers into the plush material. If Philip lost then that meant Amelia would have changed. Colin couldn't stand the thought of that. He didn't want to be right.

Suddenly, the room felt too small and hot. He felt as if he was going mad. He strode toward the door and threw it open with a bang. Gripping the banister, he took long measured breaths. If Philip won the bet, Colin had no doubt that Amelia would become Worthington's wife, unless the man was a complete and utter fool, and as much as he hated to admit it, he didn't think Worthington was that stupid.

What a bloody, impossible predicament he was in. The idea of winning the wager made him sick and the idea of losing the wager made his blood run cold. He didn't know what the hell he wanted with the exception of Amelia in his bed, and that was the last thing he could have. At least, not yet.

Chapter Fourteen

The next morning, Amelia positioned the light-green carriage hat on her head. They had purchased it on the spot yesterday, and now she gaped at her reflection in the looking glass. Stepping back, she viewed herself in the carriage dress that had been quickly altered for her. An unstoppable grin spread across her face. If she had known years ago that taking extra care with her appearance could make her look passably pretty, she would have set her books aside and tried harder with her clothing and hair. She laughed. Her books had been her refuge when she was teased so mercilessly, so perhaps she had not been ready to set them aside until now.

Until Colin came into my life. She caught her breath on the errant thought.

Warmth blossomed low in her belly with the remembrance of Colin's sweet words to her yesterday in the seamstress's shop. The man had a way with complimenting her that made her think he actually believed the non-sense he was saying. She cocked her head and attempted to see herself as Colin had tried to paint her yesterday.

She widened then narrowed her eyes. They might be shiny, but she vowed one was slightly bigger than the other. She pursed her lips. He had said her smile was genuine, which made her beautiful. She had always considered herself sincere, but it certainly did not seem honest to dress in finery, bat her lashes, and brush herself against a man to get him to fall in love with her when normally she would do no such thing. Doubt seeped into her mind, not for the first time.

A scratch at the door interrupted further contemplation. "My lady, His Grace is here to collect you for your outing."

Amelia rushed to the bedchamber door and flung it open. Whether the gown was hers under false pretenses or not, she did like it and could not wait for Colin to see her in it. "Thank you, Lucy. Are you ready to go?"

Amelia new lady's maid nodded. "Yes, my lady."

"Then come on. Let us see how the duke likes my carriage gown." Amelia hurried down the spiral staircase without waiting for a reply.

As she neared the bottom, Colin looked up and his eyes lit, making Amelia grin. "You approve?"

He held out his hand to her. "I more than approve. I will have to beat the suitors away with a cane." A stricken look crossed his face. "We are in dire trouble, Lady Amelia, for I do not possess a cane."

Amelia chuckled, once again struck with how lighthearted Colin actually was. She set her hand in his outstretched one, and the warmth of his skin against hers, combined with the strength in the fingers that curled around her bones, sent a dizzying wave through her body. Sucking in a steadying breath, she said in as theatrical a tone as she could manage, "Whatever shall we do, Your Grace? Perhaps we should not go?"

"I've a cane we can take," Lucy said from behind Amelia.

Colin and Amelia burst out laughing at the same time, their gazes locking. He winked and she winked back, and he grinned at her.

Turning, she waved her maid forward. "We are playing, Lucy. His Grace is certainly not going to have to defend me from rabid suitors."

Lucy's cheeks reddened. "Oh, yes. How foolish of me."

"Nonsense," Colin said with a gentle tone that made Amelia's insides melt a little. The man truly cared for people's feelings whether he admitted it to himself or not.

Colin helped Amelia down the last few steps while his gaze remained on Lucy. "Lady Amelia certainly looks lovely enough to inspire dangerous devotion, so do not think yourself foolish. If either of you ladies needs protecting. I am not as soft as I appear."

"Your Grace," Lucy exclaimed. "You don't look soft at all. Hard as a rock and chiseled like a boulder is more apt. I've no doubt you could protect us."

Amelia had been thinking a similar thing, but it irked her that Lucy was apparently taken with Colin. Heavens, she clenched her teeth together. She was jealous, and she had absolutely no right to be. In fact, she should not be bitter over a man she did not want for herself. Yet, she was.

"Thank you," Colin said to Lucy, interrupting Amelia's inner dialogue. "I hope I can live up to your faith in me."

The insufferable man liked Lucy's comment a bit too much. When she was alone with him, she was going to tell him not to encourage her maid.

His gaze found Amelia's, amusement dancing in his eyes and the slightest of smiles tugging at his lips. Though he looked at her, his faint smile faded and a smirk replaced it. "Lucy, go ahead to the carriage. We will be along momentarily."

Amelia watched as Lucy bobbed a curtsy and scrambled to do Colin's bidding. As soon as her lady's maid disappeared out the door, Amelia turned on Colin. "You should not encourage her adoration of you."

"Jealous?" He quirked an eyebrow.

"Certainly not," she snapped, even though she was.

"You are changing, Amelia. Two days ago, you would have been truthful. Already you're learning to play by the rules of the *ton* and hide your true feelings. At this rate, you will be begging for my hand in marriage by week's end."

Amelia stiffened. He delivered his accusation in a teasing tone, but the fact was she *was* hiding her true feelings, and that made him correct on that account. Was she changing? She was jealous of Colin's attention to Lucy, and it was hard to think properly when the man's presence set her senses on fire. She liked him as a friend, certainly, but did she care for him as more than that? Either way, she did not like him because he was a duke, and she could not let him think he was correct about her playing by the *ton's* rules.

"You're right." She forced herself to stare at him without blinking. "I was jealous, but I have absolutely no reason to be. Flirt with her as much as you like. It is not my concern."

She swiveled away to make her way out the door, but Colin gripped her arm and stopped her flight. He leaned down, his lips coming very near her ear. "If we were to marry, Amelia, I would never cause you one moment's worry. There would be no woman but you. Once I say my vows, there will be no dallying, not that there has been of late anyway."

Her heart pounded in her ears as she looked at him. "I daresay you will make some woman very happy one day."

He stepped away, his face suddenly unreadable, and then just as suddenly his jaw set and his nostrils flared, almost as if he were engaged in battle, but with whom? Himself? Not her, certainly.

In a low, steely voice he said, "If fidelity is all you require, then you'll be ecstatic married to me."

"You've more to give, Colin."

He arched his brow high, in a mocking way.

"Do you think so?"

"I know so."

"Then you don't perceive enough. I don't want to have more to give."

He said one thing, but his gaze locked on hers, and in her mind, he was beseeching her to help him realize he wanted to give more, and that was precisely what she intended to do.

~

Carriages and people strolling who wished to see and be seen crowded Hyde Park, but Colin managed to find a secluded spot to park his cabriolet on a side path that was surrounded on one side by tall trees and on the other by flowering bushes. Once Colin helped Amelia and then her lady's maid descend, he led Lucy to a bench on which she could sit, and then he directed Amelia out to the main path to stroll among all the other lords and ladies of the *ton*. This was the best place to introduce her to men who held greater titles than Worthington, men who would trip over themselves to gain an introduction to her, which in turn would make her an Incomparable.

His gut twisted relentlessly, but he pushed on toward the path. If she changed, maybe these disturbing feelings would bloody well cease. Or he could feel the loss of who'd she had been so acutely that he never recover. He jerked to a halt, and then moved them off the path toward some flowers. He didn't know what the devil he was doing, but his gut felt better.

"Where are we going?" she asked.

"A slight change of plans," he said, having absolutely no idea what else *to* say. And to avoid any more probing questions that would require him to know his own bleeding mind, he started pointing out flowers his father had taught him about. He was surprised to learn she knew just as much, if not more, about the flowers, as he did. He stopped in front of the water and leaned down to tell her about the pink flowering plant rising from the glassy surface. He touched the leaves, and a memory of the times he would come here with his father invaded Colin. His father's unhappiness would fade for a bit here. "This is—"

"A great willow herb," she said.

He glanced up at her, barely able to see her face as he squinted against the sun. "Correction. This is a great *hairy* willow herb," he said, stroking a finger across the furs on the robust stem. "Can you see the hairs?"

Suddenly, she was beside him, kneeling. Her skirt lay partially over his trousers and her arm was pressed against his. Her fingers touched the tip of his where she had planted her hand against the ground for support. Devil take it, his body heated as if someone had turned the entire force of the sun on him. She was like the sun—beautiful, warm, and life giving.

"How do you know so much about flowers?"

She ran the tip of one slender finger up the stem of the flower. What would it be like to have those slender fingers wrapped around him? Offering pleasure and— He shoved the thought away, but his body was rigid and throbbing.

Sadness crept into her bright eyes. "My father used to have a beautiful flower garden, and he taught me all about flowers. Mother could not bear to look at it after he was gone, and she destroyed it one night."

Her audible swallow spurred him to touch her and offer comfort. He placed his hand over hers. "I'm sorry. I could send my gardeners out and have a new, magnificent garden built for you. I would personally oversee it."

She offered him a small smile that tugged on his heart. "I don't think my mother would care for that, but that's very kind of you to offer. Tell me, how do *you* know so much about flowers?"

"My father, as well. We had—still do actually—a magnificent garden, but he still liked to pile in the carriage and come for what he called a 'grand outing' here. We would stroll for hours and look at flowers, and he would tell me about each and every one of them. I think talking about the flowers gave him peace he was hard-pressed to find."

"Is your mother the expert you are?"

Colin shook his head. "She never came. It was his time to escape her, you see."

Amelia blinked at him. "Escape your mother?"

He nodded. This was the closest he had ever come to spilling his family secrets to a woman.

"I don't understand."

Suddenly, he wanted her to. He would tell her everything. "You see—"

"Aversley, whatever are you doing crouched there on the ground?"

Colin stiffened at the interruption by the deep male voice. He turned to see who it was and stifled his groan. The Marquessess of Edington and Shrewsbury stared down at him from some ten paces away. Both gentlemen were unmarried, well titled, and worth a great deal of money—exactly the sort of men whose attentions would help to make Amelia an Incomparable. Colin wanted to tell them to bugger off. Instead, he helped Amelia up and faced them.

"May I present Lady Amelia de Vere," he said

Both men nodded as Colin turned to Amelia. She smiled graciously before focusing her attention on him. "Lady Amelia, this is the Marquess of Edington and the Marquess of Shrewsbury."

The men surrounded her like vultures fighting over a dead carcass. Colin forced his unwilling legs to step back and let the gentlemen closer, but it rankled him to do so. *This is what I intended* he reminded himself. His mind, in turn, kindly whispered, *Coward.* He pinched the bridge of his nose and hoped no one else in the party would notice that he might be going slightly mad. That would certainly turn all the talk away from his mother once and for all, him becoming a raving lunatic. Leave it to a woman to unknowingly drive a man insane.

"Where are you from?" Lord Edington inquired of Amelia.

"Norfolk. Have you ever been there?"

That was it! Colin couldn't stand here and listen to Amelia and these men trade polite banter anymore, but he did have to stay here. Glancing toward the water and then back to the group, he waited for the moment they all seemed engaged with each other, and then he strolled near the water but not too far away. He was determined to distract himself, so he tried to recall as much as he could about all the flowers his father had loved so much.

Intermediate laughter trickled to him, worsening his already darkening mood. Despite the fact that he knew it would probably make things worse, he glanced over his shoulder at Amelia. She had a smile firmly in place and her gaze was locked on the gentleman, as if raptly interested in what they had to say. Her playing her part perfectly snapped his control like a twig breaking under a heavy boot, fast and hard. His blood pounded through him. He knew good and well he was being unreasonable, but he didn't give a damn at the moment.

Stalking over to the group, he interrupted Edington telling Amelia about a picnic he wanted her to come to. "We really must be going, gentlemen," Colin said, barely keeping the snarl out of his voice while gently grasping Amelia's elbow.

"We will see you at the Kendall's ball tomorrow night, won't we?" Edington inquired.

"You'll see her," Colin snapped, all his patience fleeing.

"I'll make sure you are invited to the Banbury's picnic," Edington added.

"I can collect you for it, if you wish," Shrewsbury offered.

"That won't be necessary," Colin said through clenched teeth. "I will be taking her to the picnic, and she is already invited." Or she would be. And so would he. It was a simple matter of a quick note from him, changing his reply from *No* to *Yes* and checking the box that he had previously left empty, the one that would soon indicate that he would be bringing one guest—Amelia.

"Oh, very good. Glad to see you have it all in hand," Shrewsbury said, giving Colin a look he would bloody well describe as challenging. The man wanted to challenge him for Amelia, did he? Colin would grind the little bugger into—

"Save a dance for me, too," Shrewsbury said as the men departed. Colin blinked. He'd been so occupied with his thoughts he had missed the last part of the conversation.

He swung toward Amelia. "Did you agree to save dances for both of them?"

"Yes." She watched him steadily. "Does that please you?"

The word *no* was on the tip of his tongue. He shoved the blasted thing down where it belonged.

"It is part of the plan, is it not?" she asked.

He pressed his lips together for a moment then spoke. "Yes, I suppose it is." He extended his elbow to her, not liking the way she made him feel as if he was ready to explode. "Come." No woman had ever had this effect on him. Amelia did. There was no use denying it. He needed to put order back into this day and stick to his plan for her. Every last detail of the thing—including never caring about her because to care was to be vulnerable, and he refused to be that. He'd just have to live with the consequences of his decision, no matter how painful.

"I brought you here to be seen, so let us commence making it happen."

"All right," she agreed.

Colin glanced sideways at her as they strolled and studied her profile. She had her head turned slightly away taking in the other people walking or maybe she was still studying the flowers. His gaze went immediately to her full, kissable lips. He jerked it to her neck. That was a more benign part, wasn't it? Less enticing and less apt to lead his mind to lustful thoughts. Of course, her neck had to be creamy and slender and the perfect place to begin a conquest of her body that—

His own body now strumming with need, he lurched away from her. She turned toward him, a frown on her face.

"Whatever is the matter?"

Sweat trickled down his back that was not caused by the damn heat. "Nothing," he replied, wincing at his hoarse voice. "Something bit me."

"Oh?" She cocked her eyebrows. "Where?"

"On my arm."

She eyed him dubiously. "Through your jacket and shirt?"

He scowled. Leave it to him to decide to transform a woman who paid attention to details and who he apparently wanted more than any woman he had ever desired in his life. Amelia's sharp intake of breath and her clutching his arm drew his attention back to the present. "What is it?" he asked, looking in the direction she seemed to be staring.

Colin locked gazes with Worthington. Of course. Worthington with that same chit from the Stanhope ball clinging to his arm would explain Amelia's reaction. What he could not explain properly was the twinge of jealousy in his chest. Colin clenched his teeth, and slid Amelia's hand firmly back through the crook of his elbow while gazing down at her with a seductive smile for Worthington's sake.

"Close your mouth, Amelia. Gaping will not win over Worthington. Is that Lady Georgiana?"

"Yes."

Colin took a quick assessment of Amelia's rival. Average height. Nondescript brown hair. Pretty. Though not a classic beauty like Amelia.

"She's stunning, isn't she?" Amelia said, her voice wavering.

He frowned. "The woman in the yellow dress, correct?"

"Of course. Who else? The woman who Lord Worthington is gazing at adoringly."

Colin glanced at the woman then back to Amelia. "You are stunning. She is forgettable."

Amelia's mouth parted once more. This time Colin did not mind one bit. "Close your mouth, Amelia. You're gaping again."

She snapped her jaw shut, a ferocious blush staining her cheeks. "Well, obviously Lord Worthington seems to think Lady Georgiana the unforgettable one, which makes me—"

"Foolish for worrying about him," Colin said, half joking.

"Do be serious," Amelia pleaded.

"Yes, all right." Colin studied the couple. They had paused to speak with an elderly gentleman Worthington apparently knew. Lady Georgiana may not be beautiful, but the jewels sparkling from her neck and fingers were. Colin eyed her yellow silk dress. It was clearly costly with beads all over the place. Too many baubles in his mind. Bloody distracting, but maybe that was the point. A suspicion formed then. Worthington's family had a title, but it was a well-hidden fact that they did not have much money. A plight that had made Worthington prickly as long as Colin had known him.

"Is Lady Georgiana's family well-off?"

"Extremely," Amelia murmured, tensing beneath his fingers.

Well, that confirmed his notion. Worthington was marrying for money, unless Lady Georgiana had great wit or astounding skill in the bedchamber. One conversation with the lady was all that he needed to detect wit or a keenness for bed play.

Colin squeezed Amelia's arm as he watched the other couple approach. "Act besotted with me."

Amelia nodded and smiled up at him with a coy smile that sent his blood humming again, despite the fact he knew it was an act. He was a fool.

Worthington stopped in front of Colin, eyes narrowed and a false smile on his lips. His gaze flicked over Colin before latching on to Amelia, and a true smile spread across his lips. That little twinge of jealousy assaulted Colin like an army bent on destruction.

Worthington cleared his throat. "It's wonderful to see you, Lady Amelia."

"It's lovely to see you both," Amelia responded. "Lady Georgiana, I'd like to introduce you to the Duke of Aversley."

The lady's eyes popped wide, then traveled hungrily over Colin in exactly the same way so many women's eyes had in the past. "I've heard of you, of course. I believe you are acquainted with my aunt, Lady Diana. She speaks so highly of you."

"Does she?" He struggled to keep the amusement out of his voice. "When was the last time you spoke to her?"

"At Christmas when I was in Town visiting her. She had just returned from a night at the theatre with you." Lady Georgiana licked her lips. Slowly. Purposely.

He remembered the night well. They had never made it inside the theatre. They had run into one of his mother's former lovers and Colin's mood had turned bad. Diana had refused to leave the theatre, so he'd enticed her away with the promise of a bedding she'd never forget. He'd delivered on the promise, too. Repeatedly. In the carriage. That dirty feeling he'd been trying to get rid of washed over him.

"That certainly explains why she spoke highly of me," Colin replied, wishing he could walk away from this silly chit's inquisitive stare and smirking lips. He didn't move a muscle. For Amelia, he would stay and endure the silent invitation to yet another bed.

Lady Georgiana tittered. "I adore the theatre. I find the ride in the carriage to be my favorite part."

"I find it to be my least favorite," Colin said, barely managing to maintain a civil tone.

Lady Georgiana's lips formed a pout. "That's too bad. I was hoping you would call on me after I was married and take me to the theatre."

Well, the lady definitely had an appetite for bed play, but she certainly did not have keen wit. She'd utterly failed to read that he was not interested. "I'm sure your husband would have something to say about that." Colin purposely eyed Worthington, who was shifting from foot to foot, a pinched look on his face.

Lady Georgiana snorted. "We shall see. Husbands have a way of being managed, especially when the wives bring so much to the marriage." She flourished her bejeweled hand giving Colin the answer to his earlier question.

"Georgiana, are felicitations in order?" Amelia asked.

"Not yet," Lady Georgiana said in a syrupy tone. But I'm sure they will be soon. Won't they, Lord Worthington?"

Amelia's fingers curled into Colin's arm even as her lower lip disappeared between her teeth. He wanted to shake her for caring about whether Worthington was marrying this foolish woman before them. Clearly, Lady Georgiana was referring to Worthington and herself, which made Worthington more of a fool than Colin had given him credit for.

Worthington turned a deep shade of red. "I…ah…That is, I mean to say—"

Lady Georgiana smacked him on the arm with her fan. "It seems I have taken Lord Worthington by surprise. Is that it?"

His meek nod made Colin almost feel sorry for him. Almost.

"Well"—Lady Georgiana smiled brightly—"we must be going."

"If you must," Colin drawled out, nudging Amelia to get her to respond.

"Have a nice ride," Amelia said, though there was no carriage anywhere in sight.

After the couple disappeared, Colin turned to Amelia who still stood watching the lane where Worthington and Lady Georgiana had strolled away and out of sight. "Amelia—"

"I cannot believe it," she gasped. "Do you think Lord Worthington is going to marry her?"

Colin nodded, his heart squeezing painfully with her hurt. He wanted to call Worthington out for a duel or maybe he wanted to pump the man's hand in gratitude for not realizing what he was letting slip through his fingers by letting Amelia go. "I think perhaps Worthington needs to marry for money."

Amelia jerked her head in a nod. "That would explain it. I'm just so surprised. I did not think he would truly be the sort of man to marry for money, even if he thinks he has to." She pressed her face into her hands and shook her head before peeling her hands away. "Well, I believed him to be…I don't know—"

"So much more," he blurted, wanting to stop her from pouring anymore of her heart out about the man she had thought she loved. It was painful in an unexpected, torturous way.

"Yes, that's exactly it," she breathed, clutching his arm. "But do you know what's surprising—"

"Lady Amelia!" an urgent male voice called from behind Colin.

Growling, he turned and scowled at Worthington's return. What bloody now?

Worthington strode to a stop directly in front of Amelia. "Please allow me to call on you tomorrow?"

"She's busy," Colin snapped.

Worthington glared. "This does not concern you, Aversley. Unless I'm mistaken?"

Colin glanced at Amelia even as Worthington did. She frowned and pressed her fingertips to her temples. "I don't see how that's any concern of yours. Are you not about to announce your engagement to Lady Georgiana?"

"That's precisely why I want to speak with you. Please let me call on you so we may talk in private?"

"There will be no private talking with Lady Amelia," Colin grumbled, his blood rushing in his ears. "If she wants to let you in my aunt's front door, I cannot stop her, but her lady's maid will be present with you at all times. Understood?"

"Funny that you of all men would be a stickler for propriety," Worthington sneered.

"I find I can't share your humor," Colin replied.

She turned her face from him to Worthington. "Will you be at the Kendall's ball tomorrow night?"

Worthington nodded.

"Tomorrow I'm busy, but I will see you at the ball, and if you still wish to call on me after tomorrow night, then you may."

"Excellent," Worthington said. He grasped her hand and kissed it before dashing of the way he had come.

Finally, blessed coldness seeped over Colin. It was welcome. He knew this numbness. Had lived in it and with it for years. It was caring that was too hard and painful. "Shall we go? I believe you have accomplished everything you wished for?"

"Certainly we can go, but—"

He held up a staying hand. "No need to say more. I'd rather not hear you pour out your heart in regards to Worthington."

Amelia's brow furrowed. "Yes, but Colin—"

"Aversley," a voice called loudly from close by.

He knew that cold voice. He looked in the direction his mother approached from. He had the ludicrous desire to pretend he had not seen her, but he'd never be so cowardly.

"I know you see me," she called as if reading his thoughts.

People stopped to turn and look at him, and suddenly he was a boy of ten in this very same damned park, stumbling upon his mother in the arms of another man. His aunt had been livid and made quite the scene. Heads had swiveled, mouths had hung open, and the talk among the *ton* had really started that day. Shame twisted his gut and burned it just as it had so many years ago.

Abruptly, something touching his face brought him back to the present. He blinked, and his mother was before him withdrawing her hand. "Where were you?"

"Years away," he replied, eyeing the bushes. She knew; her pressed lips gave her thoughts away. "Aversley, do you remember Lady Sara? She used to live on a neighboring estate before she moved with her father to America."

He remembered her perfectly. They had been childhood friends before his mother's affair with Lady Sara's father had caused Lady Sara's mother to kill herself. "It's been years, Lady Sara. Or do you go by a married title now?"

"No. I've never married."

"She hasn't married *yet*," his mother added, spearing him with a look.

Amelia scrutinized Colin as the two exchanged greetings, trying to decide if he looked interested in the woman or not. He did, didn't he? His gaze lingered on this Lady Sara. And why not? She had pretty green eyes and shiny black hair. But most of all, she had a sweet smile and had not declared to Colin her intent for another gentleman. Amelia should not care, but she did.

Whatever was the matter with her? Did she love Lord Worthington or not? He certainly didn't seem worth it at the moment. And Colin…Well, letting herself fall in love with a man who wanted nothing to do with love would be the epitome of foolishness, and she was not foolish. She was a sensible Elinor.

She groaned inwardly. She didn't feel sensible as she recalled her determination to make Colin trust women and want to fall in love. That had been well and good when the idea had been to change him for another woman's benefit. There was no risk in that if she failed. But to try and change him for herself, to actually hope that he could want to marry her, *her*, because he loved her and not simply because he had decided he needed to carry on his title or to simply help Philip? Well, that was likely the most foolish thing she could ever do.

When Colin's hand briefly touched her shoulder, she jerked and forced herself to follow the conversation she should have been paying attention to. The tips of her ears burned with her embarrassment. Thank goodness they were covered.

"This is Lady Amelia, Mother."

Amelia focused on Colin. The dangerous gleam in his eyes made her stomach twist. He looked angry.

She quickly curtseyed. "It's lovely to meet you."

"Likewise." The duchess barely flicked a glance her way. "Colin, I'd like you to call on me and spend time with Lady Sara."

Amelia caught her breath on the dark look that descended over Colin's face. He appeared as if was about to go to war with his mother, and her steely look and raised chin indicated she had every intention of engaging the enemy. Amelia had to do something to get Colin away.

"Oh, ouch!" She cried out and reached for her ankle. "I've twisted my ankle."

Before she knew what was happening Colin had scoped her into his extremely well built arms. "Put me down," she hissed, heat scorching her face.

"Not on your life," he said, clutching him to her like a lifeline. He dipped his head at his mother and Lady Sara, as if it were every day he clutched a woman to him in the middle of Rotten Row.

Amelia barely held in her giggle.

"Mother. Lady Sara. I'm afraid I need to attend to Lady Amelia's hurt ankle. If you'll excuse me?"

His mother pressed her lips together, giving Amelia a narrow-eyed look that made her squirm closer to Colin. Instantly, she was aware that every inch of his body was just as hard as she had imagined. The blush warming her cheeks went from blistering to down right deadly. If her hands had not been twined around Colin's muscular neck and upper back she would have fanned herself.

Colin swung them away just as his mother spoke in a sharp tone, but to Amelia it sounded more urgent than anything. "Aversley, please don't forget you have a limited amount of time to fulfill your father's dictate."

A pained look flashed in his eyes. "I haven't forgotten. Rest assured." Without waiting for a reply, he strode toward where he had parked his conveyance.

"What dictate, Colin?" Amelia whispered.

He faltered in his step, his arms tensing around her. Glancing down with a furrowed brow he said, "Nothing that concerns, you since you seem to be staying nauseatingly devoted to Worthington."

Amelia opened her mouth to set him straight—well, as straight as she could, since she was utterly confused—but her lady's maid appeared at her side, red-faced and panting. She whipped up a fan, which she vigorously began to use on Amelia.

"Did you get too hot, my lady?" Lucy asked.

Colin held her tighter as they passed by a group of people, clearly gawking at them. Amelia cringed. Maybe no one would recognize them.

"Aversley," a tall, dark, dangerous-looking gentleman called out, breaking away from the cluster of people.

Colin cursed under his breath, but all the same, Amelia heard him. She was so close to him she could feel the breath itself. "Who is that?" she whispered about the approaching man, who strangely wore a long black coat even though the heat was rather oppressive today. The garment billowed behind him, making him appear rather ominous. A little shiver escaped her.

"That is the Duke of Scarsdale. Rarely seen, but when he is, you can be sure trouble is afloat. We were once friends but not anymore."

The Duke of Scarsdale was upon them in a flash. He nodded to Colin and bowed slightly to her. When he came up, piercing black eyes caught her gaze. "I don't know you. I assure you if I did, I would be the man carrying you now instead of Aversley. You realize his heart is made of ice, don't you?"

Colin snorted, but Scarsdale's offhanded comment angered her. "All things made of ice eventually melt," she countered.

"Touché," he said in a voice of silk wrapped with thorny vines. "By the looks of you, I imagine you could provide enough heat to melt a glacier."

"Lady Amelia provides nothing but friendship," Colin said in a lethal tone. "She hurt her ankle on our walk. Mind your tongue, and your hands, or you will find yourself without either one or both."

The man cracked a smile that showed he was no angel but pure devil, though a striking one. "Pardon me. I did not realize you had changed. So she's off-limits? No sharing as in the past?"

"Scarsdale," Colin growled, the muscles in his jaw bulging on the one word.

Amelia's stomach twisted at Scarsdale's words. Had Colin shared women with this man? What sort of person would do such a thing?

"I don't feel well," she murmured, meaning it.

Colin blinked at her, surprise evident on his face. "Scarsdale," he said as way of a goodbye.

As Colin whisked her away, Amelia caught a glimpse of a gentleman lingering half-hidden behind a tree. That was odd. She squinted to get a better view. Was that Lord Huntington? No, it couldn't possibly be. The heat of the day and the awful truth of what she had heard must be getting to her. She squeezed her eyes shut, and when she opened them again the gentleman, whoever he was, was gone.

Within moments, they were at the carriage and on the way back to Lady Langley's. They rode in near silence; Lucy's humming the only thing filling the quiet. When they got to the house, Amelia didn't wait for him to hand her out. She fairly jumped out of the carriage when it stopped and raced toward the garden to be alone. Behind her, footsteps pounded, and she knew without turning that he had followed her. She flung open the iron gate to the garden and raced down the stone path to the fountain in the middle of a circle of trees.

Why was she so upset about what the Duke of Scarsdale had said?

She didn't know, but she was.

By the time she stopped, her head pounded almost as hard as her heart. Stones crunched behind her, and she swung around to face Colin. "Is what he said true? Did you—" She swallowed hard and forced herself to form the question. "Did you share women with that man?"

He glanced toward the ground and then finally back up at her. Unspoken pain glittered in his gaze. "Not knowingly. But it's nice to know you think so little of me. Not that I don't deserve it."

Such relief filled her that she flung herself at him. Their bodies collided, and she swayed backward. In a flash, he reached out and gripped her roughly to him. She splayed her hands over the ridges of his back and buried her face in his chest. It was highly improper, but she just could not seem to help herself or make herself let him go. Instead, she clung to him for a moment, counting the beats of his thumping heart and inhaling his woodsy scent. Confusing emotions ran havoc inside of her.

"I don't know what's wrong with me," she admitted.

"Perhaps you're ready to move on to loftier titles."

"Don't be absurd." She shoved him away, angered that he would not let go of his ridiculous notions about women. If she was going to make sensible—well half-sensible—decisions regarding him, she needed to understand what drove him to distrust women so. "I know some things about you," she blurted hoping confrontation would make him reveal something of himself.

He gripped her by the arms and pulled her close. "What do you think you know?" His voice was cracked, raw.

Her stomach dropped at the painful sound. "I've heard whispers. I know that you have quite the reputation."

"Yes, I do," he said, his tone flat. "I built that reputation. It was a lot of hard work. Many women lined up to use me, and I let them. Then I turned around and used them in kind."

"Why would you do such a thing? Look how unhappy it's made you."

His gaze grew dull. "Does it matter why I did it?"

"Of course it does," she cried.

He released her arm and stepped away from her. "I decided to build that reputation when I learned that the first and only woman I foolishly thought I loved had used me for revenge against my mother, who damn well does not and has never loved me."

"Oh, Colin," she softly, her heart wrenching for him.

But he gazed through her as if he had not heard her. It was a long moment until he seemed to focus on her again. "I learned several very important lessons in the years I built my reputation. Can you guess what they might be?"

She shook her head, her throat aching with the need to offer him soothing words, but she knew he would reject the offer.

"Women do not want love. They crave money, power and a man other than their husbands to satisfy the appetites they aren't supposed to have."

"Is that all you learned?" she asked, her heart thumping in her ears.

"No. I learned very early on it was better to be numb than to feel a thing. And that's how a person turns bad, Amelia."

"You're not bad. You've helped Constance and Philip and you are kind to Lucy. The woman you thought you loved when you were young hurt you. Don't you see? You are good."

"I'm not." He shook his head. "Good people can love. I don't feel that emotion."

"You can!"

"No." The denial was vehement and revealed his fear.

"You feel something for me," she blurted.

"You're right. I do. *Desire.*"

He crushed his mouth to hers in a bruising kiss. His tongue parted her lips with force and invaded her. She stiffened in his arms. All her life she had imagined her first kiss would be wonderful and from a man who loved her.

Angry, she pulled back until their contact broke, and she blinked tears from her eyes. "Let me go." Her voice trembled on the last word.

"Amelia." He said her name reverently and gently cupped her face once more. "I'm sorry." He brushed a light kiss across her forehead. "So sorry." He kissed her left cheek then her right.

A pleasant tingle began in her stomach and spread through her body as his lips moved to her neck, leaving her with a heady sensation. He lifted his face to look at her.

"I didn't mean to hurt you." His lips recaptured hers, but this time it was slow and thoughtful. The gentle pressure of his mouth against hers increased bit by bit until she thought her frail composure would shatter like glass. She opened her mouth for him and invited him in, wanting the havoc and chaos he created within her. His tongue swirled around her mouth and stoked a delicious fire.

She pressed up to her tiptoes, yearning for more of what he had to offer. He gave willingly, sucking at her lips and then lower to the hollow of her neck where her pulse beat furiously. After a moment, he pulled away and stepped back. "This is what I'm good at eliciting desire—not love."

She wanted to wrap her arms around him and draw him back to her, but she knew he would not allow it. All of his words, clearly so carefully chosen, had an undeniable undercurrent of throbbing, dizzying pain. *His pain.* She desperately wanted to help him, and she sensed from what he'd said, and what she'd seen at the park, how much pain his belief that his mother didn't love him caused him. "What makes you think your mother does not love you?"

"Twenty-five years make me think it," he said dully.

She resisted the urge to sigh with exasperation. Men really were difficult at times. "You must have thought she loved you at one time."

He simply raised his eyebrows in response.

"She's your mother, for goodness sake. Of course she loves you."

"One would think, but she does not have the capacity to love."

Amelia did huff then. He was so set on this, so stubborn. "Surely she loved your father?"

He barked with laughter but not the happy sort. No, not at all.

"If you call having one affair after the other *love*, then she worshipped my father."

A heavy feeling pulled at the pit of Amelia's stomach. He'd said he'd thought he'd been in love as a young lad, but that the woman had used him for revenge; was it possible that the woman he thought he loved has used him to get revenge on his mother?

Amelia's hand fluttered to her throat, and she swallowed convulsively. "Was the woman you'd thought you loved vengeful toward your mother?"

"How very perceptive you are," he said in a flat voice.

He was putting up defenses. She understood it. Her books had been a defense, a refuge. "And that's why you became who you were?"

"Enough, Amelia." It was a harsh command. "I won't stand here and bleed for you. No matter if I wanted to tell you everything or not. I cannot—I *cannot* do it." He shuddered.

Maybe he would not tell her everything about his past now, but he was telling her enough to make her sure he could love, and if he could love then perhaps—"

"Amelia! Aversley?" Philip called, seconds before she saw him striding toward them.

"Philip, whatever are you doing here? Is Mother with you?"

He shook his head as he came to stand in front of them. "No. she said she didn't feel she was quite up to the Season, but she insisted I come to keep an eye on you and to find myself a wife, instead."

Colin groaned beside her. She pressed her lips together so as not to remark and focused on Philip. "You are sure she is well enough to be left alone?"

"She's hardly alone," Philip muttered, his face flushing. "Lady Constance and her mother have come every day to visit, and they said they would continue to come each day, twice a day. But Mother did seem better, as if some burden had lessened."

"Thank goodness for that," Amelia said.

Philip eyed Colin and then her. "So am I to expect Worthington to show up, now that I'm here, and ask for your hand?"

Amelia shifted from foot to foot. She needed to talk to Philip and explain to him how complicated things had become with her head and heart, especially since his winning the wager balanced on her staying true to her love for Lord Worthington, but she did not want to try to sort out her muddled state of mind in front of Colin.

"I'm not sure," she murmured.

Philip patted her arm, but oddly, he was staring at Colin. "Don't look so glum," he said flickering his gaze to her and then back to Colin. "I'm sure you will catch Worthington's heart and then your future happiness will be set."

Before she could think what to say to that, Colin said, "Harthorne, I have some business to attend to. Do you care to come to the club tonight?"

"Actually," Philip said, "I think I'll come with you now. I was thinking, if it's all right that I'd stay with you while I'm here. Amelia is in good hands, and I have a lot of appointments in Town. Your home is closer."

"Certainly," Colin said with a nod. "We'll come around to collect you and my aunt tomorrow night for the ball at eight."

Philip gave her a pat on the back, and Colin turned on his heel.

Amelia stood, rather stunned, watching the two men walk away. Philip was not acting himself, but rather strangely sly and elusive, and Colin...He had told her enough that she was certain he could feel love *if* he could get over his pain. The question was *could* he get over his pain and open his heart? Until she spoke with Philip—hopefully before tomorrow night—she would go along as planned, though the prospect of boring conversations and the endless fluttering of her eyelashes made her head hurt.

Chapter Fifteen

"Aversley, why do you not go and dance instead of sitting here with us while we gossip?" Colin's aunt asked loudly. The chatter of his aunt's two other spinster friends sitting at the table with her stopped abruptly, and a pale-gray gaze and a light-blue one turned to him.

"I'm fine," he said and purposely gazed in the other direction so they would quit asking him questions. He was sitting here because he could keep a watchful, albeit tortured, eye on Amelia as she danced with every eager buck that approached her, and he could contemplate what Amelia had said about his mother surely loving him because she was his mother.

He couldn't get Amelia's words out of his head. He'd thought them so many times himself before he'd given up on the notion that his mother even had the ability to feel love. For the first time, in as far back as he could recall, he wanted to speak to her and ask her again why she had treated Father as she had. Would he get a different answer now? Was she hiding something? Father, even in the end, had been sure he shared the fault for her behavior, so could it be that what had happened between them had affected her love for Colin?

"Aversley, I think you should dance," his aunt said.

He turned toward the women and smiled. They had matching curious looks on their faces. "I don't see anyone I wish to partner with right now," he replied.

Lady Chatham raised her wrinkled, bony arm and pointed toward the dance floor where Amelia was being twirled by Belford. "What about that chit? You've not taken your eyes off her all night. You watched her when she danced with the Lord Belford the last time and then Lord Shrewsbury and Lord Edington. If you keep sitting here all night she will dance with a man who will steal her right out from under your nose."

"Thank you for you concern," he managed and scooted his chair back. "I believe I need a refreshment."

The three women exchanged a knowing glance that rankled Colin before nodding to him. His aunt patted him on the hand. "Come see me in the morning, Aversley. I'd like to talk about the parties you wish for me to attend with Lady Amelia."

"Certainly," Colin replied. He strode toward the punch bowl even though he wasn't thirsty at all, but he was not going to sit around while his aunt and her friend's tried to delve into his personal life. He grabbed a glass of punch while greeting a few people he knew and then discretely headed for the potted plants toward the back of the ballroom. He found Amelia in the crowd and resumed his vigil of keeping her in his sights. The azure gown with the encrusted pearls suited her to perfection. With her light hair and creamy skin, she looked ethereal. She certainly seemed from a different world than the one he knew—to good to be true. So, surely, it wasn't true. She wasn't as perfect as she seemed. He glanced down into his pink punch and absently took a drink then frowned in distaste, swirling the liquid in the cup.

Yet, what if she was exactly what she seemed? Honest. True. And full of love. If she didn't change during the Season, yet realized Worthington was not worthy of her love, she would still need a husband and Philip's debts would still need to somehow be paid. Colin raked a hand through his hair, uncertainty strumming through him. Could he be the sort of man she wanted? The ability to open himself up to loving someone seemed impossible. Daunting. Yet...

"There you are," Harthorne said and clamped a hand on his shoulder. "I should have looked in the shadows instead of among the people. Sorry I'm late. I've been detained all day with business."

"You've not missed much," Colin said.

Harthorne frowned. "I've decided you may be right about women. I was just forced to dance with a chit who made it plain she would never marry a man whose fortune did not at least match hers."

"I'm sorry to be right," Colin said, trying to shake his distraction and focus on his friend.

Harthorne grinned. "I did receive two very lurid offers from widows, however, which made the prospect of turning jaded seem more desirable."

Colin stiffened and shrugged Harthorne's hand off his shoulder.

Harthorne's face drained of color. "Damnation, Aversley. I'm sorry. I'm not used to you being touchy, but all the same, that was foolish thing for me to say."

"Think nothing of it," Colin said and motioned to the dance floor. "Lady Amelia appears to be having a grand time."

"Where is she?" Harthorne asked, peering into the crowd.

"She's there." Colin pointed but was surprised not to see her any longer. His pulse increased a notch as he quickly scanned the perimeter of the room and swept his gaze over the dancers once more. "She was just there. Do you see her yet?"

"She probably needed air. I'll check the terrace, and you comb through the room."

Colin nodded. "If she's not on the terrace, check the gardens. If I were trying to seduce a lady that's one of the places I'd take her. It's secluded."

Harthorne's eyes bulged. "I'm sure you won't discover her there."

"I better not," Colin growled. "I won't be held accountable for what I do to any man who has attempted to seduce Amelia."

~

Throwing a wary glance over her shoulder, Amelia scurried down the dark hall and away from the hum of conversation and bright chandeliers of the ballroom. She stopped in front of moonlit room that appeared unoccupied. With care, she pushed the door all the way open and poked her head into the shadowy room. The smell of leather and musty paper filled her nose. The library! Perfect. She scurried into the room and fell into a weary heap on the settee.

Her temples were pounding from thinking on inane topics to converse upon, and her cheeks ached from hours of false smiles. Leaning her head back, she closed her eyes. Slight guilt nagged at her for dashing out of the ballroom when Lord Shrewsbury had gone to get her punch, but not enough remorse that she was going to go back anytime soon. It wasn't just Lord Shrewsbury she was hiding from; it was every gentleman she had danced with tonight.

They seemed all the same, talking nonstop of themselves, their wealth and what *they* expected from a wife, yet she knew they could not all be *exactly* the same. She also knew they were not Colin. None of those men made her feel perfectly comfortable just being herself. None of them had Colin's sharp wit or his ready, beautiful smile. She would bet the gown off her back that none of them shared her love for flowers as Colin did, either. There was, of course, no way to know, because not one of the gentlemen had asked her about herself.

Colin had been asking her about herself since the moment he'd met her. With a start, she realized none of her thoughts were for Charles. She forced herself to think on him. He may or may not have rescued her that day on the horse. She was so uncertain now. He had stood up for her to his friends, but according to Constance only because Constance had shamed him into action. He had most definitely discussed books with her many times, and with great passion and he had called her agile. Maybe Charles had simply felt sorry for her, because truth be told she was not that agile, except when Colin was leading her.

She rubbed her temples as she thought. Heavens, had she made Charles into her hero, but he had thought of her as a mere friend? Rather like a secondary character? Had she been so lonely that she created a relationship in her mind? However she had thought of him, it did not compare to the way Colin made her feel.

He stole her breath, raced her pulse, made her laugh, made her want to shout, and made her think she was beautiful. Possibly, she was falling in love with him. But could he ever love her back?

"Amelia," a voice said above her. Her heart raced as she jerked up and scrambled to her feet. The room was dark but not so much so that she could not see Charles standing behind the settee.

"Charles," she blurted, forgetting herself. She pressed a hand to her lips. "I beg your pardon. I mean, Lord Worthington."

Charles raced around the settee and grabbed her hands in his. "No, please call me Charles and let me call you Amelia. It's how I think of you in my heart."

Amelia felt her jaw drop open. She promptly snapped it shut. Maybe how he felt about her wasn't all in her head at all. "What are you doing in here?"

"I followed you."

If he'd admitted that several weeks ago, she would have jumped into his arms for joy. But now...She pulled her hands out of his and took a step back. "Followed me? But why?"

"Because you are driving me mad," Charles replied, advancing on her.

Instinct sent her scuttling backward out of his reach, but she hit her shoulder blade on something hard. A quick glance behind her confirmed she had run into a bookshelf. "Charles," she placed her hand out to keep him at a distance, and he grabbed it. She gave a tug, but he held firm. Huffing, she said, "I'm going to have to insist you leave the library at once. This is improper, and if anyone should see us—"

"Do you worry about being proper around him?" Charles asked, his tone sharp and his lip slightly curled.

"Who?"

"Aversley. That's who. Do you ensure he is not alone with you in a room? I assure you that you should. The man is a danger to your innocence, unless you're no longer innocent."

"Lord Worthington!" Amelia snapped, anger blossoming in her belly and spreading like fire through her veins. "I assure *you*, though it is absolutely none of your business, His Grace is always a perfect gentleman with me." Except for yesterday's crushing kiss followed by that lovely gentle one, but that was her secret, and in truth she had enjoyed it too much to give a fig about the lack of propriety.

"Let me go," she demanded, pushing at his hand. He did release her, but his arms came up to either side of her hips, effectively trapping her. "Whatever do you think you're doing?" she yelped.

He leaned toward her, his face mere inches from hers. "Amelia, please. I know you care for me."

She did. Or she had. She stared at his eyes, not nearly as beautiful as Colin's, and didn't feel the tiniest heart palpitation. "What of Lady Georgiana?" she said gently. Charles was like a boy who did not want to share his favorite toy. He didn't love her. "The two of you seem a breath away from the altar."

"Forget Lady Georgiana for the moment," he whispered, his warm breath wafting over her face.

That sounded like a bad idea, if there ever was one. "I think not," she replied, in what she hoped was a prim voice. "Are you or are you not going to make an offer for Lady Georgiana. Or have you already?"

"I have not. Amelia, it's complicated, but seeing you with Aversley and thinking of you becoming his makes me want to find a different solution to my problem. Kiss me, Amelia. Surely you must want to feel my lips on you as much as I want to feel yours on me."

Anger burst throughout her body like a crackling, burning log that could no longer stand the heat. She wanted to slap him not kiss him.

Before she could decide whether to do it or not, the slow creak of the door filled the room, and Colin stepped into the moonlight. The frown of cold fury he wore made her shiver. "Back up, Worthington," he demanded in a tone that brooked no doubt that Colin would physically back the man up if he did not comply.

Charles stepped back and set his hands to his hips. "Aversley, you're intruding. This is none of your business."

"Lady Amelia is my business," Colin said in a ruthless tone as he advanced in two long strides across the room. "If you ever proposition her indecently again or beg a kiss, unless you are betrothed, you better find a ship to the farthest corner of the world because I will hunt you down and tear you apart piece by piece."

Amelia's mouth went dry at his statement, even as her stomach fluttered.

"You've no right to order me around," Charles snarled.

Colin's hand flashed out, and before Amelia could squeak of fright, Charles, having been rather roughly dragged forward, stood before a glowering Colin. "I don't give a damn if you think I have the right or not. In fact, I rather find I hope you are challenging me. I will be happy to meet you in a duel if you wish it. Shall we?" Colin flung Charles away, and he went staggering backward.

He pulled himself upright and tugged on his coat until it was straight. "That won't be necessary. *Yet*. You are quite right that I should not have disrespected Amelia, but you had best not either."

"Are you threatening me?" Colin said, his tone one of sarcastic amusement.

"No more than you just threatened me," Charles snapped and thrust his elbow toward Amelia. "Come with me, Amelia. I'll ensure you get back to the ballroom safely."

Amelia shook her head. "As far as I can tell you are the only one who was putting my person in danger. Please go. I am perfectly capable of getting back to the ballroom without your assistance."

Charles scowled at her but nodded. "As you wish. However, I am going to call on you tomorrow."

Before she could tell him not to bother, he turned on his heel. She watched as Colin stalked Charles all the way to the door. Colin's back was to her, and for a moment, she feared he might simply leave her standing there without saying a word. Very quietly, he shut the door and turned to her. His face had taken on the look of a marble effigy. He paused in front of her, a grim smile spreading across his lips. "Very well played, Amelia."

She frowned at him. "What?"

"You will have an offer for your hand from him in no time. I could not have planned it better had I thought of it. Leaving the ballroom was a brilliant stroke. I suppose you knew he had been watching you and would follow."

Her stomach twisted into a tight coil. Colin thought she had planned this to get Charles alone? To what—tease him, make him jealous? Sadness filled her. Of course, he would think such a thing because he believed women were inherently wicked, and well, because she had inadvertently nourished that conviction by agreeing to be part of that stupid wager. "No, Colin, I—"

He pressed a finger to her lips. "There's no use denying it. I saw how you were looking at him."

"How was I looking at him?"

"With longing. And triumph."

Good heavens, the man was jaded and completely wrong and would never believe her if she told him so. What to do? She sucked her lower lip between her teeth and raced through possible solutions, discarding them as quickly as she had thought of them. The only thing to do was to turn the tables on him.

She cared for him, and the only way she knew to possibly get through to him was to show him, beyond any doubt in his distrustful mind and wounded heart, that she was never going to hurt him. And that if he would let her, she could love him with all her heart if only he would give her his. Yet, to accomplish her goal she needed him to see that even if she had a hundred marriage offers from a hundred dukes just as lofty as he was or even more so, she would want him. Only him. Always him.

"Kiss me, Colin," she demanded, making her first move in a plan that was sketchy at best.

"Kiss you? What for? Your prey has flown the coop."

Her cheeks heated, but she forced herself to speak. "I need to practice in case Charles and I become betrothed. I wouldn't want him to cry off because I didn't entice him."

"He wouldn't dare," Colin growled. "You need no practice."

She purposely licked her lips, feeling foolish but pushing forward. His suddenly bulging jaw muscles made her want to cheer in victory. She was getting to him, even if only to his baser side. For now that would have to do. War was often won with small maneuvers and softening Colin's heart certainly felt like combat. "You promised to transform me," she continued, knowing that would get to him. The man was honorable, whether he liked it or not.

"One kiss," he said, in a stern tone.

"Yes. Just one."

"I find you impossible to resist," he muttered.

She bit her cheek to keep from grinning and forced herself to stay silent.

Grunting, he crooked his finger at her. "Come here."

Suddenly, her legs trembled and her heart beat wildly. She judged the distance between the two of them. It was three steps at the most. Could she make it? She'd never experienced anything like the giddy anticipation racing through her that was leaving her this weak.

A devilish smile played at his lips. "Changed your mind, have you?

With that, she moved toward him on legs like jelly. His dark, glittering gaze met hers and her heart turned over in response. He slipped his hands up her arms and brought her closer to him, until her chest brushed his, and she inhaled harshly at the contact. His breath rang in her ears, sharp and uneven. The dual pressures of his warm hands coming to the small of her back and the base of her skull sent a shiver through her. With shaking limbs, she clung to him, having no desire to escape his embrace.

He leaned near, and his lips touched hers like a feather being dragged gently over her skin. "Amelia." Her name was a groan of need from his mouth.

Deep within her, raw ache sprang to life and took her breath away. Unable to form words, she twined her hands into his hair and dragged his lips to hers, a silent plea that he fulfill his promise. His lips captured hers once more, demanding this time, and devouring the little bit of self-control she had left. Their tongues met and swirled in a tangle of urgency and longing.

The pressure on her back increased until he crushed her to him so that she felt the savage beating of his heart. Her head rang with the sound until the beat of her own heart took up with his and the world seemed to slip away. She raced her hands down his neck, over his shoulders and the muscular planes of his back, just to press her fingertips against his hard body.

His mouth left hers and moved with rapid-fire precision down her neck and to the skin of her chest exposed by her low-cut gown. Every place he touched burned, and when his tongue flicked out to trace across the top slope of one breast and then the other, she moaned deep within her throat.

A loud knock yanked her back to the library and her insufficient senses. Luckily, Colin seemed fully aware of the scandal they were on the verge of. Before she had even blinked, he was across the room and behind the settee as a voice called out, "Aversley, are you in there?"

Amelia wrinkled her brow, her muddled mind taking a moment to register the voice. When she did, she gasped. Her brother! If Philip suspected what she and Colin had just been doing, he would demand Colin marry her and that would ruin everything. If they ended up married, she wanted it to be because they were deeply in love. Yanking on her gown to set it in order and running her trembling hand through her hair, she had just enough time to glance at Colin before the door swung open and her brother and Lady Langley burst into the room.

She swung her gaze from her brother's astonished face back to Colin and prayed what she had thought she had seen was a figment of her imagination. But it was all too real. Colin's cravat hung lose, his hair was nothing short of a disheveled mess that looked quite accurately as if someone had run their fingers through it, and the color she had used on her lips tonight was now smeared on his. It was the last part she had no idea how to explain. She tensed, expecting Philip to explode, but before Philip could say anything, Colin's aunt rushed across the room and linked her arm through Amelia's.

"There you are," Lady Langley exclaimed. "I've been frantically searching for you. There is a table full of eager matrons you simply must meet. They can help you make a spectacular showing this Season with just a word." Lady Langley pulled her toward the door and stopped in front of Philip, whose mouth was hanging slightly open and gaze was darting back and forth between Colin and her.

Lady Langley smiled at Philip. "You must let me take your sister with me at once. You will excuse us, won't you?"

"Certainly," Philip said and inclined his head toward them both.

As Amelia entered the hall, she heaved an inner sigh of relief. Lady Langley kept furtively looking at her, but instead of mentioning anything about the scene she and Philip had come upon, she chattered non-stop about the ladies to whom she was going to introduce Amelia.

As they drew near the ballroom, Lady Langley paused and turned to Amelia. "You should not wear lip rouge if you plan to let Aversley kiss you in darkened rooms."

Heat flamed Amelia's cheeks. "I had not intended— I mean, that is to say, I did not set out at the beginning of the evening to let him kiss me."

"I believe you," Lady Langley said with a soft smile. "Which is why I interceded before your brother made the connection or decided to do something about it like demand you and Aversley wed. That wouldn't do."

"I quite agree," Amelia said, feeling rather odd having this conversation with Colin's aunt.

Lady Langley eyed Amelia. "Aversley is not going to be easy to soften, you know."

"I know, but the thing is…I think I may be falling in love with him."

Colin's aunt frowned. "You think? That's something you need to know definitely, my dear." Her lips had pressed together in a smirk, and she was staring at Amelia in the most disconcerting way, as if she understood something Amelia did not. "I had not thought you the type of woman to let a man you don't love kiss you in the dark."

"Oh, I wouldn't!" Amelia exclaimed, shock and realization flying through her the moment she said the words. She loved him. Warmth filled her, followed by joy and fear. Her stomach flipped. "I love him," she breathed on a whisper.

"Yes, dear, I know," Colin's aunt said, patting her hand.

A dull ringing filled Amelia's ears and head. "I thought I was in love before, but that wasn't love. It was a childhood infatuation. I don't even think I really know who Lord Worthington is. But Colin—" Her throat ached with the intensity of her emotions. "I know him. He's jaded, wounded, and the best man I've every met. I'm frightened," she murmured.

Lady Langley squeezed her hand. "Love is a scary thing. I'd not go blurting you love him to him just yet, though. He wouldn't believe you."

"Yes, I know. I need to show him he can trust in me and who I say I am."

"Well, yes." Lady Langley nodded. "There is that. But he also needs to feel worthy of love. Your love, to be precise. Or he needs to want you so much he doesn't care if he's worthy or not. Have you any ideas?"

"Not a one besides showing him that I don't care about a title, just the man, by turning down other offers for my hand by gentlemen as well titled as he is. Of course, I would need some offers from other gentlemen who truly don't care for me. I would not want to hurt anyone." She frowned. "Basically, I don't have any good ideas."

"My dear, you underestimate yourself," Lady Langley exclaimed. "Your idea is brilliant!"

"What?" Amelia looked at the woman, surprised. "But I don't have any other offers. I don't even have anyone else courting me, besides possibly Lord Worthington, and honestly, he seems as likely to ask for my hand as Lady Georgiana's. And he wouldn't do anyway. If he asked for my hand and I turned him down, Colin—oh, I beg your pardon—I mean His Grace—"

Lady Langley waved her hand. "Don't be ridiculous. You may call him Colin around me. I've never been one to stand on ceremony."

Amelia nodded. "Colin would think I had changed as he predicted if I were to turn Lord Worthington down. Unless, of course, I turned other gentlemen who were better titled down, as well. So you see, my idea is not a good one."

"But it is." Lady Langley had a contemplative look on her face. "If there is one thing I have learned in all my years of watching my sister and the men who clamored after her it's that men will make fools of themselves over women they know in their hearts they cannot have, including the man I loved."

"Oh my. I'm terribly sorry." She had known there was more to Lady Langley's story than Colin realized.

Lady Langley shrugged. "It was years ago. My sister told Lord Giliford she did not love him and never would. I heard her tell him so, and he pursued her all the harder for it until she caved. Loneliness and neediness will do that to a person." Lady Langley's gaze caught hers. "Be yourself, but make clear to the gentlemen who call on you that you are not interested. I guarantee you it will make them more so."

"But what if no one calls on me?"

"Oh, my dear." Lady Langley grinned. "You do not truly see yourself or you would not have such a silly fear."

Colin darted a glance at the now-open library door, anxious to follow Amelia and make sure Worthington was staying away from her. Struggling to control his impatience, he watched Amelia's brother pace the length of the library four more times. This was bloody enough. If Harthorne was going to call him out for kissing his sister, the man needed to say so now and be done with it.

"Harthorne, let me try to explain—" Colin started then abruptly stopped himself. How could he explain to Amelia's brother why he had risked her reputation and kissed her in the library for anyone to walk in and see them when he wasn't sure himself what was possessing him?

Harthorne stopped his pacing and faced Colin. "Do you want to win or lose this wager?" he demanded.

"I don't want to win under the terms we set, and I damn sure don't want you to win and see Amelia marry Worthington."

"Would it be fair to say you hope Amelia proves your beliefs about women incorrect?"

Colin tensed. Was it fair to say that? Amelia's faced filled his head, her laughter his heart, and thoughts of her kindness, her wittiness, her smell, the very way she moved occupied his every thought every minute of every day. Breathing seemed suddenly difficult.

"Your observation is fair," he choked out. Though hope was not an emotion he typically allowed himself, it was there. Because of her. Fear sprung up in his belly, jagged and painful.

Harthorne shook his head. "Normally, what I think I just came upon would have been the end of our friendship, Aversley. You are like a brother to me, but you are not my brother. Amelia *is* my sister, and her best interest takes precedence over any friendship, no matter how deep it runs. If I didn't see the utter confusion and fear on your face I would call you out, but I do see it. You are not changing her, my friend. She is changing you. Exactly as I had hoped when you suggested the absurd bet in the first place."

"Just as you had hoped?" Colin stared in amazed wonder as Harthorne nodded.

"You duped me?"

Harthorne grinned. "Don't sound so surprised. I have always thought if you could straighten out your muddled head that you would be the only man for my sister. She needs a strong man who wants a strong woman as a wife. Now, the sooner you accept that—and the fact that you are changing—and be damned glad for it, the better. Until then, keep your hands off my sister. Do we understand each other?"

"We do," Colin replied, still struggling to believe that honest-to-a-fault Harthorne had lied straight to his face and so surprisingly well.

"Excellent," Harthorne said. "Let's return to the ball."

Colin did not have to be asked twice. He was out the door and striding down the hall in a breath. Amelia was changing him. Softening him. Making him long for things he had never allowed himself to believe possible. The question in his mind was, could he be the man he knew she wanted—a man who would give his whole heart? And if he somehow miraculously could, would she even want the tarnished, tattered thing that it was?

Chapter Sixteen

Amelia descended the stairs in Lady Langley's home the next morning with her stomach turning in circles. She loved Colin, but he may never love her. Or if he did come to love her, with all the pain in his past, he may never accept or recognize his love. For him, it was a weakness. Still, she could be his wife, his duchess. It would simply take pretending she had changed, and therefore make her brother lose the wager, but that was no way to have a marriage of love and trust.

As she neared the bottom of the stairs, the strong, sweet scent of flowers filled the air. Amelia walked into the foyer and stopped, amazed at the sight before her. On every available table were rather large arrangements of flowers that she strangely did not recognize the classification of. They flourished out of beautiful vases that looked to be cut of fine crystal and made the room appear as if washed in white, except for the center table where four other arrangements of various bright flowers sat. Amelia wrinkled her brow. Lady Langley certainly had a love for flowers.

Her stomach growled; she had dawdled long enough. Turning toward the breakfast room, she almost ran into her sponsor. The woman was leaning against a wall, an amused smile pulling at her lips. She swept her hand out toward the flower-filled room. "What do you think?"

"I had no idea you loved flowers so much," Amelia said, avoiding a direct comment on the overabundance of them.

Lady Langley laughed. "I don't actually care for flowers all that much. They tend to make me sneeze."

"Then I don't understand," Amelia said slowly. "Why did you fill your entranceway with them?"

"My dear, I didn't!" Lady Langley exclaimed. "These arrangements are for you. From your admirers."

"Me?" Amelia could not have been more surprised if Lady Langley had told her that King George himself was sitting in the drawing room waiting to see her.

"Yes, dear. They started arriving an hour ago. The ones in the center, the colorful ones, were first. All the rest"—Lady Langley swept her hand toward the white flowers—"arrived at the same time, from one gentleman. I must confess I'm dying to know who! The florist would not say, and I did not want to take the liberty of reading your cards." Lady Langley, standing by the largest arrangement of white flowers, reached over and plucked the cream-colored card from the placeholder. She smiled at Amelia. "I did, however, make sure to place this flower arrangement right here, so you could find the card and read it." She walked over to Amelia and handed her the card. Unable to imagine who would spend so much money sending the dozens of flowers, Amelia tore into the card. Bold handwriting flowed across the paper.

It was a pleasure to meet you in the park yesterday, though much too short and crowded for my liking. I intend to call this afternoon, but sent these flowers as a precursor to show you I'm not as bad as Aversley likely told you I am. I picked these flowers because they are exquisite, like you.

Scarsdale

With burning cheeks, Amelia handed the note to Lady Langley.

After a moment, Colin's aunt glanced up, an intense expression on her face. "This could be very good and very bad."

"Please explain," Amelia murmured.

"Aversley and Scarsdale have no love lost between them. I don't know all the details, but it started years ago when the boys were much younger. Fifteen, I believe. Or was it fourteen?" Lady Langley waved her hand. "I don't suppose one year matters. One of those years they had a terrible fight at Aversley's annual birthday celebration that ended in fisticuffs and Scarsdale leaving abruptly. After that, from all I could gather by eavesdropping, mind you—" she flashed a cheeky grin "—they didn't speak for years, though I do know Scarsdale tried and failed to make amends for whatever Aversley thought the man had done. I have it on excellent authority that everything exploded between them one night when Scarsdale happened to be at White's. I do believe a great deal of liquor was involved."

Lady Langley paused.

"What happened that night?"

"Scarsdale kept trying to talk to Aversley who finally snarled that he'd talk to Scarsdale the day the man gained the notice of a woman named Lady Victoria. She was a beautiful debutante known far and wide to be quite virtuous."

Amelia's throat felt suddenly very dry, remembering the exchange of words between Colin and the Duke of Scarsdale. She could only imagine what the dark gentleman with the flowing black coat was capable of. "And did the Duke of Scarsdale ever gain her notice?"

A pained look crossed Lady Langley's face. "He did. And then after several weeks of courting her, he abducted her and set off to Gretna Green. By the time her father tracked them down, her reputation was ruined, but strangely, her father did not demand Scarsdale marry her. She married a much older man, a family friend of her father's, I think."

"Colin was livid with himself for ever saying such a careless thing. He never imagined she would give Scarsdale any notice, so he assumed the lady was safe. I don't believe he has spoken more than once to Scarsdale since then, but I could be wrong," she said with a shrug. "Colin will likely be enraged when he finds out Scarsdale has turned his interest to you. He'll think the duke is merely doing it to best him."

"I think you're quite right."

Lady Langley smiled knowingly. "It's quite perfect in a strange way. No other man would likely induce Colin to examine how he really feels than Scarsdale would. But you must proceed with caution. Neither of those two gentlemen are ones to be trifled with, but Scarsdale does not seem to have the same care for limits and honor as Aversley does. If he thinks there's the slightest chance of besting Aversley, I don't doubt you'd find yourself thrown over his shoulder and riding hell bent toward Gretna Green."

"I'm not sure I should encourage the Duke of Scarsdale," Amelia said, as a knock resounded on the door and male voices floated in the air from around the corner.

Before Lady Langley could respond, her butler appeared with Charles following behind him. "Lord Worthington, whatever are you doing here?" Amelia asked, realizing belatedly how rude she sounded. "I'm terribly sorry," she added. "I'm just surprised to see you." *After last night.*

He furrowed his brow. "Why? I told you I was coming."

That was true. And she'd not actually had the opportunity to tell him not to bother. She heaved a sigh and glanced at Lady Langley. The woman gestured to the hall. "Why don't the two of you talk privately in the drawing room? I'll send Lucy in to chaperone," she said, giving Charles a narrow-eyed look that made Amelia want to laugh.

Amelia nodded and led Charles to the drawing room. Before she had time to settle on the brocade settee, Lucy scampered into the room and offered a curtsy and a curious glance at Charles. "If it suits you, Lady Amelia, I'll sit over there in the window box and work on my embroidery."

"That's perfect, Lucy." She gazed at Charles and motioned to the chair opposite her. "Why don't you sit so we can talk?"

Charles shot a look at the empty space on the settee beside her and scowled. "Very well," he grumbled. "Though, I'd prefer to sit by you."

She thought it best not to mention that she preferred not.

After he sat, he leaned toward her. "I don't have much time this morning. I've agreed to go riding with some other gentlemen, but I wanted to come and offer to marry you. I have not been able to get you out of my mind, despite the fact that I wanted to."

"How flattering," she said, allowing her ire to resound in her tone.

"Don't be tedious, Amelia. You are not at all the sort of woman I imagined marrying. Your family is not well-off by any means, and you're too outspoken by half, but we can fix that."

"It's good to know I can be fixed," she said through clenched teeth.

A crease appeared between Charles's brows as if he might have actually sprouted some sense and understood he was being an ass, but his shrug took that hope away. He pinched the bridge of his nose as if she—*she*—were the one being annoying.

Clearing his throat, he said, "I previously thought you rather graceless, but you've blossomed. Still"—he eyed her critically—"I had thought to marry for greater wealth, but I have recently been left a comfortable sum from a distant relative, which brings me to my point. Exactly how big is your dowry?"

That was his point! She almost slapped him. Her hand tingled with the desire to do so. This was a far cry from the romantic marriage proposal she had been dreaming of all these years since Charles had rescued her on that horse. How could any man who had risked his life to save her be such a shallow, cold fool? She stilled. "Charles, do you remember the day years ago when—"

"You saved my life," he inserted with a rueful grin.

Amelia sucked in a sharp breath. "I saved you?"

Charles nodded. "Well, yes, of course. Though I don't go around telling people of it, nor do I want you to remind anyone who was there about it. But I haven't forgotten how your horse spooked mine. I was on a new stallion—"

"Luther," Amelia inserted, remembering the black stallion well.

"Yes, Luther. He never did learn to listen properly. I did everything in my power not to get him to follow your horse, but the blasted beast would not heed me. Before I knew it, I was racing through the forest with the sun in my eyes. I could not see a thing. But I heard you yell for me to duck. I likely would have been dead if not for you. I was livid with you for weeks."

Amelia blinked. "You were? Why?"

"Well, your horse, of course. If you'd been handling him properly I would have never been embarrassed that way."

Amelia had the sudden insane urge to laugh at just how wrong she had been about that day. She tapped her fingers against her chin for a moment as she thought. "Do you remember how you made everyone stop calling me Tree Trunk?"

He grinned. "Of course. You were so pitiful, like a wounded puppy. I felt sorry for you, and it made me look weak to stand by and let everyone pick on you."

Constance had been correct on both accounts. Amelia sighed, not bothering to mention he had called her graceful. She did not need to hear how sorry for her he felt again. "I cannot marry you, Charles."

"Why not?" he demanded.

"You are not at all the sort of man I imagined marrying," she said, greatly enjoying using his cruel words from moments before back on him. "I think you ought to go now."

His brow came together as his eyes narrowed. "Exactly what sort of man did you imagine marrying?"

Amelia rose, hoping he would do the same. Glancing down at him, she said, "One I love and who loves me in return."

Charles stood and towered over her, glaring. "Would this Romeo happen to be a duke?"

She was not about to tell Charles her heart's secrets, but she would not lie, either. "It's none of your business."

Charles blew out a derisive breath. "You disappoint me, Amelia. If you care more about a title than a good gentleman to be your husband, the least you could do is be honest and say so."

Anger flared in her chest. "I care nothing about titles, Charles, no matter what you might think. Now, I insist you leave."

Without a word to her, Charles stormed out of the room, and she sank onto the settee with a ragged sigh. If she could not convince Charles she cared nothing for Colin's title how was she ever going to persuade Colin of the truth when he was so jaded?

~

Since Colin was arriving at his aunt's house well before the acceptable calling hour, he was astonished to see Worthington striding out the front door as Colin's carriage pulled up to the home. He quickly descended his carriage and met Worthington at the bottom step.

His one time friend stopped and glared at Colin. "Perfect timing, as always, Aversley."

"I've no idea what you mean," Colin drawled, glancing past Worthington toward the house. Had Amelia just agreed to marry Worthington? Sharp hollowness filled him.

Worthington snorted. "You know exactly what I mean. First you stole Lady Eleanor from me—"

"I did not steal her from you," Colin said, between clenched teeth. "Let us set the facts to rights regarding her. I had no idea you cared for Lady Eleanor. You had never said a word about her, and I am not a bloody mind reader. When I realized you did care for her, I ended our affair immediately, but she already had another fellow to fill her bed."

"I don't believe you."

"You don't want to believe me, but it is true. The gentleman had been in her bed, without my knowledge, before I ended things. She was after a high place in Society, and unfortunately, you could not offer her what she wanted. It had nothing to do with me and everything to do with the nature of women."

"Something we finally agree on," Worthington snarled.

Colin relaxed somewhat. "Who else do you think I have stolen from you?"

"Amelia," Worthington said bluntly. "I asked her to marry me moments ago, and she turned me down."

"And she told you it was because of me?" Colin asked, struggling to keep the astonishment from his voice and the hope squashed down.

"She said she wants love, but that's a lie. I offered her love, and she threw it back in my face."

"Maybe she does not love you," Colin said evenly, the hope despite all his efforts, growing.

"Of course she doesn't," Worthington roared. "I'm not a bloody duke."

"Did she say that precisely?" Colin asked as Worthington stomped toward his carriage. But Worthington did not look back. Within seconds, his carriage was pulling away from the house.

Colin turned and started up the steps, his heart thudding hard. Had Amelia just caused Philip to lose the wager, or did her heart now belong to him? Was he a fool to consider such a thing?

The door opened before he got to it, and the butler ushered him into the foyer and departed to announce his arrival. An overwhelming floral scent assaulted him. Colin glanced around at all the flowers in the room and paused. Who the devil would send lily of the valley's? He strolled to the open card lying on the table and plucked it up and read the note.

Exquisite, was she? Scarsdale had no bloody right to tell Amelia she was exquisite.

Anger as hot as he'd felt the night Colin had seen his mother's bedchamber door open and heard her soft laughter as she allowed Scarsdale into the room curled in his belly and lit him on fire. He threw the card on the table and stormed toward where he heard his aunt's and Amelia's voices coming from. As he turned down the hall toward the parlor, Amelia was there, resplendent in the ice blue day dress he had helped her pick out to transform her. Had he accomplished his goal? His anger deepened and stoked the flame of discontent.

He inclined his head. "Lady Amelia, Aunt Jane."

His aunt walked past Amelia and patted his arm. "Good to see you, Aversley. If you'll excuse me, though? I've the worst megrim coming on."

Colin nodded. "Likely caused by the choking floral scent filling the air," he commented dryly.

Amelia's gaze came sharply to him, but she said nothing. His aunt, however, chuckled. "Yes, well, perhaps. Lady Amelia has gained several admirers in her short time here in London, it seems."

"I see. And who might these admirers be?" Colin asked, as if the did not already know one of them.

Amelia shrugged, but his aunt grinned. "Why, your old school chum the Duke of Scarsdale is one of them. And Lords Edington and Shrewsbury are the other two," his aunt added in a silky voice.

Colin glanced at Amelia to find her gaping at his aunt. What the devil was that about? "Did you not know who sent you the flowers, Lady Amelia?"

"I knew of one of them," she said pointedly, her words laced with an underlying reprimand.

"I'm sorry, dearest." Aunt Jane shot Amelia a truly regretful look. "I'm afraid my curiosity really did get the best of me, and I peeked at the other cards when you were visiting with Lord Worthington."

Colin held his silence since he was in the same position as his aunt. Amelia shrugged. "No matter." She eyed Colin warily.

"I take it receiving cards from three gentleman with loftier titles than Worthington pleases you," Colin said, knowing full well he was leading her in the hope she would deny it. His answer was a silent, stern glare.

"I think I'll retire now," his aunt said, giving him a pointed stare. "You seem to have it hand, even if rather clumsily."

"I thank you for your confidence," he said dryly. Once she was departed, he stood in silence with Amelia for a long moment and finally cleared his throat when it seemed abundantly apparent that she was not going to be the first to say anything. "Shall we sit in the parlor and visit?"

"Certainly," she responded. "Lucy is still in there from my last caller."

"Of course," Colin replied, sweeping his hand forward to indicate Amelia should move ahead. "I just saw Worthington. He was rather angry."

"Was he?" Amelia murmured as if she did not know.

With her hips swaying provocatively as she walked, Colin found it hard to concentrate on discerning whether she was being genuine or sarcastic. Most of his energy was directed toward cooling his heated blood.

"Indeed, he was," he finally answered, unable to tear his gaze away from her softly moving hips.

He followed her into the parlor, took a seat, and eyed her.

The artful way her hair was piled atop her head with a few teasing tendrils dangling around the long, slender column of her neck made him want to unpin her tresses and see them tumble down her shoulders. The view of her creamy skin served as a fierce reminder of just how pleasing having his lips on her neck had been. He shifted in his chair to combat his growing need. "Worthington mentioned you turned down his offer for your hand. I assume this means I have won the wager?"

Damnation. He clenched his fists, suddenly understanding how much he wanted her to deny he had won and to offer a reasonable explanation.

"You assume wrong," she replied evenly.

"Are you saying you did not deny Worthington's proposal because you have now set your sights on one of the three, more prominent, gentleman who have taken a fancy to you?"

She pursed her very kissable lips before pressing them into a hard line and then sighing softly. "That's correct. I denied Lord Worthington's offer because it was quite obvious he does not love me, and frankly I realized I do not love him."

Worthington's words that she wanted a loftier title than his rang in Colin's ears. He tried to ignore it, but the layers of cynicism were damnably hard to peel away. As much as he wanted to believe, he could not. At least not completely.

He leaned back in his chair and studied her. Her color was high on her cheeks, her pulse visibly beat a rapid pace at her neck, and her hands clutched at the folds of her skirts. Somehow, it made him feel better that she seemed nervous, too. "I don't mean to play the devil's advocate"—though truly he did—"but I need to be convinced that you really have not changed who you are rather than the more readily believable explanation that it is your newfound status as an Incomparable that has caused you to deny Worthington. If you can convince me of this, then I will call the wager over and pay your brother's debts."

She took a deep breath, the full measure of it pushing her chest upward. "And how should I go about convincing you? I've told you the truth, yet you refuse to believe it. Shall I turn down another lofty lord? Five others? Ten?" Her eyes burned with anger. Or was that hurt?

The parlor door swung open, and his aunt strolled through the room followed by Lords Shrewsbury and Edington. Colin stood and scowled at the gentleman. "What the devil do you want?"

"Your Grace!" Amelia cried and popped out of her seat. "Please come in, Lord Edington and Lord Shrewsbury."

The men darted nervous glances at Colin while shifting from foot to foot. "Very well," Colin grumbled. "If Lady Amelia says you can sit with her, then who am I to stop you?" No matter how much he wanted to send them on their way. As Amelia went to sit, Edington and Shrewsbury fairly tripped over themselves to help her get to her seat. Colin ground his teeth while taking the chair opposite of everyone else. Amelia's slender body looked crushed between the larger gentlemen sitting on either side of her.

"This is cozy," Colin remarked, purposely eyeing both men. "I'm almost inclined to say it's too cozy. That there are too many gentlemen in this room. Two should leave."

"Nonsense," came a deep voice from behind Colin. "I'm sure we are all here for the same purpose. I, for one, have always loved a good competition."

Cringing with recognition, Colin craned his neck, met Scarsdale's gaze and frowned. Perfect. The day had just gone from mildly annoying to abominable. "Who let you in?"

"Aversley," his aunt snapped. "I must ask you to mind your manners no matter how difficult you may find it. This is my house, and therefore these are my guests." His aunt turned her glacial glare from him to Scarsdale, though she softened her look immediately to one of welcome. *Traitor*. "Please do come in and join us, Your Grace."

"You are kind as always, Lady Langley," Scarsdale said in a nasally voice. He took the seat right next to Colin—probably just to annoy him—and folded his arms across his chest while stretching his legs out as if he owned the damnable place. Colin extended his legs in front of him and crossed his ankles. He was sorely tempted to kick off his shoes, but, if he behaved so crassly, his aunt would probably box his ears as she'd done when he was a wild lad. Still, if anyone belonged here in this room with Amelia, he did.

Amelia cleared her throat, her face flushing as she did so. "Thank you for the lovely flowers, gentlemen."

Everyone nodded but Colin, and suddenly he felt the fool. He could have bought Amelia flowers, except he was not courting her, so why should he? Of course, she loved them, and it would have brought a smile to her beautiful face.

"I sent you the bouquet of red roses," Shrewsbury said.

"I sent you the larger bouquet of yellow roses," Edington spouted in a rushed tone.

Scarsdale smiled blandly at both gentlemen then gazed at Amelia for too long and too lustfully. Colin gritted his teeth harder.

"I sent you the thirty bouquets of lily of the valley," Scarsdale said, his voice too confident by half.

Even as Amelia smiled at the man, Colin imagined how good it would feel to get in the ring at Gentlemen Jackson's with Scarsdale and show him, punch by brutal punch, what he could do with his thirty bouquets of flowers.

"Which bouquet do you prefer?" the ever overly eager Edington asked.

Amelia squirmed, her gaze darting to each gentleman and coming to rest on Colin. "I do so like roses and the lily of the valley are quite lovely, as well, but my favorite flower is the great hairy willow herb."

Warmth seeped into Colin's body and spread through his veins. When Amelia awoke tomorrow morning, the downstairs was going to be filled with great hairy willow herb. He had never purchased flowers for a lady in his life, but he wanted to buy out all the florists in London for Amelia.

He smiled, and the one she gave him in return, full of sweet radiant joy, made his chest do that painful tightening thing it only did when she was near him.

"I'm surprised you like the great hairy willow herb," Scarsdale said, interrupting Colin's peace. He scowled at the man only to have the look returned, accompanied by a strange scrutinizing that Scarsdale eventually turned on Amelia. "That particular flower is quite ugly."

"Yes, well, better ugly than poisonous," Colin retorted. "You've filled my aunt's house with lethal flowers. Did you not know that or did you intend to kill Lady Amelia?" Colin struggled not to smirk at Scarsdale.

For a moment, the man appeared shocked with his widened gaze. Slowly, he shook his head. "I had no idea. Are they really dangerous?"

"To small children or anyone who might be inclined to eat the dark berries that accompany the flowers."

"Luckily," Amelia chirped, "I have no such inclination." She gave Colin a sideways scowl as if he had done something wrong. Blasted women made no sense.

"I'm truly sorry, Lady Amelia. I really did not know. Did you know and simply say nothing about it to be kind?"

"No," Amelia said. "I was not aware, either. His Grace"—she inclined her head toward Colin with a small smile—"has educated me about two types of flowers in two days. Yesterday he taught me the correct name of the great hairy willow herb, and today he enlightened me on the poisonous nature of lily of the valley."

"How very instructive of him," Scarsdale said, giving Colin that strange look again. "And what, pray tell, has Lady Amelia taught you, Aversley?"

Between jealousy and the desire to crush Amelia against his body, Colin's blood surged through his veins like a turbulent river. Why did a few kind words from her and one single smile affect him so? He struggled to focus on Scarsdale and his question. "She's taught me to keep my guard up higher than I had been, and for that I'm eternally grateful."

Amelia glanced quickly away, but before she did, Colin caught the tremble of her bottom lip. If ever there was an arse he was one. He hated himself, but better to hate just himself than himself *and* her, because if he let his guard down she would disappoint him, betray him and destroy him. Wouldn't she?

But what if she didn't disappoint? a voice whispered in his head.

If he wasn't careful he'd be muttering to himself soon.

Needing to escape the confines of the parlor, Colin jumped up. "We should be departing for the Banbury's picnic." Before anyone could respond he barreled onward. "Shrewsbury and Edington, you two should say your goodbyes. I'm sure you both have ladies who are waiting to join you for today's outing."

Both men shook their heads.

"Go anyway," Colin snapped, not caring how grumpy he sounded. "We cannot very well leave with you sitting in my aunt's parlor."

His aunt gave him another stern look but rose without arguing. "Though I would have put it much differently, gentlemen, we do need to be departing for the festivities if we don't want to be late." She focused on Scarsdale. "I hope we will see you again soon."

Scarsdale grinned, and before he even said a word, Colin knew he wasn't going to like the words by the glint in his former friend's eyes.

"As a matter of fact," Scarsdale said, "as happy coincidence would have it, I'm attending the same picnic."

"Isn't that lovely, Aversley?" Colin's aunt asked, turning her gaze on him. He could have sworn her lips were quivering with mirth by the upward tilt of them. What was she about today? Clearly, she did not have an looming megrim. When the silence stretched, she raised her eyebrows at him. "Aversley? Did you hear me?"

"I heard you," he grumbled. "I find certain paintings lovely. A cloudless day. A moonlit night." He glanced purposely at Amelia. "Women with luxurious golden hair and long limbs are especially lovely, but picnics full of eager suitors, like Scarsdale, does not call the word lovely to mind. I think the word is...*nuisance*."

"Really, Aversley. Your manners have not improved with the years," Scarsdale said in a mirth-filled tone before he took a step toward Amelia. "Lady Amelia, would you care to ride to the picnic with me?" Scarsdale asked, moving nearer.

If Scarsdale moved another bloody step closer to her, Colin was going to put the man flat on his back. "She is riding with me," Colin said and proffered his elbow to Amelia. "Shall we be departing?"

Without a word, Amelia slipped her hand through the crook of his elbow, and much to Colin's irritation, they departed the house as one big annoying group.

Chapter Seventeen

Colin was not sure quite how it had happened but somehow his aunt had volunteered him to give a walking flower tour to a group of the picnickers, of which Amelia was not among. He could, however, see her in the distance, strolling around the lake with Scarsdale, Edington, and Shrewsbury surrounding her and her lady's maid trailing behind them.

Swatting at the bee buzzing around his head, he barely held in his curse. He wasn't sure if it was the heat or his burgeoning temper that was making him sweat, but rivulets ran down his spine dampening his shirt and making the thing cling to his skin. He was having trouble thinking logically about flowers…or anything else. All he could think about was Amelia, and that was far from logical.

"Your Grace, what flower is that?" Lady Sara asked him.

"Foxglove," he murmured, forcing himself to look at her. When she smiled demurely, he pretended not to notice. He had no doubt that his mother was somehow behind Lady Sara being at this picnic, since she did not know the host before today. Lady Sara appearing here smacked of his mother's involvement, and the only way she could have known he was coming here would be his aunt. Colin frowned. It was a rare occasion Aunt Jane and Mother spoke a civil word to each other, but it seemed the occasion had happened.

Moving ahead a few steps to where his aunt was, he whispered in her ear, "Have you seen my mother lately?"

Aunt Jane nodded. "I saw her yesterday briefly. I went to the orphanage to see the children, and she was there."

Colin gaped at his aunt. "My mother was at an orphanage?"

His aunt nodded. "Yes. She apparently has decided to volunteer one day a week with the children."

The hostess of the picnic, Lady Banbury, strolled beside him and pointed to a tall red flower. "What is that called?"

"Dog rose," he said distractedly. He was trying to picture his mother at an orphanage, but could not quite imagine it. Yet she had been there. She gained nothing from going there, so she must care about those children. And if she cared about them, had he totally misjudged her? Suddenly, he had an urgent desire to talk to her and another to be by Amelia's side. He picked up his pace and strode to the end of the lane of flowers. *Thank God.*

"This is the end," he said, not even looking back as he hurried away toward where he'd last seen Amelia. Turning the corner, he expected to see her perhaps sitting on a blanket with the men surrounding her, but she was farther away, in a distant field of purple wildflowers with her brother, a handful of the other guests loitering around them. Her hand was raised to her face, and she stared off toward the edge of the woods. Colin followed her gaze to the forest, where three gentlemen appeared to be lined up on horses. In the middle of the field, another gentleman stood with—Colin squinted against the sun—was that a handkerchief in the man's hand?

He increased his pace to Amelia until he was running. As he neared the group, he forced himself to slow his gait, but his pulse raced ahead. Ignoring everyone else, he strode up to Amelia and her brother. "What's happening here?"

Harthorne motioned across the expanse with his hand. "The gentlemen are racing for the privilege of being able to take my sister on a carriage ride tomorrow morning in Hyde Park."

Teeters of amusement came from two of the ladies standing behind Amelia. Colin could see Amelia's back stiffen and her face flush. "I tried to stop them," Amelia whispered.

A petite lady with a head full of curly red hair moved to stand beside Amelia and leaned close to her. "Ignore those two behind you. They are simply jealous. Though, if you ask me, I cannot figure out why. The Duke of Scarsdale is too brooding for my taste. Edington not intelligent enough, and Shrewsbury without true bravery. They may all have titles, but I'd not have a any of them as a husband."

Colin instantly liked the outspoken miss. "Who might you be?"

"I'm Jemma, the granddaughter of the Duke of Rowan."

"I didn't know Rowan had a granddaughter."

"Neither did he," she said flippantly, though her cheeks turned scarlet.

"That would make you Lady Jemma," Colin said gently.

"I do not believe so," she whispered, the scarlet of her cheeks spreading to her neck.

"Ah, I see." And he did. A bastard granddaughter would be simply Jemma, but she deserved respect no matter what anyone else thought. Accordingly, he inclined his head and came up to have her hand stuck in his face."

She grinned. "If you will beg my pardon, where I come from women sometimes shake hands as a greeting, as odd as that sounds."

"There's no need to apologize," Harthorne said from beside Colin.

Colin turned toward his friend, surprised, but glad to see him studying Jemma with interest. The two exchanged pleasantries, allowing Colin to focus once more on Amelia.

He was about to speak when one of the ladies behind them exclaimed, "It's started."

Colin glanced toward the field where the men on their horses now raced toward the crowd. He did not need to watch the entire race. Scarsdale would win. That much was obvious and not surprising. Scarsdale was an excellent rider. Colin leaned close to Amelia. "Are you happy now?"

~

Amelia gasped more at the hitch in Colin's husky question than the actual question itself. Her heart thudded painfully in her chest. She swallowed, trying hard to order her racing thoughts, but it was next to impossible with him so near. He smelled of sweet flowers and sharp grass kissed with dew. A light breeze blew through his golden hair, moving a few wavy tendrils. Her fingers itched to slide through his hair. Now *that* would make her happy.

"You can't tell me all this attention doesn't please you." He waved a hand toward the riders.

His voice had taken on a hard edge, yet what sounded like uncertainty made his words rise ever so slightly. Was she starting to get through that thick skull of his? She grinned and his brows came together in a deep, furrowed frown. She leaned near him, so that the nosy ladies behind them would not hear her. The desire to tell him how she felt overwhelmed her. Now, surrounded by so many others, was not the time, though.

"I am happy because you are here with me."

He drew his lips in thoughtfully while he stared at her as if she were a foreign object he had never seen before. Good. Let him question his own beliefs, if that was his process. If she was very lucky it would lead to him questioning his heart and then finally letting her in.

"The Duke of Scarsdale has won!" one of the women exclaimed. Her muscles went rigid at the thought of having to accept a carriage ride with the man, but there was no good way to decline and still appear gracious. Walking forward and away from the rest of the group, she raised her hand once again to shield her eyes from the glare of the mid-day sun. The duke rode his horse directly to her. His stallion's black coat gleamed with slick perspiration as the animal pranced from foot to foot, snorting. She darted a glance behind her, glad to find Colin and her brother walking toward her as the red-haired lady, Jemma, led the rest of the group away.

"I've come to claim my prize," the Duke of Scarsdale said.

"My sister is no prize," Philip retorted.

Amelia frowned. She knew Philip had meant only to be her protector, but she wished he would select his words with more care.

The Duke of Scarsdale, with his dark hair slicked severely back from his rugged face and his coal gaze focused on her, did not look as if the race had taken the least bit of effort.

"Do you never get hot?" She blurted the first thing that came to her mind.

Sliding off his panting horse, he handed the beast off to his man. who had appeared as if by magic at his side. Turning, the duke smiled slowly at Amelia, showing gleaming teeth. "I assure you, Lady Amelia, the right situation can make me blistering."

"Scarsdale," Colin growled beside her. The muscles of Colin's jaw tensed visibly.

The duke chuckled. "I promise to be on my best behavior every moment I am with Lady Amelia."

"And her chaperone," Colin snapped. "She goes nowhere without her."

"Of course not," the duke replied smoothly, and rather oddly, caught Philip's eye.

Amelia would have missed it had she blinked.

Philip glanced quickly away, while clearing his throat. "I must have your promise as a gentleman that you will not abscond with my sister," Philip said. "I may have known you since our school days, but I also know of your reputation."

Surprised that she had never heard Philip mention the Duke of Scarsdale, since they had apparently gone to school together, Amelia glanced at her brother and could have sworn a small smile tugged at his lips. Something very odd was amiss.

Colin shook his head. "I'm afraid I don't share your faith in Scarsdale," Colin growled. "Lady Amelia, I truly don't think it's wise for you to go."

"You don't?" Her blood was roaring in her ears with her hope.

"No, I don't. In fact, I'm begging you not to."

"I'm standing right here," Scarsdale said evenly. "You gave your word you would ride with the winner, Lady Amelia. But if you are not a woman of your word, so be it, but I vow on my parents' graves that I will be a perfect gentleman."

Blast the man. There was no way she could say no now. Plus, if she backed out, she would look as if she did not keep her word, and she did not want to give Colin the tiniest room to doubt her. "I'll go, but only," she said, purposely eyeing Colin, "because I am true to my word."

"I want to know what time you will be arriving to take Lady Amelia out and when you plan to return her," Colin demanded.

"I'd like to know that, as well," Philip added.

Amelia had heard a tremor of laugher in her brother's voice, but a quick glance around the group showed no signs that anyone else had heard it. She wiped at her hot brow. Maybe the heat was getting to her.

Scarsdale looked thoughtful for a moment. "Is noon suitable for you, Lady Amelia?"

Never was preferable, but what was done could not be undone. Well, not gracefully anyway. "That will be acceptable."

"Excellent." Scarsdale grasped her hand, and before she could protest, he raised it, peeling off her glove, and pressed his lips to her skin. He kissed it like a man intent on but one thing—*seduction*. His dark gaze held hers, dangerous and glittering. She stared into the depths of his cold eyes and searched for a glimmer of goodness, the likes of which always shined from Colin's beguiling gaze. What she saw—deep unfathomable pain—made her gasp. He blinked and the darkness of his gaze turned frosty, his lashes lowering to veil his soul. Beside her, she could feel the tension radiating from Colin.

With a chuckle, Scarsdale released her hand, turned on his heel, and was gone the way he had come moments before.

Philip clapped his hands together, making Amelia jump. "Well, dear sister of mine, it seems you have a new, very eligible suitor. I'd not have originally picked Scarsdale for you, but he seems as if the years have taught him some valuable lessons."

Amelia was not mistaken in that Philip pierced Colin with a knowing look. Clearly, Philip knew there was no affection lost between the gentlemen, so why was he goading Colin?

"You know you should not trust him, Harthorne," Colin bit out.

Philip clasped Colin on the shoulder. "Some would say the same of you, Aversley, yet I've always trusted you. I do believe Scarsdale has changed."

"I doubt it, and I'll thank you not to put me in the same category as Scarsdale."

"In this instance, I cannot help but do so. You are both my sister's suitors, it seems."

"Philip!" Amelia cried, tugging her glove on. What was he trying to do? He'd ruin everything.

Colin's eyes narrowed. "I'll be off now and leave you two to visit."

"I'll see you at the club," Philip said cheerfully to Colin's back since he'd already turned to stride away.

Amelia watched him leave, wanting to call him back but suspecting he would not come. When he was gone, she turned on Philip. "What game are you playing with my life? Colin is nothing like the Duke of Scarsdale." She twisted her hands together, her stomach twisting, as well. I'll never forgive you if you've driven Colin away from me! I love him!" She sucked in a breath and clasped her hand to her mouth.

Her brother smiled gently. "I know."

Confusion swarmed her as she withdrew her hand and stared at her brother. "You know?"

He shrugged. "Well, I suspected. And, Amelia, you must trust me. I don't think I've driven him away. I'm trying to make the fool see what is right in front of his face, if he will only reach out and grasp it."

"How? How are you trying to do that?" she demanded, her irritation threatening to boil over.

"Calm down and let me explain," he said in a soothing voice.

Amelia took a deep breath. "This is as calm as I'm going to get, Philip. Spit out your plan before I choke it out of you."

Philip grinned. "Last night, after the ball, I ran into Scarsdale at White's."

"Why have you never mentioned his name before? How is it I did not know the two of you went to school together?"

"I suppose the occasion never came up to talk of him to you, and my friendship with him ended quite abruptly when I was much younger."

Amelia thought of Lady Langley's story about Colin's fight with the duke. Could Philip's friendship have ended over the same thing? "What ended your friendship?"

"It's not my place to reveal it, Amelia. I swore to Aversley I would take the secret to my grave."

She wanted to argue. In fact, she fairly burned to argue and learn what had happened, but she knew her brother, and if he had given his word, he would never go back on it. And that was what made her love him so. Reluctantly, she nodded. "Go on."

"I've watched Scarsdale try time and again to make amends with Aversley over the years. Some of Scarsdale's methods were badly chosen, but I believe the man was and *is* desperate. I believe he truly regrets the mistake he made and genuinely wants to somehow repair a bit of the pain he caused Aversley so long ago. Scarsdale was young and foolish when he did what he did, and normally, Aversley would see it, but it involved someone who had already hurt Aversley a great deal."

"Does this have anything to do with that lady the Duke of Scarsdale ran off to Gretna Green with?"

Philip frowned. "No. Are you listening to me?"

She glared in return. "No. I'm standing here not hearing a word you've said." She plunked her hands on her hips. "This is rather hard to follow, Philip."

"Sorry. No, the end of their friendship had nothing to do with the lady Scarsdale ran off with to Gretna Green. Their friendship ended much earlier. The Gretna Green incident was when we were one and twenty, and I do believe, in Scarsdale's defense, he thought only to get Aversley to talk to him and then ended up besotted with the lady in question."

"He told you that?"

"No and yes. Not in those exact words."

Amelia sighed. "What *has* the Duke of Scarsdale told you?"

"Last night, Scarsdale asked me if I could give him another chance, and I said I could after he confessed that what he did so many years ago gnaws at him constantly and that he would do anything to set things right between him and Aversley, but he could not think what he could possibly do."

Philip grinned. "Luckily, I could, and it had to do with you. So I told Scarsdale about the wager I made with Aversley right down to what was at stake, Aversley's opinions of women, and how I thought Scarsdale could help me, and in turn, you. But most importantly could help Aversley."

"Colin would not like that," Amelia said. She didn't particularly like the Duke of Scarsdale knowing about the wager, but what was done, was done and there was no undoing it now.

"No Aversley wouldn't like it one bit, but he'll like the regrets he has to live with if he foolishly loses you even less."

"You are a wonderful bother, Philip." Amelia hugged him. She would have picked a different way for him to show his love, but she was so thankful to have a brother that cared for her as much as Philip did.

"Aversley just needs a little push, Amelia. He's afraid. But in my experience there's nothing better to cure a man of what he fears than a bigger fear. He fears his feelings for you, but I know he fears losing you more. Scarsdale is the push. Last night, we came up with the plan for Scarsdale to appear to be courting you in earnest, and my part is to seemingly agree with it. I'm not normally one for deception, but in this case, since there is no possible way Aversley will be damaged, I think a bit of trickery is acceptable. *If* you are sure you love Aversley and won't prove him right by throwing him over for Scarsdale."

"I'd never do such a thing. I love Colin," she said, even as the words filled her with hope and fear.

Chapter Eighteen

White's was basically empty, which suited Colin perfectly. He was in no mood to make polite conversation, and the only reason he was here now and not in the comfort of his own study was because he had a thing or two he wanted to say to Harthorne. Like why the bloody hell would he think he could trust Scarsdale.

The duke's name brought Colin's other problem to his mind. After he'd left the picnic today, he'd tried and failed to see his mother. Her butler had said she was at the orphanage. Apparently, his mother now had a great desire to help others. He'd struggled all day to reconcile the image of his mother at an orphanage with the picture in his head of the cool, uncaring woman he had assumed had no capacity to love.

The more he thought about her, the more he realized with a gut-sinking sensation that his demeanor was quite like his mother's—an aloof, devil-may-care attitude. But things had once greatly affected him and hurt him. Had it been the same for his mother? Had he been so hurt by her that he refused to see the possibility that maybe she was masking pain? A twisted way to do it, but nonetheless who was he to judge?

Colin lifted his glass and took the final swig of his drink. The aromas of the barrel-aged whiskey filled his nose, and the liquor burned a path to his belly. He set his crystal tumbler down and raised his hand to indicate he wanted another dram. Within seconds, golden liquor shimmered before him once more. Harthorne would be here any second, and Colin could not figure out exactly what to say.

Why couldn't he think clearly? He wanted to demand Harthorne refuse to allow Amelia to go riding with Scarsdale, but he could not force the man to do anything in regard to his own sister. With a frustrated growl, Colin swigged the entire contents of his glass and narrowed his eyes while focusing his thoughts.

His only chance of keeping Amelia away from Scarsdale was for Colin to offer her his heart, assuming she wanted it. Devil take it, he was making excuses and he knew it. Colin took a long, ragged breath. If his mother of all people could change, he bloody well could, too. He had to face his fear, because...because—his heart exploded as he gripped his glass—he loved Amelia. *He loved her.* He did.

"Damnation," he swore under his breath. All this time, struggling not to end up a lovelorn fool like his father and Amelia had already twined him around her finger without him realizing it. His hands shook. Could he offer his heart to her? Would she want it once he told her of his past, which instinctually he felt he had to do if he meant to truly change? He needed to tell her everything, including the stipulation in his father's will. The thought made his hand shake as he raised his whiskey glass to his lips, realizing, as he tilted the glass and nothing game out, it was still empty. He grimaced at his distraction. This would not do. He needed to think carefully on how he would word telling her about the will and pick the exact right time to do it. He didn't want her to ever doubt he was asking her to marry him out of love.

He swallowed as a hand clamped on his shoulder.

Harthorne sat down beside him. "Sorry I'm late."

Colin blinked. "Are you late?"

Harthorne gave him a strange look. "Yes. Almost an hour. Did you not notice?"

"No. I've been preoccupied."

"Me as well," Harthorne said and motioned to the staff to bring him a drink.

Colin struggled to pull his thoughts away from his past and his mother and concentrate on Harthorne. "What detained you?"

"Lord Shrewsbury. He appeared at my room and requested permission to ask for Amelia's hand."

"What?" Colin growled.

"Sit down, Aversley."

Colin blinked, unaware he had jumped up. He slowly sat again. "Did you tell Shrewsbury to bugger off?"

"Certainly not. I gave the nice chap permission, and then I had no choice but to go with him to your aunt's house so he could ask Amelia to marry him."

Colin's mouth felt too dry to speak. He reached for his glass to take a drink, remembered once again, he had finished his, and swiped up Harthorne's untouched liquor. After several swigs, he set the tumbler down. His head knew Amelia would not accept the offer, but his heart reacted peculiarly anyway. "She declined the offer, I assume?"

"Of course," Harthorne said with a wave of his hand. "I knew she would, tried to convince the chap of as much, but he refused to listen, so I had to let him hear it from her lips."

Colin released a breath he had not realized he held and met Harthorne's gaze. "Amelia is not going to change."

Harthorne smiled, his eyes sympathetic. "No, she is not. The question is, are you?"

"I am going to try," Colin said, making up his mind to go see his mother again tonight. He didn't give a damn how late it was. His gut told him he'd have a better chance of understanding himself if he could simply understand her

Not thirty minutes later, Colin stomped away from the steps of his mother's home on Mayfair and lumbered into his carriage. "Take me home, Barnes."

"The duchess isn't in, Your Grace?"

Colin laid his head back and closed his eyes. "According to her butler, she and another group of women who call themselves the Angels of the Orphans decided to spend the night at the orphanage. They suspect the children are being mistreated, and they don't think the ladies currently on the orphanage committee are doing enough about it."

"Your mother? Spending the night at an orphanage?"

"I know," Colin said. "I find it hard to believe myself." Not only that she was so passionate about the orphans, or anyone at all, but that she was willing to spend the night somewhere like that. God alone only knew whom she coerced into letting her and her friends stay there.

He'd come by again in the morning, but if she still wasn't home, he would go speak to Amelia. He didn't want her to go off with Scarsdale before he had a chance to talk to her.

~

Colin awoke the next morning, and after stopping by his mother's and learning she had come home but had gone out again to somewhere the butler wasn't privy to, Colin headed to his aunt's home. He expected that both Aunt Jane and Amelia might still be asleep, but he would simply sit and wait until Amelia made an appearance downstairs.

He knocked on the door, and when the butler opened it wide, Colin caught a glimpse of Amelia on the far side of the entrance, slipping out the terrace door that led to the gardens. "I'm here to see Lady Amelia," Colin announced and brushed past the butler, not waiting to actually be let in. "No need to announce me," Colin called over his shoulder. "I saw her heading to the gardens. I'll just go catch up with her."

Colin was across the parquet floor and descending the steps into the garden before the butler likely ever took a full breath. He stopped near the water fountain and glanced around the grounds but did not see Amelia anywhere. That was odd. She had come this way. "Amelia!"

The sound of trickling water was his only returning answer. Determined to find her, he strode around the grounds, and after a few minutes, he stopped in front of the small maze his aunt had commissioned last year to replicate one of the larger ones at her country home. A woman's parasol lay open on the ground. He smiled and slipped into the maze and followed the path toward the center. Once there, he peered into the opening and breathed deeply at the sight of Amelia flapping a blanket in the air. Stepping back so as not to be seen, he soaked in the pleasure of simply watching her.

Her lovely melodic voice filled the air as she sang softly, and he smiled when she wrinkled her nose because she couldn't seem to get the blanket to lie on the grass exactly as she wanted it. She got on her hands and knees and ran her hand over the quilt until all the wrinkles were out, all the while her delectable bottom waving invitingly in the air. His desire had heated his blood by the time she sat down and opened a book, instantly laughing.

Taking a long measured breath, his chest filled with painful emotion that partially made him want to move forward and gather her in his arms and somewhat made him want to turn around and leave for fear of taking this step. He could not remember ever being afraid of anything in his life, but he was now. She laughed again as she turned the page, and the sound was so sweet, he could not stop himself from moving forward to be near her.

The smell of cut grass and shrubbery filled the mildly warm air, but Amelia's fragrant scent also lingered. He breathed deeply as he walked toward her. She was so engrossed in her book she never looked up. "Amelia," he called very gently.

Startling, she dropped the book and gazed up at him. "Colin, whatever are you doing here at this hour?"

He kneeled down beside her, so near his thigh pressed against her leg. Her gaze lowered to where they touched and then raised to his.

"Did you want to talk to me?"

He glanced around the maze, only just registering the fact that they were completely alone. "Where is your lady's maid?"

Amelia frowned. "Do you really care?"

"No. Except for the fact that it means I have you all to myself."

She batted her eyelashes at him just as he had taught her to do. By damn it had the desired affect he had instructed. He instantly became hard.

"Do you want me all to yourself?" she asked innocently.

Every second. Every minute. Every day, hour, and week. For the rest of her life. But first he had to say the things that needed to be said.

Kneeling and facing her, he cupped her face in his hands and ran the pad of his thumb over her lips. "You're so very beautiful."

She shook her head, her eyes flitting away from his.

His gut clenched, and he swallowed the lump in his throat. "Look at me, please." His voice was husky even to his ears.

After what seemed entirely too long, she focused her trusting, blue stare on him. He threaded his hands deep into her hair, glad she had not put it up this morning. The silk tresses glided between his fingers. "You *are* beautiful. I should have never tried to change you. Like most men, I was an utter fool and did not truly look at you when I first saw you. You did not need me to make you an Incomparable, Amelia. You already were one."

She raised her eyebrows questioningly, as if she were trying to decide whether to believe him or not.

For once in his life, he was going to give to a woman for purely unselfish reasons. He was going to give Amelia confidence. "Amelia, I have known a great many women." More than he wanted to recall. "You are the most beautiful I have ever encountered, not only inside but out."

No words came from her, but her eyes shimmered with unshed tears. His heart lurched, and he brushed a very gentle kiss across her lips.

She grasped his hand and pressed a kiss to it while peering shyly at him from under her lashes. "When I was younger I was teased mercilessly about being too tall. I took to slumping and slouching to appear shorter. Your words make me want to stand straight."

Something in him broke, snapped, came unclasped like a heavy iron chain being cut, and all the pain he had held at bay filled him. His past was trying to break the surface and destroy his future, but a kiss from her would stop the pain. He was sure of it. He captured her lips with his own and kissed her with all the mastery he had gained in all the years of bedding countless women. He would bring Amelia to writhing ecstasy with his kiss. He knew he could. He could make her want to bed him tonight, and then she would be his forever, unable to turn away from marrying him, chained to him by raw desire.

He'd seen the trust in her eyes. He had trusted the first woman who had ever used him and been burned for it. Changed. Scarred. His blood rushed in his ears, and his heartbeat joined the cacophony like a drum of desire, pain, and rage, mingled and beating a steady never-ending rhythm. Searching for some unknown something, he increased the pressure of his mouth until Amelia cried out and pulled away from him.

Her eyes were round, her breathing labored. The world around him seemed to stop, the pain of his past colliding with the hope of a future he did not know how to reach for or let himself have. Bitterness curled his hands into fists. He trailed his gaze to her lips, swollen and red from his savage kiss. Shame curled in his gut. Was this what he had to give her? Rage and shame? The need to cry out made his throat ache. The fear in the pit of his heart crept out and took hold of him. He was dirty, damaged, and unable to properly love another. Even now, when it was all that he wanted.

"I'm sorry," he said. Determined to get away, he rose quickly, but she captured his hand and stood.

Grasping his face, she tugged him down to her and pressed her lips to his, the kiss tender and light as the summer breeze blowing around them. "Please don't walk away from me," she whispered. "No matter your past, I won't judge you."

His body went rigid. He wanted to believe her, but it seemed unfathomable. He held her unblinking gaze. "You won't say that when you know all the details."

"I vow I will, Colin. Trust me."

He took a deep breath. "I was fourteen when the woman who wanted revenge against my mother first offered herself to me."

Amelia gripped her throat in horror. "Fourteen? But you were so young."

He smiled a merciless smile. "I was a lad, much enthralled by the idea of bedding an older woman. I thought myself special."

"But she used you," Amelia whispered.

"Yes, but at the time I thought she loved me. I eventually understood she didn't."

"Oh, Colin," Amelia started and reached for him, but he stepped back and shook his head.

"No. That's not it. I slept with her, and then there were others that following year, all while I was still bedding her." He glanced up at the bright-blue sky, thinking it should have been dark and cloudy to fit his mood. "There were four women when I was fifteen. Each of them used me. I got quite good in bed. Developed somewhat of a reputation. Around my seventeenth birthday, I realized the reputation could turn the talk in the *ton* away from how my mother was cuckolding my father with every man she could get her hands on. So I threw myself into cultivating my reputation. It wasn't hard. There were plenty of women, married and widowed, lined up to sleep with me and use me for various reasons."

She gasped, but he kept his gaze on the sky. "I told myself it was all for my father, but in the dark of night, I know I enjoyed feeling as if I were getting revenge on all the women who wanted to use me but not love me."

He forced himself to glance over at her. Tears streamed down her face. He did not attempt to wipe the tears away. She would likely jerk out of his reach, if he tried. "This is the man I was. No matter what I do in the future, the stains of my past cover me. We both know you deserve and want better."

"Lady Amelia!" Amelia's maid Lucy stumbled into the clearing and gaped at them. After a moment, she spoke. "I've been looking all over for you. Lady Langley says to come back to the house immediately. Lord Edington is here, and she's quite sure it's to ask for your hand."

Amelia scowled and glanced between Colin and her lady's maid before focusing on Colin. "Please don't leave. I—"Amelia shot an annoyed look at her maid and then faced Colin once more. "You simply cannot go. Those are no last words to leave by."

"No, they are not," Colin agreed, his chest feeling as if it had just cracked under the pressure of his love for her. She would likely tell him she could never love him, knowing his past, but fool that he was, he had to stay. After everything, the hope that she would love him in spite of himself was there.

He nodded. "I'll wait for you."

Chapter Nineteen

Amelia hurried through the terrace door toward the foyer, determined to dispatch Lord Edington kindly but quickly and return to Colin. By the look on the daft man's face when she had left him, he did not yet understand that she loved him with all her heart. As she rounded the corner into the foyer, she stopped in her tracks with a gasp. Great hairy willow herb filled the room so completely it was as if the flower had become part of the wallpaper and the fragrant scent one with the air. Rushing to the foyer table where she saw a card, she plucked it up and opened it.

I hope to always give you your favorite things.

Colin

Her heart nearly wrenched out of her chest at the sweet gesture.

She found Lord Edington in the parlor, and after listening to his proposal with as much patience as she could muster, she very gently told him she did not think they would suit. Once she saw him out, she rushed back toward the terrace and down the steps to go finish what she and Colin had started. As her shoe touched the grass, a voice called out behind her, "Lady Amelia!"

Botheration! Amelia paused in her rushed flight while gritting her teeth. She had hoped to slip away without her lady's maid accompanying her, but either Lucy had taken it into her own head to do so, or the maid had told Lady Langley that Colin was here and his aunt had insisted Lucy accompanied Amelia out to the maze. She did not care one bit for propriety or her reputation at this moment, all she cared about was returning to Colin. *Alone.*

Amelia planted her hands on her hips. "Did Lady Langley send you to me?"

"Yes, my lady. She—"

A burst of annoyance lit through Amelia like a spark taking to flame. "I am perfectly safe speaking with the duke in the maze without your chaperoning me."

Lucy gave Amelia the oddest look and lifted her hand to point behind her toward the house. "But the duke is in the parlor, my lady. I only came to tell you so."

Now Amelia was confused. She studied the maze in the distance. Colin must have gone inside as she was speaking to Lord Edington. "Oh, I see. I'll just go in to speak with him, then."

"You've no need to come to me," a male voice cut through her whirling thoughts. "I've come to you."

Twisting back around, she frowned at the sight of the Duke of Scarsdale. This was untimely indeed. He was early. "Your Grace, the Duke of Aversley is here."

He quirked his eyebrows. "Is the plan working?"

She could not help but laugh nervously when she recalled the stormy kiss of moments before, but then the memory of Colin's anguished confession made her frown. "I think so," she said, darting a glance at Lucy. Unwilling to have this conversation with her maid, so obviously interested in every word they said, Amelia pointed to a bench far enough away that Lucy could observe them but not hear. "Please do wait over there, Lucy."

The maid bobbed a quick curtsy and scrambled off to settle herself. As Amelia faced the Duke of Scarsdale he said, "So is my work here done?"

"About the work," she murmured. "I have a feeling it would behoove me to know as much as I can about Colin's past, and my brother was not willing to tell me what caused your and Colin's, er, disagreement."

"You mean the cessation of our friendship," the duke said blandly.

"Yes." If he didn't care to mince words then neither would she. Directness would get her back to Colin sooner.

"I bedded his mother, and he found out."

Amelia tried not to flinch, but really, it was impossible. For one thing, that was utterly disgusting, more so of Colin's mother than anything, especially since the duke had to have been close to the same age as Colin, since they were school mates together. Amelia swallowed hard.

"How old were you?"

"Sixteen and damn well old enough to know better. I don't offer you excuses because I don't deserve to, but I was lonely. So very lonely."

The way his voice cracked made Amelia's heart squeeze.

"My parents had died the year before, and I hated everything about life. Frankly, I did not want to live, and you are going to find this impossible to believe, I'm sure, but neither did Aversley's mother. I was visiting for his birthday, and one night when I could not sleep, I stumbled upon her in the gardens. She was weeping, and I knew that gut-wrenching sound came from deep loss."

The duke didn't say how he knew, but Amelia was sure it had to do with his parents' deaths.

"We talked all night and the night after, and on the third night, she drank entirely too much at the big celebration. I knew she had, and when she stumbled up to bed, I went to check on her. That's when she invited me in. She was swaying and kept calling me Alexander, her husband's name, and then she undressed me, and I let her."

As he made a sound of disgust in his throat, Amelia tried to picture such a young man in so much pain, and Colin's mother, obviously wracked by her own demons.

His Grace caught her gaze. "I'm sure you can deduce what happened next. That's all the sordid details. I'm disgusting, and I lost my best friend for what I did, and I also lost the friendship of your brother. Rightly so. Your brother has forgiven me, thankfully. I don't expect Aversley to do so, but I wanted to help him find some happiness since I know I had a hand in helping to cause him years of pain."

Amelia did not even realize she was crying until warm tears trickled down her cheeks.

"What's this?" the duke said, surprise evident in his tone.

Amelia sniffed. "There is so much pain, and it's so tragic what's happened to you, Colin, his mother and his father."

His Grace wiped her tears with his hand, which lingered on her cheek. "If I were a free man, and you had so obviously not already given your heart to Aversley, I'd be very crushed when you walked away from me in a moment."

Seemingly from out of nowhere, Colin loomed behind the Duke of Scarsdale. Before Amelia could make a peep, the duke was jerked around and all Amelia saw was Colin's fist connecting with Scarsdale's nose. Blood instantly appeared, but he did not raise his fists to retaliate, much to Amelia's relief. Her heart thundered as she stood there.

Colin's burning gaze cut from her to Scarsdale.

"Don't you ever touch her again," Colin snarled.

"Why?" the Duke of Scarsdale growled back. "Because you love her and want to marry her or because you *have to* marry and figure she'll do just as nicely as any other debutante?"

Amelia's split second of worry for the Duke of Scarsdale's safety at pushing Colin too far was swiftly replaced by confusion. What exactly did he mean by *have to*? Was he referring to Colin needing an heir? Before she could utter a question, Colin's fist flew through the air again, and in the next instant, the men tumbled to the ground, arms flying and legs tangled. Their bodies rolled left and then right as, punches and grunts punctuated the oppressive silence.

She moved forward to try to stop them before they killed each other, but a hand clamped on her arm. Swinging around, she stared up into her brother's grim face.

"Let me."

He let out an ear splitting whistle that caused both men to pause momentarily in their attack and when they did, Philip swooped in and tore them apart. "Gentlemen," he said, in a stern tone one would use with a child, "there are better ways to solve your differences."

As the men struggled to their feet, disheveled, bloody, and panting, Amelia stepped toward Colin. She resisted the urge to wipe away the blood trickling from his nose. First things first. "What exactly did the Duke of Scarsdale mean about you having to marry? He is referring to the fact that you need a wife to beget an heir, correct?"

Colin said nothing immediately and his narrowed gaze shifted from her to her brother to Scarsdale. Why wasn't he simply confirming what she had asked? Suddenly, her knees trembled, feeling quite rubbery, but she locked them in place and stood while her heart took to roaring in her ears.

"I don't know exactly what Scarsdale was referring to," Colin said quietly, "but I have to marry and not just to beget an heir."

Her throat was terribly dry, but she forced a swallow.

"What do you mean? Please tell me you did not lie to me, even after I specifically asked you if there was anything else you should reveal to me."

She winced at the pleading note in her voice.

When Colin stepped toward her, she stumbled backward out of his grasp. "Don't touch me," she whispered in a choked voice. "Tell me the truth if you even comprehend it."

"My father's will stipulates that if I don't marry by my twenty-sixth birthday I will lose almost all of my money."

The ground she stood on seemed to tilt, but yet she stayed upright. Somehow. Someway.

"You…you…you lied to me. I'm so stupid." She blinked because it seemed the world around her was closing in and shrinking. "I thought you might be falling in love with me."

"Amelia, I am," he started, "I did! I do love you! I want to marry you, and it doesn't have a thing to do with the will."

Colin grabbed her arm, but she wrenched it away. Her stomach clenched. How she had longed to hear him say those things, and now she could not be certain if he did truly love her or if marrying was just so he could keep his money.

"Don't you touch me. Don't you dare." She took a deep breath and struggled to gain control. "How am I supposed to believe you when you've lied to me from the very first?"

"He's telling you the truth, Amelia," Philip said.

She swung her gaze to her brother. "And I am to believe you? *You*, my own brother, who apparently knew this secret all along but helped him keep it a secret."

"Don't be mad at your brother. I'm sure he thought I told you," Colin said.

"Actually, I suspected you hadn't," Philip mumbled. "But it seemed harmless enough to me that you didn't know, Amelia."

"Harmless?" she huffed. "You thought it harmless to not know that I was no more than a pawn for the duke to not lose his fortune?"

She balled her hands into fists, wanting so badly to box Philip and Colin's noses, but she was sensible. Or at least she used to be. Her chest tightened unbearably as she focused on Colin. She stepped toward him, wanting him to hear clearly hear every word.

"Well, Your Grace, you will be pleased with yourself to know I have changed as you predicted just not *the way* you predicted. I will *never* marry a man with a title. You are a twisted, dishonest group who wouldn't know true love if...if...if it slapped you in the face!"

And with that, her sensible side fled, and she smacked Colin as hard as she could before abruptly turning on her heel and marching toward the house.

Behind her, footsteps pounded, so she swung around to be met with the sight of Colin racing toward her. She held up her hand to stay him in his progress. Thank goodness he listened for once and stopped. "Do not come near me," she said, her voice quivering. "There is not a word you can utter I will believe. I am going home, and I don't want to ever see you again."

Philip started to move, but she shook her head. She was so angry with her brother that she didn't want him around, either. "Please stay here, Philip. I know I cannot order you to, but I am so angry with you that I simply wish to be alone for a bit."

Philip nodded.

With her heart wrenching in her chest and tears blurring her vision, she hurried up the stairs to find Lady Langley and request Colin's aunt lend her coachman and carriage to take Amelia home. Now. This instant. She had to get away. She didn't care about leaving with any of her things. Philip could bring them back eventually. All she cared about was putting distance between herself and Colin immediately.

~

Colin started after Amelia once again, but someone grabbed him from behind. He swung around and glared at Harthorne while ignoring Scarsdale, who was standing there, as well. "Let go, damn it."

"I wish I could, but you have to adhere to her wishes. Just as I do. Besides, there is nothing you could say at this moment that she is going to believe."

"I have to try. I love her. I swear I do." Colin jerked his arm away, but as he turned back toward the house, someone tackled him from behind and crushed him to the ground. With a roar, he tried to flip over, but a knee dug into his spine.

"Give her time, Aversley," Scarsdale said from on top of Colin.

Colin yanked his head out of the grass, and as he did, he caught sight of his aunt's carriage pulling away down the side drive. His pulse exploded with the surety that Amelia was fleeing from him at this very moment. He bucked up and threw Scarsdale off him. Colin sprinted toward the house and didn't stop. He threw open the door from the garden and raced down the hall toward the front door, almost colliding with a servant as he ran. Behind him, footsteps pounded. He'd bloody kill Scarsdale if the man so much as breathed on him again.

Colin rounded the corner into the foyer and went sliding on the slick floor, almost crashing into the door, and unfortunately, colliding with the footman. By the time Colin was up again and out the front door there was nothing to see in the driveway except the dust from the carriage wheels and his aunt, who, turning to look at him, simply shook her head and brushed past. "Give her some time, Aversley," she murmured. "Give her time. But truly, when you do go to her, please do try complete and utter honesty."

Colin was left standing in the driveway alone. For a moment, he couldn't seem to move. Hopelessness rooted him to the spot. Even if he went after her she wouldn't believe him. He should have told her of the will from the very start. He knew that, but knowing it now didn't do him any good.

A question burned his mind as he stood there. Had Scarsdale been referring to the will? He hadn't seemed surprised when Colin told Amelia of it. If Scarsdale had known about the will,

Harthorne had to have told him. But why would Harthorne do such a thing?

Behind him, footsteps thudded down the stairs and then clopped against the pea-gravel drive. Colin tensed his fists by his sides, his body screaming. He knew it had to be Harthorne or Scarsdale or both behind him.

Turning slowly, he concentrated on Harthorne. "Did you tell Scarsdale my private affairs?"

Harthorne nodded. "I'm sorry, Aversley. I was only trying to help, but I've mucked everything up. I ran into Scarsdale at White's, and it was clear to me that the man truly wanted to make amends with you, and I thought perhaps he was just the man to make you realize you didn't want to lose Amelia or marry her, as it seemed you had convinced yourself from the beginning, simply not to lose your fortune. So I told him of the wager and of your father's will. It never occurred to me that you hadn't told her. I, well, hell..." Harthorne shook his head. "I should have kept my mouth shut. I should have never thought to manipulate you and my sister to bring you together."

Colin couldn't make himself stay angry at Harthorne. Everything the man had done had been in an effort to help his sister and Colin. But Scarsdale...

Colin narrowed his eyes on the man who had bedded his mother, and a welcome fire spread through his body. "You." He spat the word. "It's high time you got the beating you so richly deserve for sleeping with my mother and now for destroying any chance I had with Amelia."

Scarsdale's nostrils flared. "I never meant to—"

"Shut up," Colin barked, stripping off his coat.

"Aversley, you can't mean to fight Scarsdale."

Colin yanked off his cravat, the material burning his skin with the vicious jerk. "I mean to beat him to a bloody pulp," he said, never taking his eyes off Scarsdale. "Unless you're scared?"

Scarsdale answered by pulling off his coat and cravat, as well.

Within moments, both men stood shirtless with their fists up. "Harthorne, go inside and make sure my aunt is occupied, if you please. This is between me and Scarsdale."

"Aversley, you cannot be serious."

Colin's heart hammered, the beat drumming in his ears. "Deadly."

"Scarsdale, surely you have more sense than this?" Harthorne demanded.

"Not a bit. If he wants a fight, I'm more than willing to give him one."

Colin curled his lips back at the duke. "You always were so willing to give."

"At least go to Gentleman Jackson's and box each other with gloves," Harthorne begged.

"No," both men replied at once.

Harthorne threw up his hands. "All right, you imbeciles. I sincerely hope one of you doesn't kill the other. I'll be inside having a glass of whiskey while the two of you are out here pounding each other in the face. I always knew I was the smartest of the three of us."

As Harthorne stomped off, Colin faced Scarsdale. "Ready?"

"For years now," Scarsdale replied.

Colin threw a punch, straight, fast, and bone crushing, and Scarsdale's nose immediately spurted blood. "That was for sleeping with my mother."

Scarsdale wiped a hand across his face, leaving a smear of blood. He spit and then smiled gruesomely at Colin. "I deserve that. And much more."

"Shut up and fight me. If you're going to stand here talking I'll simply start punching you."

Scarsdale swung out and connected with Colin's lip. Blood filled Colin's mouth, and numbing pain danced across his tingling lips and his jaw. The expected throbbing immediately set in.

As Colin spit out a mouthful of blood, Scarsdale said, "I vow never to try to talk to you again if you can best me right here and now. But if I win, you must listen to me for no more than five minutes. Give me the chance to apologize and explain some things."

"What the devil needs explaining?" Colin growled, dancing left and right before sending his fist into Scarsdale's gut.

The duke doubled over, wheezing. After a second, he came up grim faced. He took a short, ragged breath, and said, "You'll never know if you don't agree to my terms."

"Since there is no chance in hell you could best me ever, you have yourself a d—"

Scarsdale's fist crashed into Colin's right eye before he could complete the sentence. Bright stars appeared in his eyes for a second before his vision turned blurry then black. The dizzying pain consuming the entire right side of Colin's head made him sway. He gripped his head for a moment, sure the bloody thing was about to come unhinged from his body. Once he felt certain he wasn't going to fall over, he tried to open his eye to no avail. "You jackanapes. I should have known you'd use tricks."

"You should have," Scarsdale agreed. "But you always were the more honorable of the two of us. Do you want to keep going or call me the winner?"

"What do you think?"

Scarsdale pressed his lips together. "You cannot see out of one eye. I'll kill you."

"That might be a good thing, since you've driven away the only woman I have ever and will ever love." Taking a ploy from Scarsdale's fighting book,

Colin delivered a hard strike to the man's jaw. The duke teetered, looked about to fall over, but somehow came up fast and swung out, connecting with the right side of Colin's head again.

The blow knocked Colin to the ground. A high-pitched noise commenced in his right ear as he struggled to sit up. Suddenly, Scarsdale thrust his hand at him.

"Your aunt is running this way. I do believe our match is up."

Colin nodded. His aunt would bodily fling herself between them if she had to in order to stop the fight. "Draw?"

"Only if I can have my five minutes."

"It will be the only five minutes you ever get, but since it's a draw, it is only fair." Colin waved to his aunt, who was still some distance away, to a stop. "We've quit, Aunt Jane." He swayed as he spoke. That last blow had done something odd to him. He felt as if his mind was slowing down.

"Say what you will quickly," he said, trying to focus on Scarsdale.

"I'm not offering excuses for what I did. It eats at me every day. But I want you to know that your mother...Well, I don't think she was in her right mind that night. I've thought about it over the years, and she'd had a great amount to drink, and she kept calling me by your father's name and talking to me as if I were him. I, well, hell..."

He squeezed his eyes shut for a moment, or at least Colin thought he did. Colin's vision was tunneling in the one good eye.

"I was lonely. So was she. It just happened, but it never should have and I have regretted it every damn moment since. I'm sorry."

Colin nodded, and when he did pain shot out from the base of his skull to the entire right side of his face, down the slope of his neck and then burrowed into the muscles of his shoulders. A sudden wave of nausea rolled through him. He couldn't see Scarsdale very well, but the anguish in his voice was clear, and it was the man's agony that pierced through Colin's hatred. It was time to let it go.

"I forgive you," he said right before his vision went completely black, and the outside world seemed to disappear.

Chapter Twenty

Colin heard voices as the blackness receded. He opened the one eye he could and— What the devil? He stared at his mother standing above him and shut his eye again. He had to be hallucinating. He slowly opened his left eye, but his stomach seized on itself. Saliva filled his mouth along with the bitter taste of sickness. When the feeling settled, Colin attempted to push himself to a sitting position, but his arms refused to cooperate, and dizziness overcame him from the attempt. He collapsed face-first into the pea gravel and, grunting, rolled himself onto his back. His head pounded so fiercely his teeth ached.

He pinched the bridge of his nose as he struggled to breathe. Suddenly, a soft hand touched his cheek. "Darling, what have you done?"

Darling? His left eye flew open, causing intense pain to seize his head once again, but he forced himself to try to focus on his mother. *Mother?* Had she just called him darling? She had to have been at the bottle.

"What are you doing here?" he managed to ask, though his throat felt as if someone had rubbed sand in it.

"I was looking for you. My butler told me you had stopped by. Why are you doing this now, after all these years?"

"Needed to be done," he forced through gritted teeth. Ringing had commenced in his ears, making it hard to think.

"Oh, Colin, my sweet boy. How I failed you."

Colin squinted up at his mother. All three of her. "Colin? Sweet boy?"

She flushed but nodded. "Why didn't you quit after—" She pointed to his eye.

He blinked, trying to push back the black spots appearing in his vision again. "Wanted the pain."

"But your face, darling." She touched his eye, and he jerked away. "You'll have a scar."

"Good," he muttered, his vision almost totally black now. Jesus, he hoped he wasn't going blind. The ground seemed to be swaying under him, but at least this time he was already on his back. He pressed his hands into the gravel, letting the coolness seep into his palms as he struggled to push back the consuming darkness. "Maybe they won't want me anymore."

"Who, darling? Who won't want you?"

Who indeed. He didn't know. His thoughts were too cloudy. Pictures floated in his mind one by one. Women. Countless women he had slept with. The noise in his ears roared, and his vision was black as pitch now. He gave up the fight and shut his eye. Amelia's face floated before him—sweet, smiling, lost to him forever. Her face faded, and when it was gone, he let his body relax.

~

Amelia plodded up the steps to her home bone weary and with a heart that felt significantly heavier and smaller than the day she had left for London. Colin had lied to her, and she had left him. And he had said he loved her. Her throat tightened, but she pushed back the tears that had plagued her for the past two days of travel. Surely, he had just been saying that out of fear that she was going to flee. Surely, he had not really meant it.

Thank goodness, she was home. Hopefully, her mother would be feeling immensely better and be her old chattering self.

Amelia sighed. Being alone had left her with entirely too much time to analyze everything when her goal had been to forget. Yet, try as she might to fight it, the doubt that had gnawed at her every moment since she had hastily jumped in Lady Langley's carriage seized her again. *What if Colin is telling the truth?* She tried to silence the inner voice, but it was having none of that. *Would you have told yourself the truth if you were in Colin's shoes?*

She shivered as she opened the front door, though the house was rather warm. Ever since she had fled, she had not been able to get warm. Her teeth chattered in response to her thoughts. *Would I have told me the truth were I him?* Blast that voice.

"Mother," she called, but only silence greeted her. Amelia plodded up the stairs but paused midflight. *You pride yourself in being so sensible*, that voice sneered.

"All right," she muttered, as she continued up the stairs. "I will think sensibly." If Colin loved her why had he not followed her? *You told him not to,* the voice reminded her. Yes, but if he really loved her, he would have followed anyway. He would have done everything in his power to explain. That's what she would have done if she were him and she had hidden such a thing.

If she were being logical and not thinking purely with her emotions, she could possibly understand why he might have been wary to tell her about his father's will when he had told her of the wager. A pang of regret filled her.

She paused at her mother's bedroom door. Inside, she could hear the sound of someone scurrying back and forth. Pushing open the door, she frowned at her mother, who was standing over her bed, gazing down at a pile of dresses. "Whatever are you doing?"

Her mother whirled toward her, her eyes glassy. Deep creases appeared in her brow. "What are you doing here?"

"It's a long, sad tale and one I would rather not go into right now," she said, plopping on her mother's bed.

"Has Philip won the wager?"

Amelia shook her head. "The wager has been called off, Mother."

All the color fled from her mother's face. "You have to leave at once!" her mother said, reaching out and tugging at Amelia.

"Have you been in the laudanum?" Amelia demanded, shocked that her mother was trying to get her to leave and didn't even have any questions for her.

Mother shook her head, tears pooling in her eyes.

Amelia allowed her gaze to drift around the room. The chamber was in a shambles. Rumpled bedcovers. Dead flowers in the vase. Stale water, by the smell in the air. And on the stand beside the bed several bottles littered the dark wood. The clear bottle with the red laudanum label made Amelia's stomach clench, as much because it was empty as the fact that there were two more beside it. "Mother, how much laudanum have you been taking?"

Her mother's mouth opened and closed as if she did not know what to say, and the tears in her eyes started to trickle down her cheeks. "I don't know."

"Oh, Mother!" Amelia cried, embracing her.

But her mother squirmed out of her hold. "Amelia, you have to leave."

"No," Amelia said. "I just got home, and I am very tired. And by the looks of it"—she glanced around the filthy room with a shudder—"I'm here none too soon. I will not move even an inch until you tell me what is going on."

Her mother's gaze grew wide and wild. "You must leave. You must!" Her voice had risen to a hysterical level.

Fear blossomed in Amelia's belly. Something was terribly, horribly wrong, and she did not think it was merely the laudanum. "I'm sorry, Mother. I don't wish to defy you, but I feel I must."

Her mother pulled and tugged at her hair, an expression of twisted agitation crossing her face. "But if you don't go now, he may see you."

"He who? There is absolutely no hope of you getting me to leave if you are not honest with me." Though there was no hope she was leaving anyway, she didn't think trickery in this instance would harm her mother.

Oh dear heaven! Had that been the logic Colin had used when he decided not to tell her of the will? Her breath caught. Had she allowed her anger to cloud her good sense and make her abandon a man who loved her? Or would that be *had* loved her? After all, why would he love a woman who refused to believe him and called him twisted and—

"Amelia!" her mother screeched. "This is no time for your daydreaming."

"I'm sorry," she said, mortified to have drifted when her mother so obviously needed her. Amelia shoved all thoughts of her problems with Colin away. She had to concentrate on her mother. "What were you saying?"

"If I tell you, you must promise to go!"

Normally, Amelia would never give a promise then break it, but these were not normal circumstances. Perhaps Colin had similar thoughts? She squeezed the bridge of her nose. Later. He would have to wait for later

"All right. I promise to go." *Eventually.* She sucked in her lip with guilt.

"Lord Huntington will be arriving soon, and I am trying to decide which dress to wear. Now, please..." Mother pulled her by the arm. "Go!"

Amelia gripped her mother's hand. "Why is he coming here? And don't tell me you care for him. You look scared, not in love."

Her mother's face turned a deep shade of red, and her hands twisted together. "I need to sit."

Amelia swept the gowns aside and waved her mother to the bed. "Why is he coming here?"

"I hope to convince him to bed me," Mother replied, glancing down.

"Excuse me?" Amelia heard herself gasp.

"You heard me, Amelia." Mother's voice was sharp. "I intend to seduce the man. I know you understand what that means."

Heat flooded Amelia's face as anger poured through her. "I understand," she said quietly, staring at the cascade of graying hair that covered her mother's face. "But why? Why would you do such a thing?"

"I don't want to bed the wretched man—I have to. Especially now that the wager can no longer save us. I have to make him want me still."

"Still?" Amelia felt as if the world was tilting.

"Yes. Still. We've— Well, you know what I am trying to say."

Amelia forced herself to nod. She was going to be ill. Her mother had slept with Lord Huntington.

"It was the only way he would agree not to call in the notes the bank holds over the property and all the loans your father and Philip took out. If the bank demands full payment, Philip would be ruined. *We* would be ruined. I could not let that happen to Philip. He's tried so hard to set things to right."

Amelia's heart thudded at the astonishing news. She took her mother's hand and squeezed. "Go on, please."

"I, well, I did not offer myself to him. He suggested the bank might forget the debt for a while if I, well...You understand?"

Amelia nodded once more, a bitter taste filling her mouth.

"It's been going on since almost right after your father died. I thought I would go mad with how disgusted I felt with myself, so I started taking laudanum. It dulled my thoughts and made me numb. But when the Duke of Aversley came and offered that wager, I knew if I could get you away from here, you would win the wager and we would be saved. There's no time now, but later you must tell me what happened. Perhaps we can fix it?"

"I don't think so," Amelia said, barely containing a strangled sob. Maybe, if she went back to see Colin and told him she had thought about everything clearly and how sorry she was. She trembled with fear that he would refuse to even see her. Gulping, she said, "His Grace and I did not leave things well. I cannot give you hope of an alliance." She glanced down at her hands. "I'm a fool."

A finger came under Amelia's chin and raised it until she was looking into her mother's eyes. "You are not a fool. You are in love. I hear it in your voice and see it in your eyes." With those words, heavily laden with tension, her mother stood and glanced down at Amelia. "Now you must leave! He will be here soon."

Amelia jumped to her feet, her heart leaping into her throat. "You cannot allow that man to touch you again. I won't let you."

"It makes my skin crawl to think of his hands on me again, Amelia, but what else can I do?"

Amelia suddenly remembered seeing Lord Huntington in Hyde Park and later at the ball. "Mother, I saw him in London. Whatever was he doing there?"

"I suspect he went to spy on you. He was furious when he found out you were on the marriage mart. Amelia, I am trying to seduce him into wanting me again because he decided some time back that he now wants you. I will not allow that man to touch you, but he has vowed to have the bank call in all of Philip's notes if you do not acquiesce."

Amelia's stomach roiled with nausea, but she gasped. "The Duke of Aversley will pay Philip's debts," Amelia cried out, relief flooding her. Even if he now detested her, he had set out to do all of this for Philip, after all. "His Grace would never allow Lord Huntington to ruin Philip."

"It's not only Philip's debt he is threatening us with. He has threatened to tell everyone of my bedding him."

Amelia gaped at her mother, who had buried her face in her hands. "I could live with my name and reputation being ruined, but you know as well as I do that if I am ruined you are as good as ruined, as well. For that, I fear Philip would kill the man and end up being executed himself. I cannot allow any of that to happen."

"Do you understand now? You must go!" She began to pull on Amelia to try to get her to stand up.

Silently, Amelia stayed her mother's trembling hands while trying to force down the rage rising inside of her. Anger would not help them now. Dear God. She pressed her hand to her throat as a knock resounded on the door below.

"He's here," her mother said in a horrified whisper as she yanked on a violet dress and commanded Amelia to hook it. Amelia raised her shaking hands to the fastenings, but could not get her fingers to work. She knew why. Her heart seemed to cease beating, as the terrible truth sunk in. She could not allow her mother to sacrifice herself to that man again. Amelia swallowed the bitterness in her mouth. She had no idea what she was going to do, but she would do what she must to protect her mother and keep that man's hands off them both.

"Go hide in your room," her mother hissed.

Amelia nodded, but she had no intention of doing anything of the sort. The moment her mother left the room, Amelia jumped up and tiptoed out the door. In the hallway, she grabbed their large candelabra. She would clobber the man with it before he would lay one finger on her or her mother. As she started down the stairs, the murmur of voices drifted up to her.

"My lady, Lord Huntington bade me to tell you he cannot come today or likely for a week. He took a fall from his horse and hurt his back."

Shaking, Amelia sank onto the step and pressed her free hand over her mouth to muffle her cry. One week. She had one week to come up with a plan to save them.

Chapter Twenty-One

Colin woke, stiff, drenched in sweat and unsure if it was day or night. One thing he did know for certain was he was in his bed. The smells of leather and wood in the room were familiar and the feel of the bed was unmistakably his. He blinked several times, realizing his eye only throbbed a bit. After a moment, his eyes adjusted to the darkness and his vision cleared enough that he could make out his room. The curtains had been drawn tight, but sunlight peeked through the bottom edge where the heavy drapes met the hardwood floor. So daytime it was.

He sat up, clenching his teeth and preparing for another bout of dizziness, but surprisingly he felt steady.

"Feeling better?" a feminine voice murmured from the dark corner near the window.

Colin's first thought was of Amelia, but when he looked, he saw his mother. His momentary happiness was replaced with shock, along with a vague memory of passing out in the driveway.

"How did I get here?" he asked, swinging his legs over his bed but not standing.

His mother rose and walked toward him. "Lord Harthorne helped my coachman load you into the carriage and then carry you upstairs."

"Your past lover didn't offer to help?"

She flinched but said, "He offered to help, but I declined."

Damn, he felt like the biggest arse. "I'm sorry. I should not have said that."

"No, it's all right. We have a lot to discuss, but you have every right to still be angry. I'm still angry with myself. I think I always will be."

Colin wasn't sure what to say to this woman before him. She was his mother, yet she was acting nothing like the mother he had known all his life. By God, she really did seem as if she was changing. Softening. He glanced down at his bedclothes. "Who dressed me and cleaned me up?"

She shrugged indifferently, though now that she was close, the lines of worry and the dark circles under her eyes were obvious. She cleared her throat. "I changed you and washed the blood off."

"You cared for me?" Surprise spiraled through him. "That's a first, though much appreciated. I don't mean to sound ungrateful, but why did you care for me? Do you want something?"

"I want to make amends, Colin. Nothing more."

"There is no need," he said, feeling suddenly vulnerable with how his chest suddenly ached with a few hopeful words from her. "I've turned out perfectly all right without anything from you."

She narrowed her eyes. "Yes, I can see that. You got yourself a split lip, eye, and according to Dr. Parks—"

"Dr. Parks was here?" Colin asked with a frown.

"Yes. Two days ago when you passed out, and yesterday to see how you were doing. He says your eye will heal perfectly, except for perhaps a small scar, and the concussion…well, he said we would only know if that had lasting effects once you woke and we could gauge your memory. What do you remember?" She leaned in and peered at him, the most foreign look of motherly concern on her face.

"Unfortunately, everything," he replied dryly. His gut turning with thoughts of Amelia.

His mother smiled gently. "Your aunt told me about the girl and what has happened."

The ache of moments ago was nothing compared to the twisting pain that gripped his tattered heart now. He hoped to God Amelia could somehow forgive him and find it in her heart to love him. In fact, he couldn't believe he had wasted two days unconscious. He had to go see her immediately and try somehow to convince her that he loved her and wanted to marry her only *for her* and not because of the will.

He stood up and gazed at his mother. "Why did you stay here with me for two nights?"

She came to him. "I told you. I want to make amends and you were hurt."

"No." He shook his head. He needed more than that. "Why did you stay? You did not have to. In all the years of my childhood you never raised a hand to tend to me. Why now?"

She sniffed and tears glistened in her eyes. "Because I love you."

The words were like a balm to his ears.

"You are my son. And I want to try to make up, in some small way, for what I have done to you and what I have caused you to do to yourself." She grabbed his arm, her thin fingers curling around his skin. "You won't allow yourself to love and be loved, and it is all my fault. It's because of me that you cannot trust women. When your father died, he not only left you a letter, but he left me one, as well." She glanced at the settee in the corner. "Can we please sit for a minute?"

"All right." He took her elbow, and she led him to the dark green cushions.

She took a deep breath as she sat beside him and grasped his hand. He stared at their intertwined hands, his large and hers small, and he remembered how, as a child, he had longed for her to grasp his small hand in hers. His throat ached with the old yearning.

"Tell me what happened between you and Father," he said simply, wanting to heal the pain and hoping she could shed some light that would help him to do so.

"The day I went into labor with you, we almost died. The doctor demanded that your father chose who to save—you or me. Of course, your father could not make such a choice and he told the doctor to save both of us."

Colin nodded, his chest squeezing painfully. "Go on."

His mother sniffed and wiped away a tear. "W—when it seemed we would both die, it seems your father made a v—vow to God." She took a ragged breath. "He said that if he would save us both, he would never touch me in lust again." She paused again, and wrapped her arms around her waist, deep sadness filling her eyes. "He thought he owed this to God as penance for having believed, as his father and grandfather did, that the dukes of Aversley were above the need for God's grace." She stopped again, this time looking straight into Colin's eyes. "So, he made the vow for his sin, but he believed if he ever told anyone of his sacrifice his vow would be worthless, and you and I, possibly both of us, would be taken from him." Her voice cracked on the last sentence.

"My God," Colin whispered, his throat almost too tight to talk. "He never touched you again after my birth?"

"Never." The tears streamed down his mother's face now, and it made the ache in Colin's throat intensify. She swiped at the tears. "He never came to my bed again. Yet, w—worse than that, all the intimacy that had been between us was gone." She shuddered. "Never a kiss. Never a brush of his hand against mine. And all without explanation." Colin had to strain to hear the words, now barely above a whisper.

"When I begged him to explain, he simply said he couldn't. I was sure he had found another, so I set out to hurt him or make him jealous and want me again. Anything. Anything to make him see me, because I felt invisible."

She raked a hand through her hair. "I took lovers. Countless lovers. But he never weakened. Never explained. And when I came to believe he did not have lovers, it was worse because then it was all about me. Only me. Do you see?"

Her voice beseeched him to understand. He nodded.

"*I* was the problem. He did not want me. No longer loved me. But I truly thought he stayed with me and endured me because of his love for you. I was hurt, devastated, and so very angry. I hated him and you. He held your hand, touched your cheek, and kissed your forehead. I set out to destroy him, you, me. All of us," she cried out.

She pulled her hand away from Colin and wept into her palms. "I'm sorry," she said, her voice muffled. "So very sorry. If I had only known of the vow. I could have endured it, though it would have still been awful. If I had only known..."

He slid his hand around her shaking shoulder and pressed her head down before gently running his hand through her hair and giving her, he hoped, the comfort he had always longed for from her. How wrong they had all been about one another.

"Shh," he whispered soothingly.

After a while, his mother's cries subsided, and she raised her head. "I would have told you sooner, but I knew you would not believe me. I was hoping you would see how I had changed. I stopped taking lovers and drinking. I tried to take an interest in helping you find a bride."

"Lady Sara," he said with a chuckle.

"Yes." She nodded. "It seems you were already in love with another."

"Yes, I was, and I am, but I've likely destroyed any chance with her."

"My dear," his mother said, running a gentle hand through his hair as he had dreamed of so many nights as a youth. "The only way you will know for certain is by going to her and pouring out your heart to her. As a woman I can tell you that when we are deeply in love we will forgive anything if only we can understand or feel forgiveness is wanted. Do you think you can ever forgive me for what I've done to you, your father, myself?" She glanced down at her hands. "Your friendships?"

He pressed a kiss to her cheek, a thing he had never done before. "I forgive you." The words were not uttered to calm her. They were simply true.

"But you must forgive me, too. I never saw your pain, or never bothered to look. None of us made good choices," he said, thinking how colossally stupid it had been to keep the will a secret from Amelia.

"Go to her," his mother said, pressing her hand to his cheek. "Go to her and win her back as I had hoped every day your father would try to do with me. I guarantee you, if she loves you, that is exactly what she is hoping for if she has any sense at all."

Colin grinned. "She is very sensible. Usually."

~

Amelia had never wished for anyone's death, not even Georgiana's after Georgiana had pushed her into the lake, but she was ashamed to admit there was the smallest part of her that wished Lord Huntington had died. When the knock had resounded on the door four days ago after her mother had told her of what that wretched man was threatening and what he had already forced her mother to do, Amelia had thanked God for the news that Lord Huntington had been injured, but she had questioned God's leniency in letting the evil man live, at all.

And now their time was up. Sooner than what she had expected.

Carriage wheels turning in the drive alerted her that he was here. It was entirely too bad that all the man had sustained from his fall was a nasty cut to his head. Apparently, head injuries were not enough to keep the vile beast away for very long. She fingered the note she had intercepted that he had sent to Mother yesterday telling her he would be coming to call on her today. *Call on her!* Amelia snorted. How dare the man pretend, even in a note, that his visit was merely a social one?

Amelia took a deep breath to still herself against the nerves threatening to consume her. The only way she had gotten her mother out of the house and to Constance's mother's home for the afternoon was by lying and faking a note from Lord Huntington saying he was still bedridden and would not come to call for another week. She felt slightly guilty for the lie, but it had been necessary. Just as the one where she had sworn to go back to London tomorrow had been necessary.

Nothing would tear Amelia from her mother's side. But being alone now was good. She needed to be calm when she faced Lord Huntington, and Mother did not have a calming affect. She would be livid if she knew Amelia was facing the man alone, but then again, if Mother were here, she would not present the brave face Amelia was sure they needed to show. Lord Huntington would never believe Amelia was willing to kill him to gain his silence if her mother was standing by her side shaking.

Amelia glanced at the pistol in her trembling right hand. Of course, Amelia would never kill him, but Lord Huntington did not know that, and if she needed to shoot him in the foot to make him believe the next bullet would be in his heart, she would do it.

Mother would die if she had to allow that man to bed her again. She'd not said it, but Amelia could see it in the haunting fear in her eyes. And Amelia knew deep in her heart her mother would have gladly suffered the humiliation of everyone knowing what she had done, if not for her worry that Amelia would suffer, as well. Mother saw no way out, but Amelia did. By taking matters squarely into her own hands, her mother would not be able to blame herself for whatever befell Amelia, and she would not be able to stop what she had no idea was occurring.

Hiding the pistol behind her back, Amelia took her time making her way to the door, as Lord Huntington's knocks grew louder. She paused and stared at the dark wood as a deep longing for Colin gripped her. She shoved the useless wish away. He had not come here, and he may never speak to her again even after she went to him, which she fully intended to do when this mess was sorted out.

A large lump formed in her throat. If her reputation was in tatters when she saw him next, would he believe her when she told him the truth of it? Would it even matter? His entire life had been overshadowed by whispers of his mother. It was entirely possible he would not want Amelia anymore, if he wanted her at all, if there were horrid rumors about her. *If he loves me, it should not matter to him,* she reminded herself. Yet, fear that he may no longer love her after she had fled the way she did pulsed with every beat of her heart.

By the time she turned the handle, she had to grind her teeth together to stop the terrible tic that had started in her jaw. Lifting her chin, she backed up enough to allow Lord Huntington to come in without having to turn her back. He was dressed in an ill-fitting, drab blue coat and his tight pantaloons showed every disgusting bulge. His bare head gleamed, and his dull eyes assessed her with unhidden desire. She swallowed her disgust.

"Lord Huntington, do come in."

As he stepped through the threshold, she moved back several more steps. She did not think the man would try to ravage her now, but she was not taking any chances.

He stopped in the entrance and faced her, his flinty eyes not concealing his lustful observation of her. "Where is your mother?"

"She's not here," Amelia replied, making a decision not to mince words. The sooner she was done with Lord Huntington the better.

"Did she not receive my note that I was coming today?"

"She did not," Amelia replied as nonchalantly as she could. "I intercepted the note and sent her away."

"Really? How very deceptive of you."

He took a step toward her, and Amelia gripped the pistol hidden behind her back. If he made one move to maul her, she wouldn't hesitate to shoot his foot. Maybe both feet.

"I sent my mother away because I wish to talk to you alone, and I did not want to upset her. She's told me what you have been making her do since my father's death, and she also told me how you wish to do the same with me." Amelia moved the pistol from behind her back and pointed it toward him, cursing her shaking hands. "I tell you now, I will never lie with you nor will my mother lie with you ever again." Her heart thumped wildly, but she did not blink.

"You won't shoot me," he said, narrowing his eyes and stepping forward once more so that Amelia was forced to back into the foyer table to get some distance from him. He smiled, showing yellowed teeth. The smell of sweet, disgusting liquor rolled off him in sickening waves. "You will lie with me, sweet Amelia, or I will ruin your mother, you, and your brother. She must have forgotten to tell you that."

Anger so strong it was nearly choking filled her. She rose up to her full height and tried to still her hands. "She told me. Which is why I am prepared to shoot you to gain your silence. And as for my brother, he will pay his debts." She was certain Colin would do this for Philip, and Philip would simply have to swallow his blasted pride.

Lord Huntington moved with a speed that defied logic for a man as old as he was. Her fingers stung as the pistol was ripped from her grip. He leaned closer and leered. "I like your spark, Amelia, but when I'm done with you, you will be begging me for more and not threatening to shoot me."

Amelia felt her mouth slip open, so she snapped her teeth together, but it was a second too late. He smiled, a frightening show of perverse glee. Reaching out, he yanked her to him by the crown of her hair while pointing the pistol at her temple. Though her scalp stung and tears burned her eyes, she bit her lip against crying out as he forced her head back. He licked his fat, cracked lips. "You should have never tried to defy me, Amelia."

His lips came down on hers brutally hard and crushing. Her scream was lost in his mouth. Rage exploded in her breast, and she raked her hand down the meaty flesh of his face. A fierce growl erupted from him seconds before he threw her from him. She gasped for clean air as she stumbled backward and fell to the ground. Within a breath, he loomed above her, blood seeping down the right side of his face where she had ripped his skin away.

"Spread your legs for me, Amelia."

Promptly, she clamped her legs together while placing her palms behind her on the ground to prepare to spring out of his reach, or please God not his shot, but she didn't think she'd be much good to him dead. As he lunged for her, she pushed off the floor and twisted away, but the hot, slick feel of his strong beefy fingers clamping around her ankle made her heart crash to the floor. Fear sprung up in the form of gooseflesh over every inch of her body as he dragged her toward him. She dug her nails into the wood with the strength of desperation, causing small splinters to release from a loose board and lodge under the tender flesh of her nail beds.

"Come, Amelia. It's useless to fight me," he said in a low, mocking voice. With her free leg, she kicked backward blindly and met with the hard metal of the pistol. A second later, she heard the *clank* of the pistol as it hit the ground somewhere behind them. She moved to scramble away, but he caught her leg again, yanked her back, and flipped her onto her back with a *thud* before shoving his hands between her thighs. "Let's not play any more games."

Amelia's heart ceased to beat, but her mind sprinted forward to gruesome pictures of his hands on her. She released a scream so intense her own ears rang with it.

~

Pain outlined every bone in Colin's body from his hell-bent ride from London to Amelia's home over the past two days, but when her scream rent the air, he forgot every throbbing muscle and catapulted off his horse to race up the stairs to her. He barreled through the door, hit something hard on his way with the toe of his boot, and came to a shuddering halt as his gaze locked on Amelia. For one moment, confusion reigned.

She lay twisting and screaming on the floor, her hair in disarray around her, her arms flailing in front of her, and her gown bunched up around her thighs. Reality punched him in the gut, the hardest blow he'd ever felt in his life. All the air left his lungs on an exhalation of rage and disbelief only to immediately return with a burning need to kill.

He let out a roar and kicked away the round table between him and the bastard on top of Amelia. A vase flew into the air and shattered, black-and-gold chunks scattering in front of him. He heard nothing but the thundering of blood in his ears and his own voice, wild and cursing.

He gripped the man, who was already turning toward him, and swung him around. *Huntington*! A vivid recollection of the man looking at Amelia too long and lingering filled Colin's mind. "You filthy bastard," he yelled, not bothering with questions. Amelia's torn bodice and contorted face gave him all the answers he needed.

"Aversley," Huntington cried as Colin's fist met with the man's nose. The crunch of bones shattering sent dizzying satisfaction spiraling through Colin.

"Did. You. Mean. To. Defile. Her?" he demanded, the raging river of his blood moving through his veins to make every muscle coil, jump, and prepare to kill.

"She wanted me," Huntington responded as if it were an obvious fact.

Whatever tether had kept Colin from already slaughtering the man snapped, the sound of it breaking as real as a leather whip slicing through air. A haze descended over him as he drew back his fist and delivered one vicious blow after another until the man in his grasp twitched, no more than a bloody, blithering mess. His right hand burned fiercely with the hits, but he welcomed the burn and reared back to punch Huntington again, not yet satisfied. Amelia's fearful cry slowed him, and then her words registered in his mind and stopped him altogether.

"You came!" She sounded as if she could hardly believe it.

Shame pummeled him that he had caused her to ever doubt his love. He glanced at Huntington, wanting to finish the man, but Amelia shook her head.

"Enough," she rasped as she wobbled toward him.

Colin immediately dropped Huntington, who fell like a rag doll to the ground, and then he stood and pulled Amelia to him. She wilted into him, her body shaking, her small hands grasping at his arms, and the muffled sound of her tears breaking him into a thousand jagged pieces. Her smell, so sweet of lavender, lingered on her, but stronger than that was the overpowering scent of Huntington's sweat and lust as it assaulted Colin.

He cried out in rage, and Amelia's voice joined his—a strangled cry of shame he knew far to well. "No," he cried sharply while running a hand down her matted hair then cupping her tear-streaked face in his hands. "Don't you dare think you have any fault in this. Whatever this man has done to you, you are not to blame."

"I am!" she mumbled, shaking her head and then burying it in his chest. "I'm foolish. So foolish. I thought I could handle Lord Huntington on my own, so I allowed him to come in. He— That is, I— When he shoved himself between my legs, I—Dear Heavenly God —I would rather be dead."

Colin's stomach, already a hard throbbing knot of anger and fear for her, twisted mercilessly. He pressed his lips close to her ear and felt her jerk at his nearness. Cold fury gripped him once again. "Did he —I mean to say... did he have you?"

"What?" The one word was a choked whisper. She pulled back, her lips trembling and her cheeks a painful red. "Are you asking if he rav—"

"Yes," he interrupted, fearing if she said the word, he would turn around and rip Huntington's heart out with his bare hands.

She shook her head, her eyes glassy even as her gaze wandered to the moaning man on the floor. "You arrived before he had the chance."

His chest expanded with relief, and his hands shook as he pulled her face close to his and pressed his cheek to hers. He did not want to cause her fear by trying to kiss her just yet, but by God, he burned to wipe Huntington's stench off her.

"You said you allowed him to come in here? What did you mean?"

Her frightened gaze darted to Huntington once more. "He has been—" She stopped, swallowed hard so that he heard the force of it, and took a shaky breath. "He has been forcing my mother to sleep with him so that the bank would not call in Philip's notes, and he threatened to spread the rumor that my mother was a whore and ruin Philip if I would not start sleeping with him, too."

Colin curled his hands into fists. He was going to kill the bastard. He swallowed, though it felt next to impossible to do so. "Surely your mother would not let you do such a thing?"

Amelia shook her head, her brown creasing. "Of course not. She wanted to try to convince him to let her continue to..." Her voice drifted off. She grazed a hand through her disheveled hair. "I could not allow that. She was afraid for me because he threatened to tell people I slept with him, as well, even if I had not. He may still. The rumors will be terrible if he does."

The uncertain look she gave him made him unable to take a full breath. She was worried for him. Or what he might think. Was it his past she feared? His hatred of the rumors surrounding his mother and father and what he had done as a result? Or was it that she didn't trust him because he had not told her of the will?

"Amelia," he whispered, intending to reassure her, but the sounds of an approaching carriage cut off his words.

Amelia flew out of his arms and to the window. "My mother is coming! Whatever will I tell her? This may just be too much for her to handle. She's in such a delicate state."

Colin strode to the window. "Cut her off at the curve before she can see the house and distract her. I'll get Huntington out of here and deal with him, and then I'll be back."

"Where will you go? What if you're seen?"

Colin thought for a moment. "I won't be seen. I have someone I can trust at the Pigeon Inn. He will help me." Or at least he hoped he would.

Uncertainty etched the fine bones of her face.

He had a million things he wished to say, most importantly that he loved her and wanted her to be his wife, if she could forgive him and trust him, but he needed to say it perfectly, and being rushed and in the same room with the man who had almost taken her innocence was far from perfect.

She looked as if she might argue, which did not surprise him, but she finally nodded and flew out the door without a word.

Colin stood for a moment, the rush of anger and fear slowly subsiding. His body no longer pulsed with the urgent need to save Amelia, and all the aches of his unhealed injuries started to pulse. Gritting his teeth against the pain, he moved toward Huntington, grabbed the piece of garbage up under his arms and hauled him toward the door, not going out until he saw Amelia leading her mother away from the house and in the opposite direction toward the garden.

Once Colin had his horse connected to Huntington's carriage, he lugged the semi-conscious bastard into the conveyance and settled himself with clenched teeth and a sweat-soaked brow onto the driver's seat before taking off at lighting speed toward the Pigeon Inn.

The reasonable part of his mind knew he could not kill the man, as much as he deserved it, but he could make him understand that if Colin thought, even for a moment, that Huntington ever simply considered disparaging Amelia or her mother, then the reasonable side of Colin would disappear.

Love. It was already making him as foolish as his father had been.

Despite everything, he grinned as he drove.

Chapter Twenty-Two

Several anxious hours later, Amelia's mother asked her, "Are you sure you won't have any supper?"

Amelia shook her head. She had absolutely no appetite. In fact, she was sure if she put anything in her mouth, it would come right back up. She forced a smile to ease her mother's obvious worry. The circles under her mother's eyes were darker than usual, her hair appeared lank, and her gaze, though on Amelia now, flitted around the room every few seconds.

"All right. I'm going to bed."

Thank Goodness. Amelia felt as if she was going mad waiting for Colin to return, and she'd rather not have to pretend nothing had happened any longer. It was exhausting, yet she did not want to say a word to her mother about her meeting with Lord Huntington until she spoke to Colin. "I hope you sleep well."

"I won't. Every time I close my eyes, I picture Lord Huntington. Every noise I hear, I think perhaps it is him, coming here to hurt me, or worse hurt you. Part of me is glad he has not returned yet, but another part of me wishes he would return already so the awful waiting will be over."

Amelia knew exactly how her mother felt, except her worry was for Colin's return. What if he simply didn't come back? No. Impossible. He had said he would, and he had come all the way from London to talk to her in the first place. Yet, what if he returned and had decided he did not want to chance being with someone whose reputation may soon be in tatters? He had not said he still loved her. There had been time for a declaration, but he'd not given her one. Her throat constricted at the thought. No, she was being senseless. Love had done this to her.

She swallowed and stood to kiss her mother on the cheek. "It's going to be all right, Mother." She tried to instill certainty in her voice. "I truly believe somehow things will work out."

Her mother patted her hand. "Good night, dear."

Her mother departed after a quick hug, and Amelia was left alone in the shadowy study with her worries. She paced the room for close to an hour, considering every option she had. She could sit here, waiting for Colin to return to her, or she could try to find him, tell him she loved him, and that she understood why he had not told her of the will.

Rushing out of the study, she grabbed her hooded cloak and hurried out the door and toward the stable as quietly as she could. Once she had her horse readied, she walked him to the end of the drive so there would be no chance she would wake Mother. Then she set off toward the Pigeon Inn, her worry accompanying her every bit of the way.

By the time she reached the inn, her stomach was a quivering jumble of knots. She pulled her hood far over her face to hide herself from view, but once she entered the smelly, dank inn, she realized she need not worry. No one was there except a large man sitting behind the counter drying glasses. As she approached the bar, he stopped what he was doing and glanced up at her. His eyes, keen and the color of a winter sky before a storm, stilled her for a moment.

When he smiled, she relaxed at the obvious friendliness of his gaze. He stood, a tall, towering, broad-shouldered man, and set the glass down with unexpected gentleness for someone of his size. "How might I help ye, miss?" He spoke in a thick Scottish brogue.

"I'm looking for a man. A duke to be precise."

"Ye'd not be the first woman to come strollin' in here lookin' for a duke."

Heat flooded her cheeks. Perhaps this had been a dreadful mistake. Going out in the dark alone—what had she been thinking? If she was found out— She snapped the useless thought off. If she was found out, so be it. She refused to lose Colin without a fight.

"I'm looking for the Duke of Aversley. Do you know him?"

"Aye. I know him."

Now they were getting somewhere. "Have you seen him?"

"Aye. I've seen him. Have you?" The man quirked a thick eyebrow at her.

"Yes. I—" How honest should she be? She suspected this might be the man Colin had said could help him. "He was taking care of an indelicate situation for me."

"Was he now?" The man set his large hand on the bar and leaned toward her, interest obvious in his eye. "Pull yer cloak off yer face for me."

"I beg your pardon?"

"No need to beg, milady. I just need to see if ye are who I think ye might be before I tell ye what I think ye might be wantin' to know."

She immediately yanked her cloak away from her face.

"Oh aye." He smiled broadly. "Yer definitely the lady who is helping him with his devil."

"I'm what?"

"Ask him. 'Tis his story to tell. Not mine."

"Do you know where he is?"

"Aye. Upstairs using my room to wash up. We had to dispose of something messy, but I assume ye know all about that."

She pressed a hand to her throat. "You two didn't kill Lord Huntington did you?"

"No, though personally I would've done him in. Ye English let a wee bit more pass without retribution than we Scots ever would. Where I come from, we answer a wrong loud and clear. Ye English tend to respond with a proper whisper, but I did exactly as Aversley bade me. Go up the stairs to find him. He's in the first room on the left. Mind ye tell him to bring ye back down the back way if it's more than an hour. A rowdy crowd will be here by then."

She nodded and hurried toward the stairs with a pounding heart. When she reached the first door on the left, she knocked, but no one answered. Taking a deep breath, she pounded on the door once more, but impatience got the best of her and she tried the handle. It was open, which seemed an invitation to enter. As she strode into the candlelit room, the sound of a rich baritone voice floated to her and the scent of soap filled the air.

She furrowed her brow and glanced around. This was not one room but two, and though she could hear Colin, she could not see him. But the ballad he sang made her smile. She knew "Oh, Tell Me How From Love To Fly" very well. A memory flashed of her father singing it to her mother in the garden one sunny day.

As she tiptoed toward the room where his singing came from, another sound greeted her, but it was not until she peered through the door into the smaller chamber that she realized what she had been hearing was the swish of water.

Colin stood magnificently naked in a metal tub in the middle of a sparse, small room. His face, eyes closed, was tilted to the bucket he had raised over his head. Amelia's lips parted in shock as much as admiration. Warmth flooded through her, and deep within, an ache pulsed to life and awoke desire so fierce she felt as if she were suddenly fragmented.

She took each breath as quietly as possible, wanting to revel in this moment and imprint this picture in her mind forever. He stood with his legs spread apart, the muscles defined by rises and dips under the thin veil of golden hair that covered his long, powerful legs. She trailed her gaze slowly between his legs, and instantly the pulse low in her belly contracted in a wickedly wonderful way. The most intimate part of her tingled to awareness in the space of a breath.

He suddenly stopped singing and upturned the bucket, his heavily muscled arms flexing slightly with the movement, and the hard plane of his abs tensed to make a ripple over the ridges of muscle and skin. Water swished out of the bucket and over his hair, washing it in a dark-gold wave back over his forehead to expose his strong jaw line. Streams sluiced down his broad chest and trailed in tempting, glistening rivulets all the way down his legs to disappear into the tin tub.

She sighed with pleasure, realizing when the sound came out that she had made the noise out loud. He lowered the bucket as his eyes flew open. His hazel gaze met hers. Cocking his head, he squeezed his eyes shut then slowly opened them again and stared.

"For a moment I thought I'd conjured your image, because of my anticipation to see you, but I can hear you breathing, so unless I've run mad, you are real. Here. And standing there, staring at me naked."

A blush seared her face, and she immediately turned away. "I'm sorry. I was taken by surprise."

Water sloshed, and his feet padded against the floor, stopping directly behind. The heat of his body enveloped her, and the scent of soap surrounded her. He bent his head low, so that droplets of water from his wet hair dripped on her shoulder and soaked through the thin material of her cloak and gown.

"Pity," he murmured in deep seductive voice that made her stomach flutter. "I was hoping you were standing there so silent and secretive because you were admiring me. If I came upon you naked and bathing, I know I'd stand there like a statue drinking in your beauty for as long as I could."

She swiveled toward him, and she was almost too close to him to complete the turn. The minute she faced him, he raised his arms to either side of her shoulders and pressed his hands against the door as he closed it. She leaned away, her back touching the wood, to gaze up at him. "I *was* admiring you and drinking you in."

"That's better," he said with a lazy alluring smile, but then his face grew serious. "Amelia, please say you can forgive me. I vow to God that I love you. I was stupid and untrusting, but I will never keep a secret from you again."

Her heart expanded with all her love for him. She cupped his cheek. "I will forgive you if you can forgive me for so being so silly and running away from you. I should have not let my anger get the best of me. I used to be so sensible before I met you. In fact, I had a secret habit of referring to myself as an Elinor."

"From *Sense and Sensibility*?"

Amelia blinked at him in surprise. "How did you know that? Have you read it?"

A flush covered his face this time. "You must swear never to divulge my secret, my dear. It will destroy my reputation as a cold hearted rake."

"Then I shall shout it from the rooftops," she teased.

"Little minx." He brushed his lips over hers then slowly traced his tongue over her upper lip and then her lower one.

When he drew away, she traced a finger over her tingling lips and stared at him.

He raised his hand and gently brushed her hair out of her eyes. "You are looking at me like you are wondering something."

Now it was her turn to blush again. She was thinking that if she were to write a romance the hero would dash right back to the heroine, not take a leisurely bath. Maybe her hero had a good reason. "Why didn't you return to me right away?"

"I did not think you would want me returning to your home with blood on my clothes, as well as my person. That would make for an awkward presentation when I asked you to marry me."

Amelia's chest expanded, and she fought back her smile. "Does this mean you love me still with *utter* devotion?" She loved that she could tease him, but truly she wanted him to say the words again.

"God help you, I do. I love you madly. Senselessly, yet sensibly. You are stuck with me, I'm afraid. That is, if you love me the same as I do you."

"I do, Colin." She stood on her tiptoes and crushed her mouth to his for a long lingering kiss. "I love you so very much it scares me."

"I've a healthy dose of fear over loving you, as well, but I fear not loving you more."

Amelia pressed her cheek to his chest, hearing his thundering heart beneath the taut muscle. "I have loved you since that day at Hyde Park—likely before—and once I realized what true love was, what it felt like, I knew there was no other man for me but you. And it had positively nothing to do with your title or wealth, but everything to do with your heart, mind and soul."

His lips brushed against hers as he spoke. "I love you because you are loyal."

She frowned. "*Dogs* are loyal."

His eyes flashed with humor. "True. But I would not sleep with a dog."

"That's very good to know."

"And dogs are not so beautiful that my heart constricts when I look at them." He kissed her forehead. "A dog cannot put me in my place with a witty rejoinder, or dance with me, or stroll and talk of flowers, or simply hold my hand. A dog cannot understand my wretched past and forgive it and still love me, despite all my flaws."

"My love," she breathed the words into his mouth as her arms skimmed up his naked torso and clung to his slick shoulders. "I love you all the more because of your flaws and your past. Not in spite of them. Both have shaped you into the man you are. I'd not have you any other way."

He slid his arms around her and gathered her tightly to him before burying his face in her neck. His warm breath tickled her skin as he spoke. "That's very good to hear because I cannot imagine my life without you."

Heat radiated through her chest, leaving her breathless and tingly. "Colin, I don't want to go home just yet."

He pulled back and grinned down at her. "You want to watch me bathe some more? I'll need to take my towel off." His voice vibrated, and he glanced down at the towel tucked around his abdomen.

"I'll take that off for you," she replied, pouring every fraction of her desire into her tone. "I want to bathe *you,* and then you can bathe *me*. Let us wash each other clean, and then we will begin again. New. Tonight. In each other's arms. Replacing whatever came before with only memories of us."

~

The tension that had been a constant part of Colin's life for as long as he could remember faded with her words. He pulled her to him once again, marveling at how soft her body was. He'd never taken the time to enjoy the simple pleasure of holding a totally clothed woman; before Amelia, he had not seen the point. His eyes burned suddenly. Bloody hell. The woman had reduced him to near tears. He quickly blinked, until his vision cleared and he could focus on her.

"Amelia, I love you. I never thought I would want to love a woman, but all I can think of is how I want to hold you close and cherish you forever. I've turned into my father, only now I realize it's a very good thing indeed to love another so intensely that it touches your soul. Though I vow I will never do to you what my father did to my mother."

"What do you mean?"

Colin quickly told her all his mother had told him, wanting to have nothing but truth between them.

"Oh dear. How awful for all of you." She ran her hand over his lips, softly, reverently. "I feel certain your father had many wonderful qualities, and he obviously loved your mother to depths that tortured him, but promise me you would never make such a vow."

Colin brushed a hand over her high cheekbone and down to the base of her neck to the spot where her pulse beat. He gently laid his fingers there, savoring the strength of the woman he adored. "The only vow I will ever make is this one. I promise to always and forever love you, worship your body, and share all my fears with you. Every annoying one. And if there ever comes a time I feel the need to make a promise to God, I will carefully word it and make certain you approve."

"If I'm not available?"

He chuckled. "Minx. You've thought of everything. I'll ask..." Who could he ask?

"Your mother," Amelia supplied. "She above all will understand the importance of properly worded promises."

Colin's heart squeezed painfully. "Thank you, Amelia."

"For what?"

"For accepting not only my jaded, used self but for accepting my mother and all that goes with her."

She crooked a finger at him. "Come now with me and accept what I have to give you." She brushed past him, her cloak falling in a dark puddle at her feet. When she reached the tin tub, she paused, lifted her hair and glanced over her shoulder at him. "Will you unhook me?"

He walked slowly to her, his heart thundering like he was a green lad about to lie with his first woman. The notion made him want to throw back his head and laugh with gratitude. He lifted his trembling hands to her fasteners and paused, a smile stretching his lips. Never had a woman made him tremble. He savored every hook down to the very last one that rested at the delectable curve of her bottom.

Slipping his hands under the shoulders of her gown, he slid the garment down her delicate skin and let it fall to her feet. She stepped out of it and turned to him, her arms not coming across her chemise-clad breasts in the protective manner he was expecting but opening wide and welcoming. "Come to me, Colin. Hold me and love me. Make me yours."

Within moments, they stood face-to-face, completely naked, and she raised her glorious, trusting face to his. "You are beautiful, Colin, but here"—she placed a warm palm on his heart—"is where you take my breath away, and all my love with it."

A frantic need to have her came over him. He pulled her to him and plunged his hands into her luxurious hair. Their lips met in a frenzy of exploration, need and desire. He skimmed his hands up her slender stomach and spread his fingers wide, enjoying the silky smoothness of her skin. His body grew hot as he swirled his fingers around her hard nipples, and she moaned in response.

Pulsing need sent him bending toward her breast to lick the tip of her nipple, round and round with his tongue. A painful yet pleasurable ache took hold of him, made all the sweeter by the mewling sounds she made when he took her nipple into his mouth and suckled like a babe at the breast of life. His pleasure was so intense that he realized he needed to slow greatly to hold back his climax.

He drew away and cupped her breasts, flicking her nipples with his fingers, and then squeezing the tips with just enough pressure that ragged moans came from deep within her throat. She threw her head back, and when she did, he slid his hand down her spine to embrace her and hold her upright. He took her hands, which had been bunched against his chest and encouraged her to explore.

She did, at first touchingly naive and hesitant and then becoming bolder with her caresses before surprising him by sliding her hands between his legs. Her long strokes started gently then harder and faster until, before he realized what was happening, he was the one moaning as wave after wave of pleasure rolled through him, tightening his body into a band as taut as a bow, and then all at once the tension released with a climax that left him momentarily weak.

When he came back to himself, she helped him into the tub and then bathed him with so much care that waves of gratitude washed over him, just as intense as the pleasure he had just experienced. When she was done, she rose and silently handed him the washrag.

He knelt by her feet and slowly worked his way up her body, inch by worshipful inch until he came to her breasts and lathered them first with the cloth and then his hands.

The contact of her skin to his was driving him mad with desire. His body strummed with the need to be inside of her, and by the wild look in her eyes, she felt the exact same way.

When Colin ran his hands down her slippery body, around her waist, and over the curve of her bottom to cup her under her legs and lift her to him, she was not at all sure what he wanted her to do, so she looked to him for guidance.

He ravaged her mouth as he hoisted her to his waist. Between kisses, he pulled back and spoke. "Wrap you legs around my waist and your arms around my neck."

She did so immediately, and he lowered them into the tub so that she sat over him with her legs spread wide. He gently cupped her neck as the other hand came between their bodies, and his fingers found her sensitive spot and began to move back and forth with a rhythm that drove her to distraction. Unable to sit still, she pressed toward him, wanting him to increase the pressure and the speed. His acquiescence to her unspoken desire was immediate. His fingers moved expertly, rubbing in tiny circles that made her certain every ounce of blood she possessed was pulsing between her legs.

"Colin!" she cried out, certain she was on the edge of something wonderful. Water swished all around her, and with the swirling movement, he entered her in one long, swift stroke. The momentary sharp pain was lost among the thousands of splendid sensations he caused every time he slid out almost to his tip and back in. When he moved, her world seemed to move with him, until she was no longer certain where reality ended and the dream of the moment began.

Her body clenched, and then heat, invasive and exquisite, swept over her and took all the energy she had with it as the flame burned bright and died slowly, leaving her panting, sweating, and spent. She collapsed onto his chest, water lapping up between their bodies. He wrapped his arms around her tightly and pressed a kiss to her neck and then her lips. "You have all of me now," he whispered. "Even after death takes me, I am yours."

A spasm shot through her straight from her core to her heart. "I should not want it any other way. As you are mine, I am yours. This is my vow to you." She sealed the promise with a searing kiss.

World of Johnstone Teaser

Available Now

A year after her husband's tragic death, all Lady Julianna Barrows wants is to be left alone and forget that most of her heart went with him when he passed. Instead, she finds herself the subject of many a matchmaking scheme and lurid offer to ease her widowhood, as well as save her fading fortune. Desperate to avoid having to remarry, she takes on a position as a tutor, only to discover that the man she's helping unexpectedly stirs her heart and passion.

Nash Wolverton boxed his way out of the London slums and into immense wealth, but he couldn't care less about Society's approval. Except he has his by-blow daughter's future to consider. To ensure her acceptance into Society, he'll endure anything—including procuring a tutor to transform him into a gentleman so he can secure a suitable, boring wife.

Yet what he wants changes the moment he hires Julianna. She may be a lady, but she's far from tedious. Bold and compassionate, she is nothing like the women of the *ton*. Suddenly, she's elicited a simmering desire in him, and even a longing to love and be loved that he always thought out of his reach. Knowing what he planned to settle for can now never be enough, he vows to win her love. But as the walls she's built begin to crumble, Julianna's fears threaten to tear them apart and she alone must decide if protecting her heart trumps breaking Nash's.

Also Available

BARGAINING WITH A RAKE (A Whisper of Scandal Novel Book 1)
CONSPIRING WITH A ROGUE (A Whisper of Scandal Novel Book 2)
DANCING WITH A DEVIL (A Whisper of Scandal Novel Book 3)
A WHISPER OF SCANDAL TRILOGY (Books 1-3)
WHAT A ROGUE WANTS (Lords of Deception Book 1)
THE REDEMPTION OF A DISSOLUTE EARL (A Danby Family Novella 1)
SEASON FOR SURRENDER (A Danby Family Novella 2)
ECHOES IN THE SILENCE (THE SIREN SAGA) BOOK 1

ANTHOLOGIES

A Summons From Yorkshire
(Regency Christmas Summons Collection 1)
A Gentlemen's Pact (Regency Christmas Pact)

All books are available as e-books and print books at all major e-book retailers.

About the Author

Julie Johnstone is a best-selling author of Regency Romance and the author of a new urban fantasy/paranormal romance book. She's been a voracious reader of books since she was a young girl. Her mother would tell you that as a child Julie had a rich fantasy life made up of many different make believe friends. As an adult, Julie is one of the lucky few who can say she is living the dream by working with her passion of creating worlds from her imagination. When Julie is not writing she is chasing her two precocious children around, cooking, reading or exercising. Julie loves to hear from her readers. You can send her an email at juliejohnstoneauthor@gmail.com or find her at www.juliejohnstoneauthor.com, or on Facebook at authorjuliejohnstone and juliejohnstoneauthor or at twitter @juliejohnston.

61227773R00146

Made in the USA
Charleston, SC
17 September 2016